THE
NAME
CURSE

ALSO BY
BROOKE BURROUGHS

The Marriage Code

THE
NAME
CURSE

BROOKE
BURROUGHS

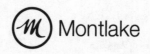 Montlake

Published by Montlake, Seattle

www.apub.com

Amazon, the Amazon logo, and Montlake are trademarks of Amazon.com, Inc., or its affiliates.

ISBN-13: 9781542029322
ISBN-10: 1542029325

Cover illustration and design by Liz Casal

Printed in the United States of America

For my parents, who initially inspired a love of the great outdoors in me when they took my terrible sixteen-year-old self on an epic two-month journey across America.

CHAPTER 1

Great-Aunt Bernice had been haunting Bernie Purcell ever since she departed this world fifteen years ago with a whiff of Chanel No. 5 and a reputation—if you believed the stories—that rivaled that of Mata Hari. And every time Great-Aunt Bernice was mentioned, which was almost daily because she was her namesake, Bernie felt a little ripple going through her body, reminding her of who she was, and who she wasn't. Especially during every conversation she'd ever had with her mother, who seemed to relish using her full name in spite of the fact that Bernie had asked her not to. Repeatedly.

"Bernice!" her mother said with a sigh into the phone, as it seemed she did every time they spoke, a little hint of exasperation but with the mollifying exhale of a woman doing yoga to try to keep her sanity.

Even though she was on the phone, Bernie's hand went to her hip in practiced defiance. It was as if every time she and her mother spoke, Bernie was transported back into adolescence. Back into a time warp of acne and hormones and thinking she was right, although down deep she knew she wasn't.

But this time, she was. "Mom, you know I prefer *Bernie*." Why did they have to keep going over this?

"It's a family name, and you should be proud of it. My aunt Bernice was a stunning woman."

"Aunt Bernice was a nutjob." She didn't add that her great-aunt had also horribly frightened her as a child. When Bernie was little, Great-Aunt Bernice would swoop into town a few times each year with her peacock-toned wide-sleeved caftans, raspy voice, and fuchsia lipstick. She'd remind Bernie how thrilled she was that they had the same name, how they were so much alike, how Bernie reminded her of herself as a child. Child Bernie tried to keep her distance from the hot-pink talons that seemed to grab onto her constantly, unable to process that just because they had the same name didn't mean she would soon also end up with a wild mane of hair and a voice that sounded like rocks tumbling.

"She lived a full life. There's a difference." Bernie could see her mother shaking her head at the phone and rolling her eyes, as if they were face-to-face. Bernie wasn't going to list the various ways that Aunt Bernice had almost killed herself doing wild stunts, but she had stored them away like little alarm bells ready to be called upon, harbingers of what could become of her. Slipping off the Great Wall of China, luckily in a soft bushy part. Getting bitten by a rattlesnake while hiking the Appalachian Trail and then being confined to the hospital for a month. Having a gun pulled on her while accidentally having an affair with a mob boss while living in Sicily in the sixties. And then, what had finally done her in was a sad mopping accident where she slipped on her kitchen floor and broke her neck. Of course she was ninety-six by then, but still.

"Whatever you say, Mom."

"I always thought you would be more like her. Especially when you were younger. You were so full of spirit. Such an adventurous kind of girl . . ." She punctuated the insult with that sigh again.

Bernie opened her mouth to protest. Her mom always said she loved her, and was proud of her, and all the good, right things that a mom should say. But then her voice would get that airy, wistful sound when she'd mention how different she used to be, and Bernie would get a little hollow feeling in her chest, a feeling that said she was a disappointment. It wasn't her fault she wasn't a full-on, careening wild woman like Aunt Bernice, or even like her mom for that matter. A woman who had left their hometown of Portland when Bernie's dad died and moved to Bend to work as a florist on a sustainable farm. A woman who didn't care about practical things like money and retirement funds because she believed in things like karma and living off the earth. A woman who could just move on after her husband died and never look back. Whereas Bernie had contentedly moved into the house her mom had abandoned five years ago, after her dad passed away, reclaimed her old bedroom with its frilly high school decor, and relapsed into a world where she could rewind the present.

"Mom . . ." Bernie didn't know what to say. She didn't want her mom to make her feel bad about being someone who liked returning to the place where she grew up. She didn't have to escape the memory of her father like her mother did.

"Look, let's get back on topic. I agree with your manager. It's time to take a vacation. As someone who now feels like she's on a permanent vacation, I think it's a grand idea. Just what you need."

This was why Bernie had initially called. She thought she'd go down to the farm for a week. Maybe help her mom pick flowers. Lie around and read. Let her dog, James Brown, run through the fields. "Okay, well, I could just come down there for a little while . . ."

"Bernice—Bernie, you have the gift of forced vacation. Why don't you go somewhere? You should get out of that *house*."

Bernie's eyes fluttered closed. Her mom's tone made it sound like she was living in a dilapidated shack. Or a part-time brothel. "You mean, *our* house? The one you raised me in?"

"I'm just saying you could do a lot with that time. Go to Europe or Hawaii or *anywhere* in the world."

Bernie sighed. The thought had run through her head, but she'd already consulted with Tabitha, her best friend, who was unable to join her. "I'm totally cool with taking a vacation—it's just hard when you're single."

Her mother hummed her disappointment. "You could go alone."

That was ridiculous. "What am I going to do? Eat dinner by myself every night? Hang out on the beach alone? I'll be targeted by a serial killer." She braced herself, waiting for another comparison to Great-Aunt Bernice, who seemed to have taken only exotic vacations on her own.

"Honey, I think you're overreacting."

They could agree to disagree, as they did on basically everything. "But really, what do you think about me coming down there in a few weeks? I can help out maybe. Do some gardening. Make some flower arrangements or something." She tried to sound hopeful, helpful, all the things that would make her mom agree. But instead her mom just laughed.

"You don't exactly have what I would call a green thumb, sweetie."

"Well, it's never too late to learn. I have a houseplant." Bernie glanced over at the withering money tree in the corner of her living room, the leaves tinged a crisp brown at the tips. The person who'd sold it to her had said it was impossible to kill, and yet . . .

"Having a houseplant and getting your hands dirty are two very different things, but sure, if that's what you want. You're always welcome." Her mother's voice couldn't hide the hesitation, though. "Are you sure that's really what you want?"

She'd mentally gone through the rest of her close friends. She wasn't sure if she could go with Rachel for a week anywhere. Deb snored, so they couldn't share a room. With Rob, it would just be too weird. And she wasn't desperate enough to start rekindling a pseudo-relationship with her last ex just to take a trip somewhere.

"I don't have a passport, so . . ." It was a legitimate excuse.

"You're just like your father now! I don't understand what happened. Such a homebody." She had always complained about his placid immobility, like it was a self-inflicted wound on both of them.

Bernie winced at the way her mom compared her to her father. Like it was such a bad thing. In fact, it was the only time her mother ever brought her dad up since he'd died when Bernie was twenty-two. Like she'd wiped away all the joy the three of them had once shared. Sometimes it felt as if her mom had counted up all the things that annoyed her about her husband when he was alive, like beads on an abacus, and then flung them at Bernie during every argument they'd had since. But in fact, Bernie relished the commonalities she could still find with him.

"You know, we have a big, beautiful country you could travel in without a passport. Go on an adventure."

Bernie sighed, the visions of where she could go bubbling up inside her like the feeling of being sick. Their beauty and temptation a threat. Hawaiian beaches, a mountainous road trip through state parks, cruising down Route 66 with James Brown. Going on an adventure was tempting. She could feel something inside her start to tease out the possibilities just at the thought. Then that feeling soured as she remembered the last time she'd gone away. The idea of her world completely crumbling under her again was like a threat that did the worst kind of taunting.

But she knew she needed to appease her mother, or else she'd never hear the end of it. "Okay, I'll think about it. I have enough vacation time, so I could come see you and go somewhere."

"Are you bringing James Brown with you?"

"Yes, he is coming." Bernie bent down to pet her fawn-and-white boxer, who was doing his namesake wiggle since she was standing in the kitchen and he apparently thought he was going to get some food. "He loves to run around out there."

"Okay, well, just let me know what dates you're thinking about."

"Will do." They said goodbye, and she sank down against the cabinets and scratched her dog behind the ears. Would it be weird if she took a road trip with her dog? Where would they go? It wasn't like many hotels would actually take her muscly, eighty-pound boxer.

She sighed and squeezed his face between her hands. "I can't even go on vacation with *you*."

Bernie had laughed when her manager had told her she needed to take a vacation earlier that day. She had completely thought it was a joke. No one at a company asked you to take a vacation. They usually wanted you to work as much as you could.

"No, I mean it, Bernie. You haven't had a break in two years. It's time, don't you think?" Rosalie, her manager, had tilted her head and given her that judging squint that told Bernie if she knew what was best for her, she would take some time off.

"Okay. Well, when?"

"Soon. There are five months left in the year, and if you don't take at least twenty days of what you've stockpiled by then, you'll lose them."

"That's four weeks." She had no idea what she would do with four weeks with nothing to do.

"Yep. Do you know how many people would kill to be in your position? Go do something fun. It's my job to make sure my team is healthy, happy, and gets enough time off. It will be refreshing for you. Then you can come back and tell us all about it."

It felt like an unwelcomed gift. Like her manager had just given her a wine-shaped box, but inside was a gray toothbrush. Similar to how she'd felt about her mom visiting six months ago, the first time she'd been back to the house after moving out. Bernie had assumed the world would feel right again with her mom back. Maybe her mother would remember how much she'd loved the house, and they'd bond by taking a weepy stroll down memory lane.

But instead her mom had entered the house looking around suspiciously, as if she was searching for ghosts, and blew her hair out of her face, exasperated and sighing extra (which Bernie didn't even think was possible) as she tried to get comfortable in a space that should have felt like her real home. She'd burned sage in every corner of the room to clear out all the "bad technology juju." Bernie's beloved frozen pizzas and Diet Coke had been replaced with new, greenish things with ecopackaging made entirely of plants. Bernie would go with Rachel sometimes to their favorite vegan restaurant, but that was outside, and this was in her house. It was like her kitchen and her life had been taken over by a fairy godmother on a juice cleanse who shoved glasses of forest-green liquid in her face every morning, when Bernie just wanted a coffee with her mocha-flavored creamer and didn't care about its unpronounceable ingredients.

But she could deal with her mom if she went to the farm. She just didn't want her trying to change the life Bernie was fine with living, just the way it was. Well, at least for the most part. The fact remained that Bernie was, at twenty-seven, in a job that was tolerable and paid the bills, yet she couldn't even find a date to go on vacation with.

◆ ◆ ◆

"Don't hate me." Those were the first words out of her mom's mouth when Bernie answered the phone a few days later. No "hello"; no "Hi, it's me"; no "How's my sweet girl who's ready to come to my hippie commune for a few weeks?"

"That sentence does not bode well for me, does it?" Bernie said, rolling away from her desk and then walking into the kitchen at work to grab a coffee.

"Well, I think it does. I bought you a Groupon."

A Groupon. A seemingly innocuous gift, although purchased by her mother, so who knew what would lie in Bernie's future? Maybe it was a spa day or dog sitting. Those were things she could actually use.

"Okay. Cool. What's it for?"

"I bought you a vacation."

"Really? A vacation?" Her finger froze in front of the coffee-vending machine.

"Yes. I thought to myself after we spoke the other day, Bernice—Bernie, sorry—would never do this for herself. Therefore, I'm just going to help her out. Give her a little nudge."

Her mouth opened to say she didn't need a nudge. That she was perfectly content with the staycation and farm trip she'd planned, but this was a really nice gesture, even if she and her mother seemed to exist on different planets most of the time.

"And it's a group thing, so you won't be alone," her mother continued.

"Oh. Well, that's very thoughtful of you." If Bernie was going to go somewhere, then maybe this would be the perfect solution. She didn't know where to go, what to do, or how to plan it on her own. And she wouldn't be the lone woman eating at the same table every night.

But what kinds of group vacations could a person buy on Groupon, and would they be good? Though the bigger question was: What kind of vacation would her mother, self-decreed patron saint of herbs, flowers, and pollinating insects, buy her?

Maybe this was too good to be true.

A rush of breath sounded into the phone. "Oh, good. I thought you were going to freak out, and it's nonrefundable, so I was a little worried." She said the word *little* in that tinkly voice that told Bernie it was both expensive and that she'd been more than a little worried. And yet she'd bought it anyway. Such a typical mom move.

She silenced her rebuttal. "Nah. Of course not. It was really nice of you to think of me. Where is it a vacation to?"

"Okay. I saw this and thought it would be perfect for you. You are always at work and don't leave the building all day, so it has some sunshine. I mean, you really need to watch your vitamin D levels, since we live in the Pacific Northwest."

Sunshine = beach. This was sounding better by the minute. "Don't worry, I take a vitamin every day." Well, that was almost true. She'd at least opened the bottle of vitamins her mom had given her last year. And when she remembered, she took them. So . . . she'd taken about five.

"Good girl. And then it has some nature. You do, after all, have a creative job, and I've read that being outdoors can be very stimulating for creativity. When you get, you know, in a dull spot."

"A dull spot?" Like her mother knew anything that she did in marketing. And the word *creative* might've been a little too generous for the work that Bernie did. It was more analyzing data for their customers to figure out how to get them to love her company's clothing brand even more.

"I just thought maybe your manager wanted you to take a vacation because of that. I don't know! Just my thinking." She could see her mother throwing up her hands at the speakerphone.

"I don't think that was it. I literally have too much vacation. It's not like we're *Mad Men*." Bernie smiled, imagining what her mom thought she actually did. But sun and nature didn't sound bad at all, and in fact she was starting to conjure up visions of drinking from halved pineapples with little umbrellas while staring at the ocean, which would be amazing, although probably out of the budget potential of either of them. "But I appreciate the consideration."

"Anyway, the third thing was that you walk everywhere. I know you love walking. You walk to work; you walk the dog; you walk to restaurants and to get coffee. I mean, you hardly use your car. I'm very proud of you for that. You're a real woman of the earth. And I thought this fit that."

Bernie almost coughed out her coffee at that. It was true that Bernie walked everywhere. But the phrase "woman of the earth" was beyond a stretch. She worked for a boutique clothing company and had curated a collection of cute but comfortable shoes to do all that walking. She owned nothing in the earth tones of beige, brown, or khaki.

And "woman of the earth" was a flashing red light in her brain now. Her mom hadn't said bright floral prints or cute sandals or leis. Now, instead of picturing a sunny beach with thatched huts, she was envisioning no running water, a stream she would have to bathe in, and possibly having to sleep in a tree.

She took a deep breath.

"Well, Mom, you've stumped me. I'm dying to know what this vacation is." She closed her eyes briefly and said a silent prayer. *Please let there be toilets.*

"I got you a hiking trip to Denali!"

"Oh . . . wow." Bernie tried to gather what that meant. She knew Denali was a mountain. It was in Alaska. It was not a beach. There were no pineapples to drink out of. And the rest was . . . questionable. Toilets, questionable. Beds, questionable. Showers, questionable.

"So what do you think?" Her mom sounded so excited, and it was very kind of her to think about Bernie, even if it did border on meddling, so she didn't want to disappoint her. Her mom had sounded relieved when Bernie hadn't automatically protested, and she had mentioned "nonrefundable."

"I'm definitely . . . curious. I've never been on a big hiking trip like that."

"I know! That's why I thought it would be so good for you. Plus, it's in the US, you know? My friend Fran told me about how she got a Groupon to Italy, but then you don't have a passport. And there were a lot of trips to Europe—Spain, France, Austria—but then I saw this, and it just screamed you!"

"Yeah." Bernie swallowed. Swallowed the words she wanted to say, her dreams of a vacation doing nothing, and the reality of not having running water. This was not the first time her mother had given her a gift that "screamed Bernie." Usually Bernie shoved those handcrafted blankets, hemp tote bags, and silver rings claiming mystical powers into a drawer, but a hiking trip was a little too abstract and big to shove somewhere. "It's just so, so . . . thoughtful of you."

"It was such a good deal I had to get it! And don't worry: it's not one of those hard-core hikes to the summit where you have to wear snowshoes the whole time and parkas and where people can die or freeze to death."

Freeze to death? That was a trip that people paid money for?

Maybe she needed to investigate this further. After all, her mother was the nature child, not her.

"Mom, are you sure *you* don't want to do this hike?" She could pawn it off on her mother, convince her to go instead.

"Honey, I'd love to go with you, but you know my hip hasn't been the same since I broke it."

Bernie didn't bother clarifying that she didn't mean "with" but meant actually "instead."

"I just can't walk eight miles a day up a mountain, you know?"

"Eight miles? A day?" Bernie asked for clarification to make sure she'd heard her correctly.

"Well, that's the average, but you're easily walking five every day now. It shouldn't be any real work for you to do. You're young and healthy and fit. I called the company and had them hold a spot for their trip in two weeks for you. I can totally watch James Brown while you're gone."

"Can you send me the information?" Bernie cleared her throat and tried not to sound gloomy, but she had to find out exactly what she was in store for.

"Yes. As soon as the satellite internet kicks back on, I'll send it right over."

And just as her mom spoke, Bernie also realized that if she went on this trip, she would likely not have any connection with the outside world for a week.

Could she do it?

CHAPTER 2

"I think this is the perfect opportunity! You can finally put your house on the market." Tabitha grabbed Bernie's arm in the middle of the sidewalk as they headed out to get coffee.

Bernie hummed. This was the yearly discussion they had. Bernie should sell her house. At least rent it out. It was too big for her; she could get a lot of money for it and downsize. And then the conversation would deviate into Bernie just insisting she needed to fix it up first. A task that had never happened. Granted, she needed to do something with the place—update the furniture or paint the walls—but something always came up. But she could see the ten-year-old stain in the carpet from a Christmas where her dad had dropped a pot of tea that no one had been able to remove. Bernie was sick of looking at the stain, too, its pale-brown smudge against the light-green pile. But then when she looked at it, she remembered her dad, how he did his signature *whoops* look with a downturned grin and a shrug, and everyone had laughed, high on sugary cinnamon rolls.

But did she really want to be clinging onto memories tied up with brown stains?

"Maybe. But I couldn't fix it up in two weeks before I leave . . . ," Bernie said, but the words masked that familiar swirling pool of dread that spun up in her stomach every time she thought about selling the house. Her house. Her mother had abandoned it, along with all its memories, so how could Bernie do that, too, even if it might be the best, most logical thing to do?

"Bernie, this neighborhood has seen tremendous growth over the past year. Putting my real estate agent hat on for a moment, I think you could sell it for upward of nine hundred."

"Thousand?" Bernie stopped walking, trying to imagine what her mom would say if Bernie passed this information on. Would she wave her hand dismissively and say she was happy with her farm life? Or would she take the money and disappear, buying all the European Groupon vacations she could gobble up and live her free-to-be-you-and-me life on another continent?

"Yes. Three bedroom, three bath, in good shape, and in walking distance to this?" Tabitha's arms gestured toward the main street they were approaching. "Totally."

Darling restaurants with striped awnings and wicker patio sets on the sidewalk. Small houses converted into boutiques that sold a cute mix of vintage and designer clothes. At least two pet stores that she and James Brown took Saturday-morning walks to.

Bernie was still processing as Tabitha continued. "I know you have issues letting go of that place, but as your friend, I think it would be good for you. As your real estate agent, I can fix it up while you're gone, take some photos, get the listing ready. Then no commitment needed—we can decide when you're back if you're ready for me to list it."

"Let me think about it." This was Bernie's standard response when Tabitha brought up selling the house. A topic she wasn't 100 percent ready to discuss.

As they rounded the corner on Northwest Twenty-Third, Tabitha spotted a lone table in the midst of the crowd in front of their favorite coffee shop. She ran-walked to grab it, and Bernie opened the door. "The reg?" she asked her friend.

Tabitha gave her a thumbs-up, and Bernie went inside the blue-walled café to order two coffees and whatever cake looked good that day. Waiting in line, she tried to imagine a new life in a new apartment. Maybe one of those new condos they'd built out of a warehouse, with a dog park in the back. Or someplace closer to her office. Decorating it so it felt like her, instead of staring at the nineties floral wallpaper in the kitchen that she imagined covering up nearly every morning while drinking coffee. But for some reason, she could never change all the little things she'd have to do to really make her childhood home a house that fit adult Bernie. Because then it wouldn't be her childhood home anymore, and all those childhood memories would be gone.

Bernie pushed the door open with her back and carried a tray out to the table, where Tabitha stared at her phone, likely plotting out the quick sale of Bernie's home. "Thanks, babe, this looks awesome." She took a drink of her coffee. "Okay, not to be all pressure-y, but I did see this cute house down the street from me on my way to yours, and just take a look."

She thrust her phone toward Bernie and started flipping through the pictures. Small house, modern, patio, cute backyard, and down the street from Tabitha. Bernie tried to imagine her life living in a house like that. It looked perfect for her and James Brown, but it wasn't *home*. "Oh, it's also two blocks from the dog park. See, perfect?"

"The house, this trip—it's too much at once. That's a lot of change to deal with." Bernie dug her fork into the banana cake, took a bite, and then a deep breath.

"But won't it be *fun* if we're neighbors? Change is good. Getting out of that house will be good. Going on this vacation will be good. You need a shake-up."

She stared at her friend, who was giving her that squinty, judging look. Maybe she needed the external force that was Tabitha applied to her reluctant logic to separate herself from the house. Because it was time to change. At least if she was being forced to go on a hiking trip, she wouldn't have to watch her house go through one of Tabitha's famed real estate makeovers. And if everyone was correct, Bernie would return to Portland with a clear mind infused with extra oxygen from all that nature and know if selling the house would be the right thing to do.

"Okay."

"Okay what?" Tabitha asked.

"Okay, we can try out your plan. No commitment, but you can get the listing ready." The pit in her stomach bottomed out as she said the words, and she tried to appease it with more cake. "I can decide for sure when I'm back."

When she was back. As if she'd already decided to go. Tabitha said she needed a shake-up. Her mother and Rosalie clearly agreed. And Bernie didn't necessarily disagree with them. Perhaps the onslaught of change would help her make the decision about the house, and she'd see how she felt being away from it, her life, and the city she hadn't left in so long.

"I think it's the right thing," Tabitha said, as if she could hear her thoughts and knew Bernie needed a nudge of encouragement.

Bernie hummed in response, and Tabitha gave her another judging look.

Bernie leaned in her chair and half groaned, half sighed. "It's just a lot at once."

"No pressure from me on the house, but I think you'll be excited about your options when you get back. Just go on this trip, enjoy yourself, and leave the rest to me. What's the worst that could happen?"

"I won't poop because there's no bathroom, and I get toxic backup disorder."

Tabitha gave her that through-the-eyelashes glare she was close to patenting. "That's not a thing."

"I could get eaten by a bear."

"Bears eat blueberries and fish."

"They could also eat young ladies named Bernie."

"You're the only lady named Bernie I know."

"Exactly!"

As they walked down the street, stopping in the cute little boutiques along the way, she started to look forward to the upcoming trip. Maybe by the end of it, her mom wouldn't think she was a lost cause. Her manager wouldn't think she didn't have a life. She'd be with some cool people, maybe from all over the world, who were all captivated by the same breathtaking views in the pictures.

Although if they had to sign up for any vacation at all, she wondered what kind of people would choose a weeklong hike in Alaska as their dream vacation. Probably the kind of people her great-aunt Bernice would be proud to call friends.

But she'd try. She'd try to leave and not feel like she was going to regret leaving.

CHAPTER 3

Matthew Hildebrandt sorted his outdoorsy clothes on his bed in big sloppy piles and stared at them. "Is that really all I need?"

His roommate, Jess, put her phone away and peeked around his large frame. She shook her head. "Beats me. I mean, they just said you need hiking clothes, right?"

"Yes. And I packed some meal-replacement bars because I don't trust people who say they are going to feed me for a week."

"Completely understandable." She studied him, and he had the distinct feeling Jess was thinking about how they had ordered pizza the night before for "both" of them, and how somehow he'd eaten almost the entire thing when she had left the room to take a phone call from her girlfriend. It wasn't his fault that he was six foot two and still had the appetite at twenty-eight that he'd had at fifteen. She'd said she was fine but had wrinkled up her face as she'd stared at the one piece left, and he was pretty sure he'd hear about it again.

"Did you know the average adult human male burns approximately five hundred calories per hour of hiking? On this trip that will equate to over four thousand calories a day."

"I don't think you have enough bars."

"I'll live."

"I'm not sure why you're growing a beard for this, though." She rubbed her hand along his jawline.

"Well, I figure that if I'm not going to be shaving for a while, I might as well embrace the Grizzly Adams look."

"It's a week, right? Not six months." She looked down at the clothes and back up at him. "I have this feeling you're going to show up at the front door in a week with this even bigger beard and suspenders and a plaid lumberjack shirt and tell me you've given up bathing and are going to be a mountain man. 'Fuck LA! What did it ever do for me?'" She said the last two sentences in a deep, gruff voice that was apparently supposed to be his, along with putting her hands on her hips and sort of caving in her chest as she walked out the door.

"Hey, I don't sound like that!" he called after her. He didn't cave in his chest.

Jess turned around and stuck her bottom lip out and thrust her shoulders forward more, shrinking her down to almost five feet tall.

"I don't pout either!"

She turned and walked down the hall bowlegged, and then he heard her laugh from the kitchen.

"I'm not a pouter," he mumbled to himself.

Whatever. LA hadn't done too much for him *lately*, but overall it had been a great choice moving there after college. Maybe it was a little bit true he'd been bitter the past few years. The last four sitcoms he'd worked on had been a bust, and in his head, they'd even sounded stupid, but a job was a job. Producers or other scriptwriters he'd known had pulled him onto the projects and convinced him that this was "the one." The next hit, the next *Friends*. Everyone wanted to be *Friends*. But in the past two years, he'd written his heart out, only to have a producer say the script, the characters, and sometimes even the ideas needed to be changed and forced him to make his writing cheesier, more clichéd. "Isn't that what we're supposed to be avoiding?" Matthew had asked. "Aren't we supposed to make it more original?"

The last producer he'd collaborated with—*collaborated* being a very loose word—had told him no. "You think people watch the Kardashians because they want originality in programming? Uh, no." She'd thrust the script back at him. "Change it."

His agent, Jude, had tried to appease him, his mantra to Matthew now "It's just one show. There are so many options out there. You'll find the one."

And now he was living in a hamster wheel of scripts he didn't like and shows he wasn't proud of, constantly chasing cheese he didn't like the taste of either.

So maybe he was a little bitter. Which was easy to happen when your dreams slapped you in your face. He couldn't blame the recent bitter taste of life on his bad luck with work completely, though.

His phone rang, and he dug it out of his pocket. He was almost sure his mother was again going to question why he was going on this trip. She didn't understand his summer bucket list adventures that he took every August to reset his brain for the upcoming frenzy of pilot-season scripting.

"Hey, Mom."

"Hi, Mattie." She sighed. She always seemed to be sighing when they spoke recently. "Are you getting ready for your big trip?"

"Yes, just looking at these small mountains of clothes I have to stuff in a bag the size of my pinkie."

"Well, you *are* a big boy. So what are you doing again?"

Now it was his turn to sigh. "I'm going to Alaska to hike for a week. Get some fresh air and hopefully some fresh ideas."

"I hope this doesn't have anything to do with your father. I know you've been spending more time with him." Her tongue made a little clicking sound against her palate—a true sign of skepticism she probably didn't even realize she made. He grabbed his mini notebook with the "Mom notes" section and scrawled a note about the click for the Mom character he was constantly shaping in his mind.

"Nope. Nothing to do with him, Mom. I do this every August. Remember, last year I went on that Route 66 road trip?"

"Okay, just making sure you didn't need distance from him or something, because you could always come here. It's not like he was around when we needed him. I mean, having a relationship now is beyond considerate. Beyond polite. Which is really all I think you owe him. Maybe."

"I know." He almost inserted that, since his dad got sober five years ago, he'd turned a corner and had tried to make it up to Matthew. After years of Matthew not having a father in his life, his curiosity had gotten the better of him, and he'd agreed to have dinner with him for the first time two years ago. His dad cried over his pasta at Matthew's favorite Italian place, and it was like he could feel his dad's guilt seep into his chest. The deadbeat-dad fortress he'd built up around him started to crumble in that moment, despite him thinking he'd never forgive him.

Well, he hadn't completely forgiven him.

"Can you text me from the mountain to let me know you're okay?"

"I don't know when we'll have service, but I'll text you when I can. Send you a picture."

"That's all I ask for! I love you."

His father had asked him to forgive him for destroying his childhood, and the woman who raised him just wanted a photo. He could only shake his head at the irony.

"'Kay, love you too."

He slumped down on the bed, staring at his phone. There was a text from his dad from yesterday, wishing him luck on his hiking trip. He'd told him about it last week, when he'd accompanied his dad to a doctor's appointment at the hospital.

It was the first time he'd gone with his dad to one of his appointments, and he felt uncomfortable in the narrow room with machines that looked like robots with tubelike tentacles ready to capture their unsuspecting patients. He felt like he was playing the role of dutiful son, when in reality he'd regretted agreeing to come.

"He told me a little about your past," the doctor said to Matthew after his dad had gone to the restroom. The doctor's lips pressed together, unable to say more than what was on his mind. Probably part of the oath. *Thou shalt not express one's opinions about asshole, deadbeat fathers.*

As he'd walked away, Matthew was curious exactly what his dad had told his doctor. He wanted to run after him and ask, see if it was the truth or some fairy-tale fabrication of a man down on his luck who couldn't find his way in the world. Matthew would tell him exactly how it had really gone. His father was a drunk who ruined not only his own family, but a few others as well, as he seduced other women away from their husbands and kids. Like he couldn't stop at destroying theirs; he had to destroy other families too. At least two kids had beaten Matthew up in middle school over it, and, fortunately, the summer before tenth grade, he skyrocketed to become the tallest kid in high school, and he just had to frown at someone the right way to make them run off.

But his dad had been apologizing for five years now. He'd moved to the outskirts of LA, partly to be close to Matthew, and partly to be close to good doctors. And now that they lived near each other, his dad had at least been trying to make it up to him. Not that you could make up for a person's childhood, but Matthew had to admit to himself that his dad wasn't the asshole he was fifteen years ago.

Groaning, Matthew looked at the clothes around him. Maybe this trip would be an escape from everything that hadn't been going so well. His life always seemed to be on some circular path, with August being a much-needed break where he could take off for a few weeks and do something just for him. Like a brain reset. His trips had become a habit over the past four years.

The first year he'd gone to Peru with some of his coworkers from a failed pilot, the first that he'd worked on. He'd moved to LA the year before, and during the climb up Machu Picchu, he realized how desperately he'd been craving the silence that only nature and trees and mountains could provide. Growing up in Michigan, he'd always had the lakes, the trees, and a place to be alone when he craved solitude. It was after that initial trip when he'd had his first scriptwriting success with *The Unbreakables*.

So now it was a ritual. Every August, like clockwork, he took a new trip, reset his mind, gained some clarity, and hoped that the break would inspire him like the first one had. Help him figure out a new story, a new script to pitch, amid the silence and peace. And while he had yet to find the success he was looking for, Matthew always found a new job when he returned from his trips.

◆ ◆ ◆

Matthew deplaned in Anchorage, and after exiting the airport walked outside and took a deep breath. The air was like actual oxygen, not the fifty/fifty smog/air cocktail he had to regularly breathe in Los Angeles. In fact, he hadn't realized how bad the air/smog actually was until he stood there, and with each inhale, the air felt clear, clean, and cool entering his lungs. Mountains surrounded him, and already he felt better, somehow, about life and the decision he'd made to come here. Yes, this was exactly what he'd needed to clear his head. If anything could do it, this air could.

He took an Uber to the hotel and looked around reception: a few other thick packs were strapped to people's backs or resting on the floor, like fat, overstuffed sausages of a week's survival. He checked in and climbed up to his room and took a hot shower, relishing it and taking his time, knowing it was the last one he'd get for a while. As he emerged from the steam, his phone rang, the familiar warning beep of FaceTime. There was only one person who called him on FaceTime.

He picked up the phone, towel slung around his waist, and deliberated for a moment before answering. It was like when he'd boarded the plane in LA, that world had disappeared, and he'd taken conscious steps upon arrival in Alaska to wash it completely off. Now his father was here on his phone like an additional oily layer of guilt and distaste shimmering in a ghastly way all over his clean slate. But he wasn't going to talk to him for at least a week. He might as well answer and get it over with. It was his vacation tax.

"Hi, Dad." The word *Dad* still felt weird coming off his lips, like it was something between a curse and a royal title for someone who'd cheated his way to the throne. But his father looked better than the last time he'd seen him.

"Hi, Matt." Funny how neither of his parents called him Matthew. When they'd started speaking again a few years ago, his dad had assumed he went by Matt, since that was what his dad preferred to be called, and Matthew had internally grimaced but never bothered correcting him. Probably because he assumed his father would leave again, just like he did when he was twelve. "I was lying here thinking about your big trip this week."

"Yeah, I'm in Anchorage now. The hike starts in the morning." He rubbed at his jawline, which was becoming a new habit. The speed at which his face had raced toward beardom was alarming.

"I hope you have a good time, and watch out for bears. I just saw in the news some guy in Canada got killed by one."

"Okay, thanks. Nothing like a tale of a bear mauling to kick off a hike."

"He was trying to feed it a fish or something. So don't do that."

"I can assure you I won't. We only feed bears honey on hikes. And only bears named Pooh."

"Mmhmm." His dad nodded slowly as if he was deciding whether Matthew was trying to be funny or make fun of him. His dad's face held on to an expression that was familiar from when he was a kid. Eyebrows hunched down in thought, his bottom lip falling just a bit. Normally Matthew recollected his dad making this face when he was hungover, too tired to be at one of the extreme ends of his personality, Mr. Angry or Mr. Party.

But then the expression disappeared, like his dad could read his thoughts and needed to banish the memory as well. "The good news is that there are only approximately three human deaths caused by bears each year in the US."

"That's reassuring," Matthew said, muting the TV and flipping through the channels.

"You wouldn't believe the animal that's responsible for the most deaths each year."

"What is it? Sharks?" He'd landed on an advertisement for *Shark Week*, coincidentally.

"The mosquito. But that's worldwide. Not just here."

"Huh. I guess that makes sense." A random fact that would be useless in Alaska, but that was his dad.

"Okay. Well, I'll let you go. I just wanted to say hello. Be safe."

"I will, thanks. Bye."

As Matthew's thumb hit the end button on the phone, his dad said, "I love—" but it was too late. Now what was he supposed to do? Text him an apology for hanging up on him? Plus, it wasn't like he wanted to say it back. He'd probably avoided making it more awkward, like he'd have to grunt something vague or launch into an explanation how he wasn't ready for the L word.

Matthew wanted to believe his dad had changed and realized the error of his ways, meaning really the error of his life, but at the same time, how could someone be the definition of a deadbeat dad for so long and then want to be an advice-giving, caring, loving father?

He lay back in bed and ordered a burger from room service, then flipped through the channels before giving up and going through his mini notebook, searching for some spark of an idea that might inspire him at the start of this trip. He did his best work after a good night's sleep, right before dawn, when it was peaceful and quiet and his nighttime subconscious could do its work. He'd had his favorite show ideas in those moments. Even though they'd be hiking for hours each day, he'd been assured they would have plenty of downtime to just enjoy the scenery. Time early in the morning to relax and have coffee and think about the day.

He just had to hope that his tentmate didn't snore.

CHAPTER 4

Bernie trudged along, with her pack on her back, and pressed the button on the elevator. As she waited, she examined her reflection in the mirror in the hall. She'd put her hair in twin braids over each shoulder, hoping that would keep it from tangling over the next week. And she wore her tinted sunscreen and pink-hued lip balm—more sunscreen— so she felt like she was ready for the full sunny days ahead.

She peered down the two flights of stairs to the lobby, where a handful of people with backpacks stood around talking. It must be her group. She didn't need to wait for an elevator anyway. She was going to be walking for eight miles a day. Might as well start now. She trudged over to the stairs and gingerly crept down one at a time, worried that if she tilted forward just a little too much, she'd fall face first, her hefty pack overpowering her and somersaulting her to a sad, tragic end. Her mother would never forgive herself for buying the Groupon of Doom.

Three steps from the bottom, almost successful! Then her foot missed the edge of the next stair, and she clutched onto the rail with both hands, trying to hold herself up. But the weight of her pack was too much. She slid backward down the steps, juggling the remaining stairs with her feet, but she couldn't get a grip, even with these stupid boots that Duke, Tabitha's boyfriend, a rabid outdoor enthusiast, had sworn would hold on to anything. She shrieked and landed on her back. Well, her backpack.

This was not what she had been imagining as a fresh start with her open mind. She cursed the boots that didn't allow her ankles to flex even at a natural angle so she couldn't get her footing on the stairs. Cursed the pack that weighed her down, even though it seemed like nothing was in it. She was stuck on her back like one of those poor summer beetles, legs flailing on the sidewalk, unable to flip over, dooming themselves to a pathetic, embarrassing death. She would definitely help one of them next time she saw one.

Footsteps ran from behind her, and a scruffy blond guy leaned over her, laughing. Laughing? "Looks like you need help." He held out his hand, and she grabbed onto it, only because her backpack was over a foot deep and she didn't want to face-plant on the hard floor if she twisted herself over.

He hefted her up like she and her backpack were made of air. "Thank you. I slipped." She shrugged off the pack and decided to drag it around until she absolutely had to wear it again, the traitor. This was what being open to change got you. She could practically hear Great-Aunt Bernice mocking her from the beyond.

"Are you with the Trail Adventures group?" he asked, this man who was small and lithe and looked like he should only be able to pick up a feather.

"Yes, I'm Bernie."

"Bernie?" He had a little squinting look of concern as his face scrunched up. "I thought you were a guy." Bernie's mouth had opened to ask why exactly he thought she was a guy when he continued. "I mean, when I saw your name on the guest list."

"It's short for Bernice."

"I see. Well, that makes sense. I'm Trevor, one of the guides. And that's my partner, Sheila, another guide." He pointed at a woman adjusting the pack on a guy a foot taller than her. "We can help fix your pack so it doesn't offset your balance." He patted it like it was a loyal dog at her side.

"This must be the rest of the group?" She looked around at the people in the small crowd, a few of them applauding as Bernie walked toward them. One of the women shrugged and laughed. "Hey, someone had to take a nosedive first."

Bernie made a conscious effort to swallow her embarrassment and took a small bow. "Happy to provide your entertainment for the morning. For my lunchtime performance I'll be eating my pride." At least that got a few laughs out of the group.

"So I think that's everyone." Trevor clapped his hands together. "We're going to use this meeting room over here for a brief orientation, if you want to follow me." He walked over and whispered something to Sheila, who in turn gave Bernie a look with her eyebrows raised.

What she'd done hadn't been so horrific that she deserved raised-eyebrow stares. They were like the opposite of Tabitha's dipped-chin looks but meant the same thing. An expression that was on the *Really? Seriously? I can't believe this!* spectrum.

Did she look like she didn't fit in with the others as much as she felt that on the inside? She glanced down at her outfit, which was basically the same as everyone else's. Tabitha and Duke had taken her to REI, outfitted her, and given her instructions on how to break in her hiking boots in a week (which had involved some very disastrous outfits and multiple eye-rolling comments at work), and now she looked like everyone else with their weird waterproof clothes and layers. So why would Sheila stare at her like that?

She filed behind the crowd and, as she took a chair, realized that she was in a world of couples. She knew this world. There were Sheila and Trevor, with their whispering and shared looks. Couple. The woman who'd shrugged at her and another woman with her, their heads bent together, smiling. Couple. A beardy man and a ruddy-cheeked woman who looked like they'd just come off another hike, in matching polar fleece vests. Definitely a couple. An older woman who looked like she could be her mom's doppelgänger and a man with tiny round spectacles who smiled at her with that deep love stare. Bernie's heart did a little fluttery thing just at the sight of them; they were adorable. All she wanted in life was a man who could look at her like this man looked at his partner. Was that so much to ask?

And then to her left was one other man. Ostensibly single like her. Two lone singles in a horde of couples. He was the tall guy, with dark hair and a beard, who'd had Sheila adjusting his pack. Two single omens. Reminders to the couples of what could happen to them if they broke up and were forced on lone vacations.

This was her uncomfortable comfort space. She was constantly around her coupled-off friends, and there always seemed to be one single dude, too, milling around, the leftovers of someone's broken relationship. Like a token offering to Bernie's assumed loveless heart. Once, even her friend Deb had brought her ex to a party and practically threw him at Bernie's feet, saying, "It didn't work out with us, but I think you're perfect for each other." So awkward. Deb pranced away and the guy said, "It's literally been three days. She kind of broke my heart."

Bernie sighed, remembering how they'd gotten drunk together while exchanging dating horror stories. This new plaid-shirt guy looked at her. She hadn't realized she'd been staring at him still, and she jerked her eyes back to Trevor.

"First of all, welcome, everyone!" Trevor said in a voice that made her wonder how much coffee he'd consumed that morning already. "Sheila and I are so happy to have the privilege of showing you our beautiful state of Alaska, and specifically Denali. There are so many gorgeous things we're going to see over the next week as we hike through icy rivers, traipse through the greenest grass you've ever seen, walk through our glorious summer tundra, and take in the mountains. And glaciers! It's just so exciting. I can't wait."

Bernie was still blinking herself into reality at the phrase "hike through icy rivers." What waterproof pants would protect her from icy rivers?

"As you know, we've got equipment for you that we'll pack together this morning. We have your tents and tarps." He bent down and held up a tent. "We've got your bear cans." He gestured to a plastic canister and opened the lid, showing food stacked inside it. "This is how we'll carry our food throughout the trip. It's called a bear can for a reason." He laughed, along with everyone else except Bernie. Because bears! "And we've got all the cooking equipment and utensils, which we'll distribute evenly."

The traitorous backpack propped up against the chair had room in it. She'd read the instructions, she knew that she needed space, but eyeing all that stuff next to him made her wonder if she'd really packed too much after all. She'd tried to adhere to their strict packing guidelines, which, aside from outerwear, amounted to two shirts, two pants, four pairs of socks, and four pairs of underwear. Although to be fair, that was one thing she just couldn't get on board with, so she'd packed two more T-shirts and socks. And extra underwear. The smallest she had.

She raised her hand. "Excuse me, Trevor. What if we don't have enough room in our packs for all that?"

Trevor clasped his hands in front of him. "Well, that brings me to my next point. Thanks, Bernie. You'll be sharing the load with your tentmate."

Tentmate? Bernie looked around at her traveling companions again, none of whom seemed to be surprised at all by this news, until her eyes locked with tall, dark, and barely beardy. They both pulled a Sheila and raised their eyebrows at the same time as he, like Bernie, seemed to take in the reality of their tentmate situation.

Sheila appeared at Bernie's side. "Bernie, meet Matthew. Um, so this is a little awkward, but I hope neither of you mind . . . Bernie, we thought you were a guy so didn't think there would be issues bunking with Matthew."

"Oh." So that's why Trevor had so pointedly said he'd thought she was a boy. The one time her mother actually used her preferred name to sign her up for this trip—this was what happened. Not that she should be surprised. It was just another unfortunate facet of being deemed a Bernice. When she was a kid, it was getting teased that she had a ninety-year-old grandmother's name. Or being a girl who could never get any crappy keychains or magnets with her name on a rainbow or a state outline. So she'd changed it to Bernie. And now everyone thought she was a man. Which normally didn't matter, until now.

But how bad could it be? She assessed the situation. Apparently they wouldn't be changing clothes often, so not too much risk of a strip show. They had individual sleeping bags, so they wouldn't have to cuddle up on a bed together. He didn't look especially thrilled, either, so he probably wasn't planning on molesting her in her sleep. Besides, Duke had made her take his camping knife, which she'd laughed at, but now maybe it made her feel a little better. Just in case.

"So, is there any way we can get another tent?" her new tentmate Matthew asked, without even acknowledging Bernie's presence next to him.

Bernie's eyes darted toward him. For some reason, she felt offended by his comment. Like, did she look like she was going to force him into some kind of wild Alaskan rapture while hiking and not being able to bathe? (The answer was no.)

Sheila stretched out her lips in that look that's best described as an unfortunate smile. That look that says, *Oh, aren't you funny?* and *Bless your heart* all at once. "No, we only have the ones we have. Sorry!"

Bernie nodded slowly, and Matthew rolled his eyes.

As Bernie turned to tell Matthew in mutual commiseration that yes, this was awkward, but she'd get over it, they were both adults, and that it was nice to meet him, he spoke instead. "You don't snore, do you?"

"What?" She shook her head. That was the last thing she'd thought of. "No. Do you?"

"No."

"Okay." So much for getting to know each other like normal people. It already felt like they were fighting, and they'd barely spoken. Here was more proof that men were a special breed of inanity. And everyone wondered why she was single.

"Okay."

Sheila's head volleyed between the two of them. "So it's okay?" Before either could answer, she said, "Great! I'll grab your stuff." She pushed herself up and walked to the front of the room to the pile of things.

Bernie didn't know what to say. The feeling filling her up at the moment was like wiggling in an uncomfortable chair. No matter how she shifted and slid around, she couldn't find any way to sit with herself to get comfortable. Or sit near him, apparently. Out of the corner of her eye, she saw him look straight ahead, watching Sheila.

"So how 'bout those bear cans?" Bernie said to him, trying to break the ice with a joke.

He opened his pack, seeming to evaluate how much room was inside. "They'll definitely be useful when we see a bear. The last thing you want is for a bear to smell your food. Bears don't attack humans if they just see them, but if they smell their food or get a taste of it, that's when it goes downhill."

"Oh, okay . . ." Well, there was breaking the ice, and then there was getting a serious diatribe on bear-related food safety. Lighten up maybe? Get a sense of humor perhaps?

"Have you ever been on a hike like this before?" he asked.

"Um, no. I've actually never been hiking really. But I walk a lot, so I'm sure it's kind of the same."

He laughed, but it was one of those dismissive laughs that Bernie's older know-it-all cousin had given her way too many times when she'd been a kid. Like when her cousin had asked Bernie to describe what she thought a hand job was. The kind of laugh that turned into a sigh and basically meant, *Oh, you poor, poor, naive little girl.* A thought that probably echoed Matthew's thinking at this very moment.

"I hope you broke in your boots at least." There was something about the way he talked that made everything sound like a lecture.

"I did." At least she thought she had. She'd gotten in a good five miles in them over the last four days, and her toes were a little sore but not unbearable. Anyway, she wasn't going to give this know-it-all any satisfaction that she might not be completely prepared.

"Well, that's good. I'm going to help Trevor." He popped up out of his seat, and Bernie had to wonder if he was trying to escape her presence already. Trying to distance himself from the tentmate who'd never been hiking and potentially had foreseeable boot issues. Distance himself from the awkwardness of the two of them sharing a tent. It was like he could see through her already.

This was going to be a long week.

CHAPTER 5

Matthew should have known that this trip was not going to go as planned. That his restful week of peace and reflection would be upended by the one person in the group who looked like a picture-perfect example of the game, "Which one of these things does not belong with the others?" Not only was Bernie the only person who didn't know how to operate a backpack, but she clearly had makeup on, had done her hair that morning, sported brand-new hiking boots and new clothes, and had never been hiking before. How was that even possible?

And what was more impossible was that he was going to be her tentmate.

It took him back to the last time he'd gone camping with his ex, Veronica. A weekend that had ended their relationship. A weekend that felt like she was trying to emphasize her helplessness on all things nature. Matthew had grown up camping, and every summer, his mom had sent him to Scouts camp. He realized not everyone had this experience, or luxury, and he'd been patient. Even though Veronica had insisted she wanted to go, everything had been accompanied by a whine or remark on how there was dirt everywhere. She screamed when she saw a bug. It was camping, he'd explained over and over. After the first night, she'd made him take her home. As a struggling actress, she'd embraced the role of "silly girlfriend in the woods." He couldn't take it anymore.

He looked over at Bernie as Sheila tried to fit the tent in her pack. Her pert little nose scrunched up in confusion, and she had lip gloss on her frustrated pout, shimmering from the overhead lights. No one should have lips that shiny when they were hiking. He could see how she might be one of those people who was doing this for the Instagram story. She shook her head at Sheila as she tried to explain something. This was going to be him. Constantly explaining to her for a week. He sensed the remnants of frustration remaining from the Veronica trip creeping up into his shoulders.

Maybe, if anything, this trip would give him new perspective on patience and forgiveness and would provide inspiration for a new script. Because the thing was, this situation was a comedy gold mine. If it were happening to anyone else other than him. A big if.

"Matt, were you able to pack the bear can?" Bernie called over to him.

"I go by Matthew." He wanted to get that straight first.

"Okay, *Matthew*." He swore she rolled her eyes. "Did you pack the bear can?"

"Yes. I've packed the bear can, the tarp, and the toilet supplies. Can you not fit the tent in your pack?" He walked over to where they squatted down next to the pack. Something made from lace peeked out the top. He swallowed and tried not to stare at it. How was that camping appropriate?

"I think we'll get it," Sheila huffed, her arm deep in the pack. Then, as if reconciled to the fact that the overpacking might win, she rested back on her heels. "Actually, I think we'll need to reorganize. Matthew, you pack the tent, and then Bernie, you take the bear can. You can strap it to the outside."

He sighed and unpacked the bear can and thunked it down next to Bernie. The tent slid in the spot of his bag effortlessly.

"See? Perfect." Sheila left them, and Matthew wondered if she dealt with types like Bernie all the time and had cultivated a perfect veil of calm despite the adversity of nonhikers.

Bernie hefted her bag up with the can attached to the outside with a carabiner and groaned. "Oh my God. So heavy."

"Your back can take more than you think it can."

"Let's hope so. I don't want to risk face-planting again, especially in the bed of an icy river."

Matthew tried to contain his laughter, because he could already see it happening.

"So, my tentmate, Matthew, where are you from?"

"LA."

"Oh." Her head sort of retracted in her neck. "I thought you were like from Montana or Idaho."

"Why?" This would be good.

"You just don't seem like an LA person."

"Do you know a lot of LA people?" he asked.

"My manager is from LA."

That was one person. "Where do you work?"

"At a clothing company."

"That makes so much sense."

"Why?" Her face scrunched up in confusion, as if she really didn't know what he meant.

"Because . . ." He gestured up and down, unable to put the words together. "It just all makes sense now."

"Because I have clothes on? Yeah, so does everyone. We're not vacationing at a nudist colony."

"But they're all so matchy-matchy."

"You mean because I appreciate the principles of the color wheel so I don't look like shit? Oh, okay." She raised her eyebrows and studied what he was wearing.

He looked down at his clothes. What was she trying to say? The clothes he had on were functional and worn and comfortable. He'd had to put a lot of thought into the minimalist items he could pack. "I don't look like shit."

"I didn't say that."

"Yeah, but you insinuated it."

She squinted at him and shook her head like *he* was the one who baffled her. "How? I was talking about me."

"With your eyes."

"Oh my God." She pinched the bridge of her nose and muttered something under her breath that sounded like "fucking Groupon."

Sheila clapped in front of the room. "Okay, everyone. Packs are packed!" The group cheered, except for the two of them. "Now we're ready to get in the van and go to the trailhead. Last call for toilets!"

Bernie groaned beside him.

Trailhead. It hit Matthew just then. They hadn't even started.

CHAPTER 6

Bernie fortunately found a seat in the van next to Shalini and Diana, whom she'd been eyeing ever since she'd found out about Matthew being her tentmate. Yes, it was probably inappropriate to ask two other women who were obviously a couple if she could crash in their tent, but in the brief time she'd been around him, she could tell this was just not going to work.

She always hated it when people asked her what she did for a living—like where she worked or what job she had solidified her identity—rather than asking what she was into, or what made her excited about life. She resisted informing Matthew that she had not been a fashion major in college or anything but in fact did marketing analysis. With data.

And now Matthew had been added to Bernie's data points as someone definitely in the bottom-left quadrant of any X-Y matrix she'd ever examined.

"So where are you two from?" Bernie asked after they'd made introductions.

"We live outside Seattle," Diana said.

"Oh, cool! I live in Portland." This was looking good. They were practically neighbors. Maybe these two constantly grinning ladies would take her on as a pity case.

"Well, technically we live on one of the islands outside Seattle. We just bought a house there."

"How amazing to live on an island!" Bernie said. "I bet it's just so chilled out there."

"It is. We have a lot of change going on, so this is a sort of celebration," Shalini said, and Diana elbowed her.

"This hike?" Bernie said, thinking of not only her attempts at changing to be more open minded but also the commitment of hiking being a way to celebrate anything. Maybe being released from solitary confinement so you can feel free in the wilderness and big open spaces.

"Well, what came before this hike." Diana held up her left hand to show a glimmering diamond ring. "This is our honeymoon."

"Oh! Congratulations! That's awesome." She gave them a big smile. Well, that attempt at tent crashing was a fail. No way was she going to ask a couple on their honeymoon if she could sleep with them.

They chatted with Bernie about their first hike together, on Mount Rainier, and reassured her, just like everyone else had, that they would all be stinky and dirty and no one would care. The beauty and the peace would make up for it. That it really would cause you to look deep inside and just realize how big the world was. Then the van stopped.

"We're here!" Trevor said, sounding way too excited. "Say goodbye to wheels. We won't see this van until Saturday, when it'll take us to our hotel for the last night."

Bernie practically salivated at the idea of a hotel, and she hadn't even camped one night. It wasn't so much the idea of camping. It was more about camping with Matthew. She turned around; he was two rows behind her, chatting it up with the older couple who looked deeply in love. The couple laughed at something he'd said. They all seemed to be getting along just fine, while Bernie and he were at odds. Mr. Serious. Mr. No Sense of Humor. Mr. Let Me Educate You.

Maybe he was going to ask them if he could stay in their tent, much like Bernie had wanted to do with her new friends. He could pretend like he was their adopted son, snuggling in between them and helping keep them warm on the chilly nights. Maybe he was working out a barter system, like he'd carry their tent and bear can for them in exchange for a cozy spot for one.

Their eyes locked, and Bernie twisted back around fast. Her face felt hot and her heart was racing, like she'd been busted. But for what? Now she felt like she needed to explain why she was looking at him, but how could she explain it? That she was merely examining his potential to seduce this older couple by acting like their son? That wouldn't be an awkward thing to say at all. Did she really want to make it more uncomfortable than it already was?

She flowed out of the van with everyone else and put her palm against the side of it, wishing it well and a speedy return to pick them up in a week's time. She grabbed her pack off the ground, strapped it on in all the right places like Sheila had shown her, and joined the group.

It was a beautiful day. The sun was out, and the grass on the hills around them was dotted with tiny flowers. It wasn't at all what she'd imagined Alaska would look like. The mountains with trickles of snow in the distance, the blue sky, and the warmth of sunshine on a slightly cool day were all perfect. Nothing like the gray and white and cold she'd imagined when her mom had announced the surprise Groupon to Alaska.

"Okay, now that we're packed and ready to go, we need to go over some bear-safety rules. Bears don't usually bother humans, unless we surprise them. Or have food, hence the bear cans. So we're going to be extra conscious when we walk through trees or scrub brush to make a lot of noise. So when you hear me say, 'Bear noise,' I want everyone to go like this." Then Trevor shouted some loud nonsensical words like an adult baby learning how to talk.

He quieted down and clapped. "Okay, now everyone try it. Bear noise!"

Everyone started their goo goo gah gah bawl, and as a group they sounded like zombies approaching a crowd of humans, hungry for brains. Bernie laughed. Bears, people, everything would run.

"Bernie, everyone has to do it," Sheila said.

She nodded and joined in, although she felt ridiculous. Maybe if she had some torn clothes and fake blood dripping from her mouth like an actual zombie, it would feel more natural. She couldn't help but yell out, "Brains!" in the midst of all the babble.

"Okay, gang, that's great." Trevor applauded and everyone laughed. "The next thing is, if you actually see a bear, you have to do something like this." He zipped up his posture and held his arms straight over his head and made his legs stiff and started to walk like Frankenstein's monster. "Now you all try. You want to make yourselves as big as possible so they don't look at you like you're food."

Everyone held up their arms and walked, and Bernie took a deep breath and followed suit. She looked over at Matthew, who really didn't need to make himself much bigger because he was already gargantuan. He got into character and seemed to be adding a roar onto his bear walk. Based on what he'd told Bernie earlier, she was sure he had some specific bear techniques he was just dying to put into action.

"Good. Great job, everyone. You've all really found your inner bears," Sheila said. "Now, who's ready to start our hike?"

Bernie looked around as everyone cheered. Except for her.

CHAPTER 7

Peace and quiet and time for reflection in America's majestic natural wonders. That was what had drawn Matthew to the brochure for this specific hiking trip. He probably should have just planned a trip on his own. Although he knew that wasn't always the safest. Denali had been on his bucket list of places to hike, and hiking alone was just ripe for some kind of horror story. Ice that gave way. A hungry wolf pack that sniffed you out. An accidental slip that turned into a broken leg, and you couldn't make it to the end as fast as you should have and ran out of food. Not enough warning or manpower to scare off a bear. Plus, he'd seen that movie where the guy had to cut off his own arm after getting stuck in a rock crevice.

Maybe the chatter would die down. But right now, the crowd around him was a cacophony of getting-to-know-you's and playing six degrees of separation with anything people had in common. Harold and Becky, the older couple he'd sat with in the van, seemed nice, and they were the kind of people he'd expected on this trip. They both had that patient, slow way of talking that made even a story of choosing bread at the grocery store sound like it was a high-stakes event that deserved careful unraveling. It reminded him of his grandfather telling tales over the dinner table when he'd been alive. These two had recently retired in Arizona, and they had a passion for driving their RV around the country, exploring the national parks along the way. Matthew tried to fathom driving an RV from Arizona to Alaska, as they had just spent the last month doing, but couldn't, since he could hardly bear his daily commute back home.

Right in front of him, though, was Bernie and the couple in the matching turquoise vests, and she was hamming it up with them, laughing and hooting at something the man had said. He shouldn't be surprised; they had all clearly shopped purposefully for this trip. She'd found her camp-fashion soul mates. God help him if he ever shopped for matching clothes with a woman.

Well, his peace, quiet, and reflection would have to wait. He lingered toward the back of the crowd to try to catch a whiff of what a lone hike might have felt like. The color of the grass was a spectrum of green. Bright and electric chartreuse, dark shadows of British racing green, movement in the wind that blew a hue almost turquoise into the blades of grass. It was knee high and soft and waved in the breeze that coasted around the mountains.

Specks of tiny pink flowers clustered in spots like little bursts of contrasting color. Larger, almost purplish flowers that came up as high as his thigh topped the grass on occasion like spindles. The mountains around them in the distance were almost periwinkle and had ribbons of white snow in the long slender crevices. So long and deep he imagined what it would be like to get a sled and just slide down them. It was moments like this, the beauty of this natural world, that people rarely got to see. Most people never got the chance to witness it because they didn't leave the city or they lay around like sloths, watching the stupid shows he'd been writing.

Where it was untouched by humans, by industry, by pollution— that was where he could really marvel at nature. It was moments like this when he could see the evidence of something truly divine, some greater being that had constructed this palette of contrasting hues using a giant crayon box to color this world around them.

"How's my tentmate doing?" The voice from the right caught him off guard. He hadn't realized that Bernie had slowed down and fallen back from the rest of the group.

"Just admiring the view," he said.

"It's really pretty. Reminds me of my mom's farm."

He stopped walking and looked at her again. She seemed sincere as she looked around at the scenery and then back at him. He couldn't imagine any farm mimicking the splendor of an Alaskan summer. Or maybe this was the only comparison to the outdoors she had to work with. This, and a farm.

"What?" she asked, squinting at him.

"Nothing." He shook his head and kept walking. This woman clearly thought anything green looked like a farm. She was a city girl through and through.

"You looked at me like I just told you I was going to tie you up with all that toilet paper in your backpack."

He stifled a laugh. That was unexpected.

"Oh my God, he almost laughed!" She threw up her arms and shouted it, although no one was around to listen.

"We should catch up with the rest of the group," he said.

"Why? Are you really worried I might try it? I did hold the record in seventh grade for most expansive and thorough house TPing."

"I don't doubt it."

"There was a mansion near my friend's house, and I wrapped it up like a Christmas present at the mere age of thirteen. Think about what I could accomplish now. That house was almost as big as you."

"If you're trying to intimidate me with your tales of toilet paper mastery, it's definitely working, but mostly because I'm worried you'll waste all the toilet paper we have."

"Speaking of which, you know as a woman, I do probably need the majority of the toilet paper. I say we do an eighty/twenty split."

Matthew opened his mouth to protest. No way was she taking all the toilet paper. "Guys need toilet paper too. I mean, how much are you planning on peeing? You'll probably sweat most of it out."

She groaned. "Don't remind me. My four shirts are already crying out for help."

"Four shirts? You were only supposed to bring two." He stopped walking. "Wait, is that why you don't have room for our stuff in your pack? Because you overpacked? I thought you were just inefficient."

"Wow. Please stop with all your compliments. I just can't handle the kind generosity you're giving to me, a mere stranger. They're half the size of yours anyway, so it evens out." Bernie huffed out that little coughing sound he was too familiar with when women were pissed. It punctuated sarcasm like an irritated exclamation mark. She sped up and walked toward the rest of the group, which was now a good five hundred feet ahead of them.

She could be angry with him, fine, but what he'd said was true. She'd packed double the amount of shirts in the packing list. They had to share. She could have mentioned it earlier, and they could have worked out a system or something instead of her just not having enough room.

Maybe he could build his own tent out of the toilet paper.

CHAPTER 8

That was the last time Bernie was going to try to build a bridge between her and Matthew. *Maybe we got off on the wrong foot. Maybe it's as awkward for him as it is for me. Maybe I should make the first move.*

Well, that move was the wrong move. Matthew was an asshole. He'd distanced himself from everyone and had already insulted her, and it was just day one.

Maybe he thought he was better than her, and everyone else. Just because he had clothes and gear that had been broken in and he looked like an overgrown Boy Scout did not mean he could treat her like that. This idea of being open to change was not doing her any favors. It was failing her on this trip. It was failing her with Matthew. And it was failing her with this bear can, which flopped from side to side on her pack and wouldn't stay in the same place. She'd tried to shift it, tie it down with what she had, but it refused to be tamed and continued to bounce around in the most annoying way.

She caught up with the polar fleece twins, Gretchen and Jay.

"Hey, guys," she called out breathlessly after chasing them through thigh-high weeds. If they'd been on her mother's farm, her mom would have asked Bernie to hack them all down, except the bright-fuchsia fireweed. "Gretchen, can you unhook this stupid bear can off my pack?"

"Sure." She sounded surprised but took it off. "You need something out of it?"

"No, I'm just going to carry it. It's driving me crazy."

"Ooh, are you sure?" Jay asked, his lips curled in an exaggerated frown. He had one of those voices that always sounded like he was concerned. "It will probably make your arm sore."

"I'll be fine. It's just for a few more hours, right?"

"Yeah, we have a few hours till we set up camp, I think." Gretchen handed her the plastic tub holding Bernie's and Matthew's food. Gretchen had one of those voices too. They were from Minnesota, and that was when Bernie realized that it wasn't concern, necessarily; it was just the way they pronounced their vowels. She liked it. If she ever needed a respite from Matthew and wanted to feel like someone was consoling her, she'd just hang out with them.

"It's not really heavy." Bernie tried to prove to Jay she could carry it by bouncing it up and down a few times. "I'll be fine. Anything's better than it hitting my arms with every other step."

She walked along with the two of them for a while, chatting about their backpacking trip up Mount Kilimanjaro last year, their trip in the Himalayas a few years before that. It was becoming increasingly clear that not only was Bernie with a whole horde of hiking enthusiasts but also that she was feeling more and more like a third wheel as she forced herself onto these coupled pairs. The one feeling she'd thought she would escape on this trip was sneaking up on her. She was used to being the odd woman out in Portland, but she didn't expect it on vacation. But the alternative was either walking alone or walking with Matthew.

She turned around and saw his tall figure a hundred feet behind her. He seemed to be taking his steps easily, like he was strolling through a forest instead of four-foot-tall weeds. He'd come all alone on this trip as well. Clearly no woman could bear to be around him. Even though he was classically attractive, with his dark, messy hair that he kept running a hand through every time they were talking, his interestingly curved lips, and eyes so dark they were almost black and that seemed to be staring a hole in her head when he looked at her. Maybe he was just interesting looking. If he had a personality to match it, he'd be a nine. But being an asshole brought the hotness score much lower, like maybe by eight points. A definite one.

Right now, she'd much rather be with her mom on the farm, even with their clashes. Or taking one of those DIY classes Deb dragged her to every other month. Maybe even finally prepping her house for real estate photos, like Tabitha was probably doing at this very moment. A little weepiness inside her slowed her pace as she realized the group tour was more of a lone journey. Being alone in a crowd made you actually feel alone, whereas if you were alone by yourself, you were just you.

She snuggled the bear can in her left arm like a baby, a literal food baby, and pulled out her phone to text Tabitha, her mom, anyone, but it just said "No service." She should have expected this. She'd been told there wouldn't be service, but that didn't make her hope any less for it.

Two hours later, she reached everyone else at a clearing, where half the group was setting up tents and the other half was sitting around, relaxing on the few large rocks that jutted up from the earth. The grass was lower here, with occasional stalks of weeds sprouting up, and the hills nearby had tiny hats of snow just on the tips. A stream ran in between the hills and the campsite, but there weren't any trees nearby and she really had to pee.

Sheila was setting up her tent with Trevor. Bernie dropped her pack and bear can and ran over after stretching out her shoulders, realizing how good it felt not to be wearing it. "Hey, Sheila."

She turned around midpole and smiled. "Hi, Bernie, how's it going?"

"Good." She squatted down to get close to whisper in her ear. "Where are we supposed to use the bathroom?"

"Oh! Number one or number two?"

Bernie was so taken aback by the question that she paused and debated whether to answer in a toddler voice. "Um, just one."

"Well, I would walk over in those tall weeds, kind of where we came in, but you know, watch where you step."

She almost asked why but resisted. She could assume that the answer to the question would be, "Because the last group, or someone from this group, could have gone number two and didn't bury it like they're supposed to."

She got as far away as she could so that the rest of the campers were just sticks and shadows to make sure no one could see. She found a nice empty spot amid a circle of weeds and tried not to think what a perfect place it was to use the bathroom that probably everyone went here. She was keeping an open mind and not worrying too much about her pee, everyone else's pee, the insects that were milling around, and where she would bury the used toilet paper if she opted to use it.

She squatted and watched the group, just to make sure no one was turning around or coming toward her. But that was when she heard the rustle behind her.

"Uh . . . whoa!"

Bernie gasped and stood up while pulling her pants up in record speed. "What are you doing?" She turned her head around and glared at Matthew, who was shielding his eyes weakly with his hand.

"I was joining camp! Why are you peeing on the trail?"

"I'm not on the trail. Sheila told me to come here."

"No, Bernie. This is the trail."

Her gaze followed the tents to where Matthew stood and then to where she had squatted. The perfect little place she'd found had less grass because it was indeed the place she'd walked through; she'd just entered it from a different angle.

"Oh my God. Could you just . . ." She waved her arm in front of her so he would go and not make eye contact with him again.

"Yeah, yeah . . ." He scurried past her. She felt sick. What had he seen? How much had her shirt covered?

When he was finally at camp, she started on her way back, to give them ample walking distance. Not that she could forget what had happened, and not that five minutes would matter. There was no way this could get worse.

She looked back toward the trail they'd come in on. If she just took off running, could she make it back to the drop-off point and cell service and Uber someone to come get her?

CHAPTER 9

Matthew had the tarp down for the tent when Bernie joined him at camp. He felt bad; there was no other way to explain it. He could tell she was embarrassed, but he couldn't have helped seeing her. She was literally right in his path. As soon as he saw the bright jacket and the butt hanging below it, he'd said something. Well, almost as soon as he saw it. It had taken a minute to register what was happening.

"How can I help?" she asked, her voice flatter than normal. She stood there looking at the poles and the tent around him, but definitely not *at* him.

Might as well just confront the situation head-on. "Hey, don't worry about it," he said. "I'm sure you'll see my butt at some point on this trip too."

"Oh my God. You saw my butt?" She was definitely looking at him now, her eyes big and shocked, staring in disbelief.

"Well, I mean yeah." Maybe it was better to just lie about it, from the look on her face. "No, not really."

She groaned and crumbled on the tarp, like her body just sort of fell. "I thought my shirt was covering it."

"Look, Bernie, this is camping. It's awkward and close, and you get down to nature in a lot of ways. Like using the bathroom in the woods and seeing things you wouldn't normally see. No one thinks anything about it. You can ask any of them." He gestured to the rest of the campers.

"I'm not asking anyone about it. I don't want anyone to know."

"Well, look, *I* don't care, okay? Let's just put the tent up."

She sighed and looked at him with some mix of sheepishness and suspicion. "Okay." Her voice was quiet, which made him feel worse about it. Maybe he should cut her some slack.

He laid the tent out on the tarp and grabbed a pole and started pushing it through. "You can take a pole too."

She picked up a pole and jabbed it through one of the holes on the other side of the tent. It flew through the sheer material and narrowly missed Matthew's eye by two inches.

"Whoa! Be careful where you're sticking that thing." Okay, so the option to cut her some slack was not the best one. She clearly needed help and guidance and careful observation.

Bernie looked up, her eyes soft. He should be the one upset, not her.

"I don't want to lose an eye on this trip," he said.

She nodded. "Sorry," she said in a creaky low voice.

She couldn't be this upset about him seeing her pee. "Look, if it makes you feel better, I'll take my pants down right now and bend over so you can see my ass."

"What?" She choked on the word.

"Just so we're even. To make you feel better."

She laughed, which at least wasn't a sob. "That would not make me feel better. But thank you for the offer."

"Okay, just let me know. It's up for grabs."

"Your ass is up for grabs?" she asked in joking disbelief, sliding the next pole in a much gentler fashion.

"Well, yes, I suppose on all accounts it is." His girlfriend was no longer his girlfriend. No one since had claimed his ass. "Okay, let's get the spikes down."

After he'd put his in, he came around to her side to secure them, but they were already in, the hooks flush with the ground. "Oh, you're done?"

"Not all of this is completely lost on me." She stood with her hands on her hips, admiring her work. She had a streak of dirt across her forehead. Dare he point it out? He decided no, since she was still reeling from her self-conscious squat on the trail.

In the middle of the tents, Trevor had started a fire, and Sheila was cooking something in a pot.

"Dinnertime!" Matthew was starving. He'd eaten one of the extra protein bars he'd packed on the hike and was already wondering how much dinner was going to come out of that small pot for ten of them.

"I wonder what it is." Bernie peered suspiciously at the pot.

"They're supposed to have good food. Probably chili or some kind of stew."

"Chili?"

"It's camping. It's not like they're going to serve duck breast stuffed with foie gras and roasted potatoes."

"Oh, that's a bummer. That's what I eat every Sunday night for dinner."

He almost grinned at her sarcasm. At least it was better than a pouty "I can't pack my bag and have never been on a hike before; I just got my hiking boots last week and tried to break them in over four days" Bernie. He looked down at her boots. "How are your feet?"

"My feet? Fine. They're going to walk over and see what's for dinner." She pivoted and strolled over to the campfire and then laughed about something with Shalini and Diana. As he watched her with them, suddenly so cheerful, he had to wonder if her joy was a result of being able to get away from him.

◆　◆　◆

Bernie was not going to admit that her feet were less than fine, to Matthew especially. The boots were doing something vicious to the outer edge of her pinkie toes. Also her right forearm was starting to ache from carrying the stupid bear can. Just as Jay had warned.

"Hi, Sheila, do you need any help with dinner?" Bernie asked, peering into the pot. Indeed it was chili.

"Thanks, Bernie. I'm good here. We'll each take turns cooking meals. But if you wouldn't mind telling everyone that dinner will be ready in five minutes and have them bring their mug, that would be great."

Trevor popped out from a tent and kneeled down next to Sheila with a bag of crackers and some cheese. "The only night we get non-freeze-dried cheese." He grinned and offered Bernie a piece.

"Thanks." She stuck it in her mouth and let the creaminess melt on her tongue, knowing that whatever freeze-dried cheese tasted like, it most definitely wouldn't be like this. Probably more of a dissolving sensation, because it would have the consistency of paper. She should cherish this cheddar as potentially the last nonpowdery substance they referred to as "food" she'd get to eat for a week. Surely being open minded about freeze-dried food didn't count toward her attempt at change.

Bernie strolled around the tents. The sun was still bright, even though it was heading toward evening. She pondered whether every day would be like this. Hiking for hours, then finding refuge at a camp by a trickling stream that everyone washed their face in. Eating copious amounts of chili and then hoping your tentmate, or yourself, didn't have a gaseous eruption. Sitting around the fire listening to everyone's camping experiences while you alone had nothing to add because you hadn't left your home state for five years.

She stood near the first tent she came to. "Knock, knock. It's Bernie."

The top unzipped, and Diana's head popped out. "Hey!"

"Sheila wanted me to tell you dinner will be ready in five and to bring your mugs."

"Lovely. Thank you." Shalini's head appeared next to Diana's so that it was just two heads surrounded by tent. "How's it going with Matthew?"

Bernie had a number of ways to respond to that question, all along the spectrum of *Not great. Could be better. I think he hates me. And, oh my God, could I please stay with you, pleeeeeease? It's that bad.* "Um . . . could you clarify that statement?"

"We just thought you two looked cute together," Shalini whispered.

"Oh." Not what she'd expected, and she was in fact speechless. The serious man with no smile was somehow a cute match for her? She liked to think of herself as someone with effervescence, and he was just plain flat.

"Just ignore her," Diana said. "She's a consummate matchmaker. Shalini can't help herself."

"We wouldn't be together if I weren't." Shalini raised her eyebrows at her wife.

Diana grinned and kissed her, and they looked so cute and were giving each other that little dreamy love look so much that Bernie felt like she was intruding on a private moment. Or maybe it was just that this was the second love look she'd seen today, and she was becoming increasingly jealous of all the love around her when she was trapped in some kind of mini hell.

"I'm just going to tell everyone else about dinner." She moved on to the rest of the tents, letting the group know to grab their mugs and meet at the campfire, until she got back to her and Matthew's tent. She stopped at the entrance. He'd put her pack inside, and she wasn't sure if she could just go in. It was an extremely small space for two people, especially considering he was abnormally long.

"Matthew?" Bernie called through the nylon.

The zip hummed down and he opened it up. "Feel free to come in," he said.

She squatted down and stared into the bright-orange dome. His face was glowing from the walls of the tent, which made him officially look like the devil. His stuff was spread out in neat little stacks on one side, and he'd laid out his sleeping bag already. It was like in college, when she'd arrived at her dorm for the first time and her roommate had already claimed a side and put her stuff up everywhere, and Bernie had to fit in the crevices where she could. But this time around, where she could fit was so small. His body filled up two-thirds of the tent, and she'd just have to cocoon herself up against the nylon wall and hope a bear didn't walk too close, trip, and accidentally rip the nylon with its claws, maiming her face in the process.

How were they going to sleep in this tiny tent together? It was practically the size of a twin bed. Face-to-face? Foot-to-face? Did she want to breathe in his morning breath or his unwashed feet?

"I just wanted to change my shoes." At least she'd be able to put her sandals on and release her pinkie toes from their web of torment. "Also it's dinnertime."

"Good, I'm starving."

"You were right, it's chili."

"It's always chili."

Bernie wasn't going to care that she had to eat chili for a week straight. This week was not about food; it was about . . . taking a break from work? Making her mom happy? Figuring out what to do with her house? Trying to prove to herself she was ready for the change everyone else had seen she needed? Maybe it was all those things, but she was starting to wonder if she'd been bullied into it all by the three people she interacted with most in the world: her manager, mom, and best friend. And what did that mean, that they'd all encouraged her to do this, when she'd been less than joyful about it?

57

She slid off one boot at a time and unrolled her thick hiking socks from her feet. Yes, her feet hurt, but she didn't know that her tiny toes were going to be red and swollen and on the verge of blistering.

"Uh-oh." Matthew sat folded up like a lawn chair, trying to fit his long body in the two-person tent, sort of squeezed against the sloping side to give her room. Or maybe he just wanted to see the proof that his suspicions were right and that she'd lied to him. "Someone's hiking boots were not broken in."

"I thought they were. I seriously wore them for a week straight." Well, almost.

"Sometimes it depends on the boots." His face smashed into a pensive look as he stared at her. He must have been thinking, *I was so right. This is a woman who can't get her shit together and is not prepared at all for hiking.* Even though he was right, he didn't need to be rude and rub it in her face. "If I give you something to help, you have to promise you'll use it wisely."

"Sure. Yes, please, anything." She didn't want to sound too desperate, but there it was. They had a week of hiking to do, and she couldn't do anything about these shoes. It wasn't like she could just walk barefoot across Alaska.

He reached into the bag, his hulking body bent over, now really taking up the tent. Briefly Bernie tried to picture the logistics of how they were going to get ready in the morning together, both of them sliding in and out of their clothes modestly, with their sleeping bags and packs taking up the rest of the room.

His shirt slid up as he was reaching into the depths of his bag, and she couldn't help but notice the indention in the side of his waist where his abs curved in and his hips swept down.

He twisted around fast and caught her staring. He glanced down where she'd been looking and then gave a self-satisfied smug little hint of a grin to himself. Bernie mentally groaned.

She wanted to tell him to get over himself. That his hip was staring her in the face. That she'd been merely examining it objectively, like a doctor, like it was a data point. That regardless of what he was going to give her, his prior behavior discounted his attractiveness and the allure of his V cut heavily.

He pulled out a ziplock bag and threw a small package at her. "It's a blister pad. Use it wisely."

She cleared her throat to rid it of all the words that wanted to come out. "Thank you."

"Just put them on in the morning before you put your socks on, and give your feet a rest tonight."

Thank God it was back to no-nonsense, advice-giving Matthew. She couldn't take another look of the fleeting smugness that he'd given her a few minutes ago.

"Grab your mug and let's eat." He said it like both of them were going, but he crawled out of the tent and walked away.

CHAPTER 10

The group had dinner in a large circle, with Trevor as the chili master, doling out scoops in their mugs. Matthew, starving from that day's hike, ate his chili in silence. Bernie sat between Diana and Becky, and randomly, cackling laughter would erupt from her mouth between bites at something someone had said. Trevor and Sheila, apparently making a point to be good hosts, interjected questions here and there to the quiet ones, making sure everyone felt included.

"I'm just glad on this trip we don't have to store all our poo in a can, like you do mountaineering," Shalini said.

Even though he wasn't making an effort to listen in on their conversation, the group was pretty quiet, so it was hard not to hear what the women across the circle were saying.

"Like, a poo can?" Bernie half asked.

"Yes. You have to essentially carry another bear can, but just for your poo."

"Ugh!" Bernie squealed. "Carting around my used toilet paper is bad enough."

Jesus. Bernie was practically vibrating with shivers of disgust while her new BFFs laughed.

"Thank God I'm not getting my period this week." Bernie was loud enough that everyone must have heard, and the girls erupted in giggles.

That was enough for him. He did not need to know these details about his tentmate.

"So, Matthew . . ." Trevor turned his high-wattage smile on him. "What made you decide to come on this trip?"

It was like everyone went to complete silence; Trevor's smile had turned the spotlight on him. "Um . . . it was just on my bucket list, you know?" There was no way he was telling this group that he'd wanted to come to clear his head, reinvent his career, and reevaluate his relationship with his father. They were strangers, and that would be way too personal.

"What other stuff have you done that's on your list?" Sheila asked.

"I've completed a marathon, and a three-hundred-mile bike race. I rafted the Grand Canyon—that was cool. I swam with the turtles in Hawaii . . . you know, things like that." He didn't want to turn this into the Matthew show.

"Oh, I did that in the Grand Canyon too. Such views!" Jay said.

"I swam with the turtles in Nicaragua; it was amazing!" Shalini added.

"What else is on your list to do?" Sheila asked.

Matthew had always thought of a few things he'd wanted to do. Eventually. Pie-in-the-sky-type things. "I'd love to climb Mount Kilimanjaro, but that's up there. I don't know if I'll make it all the way to Africa, you know?"

"Oh, Gretchen and I climbed Mount Kilimanjaro last year for our big vacation," Jay said, almost choking on his chili.

"That's awesome, dude. I'd love to do the Seven Summits." Trevor nodded in appreciation.

"There's a lot just in our own country you can see and do," Harold said, followed by a grunt.

Matthew expected an epic cross-country RV tale to come next, but Gretchen started speaking while Harold's mouth was just opening.

"Mount Kilimanjaro was amazing," Gretchen added with her quiet, soothing voice. "The view from the top is just splendid." She clapped her hands together.

Harold lay back. "I don't know. Seems like a long flight for a hike."

Matthew held back a laugh as Harold, the man who'd driven a month from the bottom of the country to the top, complained about a mere flight on a plane.

Trevor and Sheila jumped in with the merits of air travel, as they took flights down to the continental forty-eight states practically each month, and a little glowing nugget of a TV pilot started growing in his head. Sheila and Trevor were practically caricatures of trail guides. Two guides who are stuck with an adventure-loving hiking group because of a snowstorm? They lost their compass? They took a wrong turn? *Lost* meets *Portlandia*. Maybe that was how he could pitch it.

He swallowed the last bite of his chili, wondering if that indeed could be the premise for his next show. He pulled his mini notebook out of his pocket, scribbled "Sheila and Trevor take on the trail" on one of the pages at the beginning of the notebook, and jotted down the idea. It was a personal record to get started on a new TV idea on day one of his trip.

◆ ◆ ◆

Bernie was thinking about a bucket list she might have had once upon a time. She remembered how, when she'd studied Antarctica for a paper she had to write her first year of college, she'd initially wondered, *Who cares about Antarctica?* and then ended up being fascinated by it all, even the fungi that survived there. That class had made her actually declare her major in geography, until her dad told her it wasn't practical at all. The next semester she'd changed it to marketing. That little spark of wonder about the world fired up again, a tiny flame that she'd once had years ago.

"What are the Seven Summits?" Bernie asked when Harold had settled on losing his flying versus driving argument.

"It's when you summit the tallest mountain on each continent," Trevor said, his face lighting up. "You know what? The oldest woman to summit Denali was also named Bernice."

Something froze within her. It couldn't be. But as Trevor said the words, a memory surfaced from her childhood. Sitting on the porch at her cousin's house at a family reunion. Everyone celebrating some kind of milestone that Great-Aunt Bernice had achieved. Bernie was more preoccupied with eating the strawberry shortcake and playing Uno with her cousins than why her great-aunt was wearing a big paper tiara that said "Congratulations" on it.

"Oh?" Bernie took a breath. "Do you know her last name?"

Sheila scrunched up her face and bent over, looking up at Trevor. "Love something? Lovelace?"

"Lovejoy?" Bernie asked, her eyes closing as if she could hide from this fate of fates.

"Yes! That's it." Trevor slapped his leg. "Have you heard of her?"

"Um, yeah . . . she's my great-aunt. I'm named after her."

"Wow!" Gretchen said with her elongated soothing vowels. "That is just the coolest."

"But you didn't know she accomplished this until now?" Harold said, looking amazed, just as Becky asked, "Is this your trial run before you try to mount the peak?"

"Honestly, I haven't thought about it." Everyone was staring at her with such wide, glittering eyes and big smiles that she felt like an imposter celebrity in their midst. Well, except for cynical Harold, and she couldn't blame him. "I didn't remember she'd done that. She did a lot of things in her life."

"I think she was seventy, if I recall." Sheila squinted like she was trying to remember. "What an honor to have someone like that in your family."

Bernie nodded, her lips tight. She couldn't escape her great-aunt's legacy, even in Alaska with a group of strangers.

As everyone sat in the circle, talking about how amazing her great-aunt Bernice was, a black hole of doubt spread inside her, swallowing her up, making her feel so small that she wished there was an actual black hole so she could just disappear. Aunt Bernice had done another remarkable thing she'd forgotten about, yet Bernie was the only person in the group who didn't have a list of destinations she could run off on her fingers. It was embarrassing. She always felt the same right after one of her mom's lectures about how she needed to embrace her youth and live her life. Like Aunt Bernice.

Eventually the topic changed to more bucket lists and more trips that sounded amazing, with Harold playing the part of skeptic and Matthew being awfully quiet. She slipped away, telling Becky she was tired, even as Becky's eyes fluttered awake themselves.

Aunt Bernice was like a looming shadow that followed her everywhere she went. Tsk-tsked her at every insufficient, normal decision she made. Crept up on her like a tiny, gray-haired angel and whispered in her ear when Bernie didn't choose the out-of-the-ordinary, atypical thing. A ghostlike shadow that reminded her of every type of disappointment she'd been to her mom the past few years.

Sure, when she was younger, she'd had all kinds of desires and dreams. When she'd gotten into college across the country, her dad had encouraged her to go. No matter that he'd been sick. She'd told him she was fine staying in Portland and going to community college, but he'd given her a hug and told her, "I would never want you to give up your dreams for me. My dream is simply for you to be successful." If only she'd known what she'd regret by leaving.

"Knock, knock. You're not naked, are you?"

Bernie had found herself groaning at everything Matthew said. Whether it was crass like this, obnoxious like him showing off all his travels, or just plain boring and pedantic. Hopefully she wasn't in store for another mansplaining diatribe on random bear facts and figures.

"No." She tried to make her voice sound as annoyed as possible. Just so he knew.

He unzipped the tent and crawled in. She had to scoot back because his presence was like Gulliver invading a town. She scrunched up against the side of the tent on her sleeping bag. He sat down, cross-legged and facing her side, while he rummaged through his pack.

"This tent is small," she said.

"The understatement of the century."

"What if I added that it's so bright out I don't know how I'm going to sleep?"

"Then I would say that everyone is also thinking this. Unless they brought these!" He held up an eye mask.

That would have been a good idea, because she didn't have anything that could wrap around her head and that also wouldn't suffocate her. Alaska in the summer was twenty hours of daylight. She should have thought about this. The sun glowed through their tent, making it look like a giant orange lamp. She was a moth, buzzing around, trying to figure out how to escape, ready for the burn that would be her eventual demise.

She sighed. Her legs were tired. Her feet hurt. And she craved sleep like it was an elusive cocktail that could make this trip and her problems disappear. The main problem of which was lurking next to her.

"How are your feet?" he asked.

"They're feeling better now that they're not in the straitjackets they call hiking boots."

He almost laughed. It was like a half laugh-snort.

Matthew wiggled into his sleeping back and put the mask over his eyes. "Good night."

"Good night." The width of his shoulders took up two-thirds of the floor space next to her head. Bernie folded herself into her bag and closed her eyes. Her feet felt like rocks, and her legs seemed to weigh three times what they usually did, logs that she couldn't bear to even lift again. She couldn't relax, even through the exhaustion. The orange glow permeated her eyelids. Also, most people had brought a sleeping pad, she'd noticed, and she had nothing. The ground was hard, like a bed of stone. She should have prepared more. Or shouldn't have tried to embrace this "ready for change" idea. Because now she was stuck in the middle of the wilderness with no escape in sight.

She turned on her side, crushing her shoulder, and gave up. She opened her eyes and jerked more awake because Matthew's face was a foot from hers. This was too weird. She needed something to cover her eyes. And also needed to not breathe his breath while she slept.

Feeling like a caterpillar, in her sleeping bag she inchwormed herself over to her backpack, wondering if she could fashion a sock wrap to cover her eyes.

"What are you doing?" Matthew groaned. "I'm trying to sleep."

"Me too. But it's too bright, and I need to find something to cover my eyes."

He sat up, ripping off his eye mask. His brows furrowed as he looked at her with half-closed, grimacing eyes, his lips pulled down into a frown. His gaze didn't break from hers as he reached into the pocket of his bag and pulled out a blue bandana and threw it at her.

She picked it up. "Thanks." How did he have this unique ability to make her feel small while simultaneously doing her a favor? Smaller than she was already feeling after dinner.

"Go to sleep." He put the mask back on and collapsed on the ground. "Bernice."

The way he said her name, as if he were completely aware of the giant schism between who she was and who her great-aunt had been, made her feel like he'd heard her internal dialogue, made up a hundred mocking jokes about her, and spouted them out with that one word that was her name.

She thought about what she could say, but his breathing deepened and she could tell he was already asleep, which was probably for the best.

She wrapped the bandana around her head and lay down. It smelled like the forest. And what she guessed was his detergent.

The bandana blocked out the light, and she found herself drifting away with the scent, like a box of cigars left in the woods blowing in a mountain breeze.

The heavy logs of her legs rolled away into sleep. The rocks of her feet planted down.

And the sound of Matthew's heavy breath mimicked the windstorm sound on her white noise machine.

CHAPTER 11

A pot banging against something like a rock was what woke Matthew up. He felt warm and comfortable, cozy really. He didn't want to get up—a rarity when camping. Once, when he'd worn the sleep mask, he'd accidentally slept twelve hours. But he hoped that sound was someone making coffee, and that was what he'd been looking forward to. A cup of coffee and some creative brainstorming time while gazing at the tundra before everyone else was up and chatting away.

But something else was going on. There was a huge weight at his side, like a bear cuddling up against him.

He slid his hand out of the sleeping bag and removed his eye mask. Bernie was tucked up against him, like she'd tried to burrow inside his bag in the night, the bandana still covering the top half of her head. Well, this was awkward. Maybe she'd been cold? Or trying to grab a piece of his sleep mat, since she didn't have one? He was ensnared between the tent wall and Bernie's body. On the other side of her was a full foot of space. He gently tried to nudge her over, which didn't work. He nudged a little more forcefully, and she rolled over on her back, her mouth hanging open, some drool on the precipice of her lip. Her body tremored, and she started swatting at her face. He couldn't help but laugh, and she jerked and pushed the bandana up.

"What? What happened?"

He shook his head. "Nothing. Just some drool."

"What?" She smeared her hands over her face and lay back down in her sleeping bag, twisting to the other side.

"And you were trying to cuddle with me." He just couldn't resist.

"No, I wasn't."

"You most certainly were." He crawled out of his bag and grabbed a shirt to go dry his face with, after he'd washed it in the stream.

"Well, *you* were snoring last night."

"I don't snore."

"You sounded like the winter-storm setting on my sleep machine."

"What?" That was impossible. He would have been told by now if he snored. "You're just saying that because you're embarrassed for trying to snuggle with me."

"Not embarrassed," she mumbled.

"There's a term for that, you know? It's called *parasomnia*. A disorder that makes you do things during your sleep that you normally wouldn't do. Maybe you have that," he said, getting up.

Still cocooned in her bag like a nylon caterpillar, she rose up on her elbows. "I don't have a sleep disorder, but thanks for another one of your random facts."

"Anytime." Maybe it wasn't a sleep disorder, but something odd was going on in that brain of hers.

He laughed freely as he stepped out of the tent so Bernie wouldn't see what Veronica had once deemed a horror show—the way he normally smiled. He could hear her voice even now mocking him, telling him to show less teeth, or dragging him to a mirror and giving him her practiced wannabe-actress-closed-mouth grin. "Smile like this."

He sighed. The memories of her criticizing him always quieted any laughter from escaping his mouth.

Outside, the brightness of morning was too similar to the brightness of night. It was weird, missing the dark like that. Like they were living in perpetual daylight, the sun striking with a cool warmth constantly. But it was beautiful and misty this morning—the mountains, the stream, the tents dotting the landscape. He stretched out and grabbed his small notebook and his mug, still smiling to himself about Bernie's face cuddling into the nylon of his sleeping bag, more convinced than ever that he didn't snore.

"Morning, Trevor," he said after reaching the small clearing where they'd had dinner last night. He could smell the coffee, like a beacon calling him to the tiny fire, where the percolator was still steaming.

"Well, hello! Beautiful morning, isn't it?" Trevor looked around, like the kind of person who'd never seen such a view, although last night he said he'd done this hike at least twenty times.

"Yeah, it is. I'm going to grab a cup and disappear for a little bit."

"Sure thing, man." Trevor nodded. "Breakfast should be ready in thirty."

"Great, thanks." He filled his mug and walked toward the stream, where a few big rocks jutted out of the landscape and would be perfect for sitting on. The coffee burned his throat, but the contrast with the cool wind blowing through the hills was great. He took the mini notebook out of his pocket. Surely if Bernie was going to jot down her thoughts, she would have brought a giant notebook, an assortment of rainbow-colored pencils, and something with a unicorn on it. She just seemed like that kind of person.

He was liking this pitch idea of the forlorn hiking tour more and more. Trevor and Sheila were great examples of stereotypical nature people. The rest of the group could be amplified and made into even better characters. And then there was Bernie. How did she not know that her great-aunt, her namesake even, had accomplished such a feat?

The more he thought about it, the more he realized she was the perfect comedic heroine in distress. Even the story of her great-aunt fit in perfectly. This character could be the downfall of the tour—always getting into some kind of trouble, not knowing what she was doing—and ripe with perfect opportunities for calamity. Hell, on just day one, she'd gone to the bathroom in the middle of the trail and exposed herself to a virtual stranger. They had five more days. Maybe just by observing Bernie, the pilot would write itself. Rather than basing the story on Sheila and Trevor, what if he focused on Bernie as the main character?

The Chronicles of Bernie, he scribbled on a blank page of his notebook. It had a nice ring to it.

"Someone's having a good morning," a voice behind him piped up.

Matthew hadn't meant to laugh out loud, but he couldn't help it. Harold was walking behind him, heading toward the stream.

"Sorry. Just trying to get some thoughts down about this new pilot I'm thinking about."

"Pilot?"

"I'm a scriptwriter for television. Mostly comedies."

Harold put his hands on his hips and seemed to examine Matthew. "Huh." But he didn't say it like a question, although Matthew could see questions spinning around in his mind. "Anything I've heard of?"

The past four shows Matthew had worked on had flopped, so definitely not those. They never made it past the pilot. "*Seinfeld*?"

Harold was paying attention now. "You worked on *Seinfeld*? Aren't you a little young?"

"Just kidding. But I grew up on *Seinfeld*. That's why I write comedy."

Harold patted his back with a weary sigh that made Matthew feel more like he'd just said a relative had died instead of cracking a joke and then made his way toward the stream. Harold bent down and washed his face in the mountain water. Matthew should go ahead and do that too. He might have Bernie's dried-up drool invisibly tattooed on his cheek. He laughed and wrote it down in his notebook. Her series of unfortunate events would be perfect fodder for this idea he was already planning to pitch when he got back to town. Initially Bernie was a curse, when in fact she might just be the creative spark he needed.

Once his mom had told him that if he just stopped thinking about something, it would help him process it. That his brain would do the work for him when he wasn't paying attention. He'd been so occupied with dealing with his dad over the past few years that he hadn't been able to let everything else take the forefront. It was truly a gift not having cell service. That absence might be the thing he needed to let this story idea unfold and give him a script that could actually make it past the pilot and into episode two.

CHAPTER 12

As soon as Matthew was out of the tent, Bernie wiped her face with one of the towelettes she'd packed and slathered on sunscreen. The light outside was eerie, a constant daytime. During an apocalypse, it would be like this everywhere, not just Alaska. Like the earth had spun off its axis, the sun got too close, and they were all on the brink of sizzling up. That was what this was like. Just not natural.

Portland was fairly far north, and she luxuriated in the late-summer nights, often forgetting even to eat dinner until nine because of the late sun still shining bright. But all day and most of all night was weird. Maybe Bernie was so out of touch with nature that actual natural occurrences seemed weird.

Another natural occurrence was apparently to cuddle up to any sense of warmth near her in the middle of the night. She remembered waking up, her back hard against the ground, the thin down of the sleeping bag a feeble cushion for her body. It was cold, colder than she'd anticipated, since yesterday's weather had been perfect. A vague sense of heat drifted from the left of where she lay. It could have been a fireplace, a space heater, a curled-up James Brown. But no, it was Matthew, and unfortunately her sleep brain couldn't differentiate between the random sources of heat. She'd inchwormed toward it, seeking warmth, and she'd been caught.

A line of nerves sizzled straight from her throat and shot down through her belly. How could she have done that? He'd seen her pee in the middle of the grass that day. She'd admitted to him that her boots weren't broken in, essentially giving him the satisfaction that she wasn't prepared. And after all his snide comments—and the way he almost smiled but never quite did, which made her question if he in fact had a soul—she'd cuddled up to him. In spite of it all.

Inside, she silently screamed in irritation at herself and threw the sleeping bag off her body and rolled it up. She wanted coffee and to escape the stuffiness of the tent, the space of two bodies. Outside, everyone else was waking up. She could hear their laughter and shared camaraderie of a glorious morning in the wilderness. People like her mother, who enjoyed fresh air and mountain views and their fingers feeling frigid as they sipped their first cup of hot, black coffee in the morning.

She may not have been one of them, but she would have to try.

Bernie emerged from the tent and, like a lizard, swiveled her head around to ensure Matthew was out of sight before she went to pee in the toilet-approved area, where she tried not to think about how her shoes could be walking through Diana's or Harold's pee. She then went back into her tent, where she would sleep while breathing in masked urination fumes. She just had to get over it. She needed some coffee. And she really needed to put bandages on her feet.

As she hobbled over to the campfire, Trevor was globbing oats into outstretched arms holding their all-purpose mugs. Bernie squatted next to Sheila. "Did I miss the coffee train?" she asked.

"Oh no. The coffee train is still at the station. It's the last to leave in the morning." She smiled and picked up the percolator, then filled Bernie's mug. "There's some powdered milk and sugar in your bear can if you need it."

"I'm okay." The bear can. She'd almost forgotten about it, but as if on cue, her biceps started aching at its mere mention. Maybe she could carry it on her head. She'd seen images of women carrying giant pots of water twice the size of a plastic bear can on their heads. It would help her posture, free up her hands, and make her even taller if she did run across an actual bear.

She sipped on her coffee, letting the steam warm her face. Maybe there was something about the cool morning and the hot beverage contrast that was appealing. She'd been so cold the night before, so cold this morning, that any hint of warmth felt indulgent. Apparently even if it came from Matthew. She closed her eyes and wondered if she could somehow magically banish the memory.

After saying her good mornings to everyone, she took the remnants of her coffee back to her tent and studied her pack. She needed a better strategy for sure, and apparently they had thirty minutes to get ready to leave. She rolled and squeezed her clothes so they were tightly bundled in her bag, stuffed her sleeping bag into its pouch, and tried to see if there was any chance in hell she could get the bear can inside.

After five minutes of trying, she gave up and went with option two. She took Matthew's bandana and some small bungee cords that Duke insisted she bring and then stood outside the tent, bear can on her head, and tried to fasten some kind of headpiece.

"What the hell are you doing?"

Matthew's voice behind her sounded like it was about to crack into a laugh. Could it be? She imagined a David Attenborough–type narrator documenting her tentmate's habits. *Here, you can see the elusive hiker called Matthew, a city dweller, out of his natural habitat of Los Angeles. Typically he is known for a complete lack of humor and attempts at pedantic diatribe, which bore his victims into a state of unconsciousness. But in a rare moment, oh, there it is—he almost laughs!*

She stood up straighter. Making herself larger might work for Matthew like it would work for a bear. "I'm innovating on a bear-can solution."

"Innovating, huh?" He squinted at the half-built contraption on her head. "It looks like you're about to hurt yourself with those bungee cord hooks. They are very close to your eyes."

They stared at each other for a moment. His dark-brown eyes, eyes that could be warm and cozy when they weren't chilling her with mockery and judgment, latched onto hers. Like their eyes were having the conversation, instead of words.

It's a shame you have eyes that look like they belong on a teddy bear, her eyes said.

I can't see your eyes because your bangs are always flying in front of them. But they seem kind of small and beady, his eyes would bandy back.

Correction, a zombie teddy bear that has been run over by a semi. Hollow, brain-thirsting eyes, she'd reply.

Your small, beady eyes clearly impede your vision so that you're incapable of using bungee cords properly. One snap and . . .

Okay, well maybe the conversation was in her head, but for a moment she forgot to breathe, swarmed by confusion over his stillness and her ridiculousness. Her hands released their hold on the can on her head, and just as Matthew was saying, "Well, if you want oats, it's last call," the bungee cord slipped, the can flew off, and the hooks of the cord snapped on the back of her head.

"Ow!" She clutched at her hair. Where the hooks hit her felt like she'd been shot with a BB gun.

Matthew's hand flew to his mouth, apparently so he wouldn't be caught laughing.

"Stop, it hurts."

"I'm sorry, it's just that . . ." He shook his head like it was so funny he couldn't find the words. But then he blew out a breath and seemed to collect himself. "Are you okay? You don't have a concussion or anything, do you?"

"What?"

"That bear can shot off like a missile. It's like you just turned your head into a giant slingshot."

"It's not bleeding, is it?" Bernie asked, feeling the back of her head and examining her hand for blood.

"Oh." He tiptoed over, like he was scared of what he might find.

"Just look. It's not like I have lice or anything."

"I know."

"If I did have lice, you'd get them anyway, since we're sharing a tent together."

He raised his eyebrows at her, which she was starting to understand was the way he asked questions instead of by using words. She sighed deeply. "Do you see anything?"

He peered over her, keeping his distance. "No, it's just red. But not blood red, just like you were smacked in the head by two metal hooks. Oh, wait, because you were."

"Seriously?" She flung her head back and her braids flipped over her shoulders, then saw him rubbing his chin in mock deep thought.

She salvaged the bear can and picked up the evil bungees and realized maybe it was a stupid idea. But she wasn't above trying anything out on this trip to make life easier. As she tried to figure out how to best strap her pack on, Matthew took down the tent in mere seconds and stuffed it in his bag.

"How did you learn to do that so fast?" she asked.

"I've been doing it all my life. I was one of those guys who kept being in Scouts even when it wasn't cool. I've always gone camping. It's like tying my shoes. Didn't you ever go camping?"

So he was a nerd. Funny, he didn't look like a nerd. "Just when I was a kid."

"Then what happened?"

"My dad didn't really like it, so we stopped. My mom's side of the family is the more outdoorsy one." She remembered the story of Great-Aunt Bernice going to a nude beach when she was sixty—not quite as "outdoorsy" as summiting Denali. She couldn't wait to get cell service so she could ask her mom about this fact. Maybe this trip had all been a plot from the start.

"Ah. And you take after your dad?"

"I like to think so." She wasn't sure if that was absolutely true, because up until he'd gotten sick, she'd done some pretty wild things. But she had always admired her dad, his advice, his matter-of-fact outlook on life. He'd always been her sounding board. And now that he was gone, she tried to embrace his attitude all the more, since she didn't have him around to guide her. It made her feel closer to him, doing what she thought he might want her to do.

She picked up the bear can, and they headed toward the others, who were waiting in a group by the now-extinguished fire.

"Why are you carrying the food like that?" he asked.

"Because it was flopping on my back."

He sighed. "Give it to me."

She handed him the can, and he pulled on her backpack for a minute. She heard the bungees snap tight and felt a new but minimal weight on her back.

"Better?"

"What did you do?" She tried to peer around, but of course when she turned the backpack, she felt like a dog chasing her tail.

"I used your bungees. In the right way."

"Are you sure you didn't turn me into a giant slingshot this time?"

He almost laughed, just like he had almost smiled. "I'll definitely keep that in mind for tomorrow."

CHAPTER 13

Trevor announced that in today's hike they would be traveling north and increasing their elevation. "It's a gorgeous hike. You'll see meadowlands, mountains, rivers—just amazing!" He clapped his hands together. "Everyone ready?"

The group shouted out variations on the word *Woo!* and Matthew couldn't help but glance over at Bernie, who looked like she was trying to smile, but on top of a grimace.

"Did you put your bandages on so you wouldn't get blisters?" he asked.

She nodded.

"Did you put them on properly?" Knowing her track record as of now, she could have put them on top of her feet or on the bottom, rather than where her shoes were rubbing against the sides.

All the parts of her face pinched together, and she closed her eyes. "Properly," she said nasally, "using the patented Matthew technique."

"Was that supposed to be a British accent or just a snotty one?"

"Just yours, so . . . ?"

"I could fill that blank in with a lot of words. Genius? Clever? Helpful?"

"Narcissistic?" she offered.

He almost laughed. Again. He'd need to watch that, or else he'd never hear the end of it.

They walked in silence for a while as they traipsed through the fields. Birds and butterflies were flitting about this morning, and the sun hung over them, warming his face. Eventually, the grasses morphed into larger shrubs and evergreens, and Trevor halted the group.

"Okay, everyone. Remember what we learned in our orientation? When we get to areas of trees or scrub brush, we need to make sure the bears know we're here so they don't get spooked. So as we walk through here, make a lot of noise. Have loud conversations, bang stuff, do whatever you can to make sure they can hear us."

The group erupted into a series of howls, yips, and woos. Bernie started laughing hysterically behind him. He turned around, and she waved her hand in front of her face. "I just can't do that." She looked like she was about to burst.

For whatever reason, Matthew stretched his throat out and made a sound like a wolf. "You can't do that? Just harness your inner beast."

"I think my inner beast is a squirrel."

"That's like the worst inner beast ever. Squirrels are like rats of the city." As soon as he'd said it, he wanted to smack his forehead.

"Um, I think *rats* are the rats of the city. Squirrels are woodland creatures that have slipped into the city realm."

"So you fancy yourself a woodland creature?"

"Aspiring woodland creature. I'm trying." She sighed.

"Why did you come on this hike?" He hadn't seen her take many photos, so his Instagram theory seemed potentially incorrect. "I'm assuming it's not to follow in your great-aunt Bernice's footsteps, since you didn't seem to know about that?"

"Louder, everyone! Don't stop!" Trevor called from the front. After the first bursts of noise, the sounds had died down, fizzling into laughter and then normal conversation.

"No." She let out an irritated sigh. "I didn't want to disappoint my mom!" Bernie shouted. "Or my best friend."

Not what he'd expected. "That's an odd reason to hike Denali."

"Oh, and also my manager. She sort of made me take a vacation."

"Are you one of those workaholics who loves her job so much and is so important she can't ever leave work?" He tried to picture Bernie in a suit and clickety-clack heels, marching down the hall, with her hair in a bun and a briefcase in her hand, pointing her finger at random and ordering people around. She'd take meetings sitting on her desk, her legs crossed, and when the last unsuspecting intern, maybe named Joey or Blake, remained in her office, she'd release her coiled-up hair and shake it around so it fell to her shoulders. He swallowed.

He couldn't see it—the suit, the tight hairdo creasing her brain, the orders. She had these twin braids that made him think of a sunnier Wednesday Addams. And a personality that fell somewhere on the spectrum between Arya Stark from *Game of Thrones* and a manic pixie dream girl plucked from an indie movie from the early 2000s.

"No. I just . . ." She shook her head. "I had four weeks of vacation saved up, and my manager told me I had to take some of it. So then my mom bought this trip for me, and then my best friend told me I needed to be open to change and consider selling my house, and well, here I am."

"That's just so random."

"Why? It's no more random than a 'bucket list.'" She made air quotes around the words. "Why are you here then?"

"I'm here to clear my head."

"And that's not random?" she shouted again.

"You don't have to yell it." He could hear her because they were lagging behind the rest of the group and the cacophony they produced would scare off anything within ten miles.

"Bears!" She gestured around at the trees.

"Well, I guess my career has been sort of stagnant, so I needed a change of scenery. I thought it would help." He didn't need to mention that he was trying to escape his dad temporarily.

"What do you do?"

"I write comedy."

Bernie stopped walking, and her hands came out in front of her like she was telling an invisible person to stop. Then she burst out laughing so hard that she started to tip over from the weight of her pack. Matthew bent in front of her and grabbed her forearms, pulling her back up. But now she had tears filling up her eyes, still laughing, and seemingly oblivious to almost face-planting on the ground in front of her. Her pack probably weighed as much as she did and could crush her.

"It's not that funny," he said.

"Oh yes. Oh yes, it is." She resumed walking, and then stopped and started laughing again, making her snort.

Well at least they wouldn't be surprising any bears with her cackling. Or snorting.

"May I ask why exactly you find it so funny?"

"You're like the most serious person I've ever met."

"No, I'm not."

She put her hands on her hips and cocked her head to the side, and then did the nasally voice again. "Bears are natural predators of berries, salmon, and food things found in bear cans." She took another pose and pointed, like she was gesturing to a whiteboard. "If you want to calculate the urine perimeter of the camp, travel twenty-five footsteps in the direction perpendicular to the trail." She paused again and squinted, as if she were reading something in the distance. "The air-to-smog ratio in Los Angeles, California, is 3.25 to 1.4 parts. A precarious mix of carbon dioxide, oxygen, and celebrity vegan excrement."

"What? I never said that." But he kind of wished he had. He couldn't help but laugh at the last one and put his hand over his mouth. He whooped by accident.

"But I'm sure you thought it." She smiled. "And oh my God, he does laugh. I've cracked the stony exterior of your face."

"It's not stony." His chuckle faded as he noticed her watching him. "*Stony* is a kind word."

"In what universe?"

"Well, I could have said *blank, mean, cruel.*"

Matthew sighed. He had been less than kind to her, true, but *cruel* seemed like an overreaching of her perception. "I'm not that bad."

"I've never heard you say anything nice."

He looked at her. She had nice eyes. A nice smile. Even her cackle was nice. But he wasn't going to tell her that. "Bernice . . . ," he started.

"Please don't call me that."

"Why? It fits you."

"Like I'm an elderly woman who sits on her porch, and the only movements she can muster are to knit a shawl for her cat?"

"No. It just does. Like the spirit of a woman who would climb a mountain unexpectedly. I bet no one thought she could do it either."

"Oh, I bet they did. She's famous for her random acts of inspiration."

"No one I know is named Bernice. That means it's a cool name."

"There's a reason for that. Because they stopped naming people Bernice in the first half of the twentieth century."

"Anyway, I was going to say something nice."

"I can't wait."

He took a deep breath. "Bernice, I think that one day you will be the woodland creature you so desperately want to be."

She rolled her eyes and shook her head and started walking again. They were far behind the rest of the group. But he could still catch a smile out of the side of her cheek, peeking back at him.

CHAPTER 14

Bernie trailed behind Harold and Becky as they hiked quietly through the narrow path among the high grasses. Occasionally, Harold would reach out his hand to help Becky up a steep incline, or his hand would fall on her back, not to push her, but almost to comfort her, just to let her know he was there. She'd look at him, and even though they didn't say more than a few words at a time, the smile on her profile, and the way her chin tilted up to meet his eyes, showed just how much in love they were.

She couldn't help but wonder if her parents would have been like that in a few more years. Although she doubted it. Her mother didn't talk about her dad. Bernie had seen her mother's lips moving as she worked on the farm sometimes, and she fantasized that she at least talked to the flowers about him.

What would her dad think about what she was doing now—hiking this sixty-mile trail? Like walking halfway to Seattle. He'd say it was insanity, that there was no point to it. But then he'd laugh and give her a hug. He was always like that, the more affectionate one, even though her mom was the daydreaming, follow-your-instincts kind of person. The last time they'd gone camping when Bernie was a child, her dad had pointed out the impracticality of just two nights in a tent.

Why are we living like homeless people? What is the fun in that?

My parents worked hard to send me to college so I could have a good job and provide for my family, and now we don't even have beds!

Canned food and fires in dirt are what people rely on in times of war. We have microwave technology for a reason, people!

They'd left after Bernie's mom had acknowledged she'd lost the fight and then vowed never to try to take them camping again.

The blow was softened by buying a new house with a bigger yard and space for the garden that her mom had been talking about for two years. And of course, now her mom spent practically all her time outdoors, soaking up the sun when it was out and tending to the various strains of wildflowers and native Northwest varietals for the farmers' markets.

In retrospect, it was the only fight she remembered her parents really having. Maybe that was why Bernie had been so reluctant to come. Or maybe she was too much like her father. A homebody who liked hot food and pillow-top mattresses and the craft beer down the street when she was in the mood. Who understood the practicality of carrying a bear can and shouting like a crazy person while hiking through bushes, but that didn't mean she relished it.

Maybe her parents wouldn't have been like Harold and Becky. Maybe there was a reason why her mom didn't talk about her dad. Like whenever Bernie brought him up, her mom sighed and put her head into her hands and sniffled. Like how her mom couldn't make eye contact with her when his name was mentioned. Maybe within some dark, quiet place inside her, she was content, or maybe relieved, that she didn't have to spend the rest of her life with a man who was so very different from her. Who, in her mind, kept her from doing the things she loved. And overall, she regretted their marriage. Maybe that was what the tears were about.

A sick little bubbling stewed in Bernie's stomach as she thought about it. This was why you shouldn't go on vacation alone without cell service. There was too much time to be alone with your thoughts, with no way to talk them out with your best friend, who would surely give you a hug and say you were being crazy while she forced you to eat some delicious cake.

Cake. Not chili. Bernie was positive that endless bowls of chili had never soothed anyone's soul.

It was probably almost chili time. They had to be finishing up their hike. She looked at her watch and saw that they'd already hiked six miles, which was almost the goal for the day. She turned and saw Matthew straggling behind the group, just like he did yesterday. He was either avoiding her, avoiding the group, or watching to see how much she was limping. Because even with the pads he'd given her, nothing had changed in her feet during the climbs in elevation they'd done.

She tried to remember the instructions Matthew had given her about the pads: of course there had to be only one way to put on blister pads. The ball of her left foot had something cruel growing on it—definitely a blister-type substance—and her pinkie toes on each foot silently screamed for release. There was also a new development—something on the heel of her left foot as well. Was her left foot abnormally larger or smaller than her right and she'd just never noticed? And everyone was too kind to say anything about it?

She couldn't ask Matthew for more blister pads. At this point, she'd have to wrap her left foot up completely in them like a blister-pad mummy.

As soon as they got over the next hill, Sheila held up her hands. "We're here!"

The group cheered, and Bernie almost cried with joy. Salvation for her feet was nigh. She turned and waved to Matthew with both hands, which she was sure looked like a Mayday signal and no doubt was. He had the tent in his bag, and she had to wait on him since she had no idea what made a good platform for tent setup.

He seemed to be walking in slow motion to reach her. She sat down on a rock that was at the beginning of the clearing and waited.

"Are you trying to torture me?" she asked when he reached her.

"Why would I be torturing you? Or maybe a better question is, *How* would I be torturing you at this minute?" He did that thing where he squinted at her, like he was trying to coax out the thoughts from her brain. "Oh, did you go to the bathroom on the trail again?"

"What?" At least she knew his Jedi mind tricks didn't work. "No. I just wanted to hurry and set up the tent to get ready for the evening. That stuff."

"Got a happy hour to get to?" He nodded in some patronizing way that could be described as mock empathy.

"You're hilarious." And now that he'd put the vision in her head, all she wanted was to go to the Rogue brewery and get an Arrogant Bastard Ale. Great. And also, so apropos.

He walked around in some circles, judging the ground, like how James Brown figured out where to pee. He plopped his pack down and then tugged the tent out of it.

Bernie joined him, dragging her pack behind her, since she'd taken it off already, eager for any excuse to give her shoulders a rest. She grabbed the poles and started fitting them together in record speed, sliding them through the eyelets on the tent like she was stabbing them into her enemy. Die, blister, die!

"Whoa!" Matthew ducked out of the way as one pole missed the hole and jabbed the air.

"Sorry, I'm just . . . anxious to get it done."

"I see that. Just don't blind me, ninja squirrel."

It was confirmed. She never should have admitted the thing about squirrels. But she'd had a thing for squirrels ever since she was young. One squirrel would always hang out in the backyard and come sneak sips of water out of the small koi pond. Her mother had put a structure behind it that looked like a thick rung ladder, where her jasmine trailed up and bloomed in the summer. This squirrel would come, get a drink, and then lay with its belly flat against one of the rungs, its four legs hanging down the sides, just soaking up the sunlight and the smell of the flowers in the summer.

"It's such a character!" her mom would say with a laugh. "It reminds me of you."

"Me?" Bernie would ask.

"Yes, you're always doing such funny, unexpected things."

Bernie had felt her mother's love then, just like that squirrel basking in the heat of the sun. But she had to wonder now at what her mother had said. What had happened to those unexpected funny things Bernie had done? She knew exactly what her mom was thinking about. How Bernie used to take her dolls and stuffed animals apart and then mix them up so she had new species of creatures that were all hers. She'd put on plays about the dinosaur extinction with her toys and a beach ball, and she used her dad's poker chips as a plague. In high school, she'd decorated her bedroom with funny signs printed off the internet and framed photos of animals in clothes.

And now? Her house was trapped in a time warp of boring floral prints from the nineties. The only funky thing she had was a dog pillow that looked suspiciously like James Brown. A few pieces of framed art on the walls. That was the feeble attempt she'd made at making her childhood home feel more like a home she should be living in. Because at the beginning, it had felt temporary. She'd moved back from Pennsylvania not knowing what to do, and sliding into her childhood bed had felt so right. And when Tabitha discussed selling the house, it sparked something in her, but then the words her dad had said when she'd gotten the scholarship to the University of Pennsylvania echoed in her head. In his voice.

"I'm nervous about leaving you when you're sick," she'd told him.

"I'll be just fine; don't worry about me."

"But it's so far away," she'd insisted, practically looking for a reason to stay, even though her dad had coached her on the scholarship and helped her fill out her applications.

"It's not that far—maybe four hours by plane. Besides, this is your time to live. You have to leave to get lost. But you can always come home to find yourself."

And even now, if she was being honest with herself, Bernie still felt a little lost despite living in that house.

Matthew finished pounding the ties into the ground.

"Can I go in?" she asked.

"Your castle awaits," he said deadpan.

Bernie shuffled inside the tent and dragged her bag behind her, then unrolled her sleeping bag and fished out her sandals. She really needed to pack those last so they were on top. She whipped her hiking boots off and carefully rolled down her socks in case there were pieces of flesh sticking to them. Because as gross as it sounded, that was exactly how they felt.

But there was nothing boiling out of her feet; they were just red. She had three new blisters in exactly the places that felt like they were on fire. The skin on the back of her left heel was rubbed raw. She held her poor left foot in her hands and examined it.

The nylon curtain parted ways, and Matthew's head appeared. "Ouch! I thought you knew how to put on the blister pads."

"How hard could it be?" she halfway mumbled.

"Bernice, Bernice."

"I told you to stop calling me that."

"Bernice, now is not the time to argue about such petty things. You do realize you have forty-four more miles to hike this week?"

"Is that an exact number or an estimate?" She smirked.

"Exact." He slid into the tent and yanked at his pack before unrolling his sleeping bag and pulling out a ziplock bag. He held it up to her, and she could swear a golden light was emanating from it. "You know that these are sacred, right?"

Bernie almost drooled looking at the bag of bandages. She nodded silently, entranced by the promise of cushioning and blister-free walking.

He picked up her foot and examined it.

Bernie gasped in protest. Wasn't there some kind of protocol before touching someone else's foot? Consent so it wasn't foot molestation? She was ticklish too. Hopefully he didn't have a light touch. But at the risk of scaring him off from helping her, she silenced her paranoia about her feet smelling or being sweaty. She was in need of professional help, after all.

And Matthew had the opposite of a light touch. He manhandled and twisted her foot, then examined the other one. "What's up with the left one? Is it deformed or something?"

"Hey!" It was like he could read into her secret fears.

"I'm just kidding. It's like your right one is fine, but the left one is all kinds of fucked up."

"I'm aware. It's been like this for the past few hours."

"You should have said something."

She could imagine exactly what she'd have to say. *Matthew, I'm a poor helpless woman, and you were totally right. I'm completely unprepared and have no clue what I'm doing. I'm an imbecile city girl who can't function in nature. Please save me with your big hands and blister pads!* Never!

He pulled out the blister pads and carefully wrapped one around her left ankle. Then he adjusted the one on her pinkie toe. She relaxed back on her forearms as she leaned into her sleeping bag, trying to accept the help he was giving her. On the bottom blister, the tip of the bandage was like a feather; then Matthew's thumbs were trying to get it in place, and the sensation was so ticklish that she burst out in laughter as her foot thrust forward and punched him in the nose.

"Ow!" His hand released from her foot and wrapped around his nose.

"I'm sorry. I'm just really ticklish. I was trying to rein it in."

"Oh, you were trying to do something, all right."

"No, seriously. That was a total accident. Are you okay?" He was helping her and she kicked him in the face. How did that even happen? Like her foot nerves had minds of their own.

He moved his hand from his nose and stared at his palm. His hand was so big she couldn't see most of his face. But she could see his eyes, a look of horror widening them. "Oh my God," he almost whispered. "There's blood!" His eyes met hers in a panic. "So much blood!"

Bernie's heart sped up. What had she done? Did they have a proper first aid kit? She scrambled onto her knees and tried to look.

"The blood!" he practically shouted, and then he thrust his palm in her face. Bernie screamed and fell back as she tried to clamber away. He leaned over her and laughed, his palm still wagging in her face.

There was nothing on his hand.

He fell back on his bag and shook as he laughed silently, pressing his lips together. "Oh God, that was funny." And then he sighed. "Your face!"

"I thought you were gushing blood. I thought I broke your nose."

They both lay side by side, breathing hard. Her bones ached she was so tired. Her legs felt heavy. The last time Bernie had lay like this with a guy, feeling so heavy, had been after sex. She cleared the thought from her head.

"If I promise not to kick you, would you please help me with my last bandage?"

Matthew sighed, and for a minute she thought he wasn't going to.

"Okay. Since you said please." He sat up, picked up the bandage, and grabbed her foot forcefully. So forcefully, Bernie swallowed.

"Bernice, don't move."

The rebuttal at her name was singing at her lips, but she resisted. The way he held her foot like this made her imagine how he would hold other things.

A pint of beer. He'd have to drink out of an elaborately carved stein, though, because he'd break a glass.

An ax. No question it would look perfect in his hands.

A firefighter's pole. A grip like that should not be wasted on a laptop. Or pens.

She gulped and closed her eyes.

A woman's body. Warm, thick fingers pulling her to him by enveloping her entire ass in his grip, the other hand at the base of her neck as he pulled her to him and kissed her, drowning her with his pouty frown. He was a serious guy. He'd definitely be serious about that.

Goddamn if she didn't want to think these things, but there they were. A side effect of being forced to sleep with those hands alongside her every night. A side effect of his giant male energy forced into her personal ecosystem.

He laid her foot down, and she opened her eyes to examine her now partly mummified foot. "Thanks," she managed to creak out.

"Oh, and you might want to meander down to the stream and wash those off." He pointed at her feet and waved his hand in front of his nose.

How dare he! She reached for whatever was near her, which was a rolled-up hoodie, and threw it at his head. He slunk out of the tent laughing.

"Asshole," she muttered. Maybe he *could* read her mind and excavate her worst fears.

All those thoughts about his hands were definitely just a side effect.

◆ ◆ ◆

That night, after a dinner of rehydrated pad thai that was not absolutely terrible, Bernie sat around the campfire with the rest of the group, shivering. It was comforting to know that chili was not the only dish on the menu. The extra hot sauce Sheila had passed around helped warm her up, but when she stopped moving, she realized how chilly it was. Luckily the sun never stopped shining, except when they were asleep, so at least she had the warmth from its eerie constant glow helping her not freeze.

Everyone was talking about jobs. Shalini was a schoolteacher. Diana was in her medical residency. Harold had been a dentist and Becky had been a nurse, although they were both retired. Gretchen and Jay, who had cooked dinner that night, both worked in IT, and Sheila and Trevor were ski instructors when the snow was out, which fit together like a predictable puzzle.

That was when Harold burst out with, "And our Matthew here works in TV!"

"I'm a scriptwriter," Matthew clarified, like he was trying to brush off the excitement that was swelling everyone's eyes, like they were in the midst of a celebrity.

"What shows have you worked on?" Bernie said. She'd forgotten to ask when he'd told her because she'd been blindsided by the fact that he might actually have a sense of humor. Never had she met more incongruous facts.

"Well, I don't know if you've seen any of them. The last few were trapped in pilot stage and haven't released."

"Trevor and I don't really watch TV," Sheila said, wrinkling up her nose. "We get our entertainment from nature."

While Bernie agreed that the scenery was pretty amazing, she had to make an effort to cover up a laugh at Sheila's superiority toward TV, looking like she smelled something bad.

"What are they called, so if they do release, we'll watch for them?" Gretchen asked, clearly excited by the prospect.

"One is called *Drag Under*. It's a cop show like *Brooklyn Nine-Nine* but set in New Orleans."

"So the show features a lot of drunk tourists and nineteen-year-old girls begging for beads from the cops?" Bernie said with a laugh. She could imagine a lot of unfortunate flashing jokes.

Matthew did that squinty thing again. "Yeah, something like that. The pilot was about Carnival."

"What else have you worked on?" Gretchen exclaimed.

"There's another show called *Ransom*."

"And it's funny?" Diana asked.

"Yeah." But the way he said it made Bernie think it wasn't funny at all. "It's about these friends who get in a bind when they accidentally steal these jewels and get caught up in a life of crime."

"Accidentally?" Becky asked. "I can't imagine that."

"Yeah . . . well, there's a reason it didn't make it past the pilot."

Was it her, or did Matthew look uncomfortable? He was shifting around, as much as you could do cross-legged on the mini tarp he used for a seat. His eyes looked to the ground, and he seemed to be drawing in the dirt with a stick. Like a four-year-old.

"So have any of your shows actually been released?" Jay asked. Even with that consoling tone to his voice imposed over a question laden with unspoken judgment, he couldn't hide that it was a slight. Bernie wanted to interject and ask him what he'd accomplished in his job that made him think his achievements were a cut above Matthew's writing.

"There's this show that came out a few years ago, but it just ran for one season. It's called *The Unbreakables*."

Bernie looked up. She loved that show. In fact, just a few months ago, she'd googled what had happened to it, because she couldn't find any more seasons of it and wondered where it had gone off to. That was when she'd found out it had been canceled. It had such a funny cast of characters: a band of misfits set in a midsize city, like Pittsburgh or somewhere. A loser older brother, a single mom who worked in a café, and a best friend from Australia who had some kind of odd design job that brought in large sums of money on occasion. The show had ongoing jokes about how she was possibly a high-class escort because she'd never fully admit what she did. And there was a cute French bulldog named ChiChi.

"ChiChi!" Bernie exclaimed in the quiet of the night. Apparently no one else there had seen the show besides her.

Matthew looked alive again and stopped drawing miniaturized crop circles in the dirt. "You saw it?"

Bernie nodded. She wasn't going to tell the guy who'd just said her feet smelled—even if the comment had made her sneak off and use the cleanser wipes she'd brought to wipe them down—how much she loved the show.

"Cool" was all he said, but Bernie felt like something in his countenance had been adjusted.

"I'm going to call it a night." Harold stood up and held out his arm to Becky, who followed him to the tent, their hands still clutching one another's. Everyone else started popcorning up to go to bed, and Bernie walked toward her tent. And Matthew's. It was like it had been sunset for two hours now, the sun stuck in some kind of eternal horizon.

She climbed in the tent and decided to read her book for a little while to decompress before sleeping. Matthew was talking outside to Trevor about something and laughing, and she couldn't help but pay attention to them. He laughed fully to Trevor. He must really think Bernie was annoying if he didn't think she was funny at all. Not that she was a comedian, but her father had always said she had the gift of making people laugh.

She gave up listening and had turned back to her book, ironically a love story, the last thing she should be reading, when Matthew unzipped the tent and crawled in. She tried to ignore his presence, hoping he'd just put his blindfold on and go to sleep, but it was difficult, even when he tried to fold his body up like his own personal brand of origami. Or a human lawn chair.

He thunked down to the ground, and he put his sleeping mask on. "Good night."

"Good night," she said back, glancing over at him. She could see him clearly still. The angles of his jaw, disguised by this beard that grew and expanded like moss every day. The sharp tip of his nose. Along the bridge he had a faint bump, like someone had hit him with a baseball when he was a kid, and its top became flattened out and never grew straight again. And he had very unusual lips. The curves were sharp somehow. They were almost as intimidating as his eyes. He was much easier to look at when she couldn't see his eyes. Those dark-brown wells—almost black so you couldn't even see his pupils. That must be why they were so off-putting. Why Bernie was worried he could transmit her thoughts when they locked eyes for too long.

"Are you looking at me?" he said.

"What? No!" She pivoted back to her book. Shit. How did he know?

"It felt like it."

She'd reacted too much. No one ever denied something that hard when they were being truthful. "You have a mask on. Why would you think that?"

"I could sense you were looking at me." He adjusted himself in the bag. "I just read this study about how people who are born blind have a heightened sense of hearing, smell, and touch. It was like that. I shut down sight, and my other senses are alive."

Sometimes he reminded her of her middle school biology teacher the way he rattled off useless information. But maybe he did have extrasensory Bernie perception. "Well, I'm just reading. Staring at my book."

"What are you reading?"

"Oh, it's a story about France." Which was partially true. It was a love story set in France, and she didn't want him to know exactly what she was reading.

"Like a history book? That's an odd choice of reading material."

"It's about people in France."

He whipped off his mask. "Sociology? Is that something you read about for your marketing job? Like, you have to figure everyone out to determine how to sell clothes to them?"

"It's not sociology." She set the book down and glanced over at him. "I thought you were going to bed."

"I would call it 'going to bag.' That's more appropriate, don't you think?"

"Maybe." Although "going to bag" sounded like some new trendy slang that meant you were going to steal someone away in a sack to have sex with them. That was not what they were doing.

He grabbed her book where it lay between them, her finger still inserted like a bookmark. She lunged for it, and his monstrously long arms pulled it out of her reach, whisked it up like a Ferris wheel, far far away, and read aloud. "And while Camille had missed the embrace of his arms, ensconced around her waist, clutching her tight as he had before the war, this was what they both needed now. His explorative fingers drifting inside her blouse, seeking the heat under her skirt . . ."

She frantically wiggled out of her bag and, on her knees, grabbed the book from his hand. Her face was hot. She was sure it was red. "That was a violation of tent code!"

"Sounds like Camille was the one about to get violated." He fake coughed.

"Seriously, that's rude. And you're a writer—why are you making fun of my book?" She turned on her side, away from him.

"I'm not making fun. Just wanted to see what you were reading. You were being so evasive; I knew it had to be juicy." With these last words, he leaned toward her and whispered darkly near her ear. She tried to ignore the tremble in her abdomen that occurred. That aching, ticklish feeling like butterflies in your stomach, but much, much lower. *Juicy.*

Another side effect of reading about Camille and Patrice's love affair broken by the war.

"No more book grabbing."

"Okay . . . so that's your tent code? Disappointing, but I can live with it."

"I'm sure there can be other rules."

"Okay, then my rule is . . . no snuggling with me in the morning."

"I wasn't snuggling!" Bernie's chest tightened as if even her lungs were protesting.

"Mmhmm. Sure."

There was a pause, and he rearranged himself into his bag. She turned on her back, since sleeping on her side was less than comfortable, and resumed reading. His sleep mask was now on, and hopefully he would just pass out soon.

"So you watched *The Unbreakables*?" he asked.

No luck there. She willed him to go to sleep. Just a few moments of peace.

"Yes. I saw the first season."

"Well, there was only one. I was sad it got canceled. It was a fun show to work on."

"It was funny." She almost added a snarky comment about how she was surprised he'd worked on it but refrained.

"You liked the dog?"

"I liked the characters too."

"Which episode was your favorite?"

Bernie put her book down and slid its bookmark in. She was clearly not going to read. "Um . . . the one where the son accidentally shoplifts something, and then he has to work at the Salvation Army for community service and finds such good stuff he opens his own resale shop on the side."

Matthew erupted a brief chuckle that wheezed out like the sound of nostalgia. "Yeah, that was a good one."

"So what happened to the show?"

"Oh, you know . . . everything's about the ratings and ad dollars, and the show wasn't making it. So they canceled it. It happens all the time."

"But that show was actually good. Clever, even. It's a rarity."

"Yeah, but I don't think most people want clever. They want cheesy reality. There are more TV shows being produced now than ever before, and most of them are not great. Like at the hotel, I had cable for once, and flipped through the channels and still couldn't find anything I wanted to watch."

Bernie hummed in agreement. "The same thing happened to me." Her legs and feet and shoulders were doing that thing where they finally succumbed to exhaustion against the hard dirt and sank into the ground. She grabbed Matthew's bandana, which she had kept, since he hadn't asked for it back yet, and wrapped it around her eyes. It was amazing what the body could do when it was tired. She could be on a bed of dirt or a pillow-top mattress and she would probably drift off to sleep as equally as fast.

Just as she was about to fall into the sleep zone, Matthew's voice whispered from a few feet over, "Bernie?"

"Hmm?"

"I'm glad you liked that episode. I wrote that one."

Something like an inhale swept through her body, as if it was briefly filled with life, even though she must have been on the brink of a REM cycle. But she didn't say anything. She tried to ignore the feeling, the thought that they actually might have some thread of commonality that strung them together. The countdown in her head, the Advent calendar of this hiking trip, where she ripped off another day leading to the glorious end, ticked another close to the day. A day where they hadn't actually argued. In fact, he'd laughed, even though he'd tried to hide it from her.

Maybe instead of counting down the days until the end, she should be tallying the times she could get Matthew to laugh. Twice that day had been seemingly a record. But what else could she do to distract herself from her sore feet, her aching calves, and the way her shoulders cried every time she removed her pack?

Let a new countdown begin.

CHAPTER 15

Matthew swept his coffee away to a nearby rock and jotted notes in his idea journal—well, idea mini notebook—that was somehow now damp around the corners. He opened the next few pages and started documenting the previous day's tales of woe, starring Bernie.

Reads romance novels. And gets caught. Then blushes.

Can't bandage her own feet properly and limps around—for miles!

Can't tie a bear can correctly to her pack and would rather carry it.

Thinks her inner beast is a squirrel.

There had to be something in this list that would surface. At least one character. Because who had squirrel as her bravest self? He tried to think of all the things this fake Bernie could do in his script. She was obviously ripe for calamity, but there had to be more. What were her dreams? What did she want to accomplish in life? Who did she want to fall in love with?

All the essential questions to understanding a character.

Oh, and he added to the list.

Went on a weeklong hike not to disappoint the people around her.

Because who did that? And how did she have four weeks of vacation time saved up? Granted, Matthew worked in one of the most nontraditional of jobs, but even if he worked on Wall Street, he would be taking off time for travel, for trips, for exploring the world around him whenever he could. The city could suck you dry. Even when you were surrounded by mountains and beaches, just sitting in traffic to get there could outdo all the anticipation you'd had leaving your house.

Maybe Portland wasn't like that. He imagined it was full of people who wore too much polar fleece and needed haircuts and rode to work on skateboards, craft beer in one hand and homemade granola in the other. Maybe Bernie wasn't like that. She seemed polished. He could tell she wasn't used to the outdoors, even though she was from a place he completely associated with the outdoors. And to be honest, riding a skateboard to work and drinking craft beer didn't sound too terrible either.

With this character he wanted to write, all her oddities should shine. Maybe he needed to go spelunking inside of Bernie.

Oh, that did not sound good. Spelunking in her brain, maybe?

The sound of footsteps behind him in the grass made him fold up his notebook and pen and stuff them in his pocket. Harold emerged beside him.

"Morning," Harold said and then let out a sigh that made Matthew think Harold was the kind of guy who believed in "morning constitutionals" and basking in the early-morning chill as he contrasted the heat of the coffee in his hand and the cool breeze on his face with the release of his bowels. In fact, maybe that was exactly the direction Harold had just come from.

"Nice morning, isn't it?" Matthew asked. And it was true. The sky here was a forever shade of blue, dotted with clouds. The grass that usually topped up at their knees was waving in the breeze, showing myriad shades of green. The pink and purple flowers that were embedded within, speckled like little bright mittens here and there, waved hello.

"Every day I'm still alive is a good day." Harold gave another sigh and clapped Matthew on the back.

Harold sounded suspiciously like his father.

Matthew was afraid to ask Harold the questions that were popping up in his brain. But then something inside him had to know. He could make up stories all day about how Harold was in the war and survived a close blast from the enemy. Or how back in 'Nam, he'd watched his best friend bleed to death beside him. Or how he'd lost the love of his life to a battle with cancer when he was a young man. But what was the truth? Plus, Harold had left his sentence dangling out there like he was begging to be asked.

He needed to create a "Harold's Heroics" section in his notebook for some character ideas. "Why is that?" Matthew asked, taking a warming sip of coffee.

"Well, when you get to be my age, you watch the people around you just disappear. Your friends just go. You'll talk to one on Tuesday and everything's fine. And then the next day, you get a call from his wife that he passed away in his sleep. Or someone thought they had indigestion from too many meatballs that turned out to be a heart attack." Harold let out another one of his sighs. He could patent those things. When he sighed in reflection, it made Matthew pause in reflection as well.

"Becky and I are trying to figure out what's next for us. There's a balance in life. Don't hold yourself back, and then don't kill yourself trying to live, you know?"

"Yeah, I guess so." Funny how Matthew really wanted to hear more, like his whole life he'd been missing out on anecdotes like this one.

"But it's more important to just live, you know? You never know what's going to happen. You have to seize the moment and make the most of it." And there it was. Matthew examined his life and wondered where those moments were he wasn't seizing. What parts of his life was he not living?

Harold clapped Matthew's back again, and he almost slid off the rock from the force. "I need to take a shit."

Matthew snapped out of his momentary existential crisis and laughed. "See ya."

Morning constitutional.

Sometimes he wondered, if his dad hadn't left him when he was so young, what kinds of wisdom he would have imparted upon him. What kind of advice about girls he would have offered, opposed to what his mom had told him, which distilled down to her spelling out the song "Respect," followed by "Don't get anyone pregnant!" Or even taught him how to wax a car or fix a sink? Moments he'd clung on to at his friends' houses, volunteering for menial tasks with their fathers, or crouching down, memorizing steps as they fixed some random thing in the house.

Or if his dad and mom would still be together today, if his dad hadn't been such a selfish ass. Could his mom be happy? She'd dated but had never remarried. Would they have taken trips together, like Harold and Becky did?

He looked out on the meadowlands and sighed. Harold's morning-constitutional deep thinking was rubbing off on him.

Matthew hopped off the rock and headed back to the camp. Everyone was sitting around, caps tugged over ears, hunched over steaming mugs of oatmeal.

Bernie was the only person not there. He filled his mug, took a few bites, and asked the group, "Have you seen Bernie?"

They all shook their heads, and Matthew took his oatmeal back to the tent. How could someone not have woken up by now?

"Bernie!" he called through the door. "Are you awake?"

No answer. He unzipped the tent, and it was empty. His heart thudded in his chest. Where could she be? Had something happened to her?

He stood up and eyed the grass and shrubs surrounding the camp, looking for her bright-red hat. She wasn't in the designated toilet area. He set off down the trail and called her name, feeling a little like a crazy person. She couldn't have been dragged off by a pack of wolves or mauled by a bear, could she? That was insane. But also, it was insane to wander off by yourself in a remote area of a national park.

"Bernie!"

He should go back and tell the others. Would they need to do a search party for her? This was such a Bernie thing to do, to get lost on a hike where there were tents and a trail and the smell of coffee to guide you back to camp. He'd document it in his Bernie book after they'd found her and ensured she hadn't been mauled to death.

"Hey." Bernie waved as she emerged from around the corner.

His heart seemed to stop. His frantic worrying now quickly morphed into full-on agitation. "What the hell are you doing?"

Her eyes widened, and he saw a smile spreading on her face. "I saw a rabbit."

"What?"

"I saw a rabbit near the 'toilet'"—she put the word in air quotes—"and followed it. A huge one. It had the biggest feet."

"What are you, Alice in Wonderland? I was worried—we were all worried," he corrected, even though he hadn't mentioned it to the others. "You can't just wander around by yourself out here. There are wolves and bears."

"Well, it feels like if a rabbit can run around, so can I." She joined his side and started walking back to the camp.

"I'm sure that's exactly what Alice thought, and look what happened to her."

"You think I'm going to have to take some magic pills and play croquet with a toucan? Actually, I could get on board with that, because I'm pretty sure the queen has a bed and central heating."

He could only groan.

"Is there any oatmeal left?"

"I don't know. You know, this isn't a hotel. You have to eat breakfast with everyone."

She shrugged. "I just got distracted."

When they got back to the camp, she said, "Sorry I worried everyone."

"Worried? Why would we be worried?" Diana asked.

Bernie turned and squinted her eyes suspiciously at Matthew and then gave a little knowing raise of her eyebrows, a half smile, and then turned around. "Oh, I just heard I had wandered off and could have been eaten by a pack of wolves."

Matthew should have protested. Did he say everyone was worried? Well, they would have been if they'd known a woman like Bernie was traipsing through the tundra alone. But his words had flown away. He felt like all the oxygen had been sucked out of his body in an instant. He lost all cogent thoughts to defend himself. Like all the clothes had been stripped from his body and he stood there naked, a bare man-child pouting silently and stewing in his own self-created misery.

"I just saw this really cool rabbit," she said. She poured some coffee and then inspected the oats.

Sheila nodded in some weird mutual understanding. "I bet it was the snowshoe hare. Did it have really big feet?"

"Yes!" Bernie hunched down to start talking to Sheila.

Well, now his character profile was expanding. Follows rabbits à la Alice in Wonderland.

Bernice in Wonderland.

CHAPTER 16

Somehow that day, Bernie's blisters didn't bother her as much as they had the day before. She had more than a spring in her step, like the trampled grass and occasional smooshed bright-fuchsia petals were providing a trampoline for her hiking boots handcrafted by the devil himself. Maybe it was the blister pads, or maybe it was just the look on Matthew's face when she'd busted him. Caught him in a lie. Actually shut up that smart-ass mouth of his.

It was funny how she couldn't help smiling every time she replayed it in her head. It was like a switch that got turned on. Maybe he was genuinely worried. Maybe he wanted to make her feel bad. It didn't matter. His face shone with pure panic. Like the kind of panic Tabitha had etched on her features when she suddenly realized that she'd forgotten her mom's birthday or to let her boyfriend's dog out. The fear of genuine retribution, either in the form of a pure adolescent guilt scolding or of facing explosive dog poop all over the carpet.

Now he was avoiding her. And it was their turn to make dinner that night. She had to wonder if he was planning some kind of sabotage to get her back. Not that she had done anything, but a guy like him who gave her a look like that told her he couldn't take it when he was busted.

Although if she was honest with herself, he could do all kinds of torturous things to her in their tent. He had her to himself for eight hours a night while everyone else was fast asleep. And it was so bright he could see everything. Pull a slumber party prank by putting her toothpaste in her hair. Cram all his crevices with her cleansing wipes and then carefully put them back in the plastic. Open up the bear can, set the food on her chest, leave the tent open, and then go bunk with Harold and Becky. Tower over her and suffocate her with his mouth.

"Bernie, wait up!" Shalini shouted behind her.

Relieved to have a respite from the swirly churning bubble of desire that had slunk through her abdomen again, she turned around and waved at Shalini and Diana, who were coming around the bend she'd just climbed up. "Hey!"

"Your bear can is slipping off your pack," Sheila said as they got closer and then turned her around.

"Oh, that's because I did it myself." Bernie laughed. She'd tried not to ask Matthew for anything for fear of another good scourging.

"Matthew didn't help you?" Diana asked, her pitch high on his name, just begging some other question.

"Nope."

"Oh my God, Diana, seriously?" Shalini turned Bernie back around. "You're all set now. And just ignore her. She is always looking for an opportunity to set someone up."

"Or don't ignore me and admit that I'm onto something," Diana said with a laugh. The three of them began walking up the trail again, and Bernie's face felt like it had its own heating dial. She was cold no more.

"Seriously, though, how's it going rooming with a complete stranger? A complete *handsome* stranger?" Shalini asked.

"Not you too!" Bernie wailed. They all laughed, and Bernie forgot how comfortable it could be to meet a new group of people and walk together, embarking on a weird journey. It was like starting a job, or training your dog in puppy kindergarten together, or the first day of school.

"I can't help it. She's rubbing off on me. We need some entertainment. Like we're trying to create our own reality TV show on our hike." Shalini grinned at her.

"Yeah, it would be called *Desperation on Denali*," Bernie said, laughing.

"Not like this is an *ideal* first-date setting," Diana said.

"You just have to see everyone's dirty parts and all." Shalini laughed. "I accidentally saw Harold's parts this morning."

Diana and Bernie groaned.

"Poor Harold!" Bernie said. She didn't wish that on anyone after experiencing it herself. "Matthew accidentally saw me the other day peeing, and I'm still mortified."

"Well, at least if you all do hook up, you've got the hard part out of the way."

Heat spread throughout her sternum now. "He couldn't have seen much. He offered to show me his ass afterward to make me feel better. You know, so we're even."

"Oooh!" Diana rubbed her hands together. "This is what I'm talking about. You see his ass, and it's just all over from there."

"I bet it's a nice ass too," Shalini said, elbowing Bernie in the side.

Maybe Matthew had seen everything. She tried to remember how bent over she was, how low the windchill was on her butt cheeks that afternoon.

"You know, maybe it is an ideal first-date setting," Diana said. "If you meet someone and click here—dirty, no makeup, hair a mess, few opportunities to bathe, grouchy from sleeping on hard dirt—and you still hit it off, they've already seen you at your worst. So there's no morning-after, 'Ugh my hair looks like shit and my makeup is smeared everywhere and I look like the Joker and smell like a horse.'"

"A horse?" Shalini gave her wife a weird look, and Diana shrugged in response and clarified: "Really, any barnyard-type animal will do."

Bernie laughed as they started walking up the trail together. "How did you two meet?" she asked, ready to take the focus off herself.

Shalini began telling the story of how they'd met through Diana's girlfriend at the time and couldn't resist the intensity between the two of them.

"We had to hide it from my ex after she and I broke up," Diana said, concluding the story. "Like for months."

"I can't imagine how she didn't know," Bernie said. "It's obvious you two are smitten with one another."

Diana smiled at Shalini. "I think sometimes love can be quiet. And sometimes you only see what you want to see. If you're open to love, it can find you. If you're closed off, or with someone for the wrong reasons, it's like the gates are shut."

Bernie nodded. She couldn't help but wonder what Tabitha would say about that. She'd probably say Bernie's gates were on lockdown.

She bent down to tug on her shoelaces, but carefully so she wouldn't tip over. In the distance, maybe a hundred feet away, a tall dark shadow of a figure approached. She could swear that when Matthew caught her head pointed in that direction, he stopped moving, delaying the time they would be forced to meet again.

Then there was a buzz coming from her pack.

She froze. Could it be? Bernie wasn't addicted to her phone by any means, at least no more than the average person, but the idea that they were at a point where she could actually have contact with the outside world, the one populated by friends and family, was too much of a temptation to pass up. She'd been conserving her battery to use it as a camera, turning it off every night, and she had a backup USB charger she hoped would power it for the second half of the trip.

Shalini and Diana similarly had received the same cell signal, and both clutched their phones in their hands.

Bernie grabbed it out of the pocket to her right and looked at a series of texts that had come through.

Hope you're enjoying your trip! Send me pics.

From her mom, and then five more following that were repetitions.

Are you ok? Why haven't you texted me back?

Hello, Bernie? See how I said Bernie. I'm trying.

Followed by, Oh, I forgot you might not have service. Then she closed with a picture with James Brown lounging in the sunshine in the middle of the garden.

Tabitha sent a GIF of someone being attacked by a bear. Haha. Very funny. And then another message.

Hope your trip is fun! Check out these pics of your house. I'm going to share it with some of my coworkers just as an FYI.

The pictures she'd attached were still loading due to the weak signal, but Bernie wasn't sure if she was ready to look at what Tabitha had done to her house over the past few days. And if it would entice her coworkers, who would then push it on their clients. The thought of someone else living in her house, other than her family, invoked a coating of dread that overtook her, just thinking about the decision she'd said she'd make.

But she still had four days to go. She had her feet, the rattling bear can, and Matthew to deal with for now. Bernie had ignited some level of change by coming on this trip, and look what it had got her.

All she'd wanted to do was thank both her mom and Tabitha for reminding her she wasn't alone in the world, and then yell at them, *Thanks to you, I'm being forced to shack up with a random stranger man in my tent who practically hates me.* They were partly responsible for this whole thing, after all. So that was what she texted Tabitha. She'd have to take it easier on her mom.

Immediately Tabitha texted back. What??? Forced? Are you ok?

Bernie looked back at what she'd written. Maybe it had been a poor choice of words.

I'm fine. They thought I was a boy so put me in a tent with another of the male species.

Fine. Was she fine?

Is he cute?

Of course that was what Tabitha would ask. She looked back at Matthew, who was approaching them, and waved. "There's cell service here!"

He held up his thumb in acknowledgment. Matthew was objectively attractive. Probably more so once the mountain man beard was removed from his face. He had startling brown eyes that intimidated her, since they seemed to have built-in Bernie ESP, but on anyone else they would have been a ten. A square jaw under all that face fur, and his height and strong build were the kind that made you automatically wonder what a man could do to you with that strength. She swallowed at a sudden vision of circus acrobatics that fluttered through her mind.

Maybe.

Bernie examined her battery, which was hovering over 25 percent. She texted her mom.

I can't talk but I'm fine and will call you when I'm back in the land of power grids and electric outlets. BTW, did Aunt Bernice climb Denali?

Shalini cleared her throat a little too loudly. "Bernie, your *Desperation on Denali* costar is here. Do you want us to leave you two alone?"

Bernie groaned as Shalini and Diana laughed and picked up their pace.

A tinkly little song perked up behind her, and Matthew stood there, giving her a weird look, like a side-eye but straight on.

"What?" she asked.

His eyes widened and he shook his head, but she could tell something was up. It was the headshake when you know you were in the right and were just trying to make the other person feel inferior. The eyes widening like you were feigning innocence but actually had a deep, dark secret. Or judgment. Her mom did it to her all the time.

He huffed a laugh down his throat and studied his phone.

It was always something with him.

CHAPTER 17

Matthew was not as intrigued by the cell service that had suddenly shone down on this little patch of earth as with why Shalini and Diana had asked Bernie if she wanted them to leave her alone with him. But then she ran up the trail chasing the two women, apparently eager for any opportunity to evade his presence. His snooping, which had gone on a one-man manhunt for her earlier and, for whatever reason, had made a bigger deal out of it than necessary, had made him feel awkward now. She was a squirrel, though, and there were things in this mountain that ate squirrels.

On his phone were a series of text messages from his fellow script-writer friend Ben about a new show that was hiring writers. His mom texted, asking how things were going. His dad sent an oddly upbeat message.

Go get 'em tiger.

About a mountain? Matthew could have used a "go get 'em" or two when he was a kid. Now, not so much.

He ignored his dad's text and let his mom know he was fine and operating on minimal phone battery. He told Ben he'd call him when he was back in town. After all, what could he do now? You had to snatch up writing work like a dog sniffing for scraps off the ground. You heard about something and then went after it, just in case. Because nothing was guaranteed.

Which was why it would be so cool if he could develop his own show. Pick his own cast. Oversee his own writing and characters, and not take direction from someone else who was trying to make the show like some other success. The show should just be its own success. People did that all the time, right? Why couldn't he?

He kept walking up the path, trailing a good hundred feet behind Bernie and her new friends, keeping them in his sight. He was far enough away that he could have the silence and peace he craved, although if Bernie fell into another calamity, he would be there to help out. To witness it. To gobble up those notes about her and use them for his idea. He could envision a *Private Benjamin* for a tour company situated in the mountains. Like *Private Benjamin* crossed with *Northern Exposure.*

He got out his notebook and wrote that down. So perfect. When he was back, he could start writing out a pilot script, flesh out the characters, get it ready for prime time. Or at least to pitch to some producers he knew would like it.

As he made his way to the top of the hill, he found the rest of the group setting up their tents. Except for Bernie, who was sitting on her pack, eating a granola bar.

He walked to where she had plopped down and took off his pack to start setting up the tent.

"Trevor said it's our turn to make dinner." She opened up the bear can and pulled out two packets of beans and rice. "I hope you like Cajun."

"I've had worse. One time I was on a camping trip, someone had brought shrimp alfredo pasta we had to rehydrate, and . . . well, I feel like the concept of rehydrating shrimp and cream just says it all."

Bernie looked up from the bear can, her lips turned down in a grimace. "There is a special place in hell for people who rehydrate seafood products."

He turned and smiled into his bag. "Definitely. And the people who slap the word *vegan* onto reconstituted whatever it is that tastes like meat and is made in a lab. It's just wrong." Of course he was thinking of his ex specifically for this.

"Processed food is for the weak." Although he meant it to sound funny, it came out way more serious than he'd intended.

"Wow. Are you like one of those hard-core paleo warriors who only eats raw meat and drinks the blood from newborn calves?"

Maybe this was his chance to make up for his declarative weakness statement that had made him sound like a pro wrestler in a "Beef: It's What's for Dinner" commercial. "Only on the weekends. You know, I have to let up on the bloodletting for most of the week."

"Or else your cholesterol goes through the roof?"

"It just gets completely out of control. Then I have to eat egg whites exclusively for a whole week . . ."

"And it's hard to start your morning without your egg yolk–calf's blood milkshake? Totally get it." Bernie smiled as she got out the rest of the supplies for tonight's dinner, and Matthew really had to rein in the giant, jolly laugh that wanted to absolutely burst out of him.

Her gestures were careful but curious. Her little pixie face twisted as she examined all the jars and packets that were in the bear can, as if she'd never actually looked at them. Her hair was this interesting shade of brown. Like sparks of gold and amber were sewn through it. For a moment, he wondered what it would feel like in his hands.

She turned. "What?"

He shook his head. "Nothing, was just thinking about my breakfast when I get back to LA."

Her eyebrows furrowed at him curiously, and then she shrugged it off and went back to unpacking.

What a stupid thing to say. Well, it was better than telling her he was thinking about her hair running through his hands. It would make him sound like some weird fetishist. Or a serial killer who collected pretty girls' hair to make wigs for himself.

But the truth was, Bernie was funny. They were actually kind of funny together. If Veronica and he had even loosely embarked on the kind of weird banter Bernie and he had just had, she would have wrinkled up her lips and said, "Ew!"

He sneaked out his notebook and wrote that down: another Bernie attribute for his show idea.

Jokes about bloodletting calves and eating raw meat. Hopefully he'd remember the joke when he was looking at this weeks from now and not just be confused about any cannibalistic tendencies. Who was he kidding? Of course he was going to remember all their conversations.

"Are you ready to set up the tent?" she asked and then stood up. "You know what? I'm going to try to do it myself today."

"Whoa. Are you sure?"

"Oh yeah. Let me at it." She rubbed her hands together and squatted down like she was getting ready to catch a football. Her boots were already off, and she had her sandals on.

He tossed the tent to her. "How are your feet?"

She looked down at her toes, looking a little mopey, like she'd just remembered something sad. "They've been happier. But they feel better today than yesterday, and that's really all I can ask for at this point. Thanks again for all the bandages."

"Sure." And then, at the risk of ruining the tightrope of tension between them, he added, "I wouldn't want to have to carry you or anything."

Okay, now he was thinking about carrying her. His arms under her knees and scooping behind her back. His left hand grazing her bottom. His right hand finding some secret ticklish spot that made that weird girlish laughter of hers squeak out at the most unexpected moments, like stepping over a rock or jumping over a stream. The body heat coming off her enough to keep both of them warm, even if they didn't have clothes on.

What the . . . ?

"Uh, yeah, that would be horrible. W-weird," she stammered and then shook her head.

Great. He'd just made the tension turn terrible and awkward instead of the playful conversation about him drinking blood they'd just enjoyed. Well, really, what was weirder?

"I'm going to go take a leak."

"Uh, okay. Thanks for sharing." She ruffled the tent in the air and then laid it down on top of the tarp, her eyes flashing up at him briefly, a look of confusion and/or shock in them. He should say something, anything to make him sound less like a douchey frat boy who was trying to recapture his masculinity by making gross guy statements. But his brain was empty, he was confused, and he would probably say something that would just make it worse.

He went off into the tundra and peed, and when he came back the tent was mostly up, and she was sitting on the corner of the tarp, screwing the pegs in the dirt.

"Ready to make dinner now? Mmm." He brushed his hands off on his pants.

She wrinkled up her face. "Can you at least use some hand sanitizer first? I don't want to serve everyone rice and beans and Matthew's penis germs."

He didn't know whether to laugh or be offended. "My penis doesn't have germs."

"Everyone's penis has germs."

He shook his head and rinsed his hands off with water and then slathered hand sanitizer on them. He stuck them in her face, and she winced her head away. "Happy now?"

She scrambled away from his hands and ended up falling on the ground, then closed her eyes and blew out a sigh. "Okay, well, let's get this Cajun show on the road before my inner zydeco band passes out."

"Funny." He sighed. "I didn't know that squirrels also had festive accordionists inside them." She made that screwy little face of hers, and he walked toward Trevor, who looked like he was setting up the fire. Going from one thing that burned him to another.

◆ ◆ ◆

Trevor and Matthew started the fire in what looked like an upside-down tinfoil hat. Bernie wondered, if she put it on, if it could block Matthew's mind-reading powers that defied all logic. She couldn't handle that look of his anymore. How his eyes narrowed into dark coals that burned into her. She swore that the man had no pupils. Definitely a sign of some demonic powers at work.

"What's so funny?" Matthew asked as he looked up and accidentally burned his thumb on the fire. "Ouch!"

"Are you okay?" she asked, peering over. Even though the fire was small, just the tiny warmth of it drew her body. Moths on the porchlight made so much sense now.

"Yeah," he grumbled, putting his thumb in his mouth. Bernie had so many things to say. Penis germs. Thumb-sucking. How looking up at her, wounded and soothing the tip of his thumb, he seemed almost cute and innocent.

"Okay, you two, have at it!" Trevor said, giving Bernie a wink. It felt like that wink was the kind of thing someone did when they were leaving two teenagers awkwardly alone as they embarked on a round of seven minutes in heaven.

Bernie took off her gloves and brushed her hands over the fire.

"Watch out or you're going to get burned too."

"I'm so cold I don't know if I'd mind getting a burn."

"Oh, I can give you a burn. Should the burn be why accordion-playing squirrels are not the best inner beast of choice for someone who looks like they could already get swooped up by a charming hawk? Or maybe it's which ancient Egyptian names you've given your mummified feet? You know, in case they ever break out of their wrappings and you need to appease them so they don't curse you? Should I keep going?"

"Ha. You're hilarious." She read over the instructions on the dehydrated food packets and emptied the contents into the pot. "And I don't know why my mummified feet need ancient Egyptian names. Why can't the names of mummies be Matilda and Byron?"

Matthew bent over, and she didn't know whether he was laughing or sighing with woe as he shook his head. "Bernie, I have to know. Why did you really come on this trip?"

He didn't ask it with a thick coating of sarcasm, and it didn't feel like he had a punchline ready. Maybe it actually was a genuine question.

"I told you already."

"But why did your mom want you to get out of town and do nature-y things?" He took the extra packet from her and ripped it open before dumping it in the pot.

Bernie's thighs were giving out from squatting, and she collapsed on the ground. "This might sound crazy, but I think she's always been disappointed I'm not more adventurous. More like my great-aunt Bernice. She didn't just climb Denali, but she was this wild woman who traveled all over and lived this exciting, full life, and my mom named me after her because when I was born I came out kicking and crying and laughing and was this kind of wacky baby. Always making faces and bizarre expressions, doing the unexpected and unpredictable. So from the get-go she thought I'd grow up to be like Bernice. Can you pour a little water in the pot?"

"Now I have to know more about Great-Aunt Bernice. Why was she so wild?" Matthew tilted the bottle over the beans and rice.

"Well, she never settled down, which, you know, was quite atypical for her generation. And apparently, she had this string of lovers throughout the world. She'd go on safari in Kenya, and then tour Morocco, and was this total hippie before the hippies. She even did a stint in India in her thirties. Like before the Beatles made it a thing. I only met her when she was a lot older, you know? I heard some pretty entertaining stories." Bernie chuckled, and something like wistfulness swept over her.

She could see these places in her head, the ornately carved buildings, almost sensual, like a woman's hip. Red silk and purple chiffon hanging from doorways, beads dripping down the sides like a curtain that jingled as you parted them to get through. So different from the giant cement rectangles dotted with square-shaped windows that plagued the downtown of every American city. The only places she'd ever been. She imagined the taste of saffron and turmeric on her tongue while the sand whipped across her face from a dust storm. Or silently waiting in the quiet savannah with a handsome brown-eyed man as they watched lion cubs playing in the tall grass.

"She sounds kind of awesome," Matthew said.

What was she thinking? That was not her; it was all Great-Aunt Bernice. "Essentially I've been a disappointment to my mom. She brings it up all the time. And then sighs about it like this." Bernie demonstrated one of her mother's lung-capacity-defying dramatic sighs.

Her dad had never treated her like she was a disappointment. A hollowness filled up her chest, blowing away the brief ridiculous feeling that had just been sweeping through, grounding her in reality and the present. Thinking about her dad made her sad. Then she got mopey and quiet, and she didn't want to unleash yet another burden on Matthew. Especially such a personal one.

Her dad had always been a guide to her, in a way. While her mom was off with her plants and in the garden, he and Bernie would spend time together in the evenings with her homework. He was the one who always encouraged her to be successful. He was the one who hugged her after she lost a lacrosse game. When she got a bad score on a test, he was the one who would reassure her, come up with a plan, and make sure she would be successful next time around. And toward the end of high school, when he'd gotten sick, he still helped her with her scholarship and college applications. And told her not to stop her life just because of him.

Looking back, she'd seen clearly how all the advice her dad had given her—about what to study, what kind of job to look for, what kind of life to live, how to be responsible, how to save money—had been in case he wasn't there to give it to her later.

She had to get her mind off what had happened. "Can you hand me that water jug?" she said to Matthew.

"Bernie, for what it's worth, I bet you are a lot more like Great-Aunt Bernice than you think."

"What? How?" She tried to measure ten cups of water into the pot, still wondering how this was going to feed all of them.

"Well, I don't know anyone who does stuff like this. I always do my backpacking trips solo. You have to really be brave and take a leap of faith to go on a weeklong backpacking trip. Without toilets or plumbing—most people I know would just say no. So maybe you felt guilted into going, but I think you're being hard on yourself. You still came. You're still here."

"Or maybe I'm just a wimp because I can't say no to my mom." She was a lot like her dad in that respect too. Unable to say no, to somehow do what her mom always wanted. Camping was the only thing he'd really put his foot down about after that first time, and here Bernie was, camping.

"I've only known you for a few days, but *wimp* is the last thing I would call you. Maybe *ill prepared*. But I had to practically beg you to let me help your sad little feet."

Her toes wiggled in response. Her feet felt like mummies that hadn't actually died but still couldn't break free. "They are sad, aren't they?"

Matthew laughed. "In fact, I bet we can really draw out your inner great-aunt Bernice on this trip."

Bernie groaned. "Oh my God, you sound like my mom."

"Ouch."

"No, I just mean she's always saying something like that. 'Oh, I thought you'd be more like your great-aunt. If only you were like Bernice . . .'" Bernie punctuated this with a big heavy fake sob.

"That's not exactly what I'm saying. I'm saying we can make it more like a challenge. I challenge you to find your great-aunt Bernice on this trip. Maybe this is the opportunity to see if she's really in you."

"*In* me?"

"Don't be gross." He shook his head and stirred the pot, but Bernie could tell he was on the precipice of true laughter. "I can help you see if she's there. If you do have some hidden adventuress who is just waiting to come out. It will give me a new challenge for this hike," he added. "Give me something to do."

"Okay, well, you can try. As long as it doesn't involve pushing me face-first into icy rivers or tying me to a tree coated in honey."

"No face-plants or bear bait required. You just need to get out of your comfort zone."

Bernie snorted, just to show Matthew that she scoffed at the impossibility of it all. He needed to join the Mom, Tabitha, and boss-lady club—they'd all rally around his cry of Bernie getting out of her comfort zone.

But it was called that for a reason. It was comfortable. She was fine doing exactly what she'd always been doing.

If she had little murmurings in her chest, little flutters of temptation—that sometimes she was convinced was the ghost of Great-Aunt Bernice beating at her with mothy ghost hands—that was fine. Moments like the one she'd just had where she imagined what it would be like to see the world, its ancient architecture, the desert, wild animals outside of a zoo—like she could almost smell the spice and dust in the air. They went away after a while, and she could stay right where she was. Smack dab in the comfort zone.

CHAPTER 18

"So what else did Great-Aunt Bernice do?" Matthew asked as they watched the dehydrated rice grow. In truth, he was excited about this new information. Inside of Bernie there were some genes predisposed to adventure. Maybe she thought she couldn't be an adventurer, but from what he'd seen there was some kind of odd restraint within her. She didn't bitch about the great outdoors, the lack of plumbing, not being able to wear makeup, or different, and clean, clothes, for that matter. If she didn't have some kind of inner sense of adventure, why else would she be like she was?

"Oh, I don't know what to say, really." She sat back on her heels and examined her hands, which were just as dirty as the rest of theirs. Cavewoman hands to match his own caveman hands. "She was my mom's aunt. She just loved to travel, and she never settled down."

"Why didn't she get married? Like you said, that was pretty rare for that generation."

"Yeah, there was this one guy she talked about, you know, and she'd get that far-off look in her eye . . . his name was Xavier. She'd tell stories about how they'd meet and go skiing or have picnics staring over the Seine. There's one about how they snuck into a winery and raided the cellar, passed out, and got caught by the owner." Bernie groaned and then laughed. "Can you imagine?"

The thing was that Matthew could totally imagine. "It sounds like fun. If I could go back sixty years, I would totally hang with Bernice and Xavier."

"Me too." She said it almost wistfully, and then her countenance changed, and she gave him an odd laugh. "I mean, free wine, right?"

"Yes . . . but you say you're not an adventurer."

"I'm not. I'd be the responsible one hiding behind the barrels of wine on the lookout, shouting out code word 'Ragamuffin!' so no one would get caught."

"'Ragamuffin'? That would be your code word?"

"Maybe." She shrugged. "What's wrong with it? There would never be any confusion in case shit was going down."

"Nope, that's for sure."

"What would your code word be then?" She sat up, her lips pulled into a pout, half-haughty, half-playful.

"Mr. Potato Head." It was the first thing that came into his brain out of his lips. Now he wanted to cringe.

Bernie blinked. "How dare you mock my Ragamuffin. After that."

He coughed out a laugh. "Yeah, not my best work."

"This, coming from a man who writes TV scripts for a living. Give me your all-purpose mug."

Matthew held it out, and Bernie dumped a spoonful of rice and beans into it. "Taste it. See if it needs anything."

"Did you also pack a spice rack in your bag, because even if it does need something, I'm not sure what you're going to add to it."

"Oh, I have my secrets."

Matthew was ready to ask what those secrets were. Did she have more relatives like her great-aunt? Some crazy past she was trying to make up for? A sordid tale she needed to liberate onto a stranger? But instead, he tasted the beans and rice that were edible mostly because he was starving, but with the consistency of textured paste and a similar flavor as well. "I'm not going to lie: it could use some . . ." He tried to think of the right word.

"Jazz hands?" She laughed.

"What?"

"You were waving your hands in front of you like jazz hands." She put her palms up at shoulder height and started waving them.

"Well, that wasn't intentional, but yeah, I guess it could use the equivalent of flavor jazz hands."

She nodded, her lip curled in a knowing, devious smile. "I might have just the thing."

Bernie walked toward their tent, and Matthew found his eyes trailing after her. They slid over her tight pants that cradled her calves and thighs and up to her hair, which was still in the two perma-braids that flopped around her shoulders when she walked. As he was staring, she turned over her shoulder, gave him a worried look, paused, and then said, "Stir that!"

Matthew's eyes shot to the pot, and he stirred the rice and beans.

"You were totally busted," a voice said in front of him, followed by a snicker.

He looked up to see Diana and Shalini standing ten feet in front of him, freshly emerged from the tent, their arms crossed and sly grins on their faces.

"I don't know what you're talking about," he said.

"Oh, I know that look," Shalini said.

"Takes one to know one." Diana laughed. "You *like* her." It was practically a whisper, but Matthew turned to make sure Bernie had not heard it. He'd never hear the end of it.

"You know nothing." He shook his head and for some reason couldn't stop this traitorous smile from creeping up on his face. A smile that couldn't be helped because he was in awe of such an accusation.

"Oh my God, Shalini, he is blushing!"

"Okay, that's kind of adorable." Shalini sat down on one of the rocks. "How long?"

"How long what?" His face did feel hot, but at least his smile was now swallowed up by fear.

"How long have you liked her? Was it a love-at-first-sight thing, or did it grow over time?" Shalini huddled over her knees, her arms wrapped around her shins as she tapped her feet on the ground like an excited tween.

"Over time? We've known each other three days." He shook his head.

"So it was at first sight," Diana said with a smirk.

"What are you gal pals chatting about?" Bernie said as she approached them.

"You're hilarious," Matthew said, and he prayed the two other women would say nothing. He looked up at them, and they both sat back, and while Diana said something to Bernie, Shalini whispered, "Don't worry. Your secret's safe with us."

How had this happened? Now they were harboring a secret he didn't even have. "There's no secret." Maybe he admired aspects of her physical appearance, enjoyed her bizarre sense of humor, and was constantly befuddled by how she seemed incapable of preparing for this hike in all ways possible, but she was a muse. That was it. A focal point of inspiration for what he hoped would be comedic gold.

Bernie squatted beside him and squirted a dollop of something that was an orange-yellow color into his mug. "Now try."

"Is it poison?" He looked suspiciously at the neon blob.

"What?"

"Just making sure. There are witnesses, however." He gestured his mug to the two other women. He ate the doctored-up bite and, in an instant, it had flavor—some heat, but not too much, and a tang, a flavor he couldn't put a name to. "What did you do to it?"

"Does it have jazz hands now?" she asked.

"I think so." Maybe that was the flavor that had no name. Jazz hands. "It could be described as having a sassy flavor."

"I have this special hot sauce that my friend Duke made me get. Said it was essential on any camping trip."

Duke, huh? Why did this name of someone he'd never met spark some kind of fire inside his chest? Like he could picture what a guy named Duke looked like—a fratty, obnoxious guy who smashed beer cans on his forehead and had a trust fund he couldn't access until he was grown up enough to be trusted with it.

And why was this asshole shopping with Bernie?

And why did Matthew even care? He was now taunted by the accusations of Shalini and Diana. Had Bernie as inspiration grown into Bernie as infatuation?

He cleared his throat. "Can I see it?"

She dug the tiny bottle out of her pocket, and he examined the serrano hot sauce. He was suddenly filled with angst over her relationship with Duke.

He handed it back to her, and she squirted half the bottle in the rice and beans. "Okay, you three are sworn to a secret-sauce pact not to tell anyone else about it so I can keep some for later in case the food gets really inedible. I don't have that much."

"Of course," Shalini said, and Diana laughed.

"Yeah, sure . . . so why didn't Duke come with you?" Matthew asked.

"Uh, because it would be pretty weird to go on a camping trip with my best friend's boyfriend."

Shalini made a noise like a hiccup that she was trying to swallow. He looked up, and Diana was shaking her head as if he should have known better. Shalini pressed her lips together to apparently stop from bursting out with laughter and covered her mouth.

"You've got it bad," Diana mouthed to him silently. Fortunately Bernie was too focused on the pot in between them to notice any of it.

Okay, he clearly needed to reevaluate what was happening here. His career was in a sinkhole. He needed a good story. And he hadn't slept with anyone in months. Clearly, this was what happened to you. Random sudden rages of jealousy directed at faceless names uttered by pretty, yet annoying, strangers.

"Yeah, that would be weird, I guess. So is it ready? I can tell everyone." Any reason to escape the present humiliation that Bernie was blissfully unaware of.

"Sure thing."

Matthew hopped up and practically ran to the nearest tent to tell Gretchen and Jay dinner was ready. Then he went to the other two tents. After three days together, the group seemed to be craving privacy and solace in their little tents. Or maybe they were just all cuddling with each other to stay warm. It was chilly this evening, and some shared body heat would be a welcome thing. He glanced over at Bernie. He wondered if he could proposition some body-heat sharing with her without sounding like a creep.

Nope.

Even the idea sounded creepy. He went back to the fire, grabbed the pot, and went around filling everyone's cup with tonight's dinner.

"Thanks for cooking. You did most of the work," he said as he ladled the food into Bernie's mug.

"Well, considering that cooking consisted of both of us stirring and pouring water into the pot, I think it was a team effort."

"You made it taste edible."

"That's just my sauce." Bernie winked as she said it, and suddenly his mind was flooded with sauce innuendos that sounded dirty even to him.

"Yum!" Trevor practically shouted. "What did you two do to the food? This is the best rice and beans we've had."

Sheila nodded in agreement.

"That's what happens when you cook with love," Shalini said. "You can taste it."

What the fuck? Matthew's eyes narrowed at Shalini, who stopped her riot of laughing as soon as they made eye contact. "Bernie has a secret sauce she added. That's all," he said to change the direction of Shalini's comment, only he realized too late what he'd said. He felt Bernie's gaze zoom in on him like a periscope. Diana and Shalini both raised their eyebrows at him.

"Ooh, secret sauce?" Harold asked. "What is it?"

"Do you have any more?" Gretchen asked.

Matthew looked up just as Bernie, whose fiery eyes rivaled the heat of a serrano, looked away from him. "Oh, I just had a little bit of it."

He'd obviously made a mistake. She leaned into him, and right when he was going to say he was sorry, she whispered, "And you will never get a taste of it again. Bland food the rest of the trip!"

It felt like a banishment. Camping food was probably the worst part of these long treks, and he'd just tasted a little bit of what it could be. And now, that had been taken away from him. She didn't have that much left in the bottle, and they had four days to go, after today.

◆ ◆ ◆

Bernie lay in her sleeping bag, trying to ignore the chill that always seemed to seep in through the nylon tent. No matter how tired she was, no matter how much her feet hurt, or how badly she wanted to slip away into sweet, blissful unconsciousness, there was something about Matthew lying a foot to her left, scribbling in his book, that made her nerves run raw, her legs restless, and her overall state of dirty, unwashed, love story–reading self be hyperaware that they were sharing this super close, intimate state together.

And tonight it was especially bad. Maybe it was the stupid comment about cooking with love that Shalini had made, making her a little sad inside. Or maybe that Matthew had tried to convince her earlier that day that somehow she was an adventurer. That somehow he had secretly colluded with her mother and that they were jointly trying to convince Bernie that she had the soul of Aunt Bernice swimming around inside her. Maybe even Tabitha had contributed to their en masse onslaught of character defamation.

She stared at the book in her hands, but the words were a guise for the truth of her thoughts.

Over the past few years, Tabitha and she had imbibed too much wine, more than once, and Tabitha had tried to convince Bernie to enact some of the ridiculous, childish behaviors that they'd done in their teens.

"Remember the Bra-Mobile?" Tabitha said dreamily, like they were in their eighties instead of their twenties.

"How could I forget?" Bernie and Tabitha had been sixteen, hyped up on cold brew and driving around the hills of Portland. Tabitha, whining about how she'd waited for her boobs to develop past the size of walnuts, had taken off her bra and waved it through the sunroof. Somehow that had led her tying it to Bernie's antenna, and they flew down the streets with Tabitha's bra flying in the wind.

That was when a cop had pulled them over for speeding.

"What about that house we broke into when we were fourteen? That was pretty . . . unsafe of us, huh?" Tabitha laughed at the memory.

Bernie smiled. "What was wrong with us?" This old house down the street from Tabitha had been slowly falling into a state of collapse. The back window was broken out, vines crept in through cracks in the bricks, and bats flew out of the attic slats every evening. So of course they decided to slip inside.

Bernie led the way by sliding through a basement window and then landed in a puddle of water. As soon as Bernie shone her flashlight around the basement, rats scurried about. Their tiny eyes reflected green in the light, amid the shelves of forgotten rotting things, all basking in the smell of mold and must.

As they ran up the rotting stairs, Bernie's foot slipped through one of the soft planks halfway. She screamed, and by the time they'd gotten outside, in the streetlight, her ankle had swollen up. In fact, it had never been the same since. She limped back to Tabitha's, afraid to tell her parents. Her mom would just put some kind of magical cure-all oil on it, but her dad would insist on taking her to the hospital after hearing what she'd done. And ground her. And give her that look that told Bernie, *I thought you were better than this.*

In retrospect, she could envision him telling her how fleeting life is, like he'd done from his hospital bed. How she needed to be careful and safe if he wasn't around to take care of her. She hadn't taken this anecdote to heart when she went to college, but after he was gone, she felt that emptiness like a dead weight inside her, filling her up like cold iron, how absolutely he was not around to take care of her.

And she'd always suspected she had done something to her ankle by not seeing a doctor. Yet now here she was, hiking for a week straight. If her mother had known about that night, maybe she'd have suggested a bus tour instead.

A laugh erupted out of her at the thought.

"What's happening in your book?" Matthew asked. "Did someone fart during a sex scene?"

Bernie wanted to cackle at the idea but swallowed it. She didn't want to give him the pleasure. She was still a little mad about the hot sauce exposé.

"Um, no."

Also, something about the word *sex* coming out of Matthew's mouth made her legs stiffen.

"That's how I would write my sex scenes—add a comedy twist to them. Like farting right in the middle."

"Really? Sounds like that would really resonate with your TV audience."

"You think?" His head twisted over so fast, his gaze so intense, that she thought he'd mistaken her sarcasm for truth. But then his eyes wrinkled up and a big toothy smile brightened up his face. She'd never seen him smile like that before. So genuine, so full of light, like she had some secret window into his mind.

He sighed a laugh and picked up his little mysterious idea pad and wrote something in it. It was so brief, that smile, and so real, that she tried to think why he never let it sneak out before.

"What are you writing in that little notebook?" she asked.

"All my comedic sex-scene ideas."

"A whole notebook of them? Really? What are the other ones?" She was just asking for trouble. She'd seen a glimpse of Matthew's smile; his mere utterance of the word *sex*, even though it was in the same sentence as *fart*, made her legs freeze; and now she wanted to open the window to bask in the light of his dirty, funny ideas.

"Not a whole notebook . . ." He set the pad down. "But I'm sure I can think of enough."

"Oh, I'm dying to hear. Please share."

Matthew took a deep breath and blew out the air so hard the strings hanging from the domed ceiling blew. He must have very large lungs. Which now somehow sounded dirty to her.

"Well, if I were writing comedic sex scenes, I can think of lots of things that make the act of love funny."

"The act of love?" The phrase just sounded wrong coming out of his mouth.

"Like goats. Anytime you involve a goat, there is instant humor."

"What?" She couldn't help but laugh at that.

"Yeah, or chickens. Or a lamb maybe. A buck-toothed pony. In general, farm animals make everything funny."

"Funny or disturbing?"

"Both—that's why it's funny. Or kids. It's always funny to have kids interrupt it."

"Funny or perverse?"

"If the target demographic is parents, they all groan-laugh because they can identify."

"Okay, I get it. What else?"

"A ghost. Like, if one of them sees a ghost and they're at the pinnacle of their lovemaking, then what? Do they just stop?"

"Again, funny or creepy?"

"I feel like this is a game," he said, narrowing his eyes at her. "Is Matthew funny or fill-in-the-blank adjective?"

"Funny or sad?" Bernie asked.

"If someone dies during it."

"There is no way that could be funny," Bernie said.

"What if it was a creepy old pervy man and he hired a prostitute and he knew he had a week to live and this was his last wish. And he died smiling?"

"You'd have to have a very good director." She laughed. "Okay, funny or hungry?"

"Wow." Matthew sucked in a breath. "This couple is having this romantic date, and they've been toiling over it, like a soufflé or something. But they can't control themselves, and so they just start feeding each other in the kitchen, but stuff that should be sexy but is really just weird. Like oysters that slide out of their mouths on the floor. Or asparagus she slides her tongue along and tries to eat, but it's so fibrous she can't chew it up all the way and has to spit it out."

"I hate when that happens."

"It's the worst," he agreed. "Especially if you are on a date. Like, do you just swallow it and hope you don't choke?"

Bernie started wondering what a date with Matthew would actually be like. Did he cook romantic dinners for girls? Did he make jokes the whole time? Did he put on his serious cap and lecture them with random factoids?

"What about funny or sexy?" The words just came out, like a dare. Like Bernie was daring herself.

"You don't think those ideas were sexy?" He feigned hurt and let out another of his briefest, most delightful grins.

"I'm pretty sure you can do better." Why was she pushing him to talk about sex as they lay together whispering in a tent? Somehow it felt less mischievous than it should, since it wasn't dark yet. If it were dark outside, then . . .

"Challenge accepted." Matthew folded his hands together and stretched them toward the ceiling as he cracked his knuckles. Like he was really getting down to work. "So you have this guy who is trying to seduce his lady, so he does a striptease. And at first, it's goofy, because he's a goofy guy. He flings his shirt around his head and wiggles out of his pants. He's just wearing boxers and those weird old-time garters that hold up your socks. And socks, of course. Maybe a bow tie. And his girl is watching him, mildly amused, but then he gyrates his hips and slides his pants between his legs like a rocking horse. He puts one leg up on the bed and thrusts toward her and then slowly crawls up the bed. And then, well . . . you know."

Bernie swallowed. Because the whole time Matthew had been explaining his idea, she imagined him doing that, gyrating and thrusting and dancing with his hips.

"Yeah, I think that could work." Her voice sounded thick. She put the bandana around her eyes. "On that note, I'm going to go to sleep."

"Oh, okay."

Was she reading into the hint of disappointment in his voice? She blew out a breath that must have been as big as Matthew's and tried to go to sleep. And not think of Matthew's calves cradled by sock garters and old-man socks, topped off by some weird patterned boxers with corgis on them, thrusting his pelvis in her needy face.

CHAPTER 19

The smell of coffee was filling her immediate surroundings. She blinked her eyes open, but the kerchief battened down her eyelashes. She stretched out, feeling so rested after last night. Maybe camping wasn't as horrible as her father had always said. Maybe there was something about living without the trappings of civilization for a period of time to reflect on life and where you were. Although there were definitely things she missed: James Brown, a toilet, and unlimited water so she didn't think she would eventually perish if she drank too much. But the toilet situation really took care of the last bit. If her doctor ever told her she drank too much coffee and not enough water, she'd have this trip to prove that it was all okay.

"Bernie." Matthew's voice was close to her ear. Was she dreaming how close it was? Like he was getting ready to tell her a secret? Or whisper what he would do in those corgi-patterned boxers?

Ugh. She could feel a blush taking over her face. Hot hot hot.

"Yes?" she creaked out, only parting her lips wide enough to restrain her morning breath from filling up the tent.

"Everyone's up. We need to leave soon. Drink your coffee."

She slid off the bandana. "You brought me coffee?"

Matthew was squatting beside her, holding out her mug. She took it, and her eyes scanned him up and down, the tight hiking pants with their dorky shorts zipper cradling his thighs. His thermal henley, just unbuttoned enough that she could see the hint of chest hair vining up to the dip of his collarbone. God help her. And he'd brought her coffee.

She shook it off and crawled out of her bag from the waist up. "Thank you. That was nice."

Why was that so hard to say? Why did it feel embarrassing?

"Yeah, sure. No biggie." He bent down and started packing up his bag. "You must've gotten some really solid sleep last night."

Bernie hummed in acknowledgment as she sipped her coffee. Obviously she was having some kind of twisted, depraved reaction to this guy because they were bound together for a week.

But she'd been stuck with people before, trapped in time with Duke's cousin at a wedding Tabitha had forced her to come to, convinced they would hit it off. Which meant Tabitha and Duke abandoned her for two days, so she had to fumble through awkward conversations with his perfectly nice and attractive cousin, whom she still referred to as "Duke's-Cousin-What's-His-Name?" Or when she knew it was over with her ex, Kit, but went to Napa on vacation with him anyway out of guilt and managed not to have sex with him even though she'd had too much wine on more than one occasion.

Could it be that Matthew put these ideas in her head about her adventurous wannabe self and her "inner great-aunt Bernice," and she was starting to succumb to his tempting words?

"You know, Bernie, this isn't a Starbucks."

Matthew's know-it-all voice woke her out of her morning daydream. "What?"

"You've got to chug that coffee and get on with the female version of the three S's."

"Three S's?" she asked.

"Shit, shower, and shave."

Such tempting words they were. Had she seriously fantasized about him erotically dancing at the foot of her bed last night?

She swallowed her coffee, which had cooled down enough not to scald her esophagus, and climbed out of her sleeping bag cocoon and began rolling it up. She started packing her bag and felt Matthew's eyes boring into her skull.

"What is it now?" She looked up.

"You need to go eat, woman. They are going to end up tossing your oats for the bears if you don't go. Those granola bars are for emergency purposes only, and you keep munching on them like they're a five-course meal."

She huffed, ready to come back with a retort. *Woman?* Was that caveman speak, or was he trying to sound like one of her girlfriends? But she had two granola bars left. Somehow, she'd just assumed she would eat his if she ran out, which, now that she thought about it, was a little selfish. Maybe he was correct on just this one, very minor, point. "Fine."

Not the comeback she wanted. She could see him laughing quietly at her, like he knew he was right, too, when she left the tent. She searched out the leftover food and said her good mornings to the rest of the group in between swallows.

Maybe Matthew was right about her having some inner adventure diva. Or maybe it had just taken this trip and a few days of adjustment to remember who she was and what she could do. Regardless, she didn't want to be thought of as the woman who needed help all the time. Even though she reluctantly appreciated the prodding that morning.

She marched back to the tent determined to show Matthew that she could be one with nature and hike for miles on end and not have a phone or a way of contacting humanity. The world could be collapsing around them. There could be a war. Portland could have been sunk into the ground. And none of them would have any idea. Bernie would pack her bag like a champ, tie her bear can on properly, and really show him.

As she marched toward her tent, feeling glorious, the other tents collapsed, falling down like hot-air balloons landing one by one. Trevor was doing his motivational speech for the morning, and yet she hadn't packed her bag. At her tent, Matthew was standing outside, the nylon collapsing like so many others.

"Hey, my bag!"

He pointed to the ground behind him. "I already packed it."

"What?" She didn't know whether to be pissed or thankful. "Isn't that an invasion of privacy?"

He squinted at her. "Oh, thanks, Matthew, for letting me sleep in today and getting me coffee and packing my bag—of which I saw nothing private, because all I did was stuff your sleeping bag in it."

She felt her lips churning as she tried to find the right words to say. She didn't know whether she should be pissed or thankful. It wasn't like she had a diary with her. It was just that she was at the point where she was starting to accept that she could be this hiker person, and he was taking it away from her. By being nice. Why was he being nice?

"Why are you being nice?" she asked.

"I don't know if it's so much I'm being nice. I'm trying to hurry up because you slept too late. Everyone was up an hour before you. But you seemed tired. You had some drool slipping down your chin and what I would call a light-to-medium snore going."

Bernie's hand came up to her chin, like the drool was still there and she needed to cover it up. "I don't snore."

"Oh yeah, you do. Ask Gretchen and Jay next tent over. They probably heard you. You might actually be like the alarm clock for our merry group of hikers."

His eyes had that sheen behind them that turned him into this six-foot-two version of a mischievous sprite. He was joking but at her expense. She was already über conscious of the lack of running water, clean clothes, and the amount of dry shampoo she'd put in her hair. She didn't need to be told she snored. And drooled.

As if he could sense her inner dialogue, he added, "Don't worry about it. We all need an alarm clock anyway."

Bernie huffed. "And here I was going to see if you needed help with the tent."

He laughed, but just one of those brief bubbles of a laugh, and rolled the tent up in what seemed like two seconds.

"Let's go, milady."

She'd never felt less like a lady in her life. A dirty, scrubby, drooling, snoring scab of a lady. "You're hilarious."

She was walking toward Trevor and the rest of the group as Sheila passed them, examining the grounds. "Hi, you two." She might as well have winked. Why did all the women seem to know something that Bernie didn't? Yeah, Matthew was attractive. And yes, there were occasional sparks of usefulness, but then those were mixed with comments about pooping, drooling, farting, or snoring. He could be funny, but then he swallowed up his laughter and smiles like he was recovering from some kind of mild case of sociopathy.

"Do you think Trevor and Sheila will do this forever?" Matthew asked.

"Why?"

"I just can't imagine. Day after day with one other person. In the tundra. All the time. No city ever. Like, they can never eat good tacos."

Bernie laughed. "That's your concern? Tacos?"

"Look, have you had tacos in LA? If you had, you'd know what I mean."

"No, can't say I have. But I think they're sweet. If there was running water and cell service, I'd do it."

Matthew stopped walking. "You would do this? Lead a hiking tour?"

"With the right person." Bernie straightened up as Matthew actually bent over laughing. No, she didn't want to lead a hiking tour. She was a city girl, but she also felt like she had something to prove to him. His eyes were all crinkly and shining with tears. Were those tears?

"I can only imagine what would happen to your poor group."

"Really?" she said deadpan. "Well, if you were leading a tour, they'd all be wondering how they ended up in some kind of military camp. You'd be espousing your diatribes on everything from tree-leaf shape to proper tent rolling, and no one would have any fun."

"Well, I'm sure it wouldn't be as bad as yours, where people would legit get lost because you don't know how to use a compass, and they'd probably all be starving because you'd expect them to survive on granola bars."

"There is nothing wrong with granola bars. My dad used to pack them for me every day. I love them."

The words just came out of her. And maybe it was a weird thing to say. But Matthew had wiped his eyes, the pissed-off look faded from his face, and he just looked at her.

Bernie twisted around, worried that he was going to say something. Ask something. And realized they were all alone. "Where is everyone?"

"Ahead."

She marched along the trail, wondering how they'd found themselves sequestered from the group. Diana and Shalini were probably reassuring the others that it was okay to leave them alone, because their fantasy of *Desperation on Denali* had come true.

They were entering a small patch of trees. Tall spruces flanked either side of the trail. A stream was bubbling ahead. Bernie was so focused on meeting up with the rest of the group that she wasn't paying as much attention as she should have. As she stepped onto the bridge, "bridge" being a loose term for the large rocks that had been grouped together so hikers wouldn't have to wade in the water, a bear was to her right, fifteen feet away, drinking from the stream.

It was big and brown, the nuances of its hair shining in the light, and just for a moment, Bernie admired how beautiful it was. The first bear they'd seen on this trip. She'd given up on seeing any. But here it was, having a drink. It almost looked like the teddy bear she'd had as a kid, but a much larger version, with a pointy snout and glittering eyes.

"Oh shit." Matthew's voice was a whisper behind her.

That snapped her out of it. Bernie puffed up and stretched her arms over her head and made the loudest noise possible. The bear noise that Sheila and Trevor had taught them. She embraced her inner bear and stomped her feet up and down on the rocks as she crossed the river, her eyes not leaving its sight.

The bear seemed startled. If it were a human, its head would have retracted into its neck and said, *What the fuck are you doing?* It almost made her laugh, this ridiculous scene. Adrenaline must have been flowing through her, because she'd never felt like this before. So alive and confident. Matthew was now doing it, too, this bear dance, but he was still on the shore, backing away from it. Bernie stepped across the rocks, reasoning that she could get to the other side and the bear would have less of a chance of catching her. If that was even something that bears did. But it was big. Twice the size of her at least.

The worry over the bear started to weigh on her. It hadn't left yet and just stared at them. The worry started to interrupt her adrenaline flow and poked holes in her confidence. She wavered on the rocks and her foot slid down one, and before she could feel what was happening with her legs, she felt it in her stomach, an empty sinking feeling, a foreboding of what was to come.

Bernie screamed as she crashed into the water from the shock and the sharp pain shooting up her leg.

"Oh shit!" Matthew hopped over on the rocks toward her, and the bear scurried away with big galloping steps.

Matthew reached for her. "Let me pull you up."

Bernie grabbed onto his hands, unsure if the tears were from embarrassment or her ankle. He pulled her up and she shouted, "Stop!"

"What?" He looked alarmed. "What is it?"

"My ankle." Bernie pulled her leg out of the rocks it was wedged between. "It hurts."

"Can you move it?"

She shook her head. "I don't know."

"I need to get you out of this water, though. Fuck it." Then Matthew just jumped in the stream and put her arm around his neck as he bent down, since he was almost a foot taller than her. "Just use me as a crutch."

Bernie tried to step, and as soon as she put weight on her right foot, the sizzle of pain shot up again. "I can't walk." The tears were still coming. She'd never felt physical pain like this before.

"Okay." Matthew reached down and touched the back of her thigh. "Does this hurt?"

She shook her head, and then in a second, Matthew was carrying her across the river like a bride over a doorstep.

"Oh my God. This is so embarrassing," she said through the tears. Her nose was running and she was freezing wet and crying and she'd failed at the one thing she'd tried to do, to be the adventurous hiker she'd attempted to be.

"That's what you're worried about?" He shook his head. "What if you broke your foot?"

That would be how this journey would end, of course. Bernie would break something, have to stop the camping trip, and be sent home for attempting to be an ounce of what her mother had wanted her to be. How Tabitha said she should try something new. Her great-aunt Bernice would be shaking her head at her from the clouds above, making that tsk-tsk noise with her dentures.

And Matthew carrying her through the river like he was Thor—this was all just too much.

On the grassy side of the bank, the rest of the group had come rushing down from the trail.

"Oh my God, what happened? We heard you scream." Sheila bent down and took off Bernie's pack.

"She fell off the rocks," Matthew said.

Bernie wiped her eyes, thankful that he didn't say what she was doing when she fell. "My foot got wedged in the rocks."

Trevor took off his pack and bent down. "I hope it's not broken. Let's do a test."

Trevor and Sheila began squeezing and twisting different parts of her leg from the knee down as Matthew stared at them from above, worrying at his lip. Everyone else stood around asking if she needed anything as Bernie shook her head. All she wanted was to rewind thirty minutes and start the day over.

As she lay there trying to process what happened, she realized she really, really didn't want it to be broken. She wanted to continue this hike. She wanted to continue mildly torturing Matthew. She wanted this vacation, because even if something bad had been the outcome of her fall, something had taken over in that moment. Some kind of brave, energy-fueled feeling that she hadn't felt in a long time, and she realized that she'd missed it.

When Sheila tried to take off her boot, Bernie screamed. The pain seemed to stretch out and expand around her ankle with every movement. "Let me do it." She carefully untied her bootlaces and made the opening as wide as she could, but every movement hurt. Every centimeter she tried to move her foot out of the boot was rife with sharp, shooting pain.

She sucked in a breath and looked at Sheila and Trevor. "I don't know if I can get it off."

"Okay. Let's try to walk on it," Trevor said.

Sheila wriggled her out of her pack, and then she and Matthew helped her up on her left leg. As soon as she tried to step on her right leg, the pain shot up again. But she didn't want it to be broken; she had to try to walk. Trevor was her crutch on the right, and Sheila was her crutch on the left. They tried to take a few steps, and each time, tears came to Bernie's eyes as she attempted to put weight on her ankle.

Trevor sighed and looked at Bernie. "I think your ankle might be broken."

◆　◆　◆

As many times as Matthew had thought to himself that Bernie was the personification of awkwardness on this hike, or voiced this thought aloud, even to her, he felt bad. After Trevor pronounced that she might have a broken ankle, Bernie burst into tears and, even worse, tried to hide them behind her hands. Maybe it was the pain, or her pride, but she definitely hadn't been a chicken in front of that bear.

In fact, it had surprised him. When he'd come up on her at the bridge, he wasn't sure if he was more in shock from the bear or from this manifestation of Bernie as some kind of Jane Goodall–Tarzan hybrid. It was kind of hot. Not that he'd ever tell her that.

And now, the whole thing was sad. There was no way she could hike several miles a day with a broken ankle. Even if they fashioned some kind of crutch, logic told him that if you had broken bones, you probably needed medical attention pronto.

Trevor and Sheila had stepped away from the group and made a call on their satellite phone. Shalini and Diana crouched around Bernie and were attempting to make jokes and finally got a smile to break through her tear-streaked face.

Sheila hung up the phone and came to kneel by Bernie. "Sweetie, I think we need to airlift you out of here so you can go to the hospital. There's a clearing up the path, and the helicopter will come there in about thirty minutes to an hour. I'll stay with you, and the rest of the group can go on with Trevor." She looked at the others. "I'll catch up later."

A series of "Awwws" broke from the crowd.

Sheila unhooked the bear can from Bernie's bag. "Is this all that you need to give Matthew?" she asked her.

Bernie looked from the bag to Matthew and nodded solemnly, wiped at her face, then gazed over at the ground. Matthew should be happy, or maybe relieved that he'd get to spend the rest of the trip in a tent by himself. But instead, something like panic fluttered through him. This just didn't feel right. The bear can hung like a dead, sad weight in his hands.

The group said their goodbyes and well wishes to Bernie, and Sheila said they could all send out emails after to keep in touch, but that didn't feel like enough. As the last of them trickled down the trail, Trevor leading them out from the bank like the Pied Piper, Matthew lingered.

"I'll wait with you," he said.

"You don't have to," Bernie said, not looking at him.

"That's nice of you." Sheila smiled up at him.

Sheila's phone rang, and she walked away to answer it.

Matthew bent down to Bernie. "Are you sure you're not just being a wimp?" he whispered.

That got Bernie to look at him. The expression on her face was so furious he had to laugh. "I'm just kidding. Geez."

"Not the time, Matthew."

"You're not just trying to get away from me by breaking your ankle?"

She shook her head, but it was pathetic; somehow it made him feel sorrier for her. Like she'd given up.

"You know, it was really brave what you did back there. I would have thought you were an experienced hiker."

"Stop." She sniffed.

"I'm serious. I was freaked out. It's like you saved me."

Bernie looked up at him just briefly enough to roll her eyes, but he still got a smile out of her.

Sheila then towered over them, blocking out the sun. "Matthew, would you be able to carry Bernie up the trail by chance? If it's possible—I just don't want her to put any weight on her ankle and possibly damage it more."

Matthew said, "Sure," just as Bernie said, "I can walk."

"You can't walk." He looked at her, shaking his head.

"I just need support."

"You're going to hop on one leg?"

She sighed and her shoulders fell. "Fine."

They brought her up to her one working leg, and Matthew picked her up and grunted just to piss her off.

"Really?" She looked at him.

He couldn't help but smile. What was he going to do without her for entertainment on the rest of the hike?

"At least you'll get to take a shower at the hospital. And use an actual toilet. Not wash your face in a stream. These are the things dreams are made of."

"I can't tell my mom. She'll be so disappointed."

"What? Don't be silly. Any of us could have broken something."

"You wouldn't have." She sniffled again. "You're like Mr. Adventure World Almighty Traveler Explorer Dude."

Matthew scoffed. "Uh. Well, clearly you have much higher regard for me than anyone else does. Most everyone else calls me Matthew. Or 'that guy.'"

Bernie huffed out a laugh in between sniffles. "Thanks for carrying me."

"Anytime. I get to show that my $150 gym membership is actually worth something."

Sheila stopped ahead of them at a bright-green meadow, dotted with those pink flowers that Bernie had been cooing over the first day.

"Here's your airfield," Sheila said.

"It's so pretty. I can't believe this is my last look." Matthew put her down, and she balanced on her left leg as she clung to his arm.

He looked down to where she held on. Brave, ridiculous Bernie. He couldn't imagine hiking on this trail without her, really.

"You can do it again, once you're healed," Sheila said. "I'm sure we can even work out a discount. And you'll get a brief helicopter tour of Denali."

They stood in silence for a few minutes, taking in the view. Matthew tried to sort through his very confused thought process. The whole purpose of this trip was to get the peace and quiet he'd craved, and now he could actually have it. But not to have her beside him, making her weird jokes, doing her little fluttery eye rolls of irritation followed by a smile; he couldn't imagine it. She was his new inspiration, and he had only a few days of material about her. A TV show wasn't going to write itself. Well, whatever the reason, he'd settled on one thing. He wasn't ready to let her go.

And then the whirring blades of the helicopter in the distance cut through the air.

"The pilot is going to take you to the hospital so you can see a doctor. And you can call your family or anyone you'd like to come stay with you. It really depends on what the doctor says. But we'll all be staying in Anchorage the last day, so maybe you can join us at the hotel for our departure dinner, if you're still there or if you feel up to it."

Bernie nodded as the helicopter landed in the field a hundred feet away. Sheila grabbed Bernie's pack and headed toward the helicopter.

"This is terrible," Bernie said, maybe to herself. Maybe to Matthew. "I hate hospitals." She looked so miserable as she said it, her face on the verge of crumbling again, apparently just from thinking about going to the hospital.

"Are you ready?" he asked.

She blew out a giant sigh and nodded. He picked her up.

Three more days until the dinner. Three days until he'd see Bernie again. During that time, she'd sit in a hospital by herself with no way to get around or move and no one there to help her. Just the nurses and doctor. It sounded so lonely, so very un-Bernie-like. He just couldn't let that happen.

When they got to the helicopter, he took off his pack and threw it in. "I'm coming with you."

"What?" She looked at him like he was the crazy one. And she was prepared to go it alone for three days without anyone to help her.

"You can't sit in a hospital room without anyone you know to help you."

"There are nurses and doctors."

"Yeah, but do you want to be helpless to them? Only them with all that weird florescent light overhead? Have them wheel you around on demand by buzzer? You said you hate hospitals."

Her mouth opened like she was going to protest again, but Sheila cut her off.

"I think that's very kind of you, Matthew."

"But the hike!" Bernie shook her head. "You always wanted to hike Denali."

"I did. And I'll get a helicopter tour thrown in as well."

Bernie was already being manhandled by the medic who was on the helicopter, and he was laying her down on a cot while Matthew climbed in. She couldn't protest any longer because Anthony, the medic, was asking her questions.

"Bye, Sheila." He waved from the open door.

"Best of luck. See you in Anchorage!"

The pilot closed the door, and Matthew put his seat belt on.

"Hi, I'm Robert," the pilot said as he handed Matthew a headset.

"Matthew. Thanks for picking us up."

"That sucks about your girlfriend."

"Oh, she's not my girlfriend."

Robert gave him a look, and Matthew resisted providing an explanation. Because really, he couldn't explain to himself why he'd insisted on coming with her and giving up the rest of his hike.

Robert asked Anthony if they were ready, and they lifted into the air. Matthew's belly sank. Oddly, he'd never been in a helicopter before, so maybe this was par for the course.

Robert's voice came in over the headset. "The air's a little windy today, so don't be alarmed by the rough ride."

"Thanks." Matthew looked behind him at Bernie, who was sitting up but strapped into a cot while Anthony tended to her ankle.

"How are you doing?" he asked her.

She nodded, but then her face winced up and she looked back at Anthony, who was attempting to remove her shoe.

Good luck with that. The helicopter flew into the air and then sank again, Matthew's stomach with it. This was not a plane, for sure. He'd never been carsick or sick on a plane, but this? This was something completely different.

"That damn wind," Robert said into the headset.

Matthew tried to focus by looking at the scenery outside. Pine and spruce trees, dark green against the gold and chartreuse grass. Specks of bright fuchsia dotting the ground here and there. As they elevated into the sky, the mountains and glaciers in the distance looked white, almost pale blue, such a stark contrast against the greenery they'd been hiking in. A river sliced through the trees, a blue that mimicked the sky.

The helicopter dipped again, and Matthew closed his eyes. His stomach, now empty except for whatever remained of the acid burn from his morning routine of a pool of black coffee, blenched, and his eyes searched the pocket behind Robert's seat, spying a sick bag. God, he did not want to get sick on this helicopter, especially after he was trying to help Bernie. In whatever weird way that was.

Robert was muttering something about the wind and the mountains, and Matthew just didn't care. He tried to remember what people said about getting carsick, how you just had to look straight ahead, and he tried to do that, but during the next dip and upward slide they made, things just looked worse as he gazed out the window, and he grabbed for the bag. Whatever was left of the oatmeal came up.

Thank God he grabbed the bag in time. Someone threw up on a show he'd worked on once, and they used literally watered-down oatmeal and food coloring as vomit, and well, oatmeal vomit was as bad as it could get.

He hung his head down and clutched the bag shut. A tap on his arm, and he looked up. Anthony was holding out a bottle of water, and Bernie was giving him a half-disgusted, half-concerned look. What a pair they were.

CHAPTER 20

Maybe they were even now. It was the only thought that gave Bernie some solace after Matthew had watched her commit the humiliation of the decade. Apparently, he had a weak stomach or got helicopter sick or had just become traumatized over what he'd done: hopped in the helicopter on a whim for poor, helpless Bernie. As if their joint jaunt through Denali wasn't enough for him already.

If she'd ruined the rest of her trip and disappointed her mother, Tabitha, and even herself, she at least got to say a high-elevation good-bye to the scenery she'd been traipsing through the past few days. The mountains rose up behind the helicopter, and the white snow was so close it felt as if she could run her hand through it and make a snowball. In fact, today, if she hadn't destroyed her ankle, she would have been stepping on her first glacier.

Glacier. When would she ever get to touch a glacier again?

Another pathetic tear came to her eye. She had to stop crying like this. Especially over a giant chunk of ice. That was all it was, ice. She'd keep telling herself that.

But it wasn't just ice; it was that she'd almost done it. She'd hiked for so many days straight—without toilets or plumbing or cell service—and she hadn't hated it. It had been fun. Although *fun* wasn't the right word either. *Freeing* maybe? Like she'd forced herself into this Portland cage, from which she occasionally crept to drive to Bend to visit her mom. And now she'd fully broken out of it. And liked it. She'd heard all the campfire stories of other adventures people had gone on, and she was envious, trying to picture herself doing the same things—swimming with the turtles in clear turquoise waters or standing on the top of Machu Picchu feeding the sweet, curious-faced llamas.

And now that spirit of adventure, which she'd tried to hold tight to, was gone. Was she leaving that version of herself in Denali with the bear she'd done such a woeful job of scaring off? It was over. She had to go home, and this time it really would be a cage because she couldn't walk.

Her back started shaking, and a series of sobs came out in the worst way, spewing and moaning, in bereavement for the Bernie she'd thought she might recapture. The one everyone, including Matthew, was convinced she had locked somewhere inside her.

"Are you okay?" Anthony asked her as he hovered over her foot. She nodded. After shrieking while he tried to get her boot off, it was the least she could do.

He rolled her sock off carefully, and she couldn't help but laugh in horror: (1) She was certain the smell of an unwashed foot for four days was less than pleasant; (2) that unwashed foot had also been hiking for eight hours a day; and (3) it was covered with those blister bandages.

"Whoa!" Anthony said, his head sinking into his neck and tilting to the side.

"I didn't break in my boots properly," she muttered, as if that explained everything.

His eyebrows raised and he nodded. "Can I take the bandages off?"

"Sure." It wasn't like she needed them anymore.

Every little movement hurt, even though she knew Anthony was trying to be gentle. He probably wasn't used to wimps like her but dudes like Matthew who grew beards and clad themselves in polar fleece and would still walk on an ankle if it was broken, just to check one of their boxes.

Dudes like Matthew who puked on helicopters. She turned, and he was still clutching his head in his hands, looking at the floor. The paper bag tight in his fist. Something zipped up inside her for him too. Something that was a little warm and sweet. Maybe he wasn't the perfect, unshakeable man she'd assumed he was. And the bigger question was, Why had he come with her?

A pressure on the bottom of her foot made her jerk it away from evil Anthony's grip. So quickly he had become evil Anthony.

"Sorry!" he said, freezing his movement.

"It's okay." He was just trying to help. But the pain shooting up and down her foot, and somehow also radiating around her ankle, disagreed wholeheartedly.

"Well, I think you have broken your ankle, miss."

She nodded. Of course. "Am I the first person to do this on a hike? The first hiking newbie to be rescued?"

"Oh no. Geez, we've had people break all kinds of things—legs, arms, feet—but mostly it's the lower half. Also, if you break your arm, as long as you can set it properly, you don't really need to be airlifted out. But a broken foot—you just can't walk on it. You can do even more damage."

"So will I have crutches or a . . . wheelchair?" She tried to imagine rolling around in a wheelchair for weeks, unable to do anything on her foot.

"Whatever the doctor recommends." Anthony wrinkled up the left side of his face in some kind of solidarity. Buildings appeared in the windows around her as the helicopter settled down. Even though Anchorage was a city, it was small and cozy and surrounded by a lush spread of grass.

The door opened and a few other medics appeared. They slid Bernie off on her cot, which they popped up to roll her into the hospital. She looked over at Matthew, who was carrying both their packs.

"Are you okay?" she asked, although she swore Matthew wasn't meeting her eyes.

"I'm pretty sure I should be asking you that."

"I'm already broken. Just wanted to make sure you weren't too." It was somehow comforting to be concerned about him for once, after he'd had to help her so much on their trip.

His face had a greenish-yellow tint to it. That couldn't be good. "Nothing a little toothpaste can't fix." He sighed.

Then she was whisked away on her gurney—was that what this was called? Or were gurneys only for dead people? Her leg was immovable. Which meant she was immovable. She'd seen Matthew throw up. He'd seen her scream and wave uncontrollably at a bear. Now she was helpless. He was sick.

What a pair they were.

The sterile white walls of the hospital were such a weird contrast to her life the past several days. The intercom noise coming over the speakers. A metallic voice paging Dr. Santi. The posters about washing hands that flanked the hall. The brightest lights she'd ever seen, even though she'd essentially been in terminal sunshine nonstop. It was all so constructed and electronic and plastic.

They slid her into a room and helped her get on the bed. One of the medics asked for her insurance card and ID, which Matthew fished out of her bag. He must have felt odd rifling through her pockets. Such an intimate thing to do.

Maybe Matthew felt that way too. Maybe he already regretted coming. That would explain the look on his face.

Then everyone suddenly vanished, saying the doctor would be in shortly, and she and Matthew were alone. Alone in the silent room.

What should she say to him? *Thanks for coming! Why are you here? Why did you abandon your hiking trip to come with me?*

"Are you going to tell your mom?" Matthew asked at the same time Bernie asked, "Why did you come with me?"

They both looked at each other, and Matthew said, "Uh . . . ," probably because Bernie hadn't meant to ask him such an assertive question, but that was just what came out. Maybe Matthew didn't know why he'd come either. Surely it wasn't because he didn't want to carry the bear can by himself.

"I will eventually call my mom. Oh, wait, we have service now." She remembered the answer she'd been silently waiting for from her mom, with her phone battery dead and the lack of a cell signal. "Would you mind grabbing my phone and my charger? They should be in that left pocket."

He took them out and handed them to her, and she plugged the phone into the outlet and it buzzed to life. She scrolled through all the messages.

> Oh yes! So funny, I had forgotten about that. But I asked your Aunt Barb and she confirmed. Look at both of you having adventures in Denali! See, I knew you were like your great aunt.

She should want to be happy, because now she was connected back to all the people in her life, but instead the confirmation was just further proof that she had ultimately failed the Spirit of Great-Aunt Bernice litmus test. Her great-aunt had climbed to the tip-top of the mountain, and Bernie had fallen down on it somewhere in the lower third.

"Maybe this sounds crazy, but I feel like I just can't deal with any technology past the beginning of the twentieth century." She covered up her melancholy with a laugh and put down her phone.

"I know what you mean. It lasts for like a week whenever I go on a hike like this or lock myself in a cabin or something."

"You've locked yourself in a cabin?" She wondered if he meant that literally. It felt like he wouldn't do anything just halfway.

"Yeah. Since I moved to LA, sometimes I just have to get out of there and escape."

"You don't like LA?"

"I do, but change is always nice. I like to get out into nature to write. Unleash my brain from technology."

"So you still haven't answered my question. Why did you give up your hike and come with me?"

"Did you want to be alone?"

"No, not necessarily."

"Would you rather have had me stay there and not come?"

Now he was turning the tables on her. The truth was she was glad he was here, but she didn't know why. "I thought *I* asked the question."

He leaned back against the sofa and sighed. "I hate hospitals too."

If Matthew hated hospitals, then why on earth would he be sequestering himself inside one when he could be hiking in nature? "So that really begs the question then—why?"

"I didn't want you to have to be all by yourself in a hospital without a working leg."

Bernie's face felt hot. God, was she blushing? "But won't you be sad you're not finishing the hike?"

"I hiked in Denali." He drew a big checkmark in the air with his finger.

"Got it. Well, thank you for coming. It was very nice of you."

"No worries, it wouldn't have been the same without you to make fun of."

Bernie's jaw dropped, feigning shock, and then the door opened with a knock. A small woman in a doctor's coat, clutching a laptop, came in. "Hi, I'm Dr. Peters. Are you Bernice?"

"You can call me Bernie."

"Will do." She shook Bernie's hand and turned to Matthew.

"I'm Matthew." He stood and shook her hand, and the doctor raised her eyebrows in a question, like she was waiting for something to follow that, to explain exactly who he was, but she puckered her lips together and turned back to Bernie.

"So we had an unfortunate accident, I see. And the medic wrote down that he thought your ankle was broken. So we'll probably do an x-ray shortly, and possibly an MRI. Are you in any pain?"

"Yes, it's sore, but only really bad when someone touches it or I step on it."

"Did you take any Tylenol or anything?"

"Yes, on the helicopter."

"Do you mind if I take a look?"

Bernie shook her head and took a deep breath. A look meant more poking and prodding and twisting and likely crying.

"What happened, exactly?" Dr. Peters asked.

"I slipped on some rocks and my foot got caught between them, and something happened to my ankle when I tried to get it out."

Matthew raised his eyebrows at her. It was like she could translate what they were saying. *That's all you're going to tell her?*

Then he raised his arms over his head, his fingers like claws, his mouth open, silently screaming.

You're not going to tell her you were warding off a bear like a maniac and weren't paying full attention and could have gotten us both killed?

"Last week someone came in with the same thing. They keep making these bridges out of rocks, but they can be challenging to navigate. Especially for older hikers or if you've had a previous injury."

Of course, the elderly couple on their hike were fitter than Bernie was.

"Have you injured it before?" She pressed on the bottom of her foot again, and Bernie shrieked.

"There was a rotting-stair incident when I was younger. I stepped through a floorboard. After that, my ankle has always been problematic."

"Okay. Good to know." The doctor patted her thigh like she was trying to be comforting, but Bernie swore she could feel it vibrate into wherever the broken bone was. "I'll have the nurse come and take you for some imaging, and we'll figure out what to do."

"Thanks."

The doctor left, and as soon as she did, Matthew loudly whispered, "Bernie and the curious case of the rotting-stair incident." He narrowed his eyes and started looking around the room like a spy.

"Ha ha."

"I mean, could you be more evasive?"

"It was nothing. My friend Tabitha and I used to sneak around when we were kids, and we went in this supposedly haunted house, and that's when it happened."

"Really? Yeah, because that's a totally normal thing to do when you're a kid."

"Why? I had a pretty normal childhood. What did you do when you were a kid then?"

◆ ◆ ◆

Whatever *normal childhood* meant, Matthew was fairly sure he didn't have one.

"What did I do as a kid? Like to entertain myself?" he asked her.

"Yeah, sure." Bernie shrugged. She was tucked up in that bed, her head on a pillow behind her. A blanket spread over her legs, like a queen. Like she belonged there, ready to rule over her minions. Well, if her minions were all slightly dirty and needed a shower. He would love to have a shower himself. Being back in civilization with the hospital so bright, he was hyperaware of how absolutely filthy they were. And he wasn't ready to dive into the cautionary tale of young Matthew and how his drunk father abandoned him, because most memories had a hazy filter of melancholy and absence traced over them.

"Hey, do you think we can use this bathroom?" He got up and opened the door on the wall, escaping her question. There was a shower with a seat and a curtain, and a glorious toilet as well.

"Yeah, I don't see why not. I almost want to will myself to walk over there so I can take a shower and pee on a real live toilet."

Matthew didn't bother to point out that there were no such things as live toilets. But this was coming from the same person who said her inner beast was a squirrel. "You can totally take a shower in here. There's a seat."

"Really?" She sat up in bed and stared into the open bathroom, her mouth agape. Her eyes roamed around, and Matthew could tell she was trying to figure out how to get there.

"Maybe you should wait until you get your x-ray before trying to shower."

"Well, there's no way in hell I'm getting a cast put on this dirty foot. It is getting clean no matter what."

The nurse knocked and came in and looked from Matthew to Bernie. "Ready for your scans?" she asked monotone. Weren't nurses supposed to be helpful and sunny, trying to alleviate the stress of a hospital visit?

"Are there towels somewhere, Nurse?" Matthew asked.

She opened a cabinet on the wall above the built-in sofa and pulled out a towel and dropped it on the sofa.

"Awesome." He took it, almost hugging it. "While you're getting all scanned down, I'm going to get cleaned up."

Bernie's face fell and she nodded. He could swear that she looked sadder than when he'd pulled her out of the water.

The nurse helped her out of bed and tugged her through the door as Bernie gave him a guilt-inducing stare until she was out sight.

But it was shower time. He threw off his clothes, grabbed the small toiletries bag, and sprinted into the bathroom. The hot water was like heaven itself pouring down on him, and he stood there for five minutes just letting it rush over him. His hair was stiff from the mix of sweat and fresh air; even though it was thick normally, today it was like try-ing to comb through sandpaper. His beard felt the same. In fact, he was over this beard. He'd started growing it a month ago when he was preparing for this trip, and now that it was done, he was done with it. He'd shave it off.

After washing himself down twice, he started shaving with his Dr. Bronner's all-purpose soap as his only aid at getting rid of this hairy mass on his face. Just as he was finishing up, the door outside to the room opened and the voices of Bernie and the nurse trickled in through the crack at the bottom of the bathroom door.

He emerged from the bathroom to grab some clean clothes, and Bernie was looking at her phone, a fresh white boot on her foot, securing her ankle in place. "I hope you saved me some hot water because I . . ." She looked up from her phone, and her lips paused in midsentence. She scanned him from top to bottom, and then did some kind of head shake and blinked. "What, uh . . . happened to your face?"

Was Bernie checking him out? He looked down. He was standing in the middle of her hospital room wearing only a cheap towel slung around his waist. The familiar pull from between his hips started to rise. No. No no no no. The cheap towel was thin. He ducked over to get the remaining clean clothes from his pack. "I shaved."

"Yeah. You look like a different person."

"Is that good or bad?"

"I don't know," she said a little too fast. "Um . . . neither. Just, uh, different."

He ducked back into the bathroom and took a deep breath, calming himself. Oh, that would be excellent. Have Bernie see that he was aroused by an ounce of attention from her. One calculating look at his body that he'd taken care of. He wanted it to look good for a reason. But it was no different from being at the pool or the gym. He had his shirt off all the time, but why did it feel more intimate just now?

He ignored it and threw on some clean clothes. He felt like a new person.

The air had cleared when he entered the room again, and Bernie was back to her phone.

"So how are you going to get in the shower, exactly?"

Bernie sighed and looked at the wheelchair next to her. "I can wheel myself in, I guess."

"Do you want some help?"

"Getting into the shower?"

"Yeah."

Bernie's eyes seemed to grow dark for a minute as she thought about it. Other things wanted to pop out of his mouth. *Just let me know if there's anything I can do to make it easier for you. Anything, Bernie, anything.*

"Maybe you can just help me in there, and I can do the rest."

Matthew swallowed. "Yeah, sure. I can do whatever you want me to."

Whatever you want.

CHAPTER 21

Bernie pressed her lips together as Matthew helped her into the bathroom. Did he have any idea how dirty he sounded sometimes? *I can do whatever you want me to.* Oh, she could imagine how he could help her out, all right, with this new face of his. Help her shower, help tuck her in, help take care of this weird Matthew ache that was now snaking up in her abdomen.

It wasn't her fault. If any man had emerged from a bathroom, looking like he did, with that towel hanging low around his waist . . . for God's sake, she could see the indentions of his hip bones! How was she going to say words with those staring at her? And his face! His new, shaven face. It was like a hot beardless stranger who also just happened to be named Matthew had appeared in her life to help her.

But being so close to him, he smelled clean; she almost missed the smell of him. The smell she'd grown accustomed to over the past few days. Anytime she entered the tent and he was there, or she woke up with her face too close to his neck. When he'd carried her across the river, and she'd clutched onto him, her foot dangling with pain. An earthy, masculine smell that she knew was just him.

This was New Matthew. A Matthew 2.0, who smelled vaguely of clean, herbal tang and looked really good in just a towel. She resisted lifting her hand to stroke his face and feel the bare skin of his cheek.

But Matthew wasn't hers. He was a bystander to her calamities. A man who'd poked fun at her attempt at this new adventure. He'd probably followed her to the hospital to see the extent of her mishaps.

She looked at his face, with that smile of his creeping up as she hopped and made a little wincing noise. He was her crutch. Maybe he didn't come to see her fail. Again. But why he'd come was still a mystery.

He set her down on the bench seat. Thank God she already had her shoes off, because she didn't want his face anywhere near her feet. Or at least until they were no longer dirty. He hung a clean towel on a hook that was hip height. "Do you need anything else?"

She shook her head. "Thank you."

"Anytime."

She laughed. Anytime she needed help in the shower, he'd be there? Okay, she would remember that in three, two, one . . .

He shut the door.

She could really use his help to undress herself on this seat instead of scooting around and awkwardly balancing on her good leg while removing her hiking pants. At least these had zippers up the bottom. Was it for this exact reason that Duke had suggested this particular pair? Like he knew she was destined to fall on her hike.

It didn't matter. Nothing mattered as soon as the hot water hit her. She soaped up her hair and didn't even care there was no conditioner. She was clean. Clean again! The shower nozzle in her hand was like a slow stroke of heat against her body. Is this how good Matthew had felt? What if he'd forgotten something and came in the bathroom, and she asked for some help? Would he assist her as she sat all helpless in the shower?

A knock at the door and she yelped. "Bernie?" It was the nurse.

"Hi. Yeah?"

"Do you want help? You can ask me for help. That's what I'm here for." The way the nurse said it, like she was sighing, like she was so tired of actually helping people, convinced Bernie that she'd never ask her for help.

"Oh, I'm okay. But thanks."

The door to the outside room thudded shut. And even though she was alone in the bathroom and Matthew was alone in the hospital room, it still felt like the rightness had been restored.

She jerked the towel off the rack and dried off in the steam. And then realized her fatal mistake. She forgot to get clean clothes.

Oh shit. Had that been an unconscious omission so she could have Matthew come in and see her in her towel state too?

Well, this was awkward.

"Matthew?" she shouted through the door.

"Yeah?" His footsteps neared.

"I forgot my clothes. Could you grab some clean ones for me? They're at the bottom of my bag."

There was a pause. During it, she rifled through her mind about what he could find in her bag. Dirty underwear, dirty socks. Dirty everything. He could read her book. Eat the rest of her granola bars. Nothing too bad. Nothing compared to the alternative, which would be that he'd help her, with only a meager threadbare towel wrapped around her, as she dug through her bag with a high probability of towel slippage.

"Uh, sure. How do I know what's clean? Smell them?" He laughed.

"You're hilarious." But it might be partially true. She tried to picture Matthew taking a big whiff of her dirty clothes, wrapped up in a tight ball. He wouldn't dare. He'd surely smelled her stinky self enough over the past several days. "The dirty clothes are in a ball, and I'm sure you can smell them from across the room."

A few minutes later he knocked on the door. She was behind the flimsy plastic curtain. "Do you want me to come in?" he asked.

If she weren't helpless with a broken ankle, there were so many jokes she could make, so many innuendos. She could be a tease, let him wonder. Because she was wondering. The towel slung around his hips, the trail of hair that trickled from his belly button down, down, down. She might have salivated. She might have willed that towel to collapse off him like a glacier. Just fall and crash to the ground.

She'd had no idea his jaw was so sharp at the edges, that he had these tendons that stretched at the corner of his lips down to his chin when he smiled. And somehow, he looked like a wood sprite, or some kind of playful woodland creature, with his hair all sticking out every which way and a lightness to his face, like a glow the beard had camouflaged with all its hair.

"Uh, Bernie? Hello?"

"Oh, sorry. Yes. Please." She'd been lost in thought, and he was outside the door. She adjusted herself as much as she could, but it wasn't like she could make herself more presentable. Through the few inches in the shower curtain, she watched him come in and proceed to hang a shirt, her shorts, a bra, and underwear on the hook. She groaned. For God's sake, the underwear had owls all over them. "Thanks."

He looked in her direction, and they made eye contact. His eyes slipped to the towel covering her up and then back to the hook as he finished hanging them. "Hoot hoot," he said and then cracked one of those weird half smiles at her and exited the room.

Bernie stared at the tile wall. How had this all happened? She was going to hear him hoot hooting the rest of the night. But she had bigger concerns. Her ankle was swollen to twice the size it should be. And it was red, hinting toward a purplish color. The nurse had said she could take a shower as long as she didn't put any weight on it. It was in the nurse's best interest, really. Who knew what was growing on her dirty foot? "Just have your boyfriend help you." Those had been her exact words.

Ha. Bernie hadn't bothered to correct her in fear of not becoming clean. She could do this.

After she got on her clothes, she called out, "Matthew? Could you give me the wheelchair or something? I can't hop around on this other leg." God, she was so pathetic.

"Sure." He opened the door and pushed the wheelchair to her. "Want to go for a ride? The nurse popped in and said that the doctor would be back in an hour. It's coffee o'clock."

"Okay, sure."

She twisted around so she essentially just fell into the seat, and Matthew pushed her toward the door. Normally after a shower, she'd feel compelled to put on makeup and do her hair, but none of that really mattered, did it? She didn't know anyone here. Matthew had already seen her at her worst. And she was in a hospital, where people were probably dying. She swallowed and closed her eyes softly.

But then she was flying down the hall, Matthew's steps thudding on the floor behind her.

"Sir, please slow down." A woman's stern voice behind and to her left pierced the electronic air around them.

"Sorry, Nurse!"

Bernie was convinced that Matthew had given her one of his glory-blazing real smiles, and she felt a little glow in her belly and went back to work.

"You are a freaking speed demon."

"Oh yeah! This is fun."

"I thought you hated hospitals."

"Well, maybe with you they're not so bad."

"Thanks for pushing me around."

"I'll push you around gladly, anytime." The sarcastic glee in his voice dripped into her ear, and she settled against the chair as they waited on the elevator.

As he rolled her in after the ding, she looked up at him. "Thanks for this. Seriously. This would have been really shitty if I'd had to be here alone. I'd be confined to my room. Nurse Ratched would have insisted on giving me a bath."

"Why didn't she give you a bath? I could have videoed it and everything. We could have made a million. I'm sure that's a porn niche."

"Witchy women giving other innocent, injured, helpless women sponge baths?"

"Oh yeah. I'd totally watch it." He laughed.

"You're the worst," she said as they entered the cafeteria. But she didn't mean it at all.

◆ ◆ ◆

"Actually, this coffee is the worst." Matthew sipped the weak, brownish brew while they waited on the elevator that would take them back up to her room.

Bernie had dumped so much cream and sugar in hers that it barely even looked like coffee. "It always amazes me how bad the coffee is. No matter the hospital. At least in the Portland hospital they have espresso."

"Wow. The hospital my dad goes to does not have espresso." He tried to take another sip and wondered if Bernie had had the right idea by masking the flavor of hers.

"Your dad is in the hospital? You didn't tell me that."

Matthew paused as he released the cup from his lips. He had not meant to bring up his father. In fact, the past few days, he hadn't thought about his dad because he'd been too focused on sketching out ideas for his new TV characters. This trip had accomplished exactly what he'd hoped. It had blocked out everything that was waiting for him back home.

"Yeah, he has kidney issues."

"Oh no. I hope he'll be okay."

"It remains to be decided."

Bernie looked up at him just as the door to the elevator opened. He could tell she was going to say something, probably ask why he'd made such a callous remark he wished he hadn't said in the first place. To keep her from saying it, he handed her his cup and rolled her out to the floor. "Should we try to frighten the nurses again?" he asked. "Do you think they'll give out speeding tickets?"

"I think I need a seat belt on if you're going to race me down the hall again."

Coming toward them was a sweet-looking elderly couple. The woman was pushing her husband in a wheelchair, with tubes leading to a bag of liquid on the side of it. "Excuse me, ma'am." He paused. "Are you interested in a friendly wheelchair race?"

Startled, the woman looked at him oddly, and he bent over the handlebars like he was in the starting position and winked at her. Bernie groaned.

She laughed nervously. "Oh no, I think I'll definitely lose."

Her husband looked up at her. "Come on, Margaret, let's do it! We need a little excitement in our lives."

"That's the spirit!" Matthew turned Bernie around.

"Oh my God, Matthew!" She turned to the couple. "He's just kidding."

"I got money on my woman," the man in the wheelchair said.

"Yeah, Bernie, you don't have confidence in me?" Matthew asked.

She looked up at him with her eyebrows asking the question instead of her lips. *What the fuck are you doing?* "There will be coffee spillage." She held up the two cups of coffee she was holding.

"The lady doth protest too much, methinks." Matthew shrugged and wheeled Bernie back around to the room. "But maybe I'll find another, more spirited, patient, and catch up with you later," he called over his shoulder.

The elderly couple laughed, and the man shouted after them, "I'll put five dollars on Margaret!" as they rolled off their separate ways.

"Oh my God. You're going to kill me and both of them," Bernie said, but he could tell she was holding back a laugh. "And I *am* spirited!"

"Yeah, you sure are, like a squirrel."

She crossed her arms over her chest. "I should have never told you that. It's going to haunt me for the rest of my life."

"That's right. When you least expect it, you'll be washing dishes in front of your kitchen window ten years from now, and I'll pop up and shout, 'Squirrel!'"

She squinted up at him as he rolled her into her room. "How do you know I have a window in front of my sink?"

"Everyone does." He took the coffees from her and put them on the counter, then reached toward her so she could get out of the chair and onto the bed. Her hands were warm in his, maybe from holding two cups of coffee. She jumped up on her one foot and landed with a thud against his chest.

Matthew's breath left his lungs, his body, as Bernie's face tilted up to look at him, her lips paused. They'd been this close before—hell, they'd been sleeping in the same tent for days—but she'd had a bandana around her face or she was rolling her eyes at him, or squinting or something, and he couldn't see how deep brown her eyes were, flecked by slivers of gold. And they seemed to be searching for something in his. Her throat rippled as she swallowed, and Matthew found himself still holding her hands, even though he'd already pulled her up, gravity tugging his face down to hers.

A throat cleared to his left. The nurse was standing in the doorway. "Excuse me. I just had some follow-up work before the doctor came in."

What had he been thinking? The breath returned to his lungs. The clock on the wall ticked loud in his ears again. He put his arm around Bernie's back to help her to the bed. He sat on the sofa while they talked and the nurse inspected the boot around Bernie's foot.

He pulled out his mini notebook and flipped through it. He added this whole hospital incident to his story, with the character of Bernie being brave and scaring off the bear as the height of the plot. It would make a great episode. What would happen to her if she hadn't fallen, if he hadn't had to carry her, and if she'd just saved the day? He scribbled it down.

He flipped through the pages and studied the sketch of a character he'd been building from day one, and then looked up at Bernie, who was laughing with the nurse—that goofy laugh of hers, her bright eyes, the wide grin—and a stupid ache appeared in his chest. Instead of some kind of catastrophic hero arc, this was turning into . . . definitely something else.

CHAPTER 22

After the nurse left, the doctor came in, and Matthew kept scribbling in that little notebook of his. Bernie waited patiently while the doctor proceeded to examine her ankle and then reviewed the scans. She was finally able to lay there still, mostly because of the churning in her mind over what had almost just happened. Had she and Matthew been on the brink of a kiss? It seemed impossible, but he'd just held her as she felt like one of her mom's precious peonies in his hands. She'd felt that exciting buzz of what-if sizzling lightly on her skin, her lips parting, heart racing—yes, she did want it. And then the nurse without any sense of timing had practically grunted her way into the room.

Dr. Peters sighed. "Well, I know this is probably not a surprise, but it is broken. Looking at the x-ray, essentially you've got a break on the knobby bump on the inside of the ankle," she said, pointing to what was once a small knob but was now swollen into a giant ankle lump. "And also a break at the bottom of the tibia." Her hand moved over to the front of the massive swollen ankle lump. "In the biz, this is called a bimalleolar ankle fracture, since it involves two sides of your ankle."

Bernie knew it was going to be bad, but two breaks? She felt herself swallow. A very different swallow from the *Is Matthew going to kiss me?* swallow. "So what does that mean?"

"The good news is that you don't need surgery. The bones aren't misaligned, so I think a cast will be just fine. But it's really swollen right now, and we want the swelling to reduce before putting it in a cast."

"How long does that take?" Matthew asked from the sofa. Probably so he could leave and not feel guilty. Maybe she'd fabricated the whole in-the-moment-kiss thing.

"I think tomorrow sometime, the swelling will have gone down and we can put it on."

"And then do I have to roll around in a wheelchair for months? Weeks?" Bernie asked, imagining the next month of her life being pushed around by Matthew. Wait, Matthew would be gone soon. It would be Tabitha, or her manager, or her mom? Would she have to wheel through the flowers for a month or two and work from the farm? The satellite internet there was horrific.

"I would suggest a scooter; have you seen those? You can just put your knee on a pad and roll yourself around. Some people think they're fun. You know, considering the circumstances. With a break like this, we're likely looking at four to six weeks."

Bernie nodded. At least she'd have her independence. She could scoot around with James Brown walking down the street beside her. Or him pulling her like he was a horse and she was riding in a chariot. She'd scoot from meeting to meeting. Matthew could race her by renting one of those scooters in town.

Wait. Cue record-scratch noise. There would be no more Matthew.

Something about the thought made her chest hollow out more than when Dr. Peters had confirmed her ankle was broken.

"Just keep that boot on, and I'll be back in the morning to check it out." Dr. Peters patted her boot and gave her a look of concern.

Bernie forced a smile and nodded. "Thanks." How much sorrow was showing on her face for Dr. Peters to look at her that way?

The doctor shut the door behind her, and Matthew and Bernie were alone again.

"So . . . ," Bernie started.

"So . . . ," Matthew responded.

Clearly neither one of them was going to discuss what had happened before the nurse had walked in. Bernie had been ready to kiss Matthew. Was she crazy, or was that what was going through his mind as well?

"I can't believe I have to stay here another day," she pouted. Anything to clear the air. To get things going back to normal. At least if not normal, whatever they were prekiss.

But to kiss Matthew . . . those thick lips of his, especially in full exposure sans beard. Leaning into those almost-black eyes, with that weird evil, elfin gleam in them. It wouldn't be bad. No, she was certain it wouldn't.

She cleared her throat. "You know, you don't have to stay here if you want to go hang out in town . . ."

"I could go to a hotel if you want me to." He leaned back on the sofa and crossed his arms. "But I'm pretty sure this thing turns into a bed. And what if you, like, fell out of bed in the middle of the night and couldn't get up, and the nurse call switch thing was way over there?" He pointed to the wall. "And you broke both of your ankles? And maybe an arm. That would be on me." He gave her one of those closed-mouth smirks of his.

Was it possible he wanted to stay as much as she didn't want him to leave?

"So you'll stay?" She smiled, hoping he understood that meant she wanted him to stay, even if she was scared of what was happening in this Bizarro world with Bizarro Matthew and his new, shaved face.

"Yeah." He put his little notebook down and leaned over his knees. "What if, in exchange for a free bed, I bust out of this joint and get us real, non-hospital-y food?"

At the mere mention of food, Bernie's stomach grumbled. With all the drama of her foot and Matthew, they hadn't eaten since oatmeal o'clock. "That would be beyond amazing." Camp food to hospital food was hardly an upgrade.

"Chili, right? That's your fave? And then we'll finish it off with some oatmeal?" He nodded like he knew her.

"Oh yeah. And if we could add some granola bars in there as a third course, I would be eternally grateful. I haven't had one in so long . . . ages, really. Like hours."

"Done." He poked in her bag. "Not an issue because I think you stole away with everyone's weekly supply."

"I resent that."

"I applaud it. I like a girl who knows what she wants."

Some large and fishlike feeling swam in her abdomen. Heat rose from that emotion-swimming monster and into her cheeks. She was turning pink; she knew it. The smile unable to be restrained. Oh my God. Embarrassment of embarrassments. Was she twelve? Blushing at his comment about a girl who knows what she wants?

"What are you in the mood for?" He scrolled through his phone. "Nothing less than five stars. We deserve it. Pizza, Thai, Chinese, burgers . . ."

"Burger, please!" The thought of a good, juicy burger with fries and ketchup and mayonnaise and all the condiments was exactly what she wanted. "And fries."

"Done." He stood up and studied her. "You seem like a cheeseburger person."

Whatever that looked like, she was guilty. "Yes. I want all the things."

"Nice. Okay. I'll return shortly. Unless they don't let me in. You did tell them I was next of kin, right?"

"I'm not sure if that was a question, but if they call, I will tell them you are . . . *that*." Who would she say Matthew was? Boyfriend, husband, brother?

"You better, or else I will eat both burgers." He paused in the doorway. "Wait, what's your number? Just in case?"

She smiled at him like an idiot as she gave it to him, and he typed it into his phone. He wanted her number! She knew she looked like a lovesick dork. Excited over a boy wanting her number. Even if it was just to call her if he couldn't get in.

"Your last name is Lovejoy, right?" he asked.

"No, that's my great-aunt's name. My last name is Purcell," Bernie replied, thinking of how Matthew could have inadvertently put her great-aunt's name in his phone instead of hers. If Matthew had been born a hundred years ago, surely Aunt Bernice would have been a better match for him than her. Aunt Bernice wouldn't have shied away from an almost kiss and then felt like a preteen. She would have swooned in his arms and said something straight out of a movie, like "Kiss me, you big handsome fool!" She wouldn't be obsessed with the idea of a burger at the moment, or pouting over her sad broken ankle, because Bernie was confident that women like Aunt Bernice never had accidents and survived solely on the olives in their classy little martinis. She sighed. "What's yours?"

He looked up at her and paused. "Hildebrandt."

Her phone buzzed as he called. She felt a little delirious as his number appeared on her screen.

Or lovesick. Was that really the word?

Matthew left, and she settled into the bed. Was it so bad to be smitten with someone you'd known for four days and couldn't stand for three of them? Someone you'd shared every moment with, for good and bad. Who'd been rude but also so nice. Who was snarky and also really funny. And yet he was there for her. He'd given up the rest of his vacation to help her.

And now he was gone. What if he never came back? What if he was out at the burger joint and a cute girl flirted with him and he decided he'd rather hang out there than with Bernie, who was essentially confined to a bed? She'd never see him again, and he'd be out in the world living life with a cold beer and a girl with a tinkly laugh who got to touch his face without feeling weird.

Panic fluttered inside her. She closed her eyes and sighed as she tried to remember all the things she'd learned over the years to calm herself down. Deep breathing. Visualizing placing her worries in a locked box on a shelf.

Because Matthew wasn't abandoning her. He wasn't leaving. He was going to get her dinner and then come back. He'd left the hike to help her. To be with her.

Bernie opened her eyes. And what did that mean?

Matthew sat in the Uber on the way back from the burger place. He'd walked there but then realized he was really tired of walking. Without the gorgeous scenery of the national park, the city was just that, a city. The concrete was just a gray trail his boots felt clunky against without the cushion of dirt and grass. Also, their food would be cold, and the last thing he wanted for his first nonrehydrated meal was rubbery fries and a lukewarm burger.

Even though he'd abandoned the trail, he was glad he'd come back to Anchorage with Bernie. He didn't know what it was. There was something about her. Maybe her quirks were getting under his skin. Like a rash. Or her inner squirrel was nibbling at his neurons. Because earlier that day, yes, he was quite sure he wanted to kiss her. He even seemed to miss the smell that usually surrounded her. It was too subtle, drowned out by soap. That was crazy, right?

The car stopped in front of the hospital, and Matthew thanked the driver and jogged to the door, then the elevator and back into Bernie's room. Or should he say their room.

"How's the convalescent?" he asked as she thumbed through her phone.

"If you're meaning me with the boot who can't go anywhere, she is starving." Bernie made grabby hands for the bag.

"Can I get mine out just so you don't eat both of ours?"

"Hey, that's my line!" she said, diving into the bag he tossed on her lap.

Bernie stuffed two fries in her mouth and groaned. "Oh, nonrehydrated salty fried thing! How did I ever last a week without you?"

Matthew paused midbite to watch her sort through her bag like it was a package of gifts rather than a burger from a local restaurant.

She sighed as she gazed amorously at her burger as if she were staring into the eyes of a long-lost lover. "And you, oh juicy burger with cheese and mayonnaise and ketchup!" She took a bite and closed her eyes, lost in sensation.

Matthew cleared his throat. It was a good burger. But he was jealous of it now. He wondered if she would ever look at him like that. Because conundrum of conundrums, he was pretty sure he wanted her to.

"There's nothing quite like a good burger, I guess." He realized he even sounded jealous. Like when he was a kid, and his mom watched the neighbor girl after school. He'd find them baking cookies and laughing together, a kitchen microcosm she'd never invited him into. They'd said the cookies were for him, and he begrudgingly ate them, haunted by their knowing laughs and new, shared secrets.

Bernie groaned again and nodded. "Thank you so much for going to get this. What if they gave me Jell-o or ugh, worse, tapioca pudding."

"Those do seem to be the staples, right?"

"Why, though? At least chocolate pudding, you can pretend it's mousse or something. But those weird tapioca balls?" She shivered. "They're unnatural."

He laughed. His ex used to always get bubble tea, and he couldn't stomach the tapioca either. "Yeah, and why do people drink it? Like, take a sip and then this giant mucous-like ball slides down your throat on purpose?"

"Let's start an antitapioca movement when we break out of here." She took another bite.

Matthew decided that he liked the way she said "we."

They finished their burgers, and the nurse came in with a tray of food. She set it down next to Bernie while sniffing the air. Bernie just gave her a big smile and, as soon as she left, held up the container toward Matthew, her eyes blazing with shock. "It's butterscotch. Not quite chocolate, but it's not tapioca. Yet, still pudding." She shook her head and peeled back the label. "Wanna split?"

"I'm okay. That's all you."

She stared into her pudding cup, her lashes low, and it made her appear so young that he could see what Bernie looked like as a kid. How she used to be with her childlike breaking and entering and traipsing around abandoned homes. What else had she done? And what had happened in between?

"So you told me about your previous life of delinquency that has been the ultimate downfall for your first hiking trip. I want to hear what else you did that was crazy."

Bernie laughed into her lap as she spooned out the rest of the pudding. "No. No way."

A swelling need grew inside Matthew's chest. It must have been better than he'd imagined, with that response. "Okay, I really need to know now."

"Just stupid kid stuff."

"Okay, one thing. Just one. Tell me the craziest thing you did when you were fifteen. I picked a random number to make it easy."

Bernie laughed in that way where her head tossed back, and he could watch her throat stretch. There was something about seeing all that skin: he wanted to rush her bed and just run his lips over it. That was weird, right?

"Okay, fifteen is an easy one. You got lucky."

He leaned over, his elbows on his knees. "Tell me." His voice was lower than he'd thought. Was he desperate for this, just a taste of Bernie? Yes. Yes, he was.

"Okay, so Tabitha and I . . ."

"Another story starting with you and Tabitha. Is she the instigator, or are you?"

"Oh, I think we were more like . . . partners in crime?"

Seeing Bernie's eyes squint as she thought hard about this made him think it was really her and not her friend. "Okay, go on."

"Well, on the coast of Oregon there are these crazy dunes. Like, you go out there and you would think you're in the middle of the Sahara or something. At certain spots you can stand, and there's nothing around you but sand and, in the summer, the bluest of skies above you." Her eyes got big as she sketched out the dunes in the air with her hands like she was drawing a curvy woman's body with the knife blade of her palm.

"It sounds cool."

"Oh, it is. We had this vision that when the full moon was out, we could go to the top of these dunes and see the stars, and it would be really awesome. But you need ATVs to get up there. And they don't rent them at night. So . . . we just borrowed two after they were closed."

"After they were closed?" Matthew laughed. "So you mean you stole them?"

Bernie shook her head in protest. "No, we borrowed them. We rode them earlier in the day, we didn't use the last fifteen minutes, so we came back at midnight and used the rest of the time. We just didn't let them know."

"So we can add stolen goods to your record. Breaking and entering, thievery . . . wow, you were quite the corrupt little thing, weren't you?"

"I was a kid. It's not like any of this would go on my permanent record if I had been caught."

"I like the foresight you had. 'Let me commit all my crimes before I turn eighteen so my record is clean.'"

"I'm not sure it was foresight, but yeah . . ." She sighed and looked away, staring at the space near the door. "It's all for the best that phase is over with, I guess."

"Well, I have never committed any crimes, if you're wondering. I won't be the next Tabitha in your future Bonnie and Clyde–type scheme, in case you're thinking of hiding guns in your cast tomorrow and robbing a bank."

She turned to him and smiled. "Oh my God, can you imagine? The Broken Burglar? The Cast-Away? The Hobbler? I don't think the scooter will really be advantageous to a life of crime."

"But you've given up your ways, right? Now you're just in marketing, you said?"

"Yes, I run data and analytics on marketing." Her voice changed, got more serious as she said it. Like Bernie had temporarily turned into a robot.

"Don't sound so excited about it."

Bernie's jaw dropped while her tongue made a little clicking noise, and Matthew braced himself for a challenge.

"My job is fine. It's stable and pays the bills, and I like the people I work with." She paused for a beat. "But it's not as interesting as working in TV. You're a comedy writer. You're practically a superstar compared to what I do."

"It's just different. I'm sure there are equal amounts of bullshit in both jobs. Besides, it's not like I'm winning Emmys for my work."

"But you're good, just underappreciated. I've seen your stuff, remember?"

Yes, Bernie had seen his little underwatched, quirky gem of a show. "You and like fourteen other people."

"I liked it. What are you working on now?"

Could he tell her about the show he was brainstorming, the one based on her? No way, not yet. What if it freaked her out? He didn't want Bernie to think he was obsessed with her and wanted to model an entire show after her, especially as they were just getting to know each other. "Oh, it's very conceptual at the moment."

"Is it anything like *The Unbreakables*?"

"I think it will be. In spirit. More about one character and their surroundings. Like the kind of character who's funny because you feel sorry for them. Like an antihero." Maybe *antihero* wasn't the right word. "More like a protagonist who is always setting themselves up for failure, but all you want is for them to be successful." Because unconsciously, he'd been rooting for her since day one. Well, maybe day two.

Bernie got quiet, and Matthew immediately regretted holding back. He should tell her. But it was too weird. *I've been making notes about you since we started the trip, and well, I think you would be a great heroine for this comedy of errors show I'm going to pitch. So I've been studying you. How you talk, how you walk, how you say things, and how accidents follow you around, so I can suggest the show to a producer.*

Yeah, it sounded like he was a class A, number one creeper. If the show did anything, went anywhere, then he'd tell her. Otherwise he'd lose whatever this thing was that he was hoping, deep down inside, they would be.

"So . . ." She cleared her throat. "You mentioned your dad was in the hospital? Is he okay?"

This was the last thing Matthew wanted to talk about. But there was something about Bernie. Something that made him go with her to this hospital, to sacrifice the rest of his vacation so he could follow her around, even if it was to just sit here in a sterile room with too-bright lighting and sleep on this sofa that a thousand people had already probably shed their tears on.

"It's complicated. My dad is an asshole." And that was what came out of his mouth. "Well, maybe *was* an asshole? He's a reformed asshole. I think."

"Oh." Bernie startled up straight in her bed. "Sorry, I didn't know."

He shouldn't have launched into the predicament that way. "No, I shouldn't have said that. He left me and my mom when I was a kid. If you look up the definition of *deadbeat dad* in the dictionary, there is probably a picture of him." Matthew paused, studying Bernie, wondering what she'd do next, but she sat attentively, waiting for him to finish his story. "He drank a lot and who knows what else. Made my mom miserable. She cried a lot when I was growing up. And then he was gone. And she cried more. I'd hear her through the walls of my bedroom."

"And what about you?" Bernie asked. She'd twisted around to look at him as he talked.

"What about me?"

"Were you sad about your dad? Did you know what was going on?"

Matthew thought back to when he was young, ten maybe, and his dad had come home drunk. He wasn't abusive, just sad and ridiculous. Sometimes he'd wished he had been abusive so he'd have concrete reasons to hate him. Hating someone for being pathetic was harder. It felt less legitimate.

One night, Matthew and his mom sat at the old oak table eating dinner, something typical and very American like meat loaf and peas, which made that picture sadder for some reason. His dad walked into the kitchen, flopping around this way and that. Banging into the countertops. He sat down with a bag of chips he'd grabbed and then just threw up on the table.

One of those sick laughs erupted out of Matthew. The kind when you remembered how horrible something was, and you could only laugh. "It was like finding out someone you idolized as a kid was actually a complete stranger. I was confused a lot. And then he moved out when I was twelve, which is probably the worst time for your dad to leave."

"Would you rather he stayed?" Bernie asked.

"I think it would have been worse for my mom. And he just got worse. He was homeless for a while, befriending different women at bars and sleeping wherever someone would have him. Until they got tired of him and then kicked him out too."

"Your mom told you all that?" Bernie asked, her face wrinkled up in mild horror.

"No, my dad did. Five years ago, he called me, out of the blue, told me he was sober and had a job and his life was straight, and he wanted to apologize and get to know me again."

"Oh!" Bernie brightened up. "So that's a good thing, right?"

Matthew leaned back into the plastic-coated sofa bed. "Well, eleven years is a long time to build up a grudge. So I wasn't super eager to see him, talk to him, or really think about him. I'd written him off already. It was easier, you know?"

"I can imagine. But eventually you talked to him, right? He is your dad."

Matthew huffed. "You sound like my mom."

"Ouch!" Bernie's eyes got big. As if that was the top insult he could have thrown at her.

"I didn't mean it like that. Even though my mom will still rail at all times against my dad, she agreed that he was my father and that I should at least talk to him to see if he'd changed. After all these years, I think somehow her heart is still codependent on him. Even after he pulled all the shit he did with her." Over time, the look in his mother's eyes had morphed from angry to sad and sometimes wistful as she'd turn away from him when the topic of his father came up. Like she didn't want to make eye contact and really let Matthew know how she felt.

"So now you talk in his postasshole state?" she asked.

"Yes. It took a while for me to actually engage with him again, but he lives outside of LA, so for the past two years we've been seeing each other. And now he has kidney failure."

"Oh. Hence the hospital."

"Yes. So now that we're on speaking terms, he's apologized for abandoning me multiple times. And he is sober. But then last month he asked me, 'Could I please have one of your kidneys?'"

It was the first time Matthew had said it out loud. He'd hidden this request from his mom, from his friends. And even though it had only happened recently, giving it a voice just reminded him of how much space it had been taking up in his brain. By ignoring it, there was this constant buzzing activity at the top of his skull the past week that seemed to be released when the words came out of his mouth and he saw Bernie's face turn moonlike in shock as she heard his words.

"What?" Bernie spit out the juice box she'd been drinking from on her tray.

"Wow. They really feed you like an infant, don't they?" He laughed, glad for the brief respite from the confession he'd just made. The look on her face was further proof of why he'd been pushing this decision to the back of his mind, trying to silence it, because he'd been in shock, too, when his dad had asked him. He'd only just started to come to terms with his father—listening to his apologies, trying to empathize, and figuring out how to make room in his life for him—and then boom! Can I have one of your organs? Wasn't that one way people responded to shock—by ignoring it?

She looked at the box. "I know. But it's fruit punch. It would probably be good with vodka. Which I could totally use with this story. Want some?" She paused. "Oh no, sorry, was that insensitive?"

He shook his head. "No, I would drink fruit punch with vodka with you anytime."

She sat back in her bed, and he swore a blush crept up her face. "Please continue. Uh . . . kidney donation and your reformed deadbeat dad—you could write a TV show out of your own life."

"It's a little too close to home, I think. And I don't know if there's much more to the story. Now he needs a kidney because he has to get dialysis all the time. And if he doesn't get a kidney, he has only an additional five years left to live. And now I'm the asshole who has to decide if I'm going to give it to him."

Bernie groaned in the back of her throat and lay back in her bed. "Matthew, that's horrible."

"Yep. I think that's partly why I needed this trip. To try to get some space from him. And his request. It was clouding up my brain, and I couldn't write."

"When do you have to decide?"

"I don't know. Soonish, I guess? The doctor did the blood work to make sure I was a match, and when I was, my dad looked so hopeful . . ." Matthew leaned his face into his hands and threaded them through his hair. Seeing that gleam of hope glisten in his dad's eyes when the doctor had announced the result had reminded him of when he'd been young. How his dad would squat down when he'd get home from work and stretch his arms out for Matthew to come running into them with absolute joy.

He sat back up. "I don't know how I'll ever make a decision. I've never had surgery before. There could be complications. What if something happened to me? What if my mom lost me, and my dad made it through? I feel like that would be so unfair to her."

"Wow, that's what you think about?"

"One of the things. There's nothing like hearing your mom cry all the time when you're a kid, and you feel helpless about it. She thought she was in love, and he destroyed her. She's never married again. And I think she has trust issues. And if something happened to me, because of this, I would feel so bad."

"Like you'd never make it through the bright light and just hang around on earth and torture your father with your still-living kidney? You could make it talk to him or something." Bernie's eyes glimmered with some kind of mischievous glow. He could see her with her juice box, skipping around as a kid, getting into all kinds of trouble with that exact same look.

"Yes, something like that. Or every time he peed, he'd have to see my face in the urinal cake."

She threw her head back laughing. He loved how she was so free with her laughs. "On a side note, what a weird name. *Urinal cake*. Like it's a tasty treat, if you don't pee all over it in the public restroom."

He laughed and leaned back into the sofa. "I want someone to totally make my next birthday cake in the shape of a urinal cake. That would be too funny."

"And then serve it in the urinal?"

He looked at Bernie, who was cracking herself up.

"No, Bernie, ew."

"I was just kidding. Anyway, this situation you're in is a shitty one. I had no idea."

"Of course you didn't."

"But I'm glad you told me."

"Okay, so now I told you my sad tale of woe about hospitals. Why don't you like them?"

CHAPTER 23

Bernie wasn't expecting the tables to turn on her like that. She'd been leaning into the pillows she'd missed after not having pillows for almost a week and had been completely consumed by Matthew's story about his dad. Not because of the story but because she just felt she knew him so much better. It slotted in one of the last pieces of the Matthew puzzle. And after this, he all made sense to her.

The snarky, but somehow sad, comedy writer. The guy who came on this hiking trip all by himself. She'd always wondered why, and now she knew. He was faced with the ultimate dilemma. Something that was weighing on him so much he couldn't harness his creative superpowers to work. He was kind and considerate but not necessarily all forgiving, and she liked that. It meant things affected him. Dammit, he'd followed her in a helicopter, thrown up, rolled her around the hospital, and got her food, and he had these deep dark eyes that were like pools of shimmering black oil she could easily slip and fall into.

But if she did, would she break something else this time?

He sat there expectantly staring at her with those same eyes. Because he'd asked her a question.

A cold damp cave whistled into her stomach where previously the delicious burger and its fry friends had made themselves at home.

"My dad. Also." She cleared her throat. "My dad is why I don't like hospitals. But for a different reason."

She took a deep breath. Bernie never talked about her dad. It was like he was a subject that was locked up in a childhood diary. Even Tabitha didn't bring him up anymore, unless it was some kind of nostalgia, like, *Remember when your dad yelled at us so loud for bringing that snake home from school?* This was after they'd left it on Bernie's porch and her dad had opened up the lid to the box and got bitten by the small garter snake. Or, *Remember how your dad set that ridiculous curfew for you on prom night? And we ignored it completely? And he called the cops? Yeah, that was shitty of us.*

"Okay, what is it? You've mentioned your mom, but not him. Why?"

"Because he died." She swallowed. The words just never felt real to her. Never felt final. It was almost like she could just not mention him, not talk about his passing, and he would still be there when she got home.

"Oh. Oh." Matthew fidgeted in his seat, like the uncomfortable-looking sofa had gotten more uncomfortable. "I'm sorry, Bernie. I didn't know."

No, how could he know when she never mentioned it? Even her ex had asked her a few months into dating what her dad did for a living. He had no idea and was hurt she'd never told him. And she knew he had a right to be.

"It's okay. I don't really talk about it."

"Why?"

Bernie shrugged. But she knew why. She had guilt raging inside her still, even after the past five years of trying to swallow it whole. She had let him down. She hadn't taken his cancer seriously. She'd focused on her life. He'd assured her he was fine constantly, and then one day he was just gone. And she hadn't even been there to say goodbye.

"Bernie, if there's anything TV has taught me, it's that you have to talk about these things. That's why shows like *Grey's Anatomy* have been on for a hundred years. It's just people and their problems. It's cathartic. Hell, I told you about my fucked-up situation. Don't you talk to your mom about him?"

"No. She never brings him up."

"I don't know your mom, but that seems weird. And it helps to talk about it. Why don't you? I can see you're sad about him, so why don't you talk about him and celebrate his life?"

"I know." She nodded and looked away. Also, when she thought about her dad, the burning and swelling of imminent tears crept up. Not even crept—they were just there, ready for one word, one memory, and the dam would break. "My dad was sick for a long time. He was an accounting professor. He kept his job at the college up until the very end. I was in high school when he was diagnosed with colon cancer. I'm not sure if it was hormones or not understanding or what, but it just felt like something he was dealing with, and it would be over soon. So initially we spent a lot of time in the hospital. He had surgery; then he had chemo. Then after a few years he was better."

"And then you went to college?"

"Yeah. He was still working and teaching, and when it was time for me to go to college, he encouraged me to go away, because I'd gotten into the University of Pennsylvania. He said, 'Don't worry about me. Your mom and I will be fine. It's important that you get a good education to get a good, practical job.'" She changed her voice to try to mimic her father's.

"So you left?"

"It was stupid. They had the best marketing program, and actually my dad found it for me. He was so concerned with doing what was practical and what made the most sense."

"Sounds like what I think of when I think of an accounting professor."

"I know, he was a total nerd. In retrospect, it pisses me off. I shouldn't have left."

"But your mom lives on a flower farm? Sounds like a funny match."

Bernie laughed, remembering how their mismatching sort of just worked. Or at least she'd thought it had worked. "Yeah, they were a weird couple. My dad was Mr. By the Book, and my mom was kind of this wild spirit at heart. They actually met because she was coming out of some eighties hair band concert, I think it was Whitesnake, and he rescued her from stumbling into the street when she was drunk." Bernie laughed.

"Wow, what a way to meet. Jaded over Whitesnake. So what happened when you were in college?"

"Well, I was in my senior year. Everything seemed to be fine, and then one day my mom called and said that my dad was really sick and I should come home." Here it was, that burning sensation behind her nose. Her eyes pinching. Her nose starting to run. "But before I could get there, he'd died. While I was on the plane. So if there is any advice I could give you about your kidney dilemma, now that your dad is back in your life, you should ask yourself: If something worse happened to him, could you live with yourself if you didn't do it?"

And then she did a full-on bawl. She couldn't escape the room because she couldn't move. She couldn't even find solace in the bathroom by herself for five minutes as the memory rolled through her. She'd cried over her dad before, but this was intense. Like the leg and the hospital and her broken attempt at change had all just swirled together with the memory of not saying goodbye to her dad and created a volcano of sadness inside her. And instead of Matthew leaving the room to give her space so she could have her ugly cry in peace, he'd jumped over to the bed and was sitting beside her, awkwardly.

"Hey, it's okay," he said, in a kind of gentle whisper she'd never heard from him. His hand came to her hair and was sort of petting it.

Bernie had turned her face away from him, since she couldn't twist over to bury it in the pillow. She just shook her head, even though she didn't know why.

"It's okay, Bernie."

The bed sank down with Matthew's weight, and she realized that he was lying next to her now, even though she was looking toward the door and away from him. Or whatever of him would fit on the twin bed. Her body was twisted away as much as it could, and his arm came up around her. Matthew was spooning her.

What was happening?

"Is this okay?" he asked.

And she nodded. It was all she could ask for. She snuggled up her back closer to his torso and swore that he huffed out a laugh. Dammit, he probably knew this was going to happen. But did she really care now? No. She wanted Matthew's heat and warmth. She wanted someone to tell her it was okay and make her actually feel like it was okay. Someone who didn't run away when she cried because he told her it made him feel weird to watch.

Matthew had one hand on her hair, stroking it, and it felt so good. She'd never had a man stroke her hair before. And the other arm was firmly around her waist. Snug as a bug in a rug. Those were the words that came to mind. But like a sexy bug, in an even sexier rug. And all mixed up with her dwindling sorrow and comfort from his heat.

"I can get why you would be so upset over it. You didn't get to say goodbye."

She nodded. "Apparently his cancer had come back, but he sort of ignored it until it was too late. He didn't want to bother my mom or me with it. He even snuck around to doctor's appointments. He didn't want to go on chemo again, because he hated it. His doctor advised him otherwise, but he was a stubborn man. I found all this out after the fact."

The tears started up again. "I'm sorry," she said as she wiped at her face.

"Don't be. It sounds like you didn't have closure."

She nodded. If she could just stay like this all night, with Matthew's arms around her, it felt like it could all be okay.

"So what happened then—did you go back to Pennsylvania?"

"No. I dropped out of school and helped my mom. I was not in a state to study. And then eventually I went back to school in Portland to finish up my last credits. This is actually the first time I've left since then."

"When did your dad pass?"

"Five years ago."

"You haven't left Portland in five years?"

She shook her head. "Well, I go to see my mom, and she's three hours away."

"Why don't you leave? Seems like after seeing how fragile life is, you'd want to live it as fully as you can."

Bernie shrugged, but she knew why. "I guess I'm the opposite. Maybe I've been afraid to leave."

Matthew was going to think she was a freak. Even when she said the words aloud, she realized how ridiculous they sounded. How illogical it was for someone to be scared to leave a place because she'd missed her dad's death while she'd been away. In her head, she just imagined if she left again, something would happen. What that "something" was, she didn't know. But she had left this time. She'd come here, to Alaska. Where maybe something calamitous had happened, but it wasn't so bad, was it? She looked at Matthew's hand on her stomach.

"I get it. We all deal with death and trauma differently." His hand came to her face and gently turned it toward him.

She must be red faced, red eyed, red everywhere. Splotchy, like a crying baby. "I'm sorry. I must look a mess." She wiped her eyes again. It was probably the most she'd cried since the funeral, and she hated that she was erupting now. But she had to admit that talking about it and having someone tell her that he understood why she felt that way made her feel better. Like that clichéd weight had been lifted from her chest.

"But I'm really glad you left for this." And then the impossible seemed to happen.

Matthew kissed her.

CHAPTER 24

Matthew pulled back from Bernie. It was the gentlest kiss he could muster. She'd just confessed her mixed-up feelings about her dad, and he didn't know what to do. All he could think about was showing he cared, that he understood. So he did what he'd wanted to do earlier that day. Maybe it was all the confession floating around in the room, but the only way to feel closer to her was to show her.

He wasn't sure what to expect. A slap? A lecture? She looked at him with her eyes, so sad and confused, like she was searching for something in his. But what could he explain? That he liked her. That he appreciated her telling him her story. That he knew how fucked up family shit could be, and sometimes it made you emotional and irrational. And apparently that was enough for him to think he could kiss her.

Her lips parted. Those soft lips that almost felt as good as the cushion of the bed. Almost as good as the soft curves of her body under his arm. He'd just given her a little kiss. It was innocent. It was almost the type you'd give your grandmother on the cheek. Touching Bernie's lips with his, though, felt more like gentle sparks filling up his chest. He could have not stopped. He could have kept going, but she did have a broken ankle, and he didn't want her to scramble away from him and fall off the bed. What if he'd read her all wrong?

Her hand came up and reached into his hair. This was definitely no slap. She pulled his head back down, and her lips clamped onto his with an urgency he'd never been seized with before. It was like the world around him drowned away. They weren't in a hospital anymore. There were no too-bright lights, no metallic hum of every annoying machine in the world singing into his ears. There was no echo of the hall intercom droning out its bored paging messages. It was just her and him, their bodies snug against each other, every movement of her chest against his, simmering through his legs. Their kiss made him feel like he was floating, like the two of them were wrapped up in each other, weightless.

He dare not move her hands, for they were keeping her in place; it wasn't like they could roll around without disastrous consequences. She rose up against him, her chest almost on top of his, and then hissed, "Fuck this damn boot."

Matthew laughed. He couldn't help it. He didn't care if it looked stupid. In his head, with his eyes closed, they were in this super sexy ethereal moment, but then he opened them, and there was Bernie with her leg in a boot, both of them on a creaky hospital mattress and unable to escape.

She smiled at him, so close to his face. Her eyes were bright, and God help him, he could see why she said a squirrel was her inner beast. They had this pixie gleam in them, much like a mischievous little hopping woodland creature after it had stolen some of your food.

"Well, that was unexpected," she said, her head propped up on her arm.

"Yeah, is your foot okay?"

She glanced down at it and sighed. "I don't think I can mess it up. It's like robot claws have clamped it down in place."

"Robot claws sound like a problem."

"The problem is that once I started kissing you, it was hard to stop."

"That most definitely doesn't sound like a problem." God, he could not stop grinning.

"Matthew, you're smiling so big! You never do that."

"What?" How the hell had she noticed that?

"Well, I feel like I have you in a vulnerable place at the moment, and it's been bugging me. You always smile and then hide it away, or laugh and then silence it. And you always keep your mouth closed when you do it. Except on momentous occasions when I'm absolutely hilarious and you can't stop yourself."

God help him, he laughed again. "You've noticed that?" Could it be that Bernie had been watching him as much as he'd been watching her?

"Yeah. Of course. It's just . . ." She looked away bashfully. "You have a nice smile and a nice laugh. You should unleash them."

Matthew sighed. Maybe Veronica had penetrated his psyche more than he'd wanted. "You don't think I look weird? Like, have a weird smile? Like I show too much teeth when I laugh?"

"What?" Now Bernie laughed, but it sounded like she thought he was absolutely bonkers.

"Yeah, someone told me that once."

"Well, they sound like an idiot."

Or just a super-self-conscious, hyperaware, image-obsessed actress. He huffed out a laugh. "Consider me officially unleashed. But you might regret it. I think all kinds of weird things are funny."

"Like what?" she asked.

"Like late-night Japanese variety shows."

"Okay."

"But the weird ones, like where they'll just show someone slicing onions for five minutes straight, crying. Just so bizarre." She raised her eyebrows at him. "And those old R&B songs where everything is a sexual innuendo. You know, like, 'You be the pot and I'll be your beans. Cook me all night long'—that kind of stuff."

"I can totally see that."

"And GIFs where you can put your face on something else, like another person, or a cat, or a teacup. I love those. Some people find them disturbing. I will likely send you some of me as a dog at some point."

"Maybe I'll send you some of my dog with my face."

"I will totally laugh at it and give it a hundred likes."

"I feel like it's good to know what you like. We should know what gives us joy in this world." She looked away, and Matthew had the distinct feeling she was going to add on, "before it's gone."

"Hey, Bernice." She turned back to look at him, suspiciously, since he'd broken the name rule. "I also think your name is funny."

"Ha. You and everyone else and their moms."

"And also, I like you."

He slid down a little on the cheap cotton sheets and kissed her again, gently. Her body heaved against him, and a lovely little moan escaped from her lips. And that did it for him. That moan stoked the small, luscious fire inside him, and now he wanted it all. He wanted everything of Bernie on this small creaky bed, boot be damned!

He sank his head into her neck and could still smell the essence of who she was through the soap she'd used earlier. It was almost elusive to describe, and yet he would perfectly define it as Bernie. Like her skin was made of ocean water, and a fresh breeze rolled over her every second of the day. As he kissed the soft place on her neck, he could taste the slight bite of salt that was still scattered about. And there was something darker too: he imagined it as a fiery core of bright pink and burning blue that swam around inside her under his touch. He wanted the flames to fire up her skin so she would leap onto him again.

A knock on the door made Bernie jump away from him. The nurse didn't wait for a "Come in" either. She took one step in and looked at both of them.

"I came to see if you needed anything." She collected the leftover, mostly untouched dinner tray from Bernie's side table.

Bernie cleared her throat. "I'm fine, thanks," she said, her voice a little breathless.

Her lips were swollen and her face was flushed, and there was surely no doubt in the nurse's mind exactly what they had been doing.

"You two behave, okay? I don't want anything happening to that foot before it gets into a cast."

"Yes, ma'am," Matthew said, and then saluted. The nurse gave him a disapproving look. Bernie stared at him, squeezing her lips together like she was going to burst out laughing.

As soon as the door shut, she did. "You're terrible."

"But seriously, that nurse is the worst. My dad's nurses are always so kind to him."

"Yeah, same with my dad. He always had nice nurses. And those cancer nurses have a hard job. Can you imagine having to help people every day who are so sick? And some of them terminal? This lady is dealing with the broken-ankle unit. Not so tragic. Cheer up, you know? Enjoy life."

"We're enjoying life on her behalf, I would say." Matthew's hand slid up Bernie's arm. Now it was like he couldn't stop touching her.

She played with the hem of his shirt, and slowly she slid her hand in between the thermal and his skin. Her fingers gently skidded over the skin around his waist, sliding over to where his hip bones dipped below. He took a deep breath as the sensation tightened in his stomach. "Exactly how much do you think we need to behave?" he asked.

"I sort of feel like subconsciously I've been waiting all week to misbehave with you." She pulled his shirt up, and the smile she gave him was most definitely not like an adorable woodland creature's, but more like a sly fox's.

"Somehow all those layers they recommend you hike with were covering up all this deliciousness." Her lips pranced along his jaw as

200

she traced a line with her finger, following the rise of his shirt, until he just pulled it off.

"Deliciousness?" He wanted to laugh, but everything inside him had seized tightly at the feel of her breath on his skin.

"Oh yeah, when you walked out of that bathroom, I was like, 'Yum.'" Her eyes looked up at him, bright and frisky, and her lips planted on his, and the smile that she kept drawing out of him widened and took her all in.

"You look pretty yum yourself, boot and all," he murmured against her lips, trying to keep his pelvis from taking on a mind of its own. Bernie had a broken ankle, and it wasn't like he could pick her up and toss her around like he really felt like doing. They had to stay carefully arranged on the bed, parallel units, with minimal movement, or else he might break something else of hers.

"Oh, you like my super-hot boot?" She was propped up on her left arm now, her head just slightly above his, and her voice was tangled in her breath, almost raspy, like she was about to lose it too. And God help him if the sound of her restraint or heat for him, or whatever it was, sent an aching jolt down into his hips.

All he could do was nod and choke out a yes.

She gave him a grin that made him feel like she could see right through him. Like she knew exactly how helpless he was against her lips. The way her little moans slipped out between their kissing and sneaked into his breath, making him feel like he were swallowing her whole. Because that was exactly what he wanted to do right now, as they fumbled through their clothes with awkward twisting on the bed and through her utterances of "Damn boot!" while she attempted to climb on top of him and failed.

As he slipped off her shirt and her skin slid under his, he wanted to consume her. Maybe the past few days had all been building toward this, but all he needed right now was to inhale her smell, her breath, her taste, and explore the most secret parts of Bernie that had been uncloaking themselves to him bit by bit. Take those bits and eat them whole so he could fully understand this woman by his side.

Maybe they had been revealing themselves to her as well. As she unraveled under his hands, he sensed that she was exploring herself and him in the same way at the same time.

CHAPTER 25

Bernie sighed and sank into the mattress, which was so much better than the dirt. Even though she felt as tired as she normally did at the end of a day of hiking, this was a different tired. A satiated tired. Her body finally felt as if it'd gotten what it deserved, a precious reward after the past grueling days on her feet. She glanced over at Matthew, who was staring at the ceiling with glazed-over eyes and a satisfied, smug look on his face that made her want to laugh. Maybe he felt like he'd gotten a little reward as well. She hoped so.

Not wanting to take her head off his shoulder, she fumbled for the remote on the bedside table. She waved it at him like a taunt. "Should we just totally give in to our dark sides and see if there's a movie on? Or we can watch the nature channels, if that would help ease the pain of you not finishing your hike?"

"Just totally give in to all electronic, light-up devices like deviants?" he asked, pulling her tighter against him. His bright eyes were almost sleepy, but still a little electric themselves, charged from what they'd just done. Boot and all.

"Oh yeah." She felt like a full-on deviant already. Hard-core make-out sessions in a hospital bed. Clothes in disarray around them. The blanket covering them both up as they lay in the bed, Matthew barely fitting next to her. And her boot. The damn boot. It was very hard to undress yourself or, more importantly, another person beside you, when one leg was immobile.

"Well, since we've made our departure from the trail a mere twelve hours ago, a lot has changed, so why not?"

A lot had changed, and breaking her ankle seemed like the least significant on the list. Because she was here, with Matthew, feeling so good in his arms, like it was the way it should have always been. So bizarre that she might have used words like *irritating*, *detestable*, or *despicable* to describe him until yesterday. And now? Now they were snuggled up like newlyweds in a hospital bed, and he'd just done things to her with his hands that she had only read about in books. It was like he could decode her body's own unique language; each sigh and gasp, he traced his fingertips to the source. With each rise of her chest and arch of her hips, he trailed his lips to where they were needed next.

She leaned over and kissed his cheek. A chaste thank-you for making her feel the way she felt just now. She didn't even care at the moment that she was possibly going to be immobile for three months.

Then a thought sparked in her mind. Another way to get to know the secret hidden layers of the Matthew beside her. "I have a better idea. Let's watch an episode of *The Unbreakables*. Another episode you wrote."

"Seriously?" His eyebrows had their own language too. And right now they were asking why.

"Yes. I haven't watched it in ages, and it would be fun. You can give me the inside scoop on everything."

"Well, if we can find an episode."

"The internet knows all." Bernie pulled out her phone and searched, just as Tabitha sent her a text.

What's the update with the guy? Are you going to put the moves on him?

The text appeared at the top of her screen just as she and Matthew were both looking.

"Whoa. You told your friend about me?"

Bernie felt her face heat up. "It's just that I called her when you were out getting dinner and told her what had happened. And she was like, 'Why did this guy go with you?' And I said I didn't know, and . . ."

"I see. So are you going to put the moves on me, Bernice?"

"Well, if those weren't moves we were just doing, then I don't know what that was."

"I feel like you didn't put the moves on me necessarily. It was more like you tried to leap out of the bed and then lay one on me. Like a leashed puppy who wants to lick you hello. Very subtle."

"Oh, I'm subtle? You're the one who came over and spooned me."

"I was trying to make you feel better."

"That was a move. Your thumb was stroking my abdomen."

"That was comforting stroking. Like a hot cup of tea."

"Ha! You're a hot something." She laughed and her phone rang. The photo of Tabitha's face making kissy lips at her appeared on her screen.

"Is that your friend? Can I answer it?" Matthew asked. She wasn't sure if he was joking.

"What? No way. I'll tell her I'll call her back."

Matthew tried to grab her phone and Bernie pulled it away, but his arms were too long and she couldn't really move, so he snatched it and stood up. "Bernice's answering service," he said into the phone.

"Don't listen to him, Tabitha!" Bernie shouted, laughing.

He stood a few feet away from the bed, very straight, with just his boxers on, one hand on his hips, a pensive expression on his face, like he was taking a business call. "Oh, this is Matthew. I thought you knew all about me. I'm the one she may or may not be putting the moves on."

Bernie covered her face with her hand. This was too much. "Tabitha, I'm in the bed and I can't get up—don't tell him anything!" she shouted again.

"So tell me, Tabitha," he continued into the phone, smiling at Bernie. "If your friend Bernice was going to put the moves on me, would I know it? Would you say she's a subtle flirt or more the kind of girl who will just do a full-body jump on you like a lemur?"

Bernie could hear Tabitha's laughter through the phone, even though it wasn't on speaker.

"What happened to being a puppy?" Bernie stretched out her hand. "Enough!"

"Oh, you've seen those nature documentaries too?" Matthew nodded, mock impressed at Bernie. "It is quite the full-body jump. Okay, I digress. The lady would like her phone back." He paused. "It was nice talking to you too."

The phone was in Bernie's hand, and she got it to her ear in record time. "Oh my God."

"What was that?" Tabitha chuckled into the phone. "I like this Matthew, whoever he is."

Bernie watched Matthew out of the corner of her eye. That rascally grin was back as he put his pants, shirt, and shoes on and then gestured that he was going out the door.

"Yeah, I think I do too," she said. She waved goodbye. He was leaving her so she could talk to her friend. Even thoughtful. Geez.

"So what happened?"

"I don't know. He brought back burgers, and maybe I was just so ecstatic about my first real meal this week that things just happened."

"Oh my God, Bernie! That never happens with you. You're like the pickiest person ever. See, I knew this trip would be good for you."

"Well, I did break my ankle."

"Yes, but you also met a guy."

"He lives in LA."

"So? You met a guy. And you seem to like him. It's a summer miracle!"

"Yes, but as mentioned, he lives in LA."

"You act like he's visiting from Mars or something. It's a short flight, a long drive, or you could just move. Your house is conveniently ready to be put on the market, as promised. And don't worry, I'll visit."

"What? Tabitha, you're crazy. We made out, not proposed to each other. Besides, until today I thought he hated me." Bernie couldn't help the smile from taking over her face. It was the first time Tabitha had mentioned selling her house, and she hadn't welled up with panic. Perhaps the trip to Denali was the thing she'd needed to help her look at her life differently.

"Ooh, that's the best kind."

Bernie laughed. "You're insane."

"I'm so excited for you. He seems fun too. I bet Duke will like him—they're probably both those crazy outdoorsy types. Then we can all go camping together, but you and I can do glamping in style."

"Really? You're planning our couples' vacations already?"

"Hell yes, I've been waiting for this day. Send me a picture."

"What?"

"I want to see him. Get the vibe and all. Or I'll just look him up online. What's his last name?"

A light knock at the door, and it opened. Matthew peeked through the crack.

"Hey, Tabs, I got to go, but I'll see what I can send you."

She squealed. "Okay, yay! Oh, and I want to talk more with you about your house, but I'll email you. Seriously, if you want to move to LA, I think I could find a buyer in the next week. Bye!"

"Bye." Bernie shook her head and set her phone down. This Matthew situation was giving Tabitha way too much fodder to encourage Bernie to move. But she couldn't ignore the excitement that had leaped up in her chest at the idea. But move to LA for Matthew, a guy she'd known for less than a week? That was borderline insane. Or was it? It might be the only thing she'd ever done that would make Great-Aunt Bernice proud.

"Your friend seems nice." Matthew had two cups in his hands. "Also, do you want a hot chocolate?"

"Um, yeah!" Bernie took one of the cups from his hand. This all must be too good to be real. "Thank you."

"Well, it's out of a vending machine, so don't get too excited."

"Even bad hot chocolate is still hot chocolate." She took a sip. Watered-down hot chocolate. Eh.

"Did you ever call your mom, by the way?"

Bernie slid her eyes over toward the door. "I texted her to see how my dog was doing."

"Bernie!" She hadn't realized his voice could sound so disapproving, and she almost laughed. "I'm sure your mom wants to know that you broke your ankle and had to be airlifted out."

"Yeah, but then she'd just come up here."

"You say that like it's the worst thing ever."

If Matthew weren't here, maybe Bernie would have called her. Her mom would make sure her hospital food was good. She'd somehow procure an iron to make her some impromptu grilled cheese. Or harass the nurse until she'd find the one chocolate pudding and the fluffiest pillow in the hospital for Bernie. But it would feel too much like it used to. The memories of Bernie, her dad, and her mom sitting in a hospital room for hours, waiting, would just be too much. And this time, like usual, her mom would just not acknowledge the fact that it was too similar and that her dad was gone, and Bernie would feel that awkward stirring inside her, like a scream was building but never got released.

She'd seen how her mom was. Her mom had cooed over her dad, bossed the nurses around, and got fierce with the doctor. And then once it was all over, she never said a thing about it to Bernie. Bernie had caught her at the most random of times crying on her bed when she thought the door was shut. Or cooking something for dinner and just wiping her nose on the back of her hand and sniffling.

Bernie had convinced herself that it was either (1) her mom didn't forgive Bernie for not getting there fast enough to say goodbye, or (2) that she'd had mixed feelings about her dad. They were like two different species. That was the thing that really bothered her. Had her mom taken off to the country to live on the farm because she'd finally gotten to be the person she wanted to be now that her dad was gone?

"My mom and I have a strained relationship," Bernie said. It was the easiest way to reply to the statement Matthew had made, which was really a question.

"That's vague."

She laughed. "Yeah. Sometimes I think I'm a disappointment to her in a few ways. With my dad and the whole thing about me not being a free spirit."

"Free spirit? Is her flower farm also a nudist colony?"

Bernie imagined the other older women who worked on the farm all pruning the plants and weeding in nothing but their skin. "No, although, oddly, I can sort of see how that would work."

"Let me tell you something, Bernie. I think the kind of girl that starts breaking into houses as a preteen and, in the cutest way possible, steals a 4x4 to climb up giant dunes to see the stars might be a wee bit free spirited. I'm betting you were a little crazy in college too."

Bernie tucked her cheek into her mattress. Damn this stupid boot. It made turning on her side nearly impossible.

"Okay, what did you do?"

Bernie laughed and shook her head. "Nothing. Really!"

"No one who did 'nothing' would make the face you just did. Like you just got caught with your hand in the biggest cookie jar ever."

"How have I gotten by my whole life without broadcasting tales of my sinful years, until I met you?"

"Oh, I have some ideas about that." Matthew had slid next to her in the bed and was gazing at her with his very dark eyes. Like they were pools of collected nighttime secrets, begging her to tell him all the things she'd never admitted to until now.

"So tell me, Bernie, what did you do in college that's making you blush like a schoolgirl?" Matthew asked.

Bernie laughed. "Nothing anyone else didn't do. My friends from high school and I did a reconnaissance of all the moments from *Goonies* on the Oregon coast the summer I was visiting after my freshman year. I was convinced someone had put a pirate ship in one of the caves, so we went looking for it, and I almost broke other things slipping on the wet rocks. We were not prepared."

"What else?"

"Skinny-dipping at night. That's pretty standard."

"Is it?" Matthew tilted his head at Bernie and squinted with what she was sure was total judgment.

"Everyone goes skinny-dipping."

"I haven't."

"Well, after my ankle heals . . ." She looked off, her voice soft. The sentence was left hanging in the air, much like the unasked questions of what would happen after her ankle healed. Was there a chance that she could somehow see Matthew again? After their flights in a few days, and after her three months of scootering around with a broken ankle? What were the chances he'd even remember her by then?

"Let's totally go."

"What? We're adults. We shouldn't go do that stuff now." She shook her head at him, but she couldn't help a smile from taking over her face. She should make him pencil in a date three months from now.

He sighed. "Bernie, other than this trip, when's the last time you did any adventurous stuff like this?"

She shook her head. "Years. Maybe like five years."

"But why? It seems so integral to who you are. All the stories you've told me about you are these funny, wild tales of youth. What happened?"

"You sound like Tabitha. She's always trying to get me to do crazy stuff when she's had a few drinks."

"Yeah, because it's fun."

"It's kid stuff."

"No, it's not. I'll prove it to you."

The look in Matthew's eyes could only be described as coals burning bright. She could practically see the evil elves at work in his brain, scheming as they shoveled white-hot idea after idea into his consciousness. "How?"

"I'm busting you out for real hot chocolate. This stuff tastes like shit, and I can't drink it."

◆ ◆ ◆

Matthew walked down the hall, looking for anything that could pass as a nurse's uniform. Just to prove to Bernie that this didn't have to be boring and normal. How could someone with such spirit just give up doing things that were fun and adventurous and maybe a little wild just because she thought she was an adult now? She was what, twenty-seven? And now she was relegated to some life of endless boredom because she'd "grown up"?

Well, screw that. He was going to capture that essence of her and haul it back out of her.

The storage closet was locked. The break room was filled with nurses chatting. There seemed to be no option for him to procure a set of scrubs. And if he found some, would they even be clean? There was, however, a gurney just sitting in the hall. He'd have to improvise.

Somehow no one noticed him tugging the gurney back to Bernie's room. When he pushed it through the door, she squinted at him. "What is that?"

"It's like our car."

"I have a wheelchair."

"Yes, but that's not as fun." He lifted her up from her bed and laid her on it, then gave her a kiss on the nose.

"I have no idea why we're doing this."

"To travel in style."

"I'm pretty sure there is zero style going on here."

He maneuvered the gurney to the elevator, with Bernie moaning little "oh my God's" at every turn. "I don't know why I'm letting you do this."

He laughed and hit the down button. A couple joined them in the hall, also waiting for the elevator, and they gave suspicious glances from the gurney back to Matthew. He nodded at them and looked down at Bernie, who had her eyes closed and her mouth partially open. Was she pretending that she was dead?

When the elevator dinged, the man motioned for Matthew to enter. "We'll get the next one."

"Hey, are you pretending to be a corpse on this gurney?" Matthew asked when they were inside the elevator by themselves.

Bernie opened one eye. "I would never do that."

"You were playing the part rather well."

"You did put me on a gurney."

"Everyone goes around on a gurney in a hospital."

The elevator opened on the ground floor, and Matthew headed toward the side door.

"Where are we going, anyway?"

"You'll see." Matthew pushed her outside and through the parking lot. Even though it was almost nine at night, the sun was still bright in the sky.

"I'll never get used to this sunlight. It just feels like it's the longest five p.m. ever. Where are we going?"

Matthew pushed her through the parking lot and onto the sidewalk and took a left.

"And how has no one stopped us?" Bernie leaned up on her elbows and looked around. "I mean, you're pushing a gurney down the sidewalk." She laughed and looked up at him.

The Starbucks was just a half block down from the hospital. If only he'd seen it before he'd gone to dinner, they could have had not-hospital coffee.

"Ah, I see where we're going."

"Yes, are there cup holders in that thing somewhere? They should really make gurneys with cup holders."

"I'm sure that's in the design specs for the latest model." She shook her head. "This is insane. Can you get arrested because of this?"

Matthew pushed her in the drive-through line behind a white pickup truck. "I can't just go in without you."

"The drive-through? Okay. I hope that truck doesn't accidentally hit reverse, because there is no way they can see us behind their enormous enormity."

"Good point." He leaned over and waved at the side mirror, catching the guy's attention who was driving. "Hi! Please don't hit reverse by accident."

"What?" The man rolled his window down. "What are you doing back there?"

"Just wanted to let you know I was behind you so you don't hit us. Accidentally. She's on a gurney with a broken ankle already." He practically had to yell over the engine. But the guy gave him a thumbs-up and moved on.

Matthew rolled up to the speaker.

"Hello, what can I get you?"

"Two hot chocolates?" He looked at Bernie, who nodded.

"Okay, is that all? Wait, is she on a gurney?" the woman asked.

"Yeah, but she's not dead. She just has a broken ankle."

There was a pause. "Um. Okay. Please pull around. Er, roll forward to the window."

Bernie laughed, but he was pretty sure it was in horror. "'But she's not dead'?" she said as he rolled her forward. "Very smooth."

After the truck had pulled away and they'd rolled up to the window, the woman slid it open. "Technically, I don't think I'm supposed to serve people *not* in vehicles here."

"It has wheels. I think technically it can pass as a vehicle." Matthew held out a credit card, trying to confidence-boost his way through it.

"Well, next time please just come in." She pressed her lips tight and raised her eyebrows at him—the same disapproving expression he associated with his middle school teachers.

"With a gurney?" Matthew asked.

"Well, if you can leave the gurney at the hospital, that would probably be best." She handed him two hot chocolates, which he gave to Bernie. The woman examined her with a look that made him think she wanted to ask if Bernie was there of her own free will.

After he'd paid and left her a generous tip in the box for not turning them away, he rolled back to the hospital. "See, a little fun never hurt anyone. That lady will now have a story to tell in their next employee meeting."

"I guess so." Bernie sipped one of the drinks. "So much better than the hospital machine drink that was disguised as hot chocolate. I'm afraid we might need another field trip for coffee tomorrow morning."

"Of course. So you *are* up for a little taste of adventure. You need to stop denying yourself. I mean, it's not like you're hurting anyone or doing anything bad."

Bernie sighed. "Maybe."

"Just because you're an adult doesn't mean you have to be boring. Adult just means you also have to buy groceries and take care of your dog and stuff. Doesn't mean you have to settle."

Bernie was quiet as they rolled down the sidewalk. As they entered the hospital parking lot, a security guard approached them with not a nice look on his face. Like the Starbucks lady's, but angrier. Matthew's heart raced, hoping that his stunt wouldn't prove to Bernie that a little adventure could also land him in jail for a night.

"Sir, what are you doing with that gurney?" And then he looked at Bernie with her hands full of hot chocolate. "Someone radioed me an alert saying that a gurney had been stolen off the property."

"Officer, do you want this one? No one's drunk out of it yet." Bernie held up the hot chocolate in her left hand.

"I'm not an officer, but what is it?"

He actually appeared to be interested.

"Hot chocolate." She gave him her sweetest smile. A smile he'd thought was fake the first day they'd met. "We can split this other one. I was just dying for some because I broke my ankle, and I'm sure you know how the hot chocolate tastes out of the vending machine here."

His eyebrows raised and his shoulders shrugged. "Yeah, I do." He took the cup that Bernie was practically thrusting in his face and, as if he remembered what his job was, he said, "But don't take the gurney off the hospital property again."

"Of course, Officer, we won't again. Not Officer. Sir, I mean." Bernie smiled up at him while batting her eyelashes.

"I'm going to escort you inside. Which room are you in?" He lifted up Bernie's wrist to read the room number, as if he didn't actually believe they'd tell the truth.

He led them to the elevator door and watched Matthew load the gurney inside, drinking his hot chocolate as the doors closed.

"Thank you, sir." Bernie waved him goodbye. She was all full of the sirs today.

After the door shut, in a high-pitched voice, Matthew mimicked her, "Of course not, not Officer Mr. Sir Whatever the Hell Your Name Is." He chuckled. "I see how easily you just gave mine away."

"Hey, what if he arrested us?"

"He said he wasn't an officer."

"We can share this one. I don't mind. And you're welcome for getting us out of trouble."

"Seems like it's pretty easy if you look cute and sound sweet." The last time he'd been pulled over, the cop had made him get out of the car and then patted him down.

"You say *sound* sweet like I'm not actually."

He took the cup out of Bernie's hands and took a sip. "Now, that's sweet." He bent down to kiss Bernie, and then the door opened on their floor. When he looked up, the couple who had been waiting with them earlier, whom he was pretty sure thought Bernie was dead, was standing outside again. He smiled at them and then looked down at Bernie, who was lying still with her mouth slack.

He looked back up at the couple, who had now stepped away from him, slightly recoiling in horror as they got out of the way.

Matthew sighed and pushed her through, shrugging. "I just can't let her out of my sight," he said.

Both of their mouths opened as they sucked in a lungful of air, and Matthew rolled back to the room.

Bernie's body shook on the gurney, vibrating up through his hands. She was trying to contain a laugh that seemed to want to burst through her.

"You are horrible. Evil. Those poor people!"

"Me?" She opened her eyes. "'I can't let her out of my sight'? Yeah, you didn't play into that at all."

"And here I thought I was the bad influence."

"Oh, Matthew, you might have woken up the beast."

He lifted her off the gurney and put her back in her bed. But he couldn't let his hands stray from her body. "Tell me more about this beast. Is it multifaceted? Does it have other sides to it? Is there a lusty beast?"

She hooked her finger in the collar of his shirt and pulled him down so their lips met. She kissed him hard but sweet and hummed a yes onto his lips.

CHAPTER 26

"Okay, seriously. We never got to watch *The Unbreakables*." Bernie yawned and snuggled into the crook of Matthew's arm.

He found an episode on YouTube and hit play. Bernie's laughs eventually morphed into silence. "Are you still awake?"

"Mmhmm." She nodded and slid up so her head was resting on his shoulder.

"I'm just paying attention. It's so funny," Bernie said. "Did you write it?"

He hummed a yes, and she snuggled deeper into his side. "It's so good."

Somehow he could see the vision of the next year rolling out in front of him. His own idea for a sitcom taking place, inspired by this trip and Bernie. Making decisions in the writers' room. Partnering with his favorite producer. Coming home to Bernie.

At the moment he could see it all. Touch it, even. But Bernie was in Portland with her own life. It was not like she lived in LA. It wasn't like they were even a couple yet. But something about this trip had made him feel like he knew her better today than he'd ever known Veronica. And yes, they didn't have all the silly, petty work things and in-and-out, day-to-day things, and he hadn't met her dog or her mom. But was walking through Alaska without soap or water harder than waking up and going to work and kissing someone goodbye and cooking dinner together? Yes. It must be. When he thought about it in those terms, it felt like real life was a vacation from his vacation.

He looked down at Bernie. How would they leave things in a few days? He almost asked her, but her breathing was heavy and her weight was full on his side. He pulled the blanket up around them and kissed the top of her hair. He needed just a few more minutes of this feeling before he'd give her some space and go sleep on his relegated sofa bed.

"Rise and shine." The nurse's gruff voice, somewhere between a scratched record and a longtime smoker's voice, was not the way Bernie wanted to wake up. Even the normally cheerful yet annoying "Rise and shine" sounded like she was pissed about something. She opened her eyes. The room was still dark, with the sun peaking around the corners of the blinds.

"What time is it?" Bernie moaned, rubbing at her eyes.

"Eight o'clock. I've got your breakfast here, and then the doctor should be in at any minute to examine you. Hopefully we'll get the cast on in thirty minutes, and you'll be out of here soon," the nurse snapped. She still hadn't smiled. As if the woman could hear Bernie's bitchy thoughts about her, she whipped on the overhead lights. Way too white. Way too bright.

Matthew grunted from the sofa. "Jesus, lady!" He threw the blanket over his face, and Bernie laughed.

The nurse narrowed her eyes at him and muttered under her breath, "That is certainly not my name."

"He just isn't a morning person," Bernie said, trying to commiserate with her. Even though she was pretty sure he was. They'd stayed up late. Bernie didn't know how late, but they'd passed out. She hadn't even brushed her teeth, and she could feel it. "Could you help me to the bathroom?"

"Of course. That's what I'm here for."

Bernie really wanted to ask, "Is it?" because so far, the nurse hadn't helped her with much at all. Other than delivering food she didn't really eat and interrupting her and Matthew. Possibly calling the security guard on them when they'd disappeared last night. Bernie couldn't help but chuckle as she remembered it. How Matthew and she had just had fun. Fun like kids. And also fun like adults. There was no forgetting how it had felt with his arms around her, his hands exploring her skin. She was fairly certain the need for another person's touch had never felt so in demand than yesterday, when they'd lain in this hospital bed together. And that was in a hospital bed. What could it have been like with two working legs, no stupid boot, and a large bed that actually fit two people?

The nurse loaded her into the wheelchair, and Bernie rolled herself into the bathroom. On the other side of the door, she could hear the doctor enter, and she hurried up so she could get back out there. She wanted out of this hospital. She and Matthew could get a room together tonight and tomorrow, and then join the rest of the crew for the goodbye dinner. Then they'd figure something out. Some way to see each other. Was she bananas? Did the Alaskan air have some kind of mind-altering properties in it? Because she was ready to use up the rest of her vacation for the year, taking the much-longed-for road trip with James Brown and showing up on his doorstep in LA.

She rolled out of the bathroom, without much grace, and the doctor smiled at her. "Good morning, Bernie. Let's hop back up on the bed, and we'll check out your leg."

Hop up? She must be kidding.

Matthew ran over to her. "I can help you."

"Thanks." She missed seeing the way he looked in the morning. All disheveled hair, sticking up every way off his head. His sleepy eyes, half-closed. Somehow it looked erotic on him—too much like his kissing face, with half-lidded eyes. His cheek creased from the pillow. He leaned down and gave her a kiss on her temple, and something in her melted, like her organs were pats of butter that just turned to liquid at his touch. How had she not seen how absolutely sweet he was on day one, when he was giving her a bear lecture?

He helped her get on the bed, and the nurse lifted her booted leg over and then the doctor removed the boot. "Oh, good, it looks much, much better. There is sometimes so much swelling after a break like that. But we'll get you out of here. I'm sure you two lovebirds have more fun things to get on with."

At that, Bernie's face felt hot. She'd never blushed this much in her life, and she side-eyed Matthew, who'd raised his eyebrows and was giving her this little half smile. Was that the male version of a blush? Did he feel it, too, this pull toward each other? Or was he just thinking of getting back home, to his TV show writing and his glamorous life in LA?

"Why don't you have breakfast, and we'll be back in about thirty minutes to get this done."

"Okay, thanks." Bernie smiled at her. While the nurse was a true Ratched, the doctor was beyond nice.

They left, and Bernie examined the tray of food next to her. Eggs that were surely room temperature. Lukewarm potatoes and yogurt. She sighed and picked up the yogurt.

"We're going to be out of here soon," Matthew said after he came out of the bathroom and then kissed her with a minty mouth. "Why don't you eat whatever is edible, and then we can go get a real meal. Totally gorge ourselves on warm, delicious breakfast. Or lunch, whatever you want."

Bernie looked up at him. "Are you sure you don't mind doing all this? I mean, waiting on me and helping me?" What she really wanted to ask him was, *Why are you doing this?*

"What else am I going to do?" He shrugged.

"I still feel bad you're missing out on the hike."

"Don't. Hanging out with you is more fun than hiking in the wilderness."

"You didn't think that a few days ago." She cocked an eyebrow at him.

"I'm not sure about that, actually."

Bernie opened her mouth to say something, but she didn't know what to say. Was he right? How many times as they'd been sharing a tent together had she thought about him? Hell, she'd even tried to subconsciously cuddle with him the first night in her sleep.

"Listen, you get all casted up. I'm going to get us coffee; then we'll find someplace to eat, and I can roll you around Anchorage. Then I'll see if we can check into the hotel two days early. What do you think?"

Bernie nodded. "That plan sounds absolutely perfect."

CHAPTER 27

When Matthew walked into the room with Bernie's latte in tow, she was on a scooter, her knee propped up on the small padded bench and rolling around the room.

"Don't try to steal this from me!" She smiled at him, and her eyes landed on the coffee. "Look, I can actually come to you now." She scooted over and grabbed the cup from him. "Oh my God, this is so much easier."

"Do you feel comfortable with it?" the nurse asked, looking at her tablet.

"Yes."

"Okay, well if you're ready to go, you can check out downstairs."

"Can I drink my coffee first?" Bernie asked, the cup halfway to her mouth.

The nurse squinted at her, and Matthew wondered if she was actually considering whether or not Bernie could have her coffee. After a pause, she nodded and left the room.

"Geez, Ratched is in a mood today," Matthew said.

"I know, but I don't care because now I can scoot around and have this high-tech fiberglass cast on." She pointed to her foot. "Where's your coffee?"

"Oh, I chugged it in like five minutes. I almost got another one but remembered we were going out for breakfast. Also, good news! Our hotel that we have booked for the last night has a room for tonight and Friday as well, if you want to drop our stuff off."

"Just one room?" Bernie gasped.

Matthew swallowed. Had he assumed and maybe even hallucinated everything that had happened over the last day? Shit. "Uh, if that's okay? Or you can . . ."

"I'm just kidding." She rolled a few steps closer and kissed him. Her mouth tasted like vanilla, and if he thought the coffee had warmed him up, it was nothing compared to Bernie's kisses.

"Shall we?" she asked, gazing up at him with that frisky look in her eye. Her inner squirrel had no business with him right now. It had been eaten up by a fox or lynx.

"Most definitely. Let's scoot outta here."

◆ ◆ ◆

They arrived at the hotel, and Matthew helped the Uber driver unload their bags.

"Can you believe that Saturday, two days from now, is the last day of the hike?" Bernie said. "We worked so hard for this moment. Standing here, at the foot of this hotel, with room service and fluffy comforters, I really feel proud for overextending myself just like everyone wanted me to. Really just pushed myself to the max."

Matthew looked over at her, and her face was doing this kooky cross-eyed thing as she sat on her scooter now, rolling across the pavement. He just laughed.

"What, you don't think I'm being serious?" she asked in the odd voice she'd just been doing. Like some kind of pseudo-bro voice of someone who'd just surfed a wave ten stories tall and lived to humbly brag about it.

"Bernice, you are your own character. No write-ups, sketches, writers' room mashups needed." All the things he'd written in his notebook—he didn't even need those notes anymore. This was all so much better.

"I'm going to assume that's a compliment because it's convenient. Although when my mom calls someone a *character*, she usually raises her eyebrows and snarls on the left side of her mouth."

"It's the good kind of character. The heroic kind."

"You're just saying that because I'm broken and you're trying to make me feel better."

He cleared his throat as he lugged both backpacks and leaned down at the start of the ramp to get to the front door. "Or it could be because I want to get in your pants."

Bernie's mouth opened like she was ready with a comeback, but then just one eye squinted, and her lips followed in an upward trajectory. She grinned and scooted toward the automatic opening doors.

"Speechless. A first, truly." He'd done the impossible, and he skipped up the ramp so she couldn't run over his foot with her wheels.

"Oh, I assure you I can make you speechless. In droves of speechlessness."

"Yeah?"

"But only if you're nice."

He leaned down to kiss her and gestured for her to go through the sliding doors first.

"That's what I'm talking about." She nodded in approval and scooted toward the reception desk.

After checking in and finding their room, he opened the door and let Bernie go in first.

"This view!" She stopped at the wall of windows, her silhouette framed against a mountain scape with a blue sky, fluffed with clouds. He joined her side.

"I think they put this hotel here just for this." It was like what they had been hiking through, but from this floor, they could see it all. The valleys curving in between the green mountains. The river, a thread of blue weaving in and out.

"Hey," she said softly, her finger playing at the cuff of his shirt. "I really appreciate you helping me. I mean it."

"Of course."

"What are we going to do?" she asked.

"Is your leg protected?"

"Mmhmm," she muffled into his chest, her lips sending the faintest vibration through his rib cage.

"Are you hungry? Or do you want to take a *not* nap?"

She looked up. "A *not* nap?"

"Yeah, where we lie in bed in the middle of the day but don't sleep."

She collapsed on the bed and began unbuttoning her shirt. "Is this appropriate not-nap behavior?" she asked.

"Yes." He cleared his throat. It was a lot raspier than he'd intended. She threw her shirt to the side.

"I wore my nicest sports bra. Don't make fun of it." She pressed her lips together like she was trying to restrain a laugh. She slid to the top of the bed and leaned against the headboard.

Matthew crawled up to her from the bottom of the bed. "I can assure you I won't. I'm just going to get rid of it anyway."

She began unbuttoning her shorts. "What about this? Also appropriate for the not nap?" Bernie's eyes seemed to sizzle with glee.

"Oh yes. Completely appropriate, and welcome behavior for the not nap."

"Come here then." She leaned forward and looped a finger into his waistband, tugging him toward her.

Matthew towered over Bernie, even though he was just sitting on his knees, as he slid his shirt off over his head. *Slid* was not the right word, though. It was more like *manhandled, corralled, ripped* without leaving any holes. The way he took off a shirt reminded her of an old commercial for Axe body spray, and she tried not to giggle. An easy task, considering the man before her rivaled the mountain outside the window in beauty.

She exhaled louder than she'd anticipated, and her hand came up to cover her mouth. In the bright sunlit room without any eerie hospital lighting or a twin bed beneath them both, she could fully appreciate the body he clearly took care of through his random adventure trips and, probably, overjuicing and Cross-Fitting, LA style.

His eyes crinkled at the corners at her reaction. She could only imagine what her face looked like as she admired him. She took him in like a big gulp of air and searched for all the places she hadn't been able to view in the hospital properly. The curves of his pecs. The flatness of his stomach. She stretched out her fingers, and they walked up his abs toward the dip in between his collarbones.

"This is a good look on you," she said.

"What? Shirtless?"

"Yeah . . ." She sighed and turned to the side, then stared at a framed painting of a moose. She'd never felt like she'd had to turn away from such masculine beauty before. The feelings that spiked up in her made her nervous. Desire mixed with want and worry and fretting.

"I could say the same about you."

She looked down at her leg in a cast, her cotton panties (which at least didn't have owls on them today), and the sports bra that was further from the definition of *lingerie* than the nice comforter she was lying on. It was maybe the unsexiest she'd ever looked, but Matthew's eyes—open and deep, shining with something that might be hunger or appreciation—made her feel if not sexy, at least kind of adored.

Damn, she was in trouble. They had one more day and then they were off, back to their respective homes. How could that even happen? She couldn't imagine going back to her life after this. She envisioned

Matthew, herself, and James Brown canoeing in clear blue waters, colorful fish swimming below the surface, as they made their way to a tiny island, where, upon landing, Matthew would scoop her up, even though she would be whole and castless, and then set her down on the sand, lavishing her body with attention. James Brown would go off sniffing, leaving them their privacy. Because that's the kind of dog he was.

"What are you thinking about?" Matthew said, half smiling at her. "You look like you're contemplating something. At first I thought you were upset, but then you just smiled."

Bernie was not ready to admit her imaginings to him. "Nothing." She instead pulled him down to her and kissed him, full and hard, wrapping her one usable leg around his waist for good measure. She'd keep him from leaving, however feebly she could. His lips did something to her that was transcendent. Like if she closed her eyes, her stomach dipped low and her body felt like it was levitating off the bed. All the thoughts and worries she'd had swirling around vanished, and she was only a thing to be adored, caressed, and appreciated by his massive hands.

He took his time, but his lingering made every movement feel bottomless. Like they could spend the next two days in this room and still not have explored every inch of their bodies. Every touch and breath and movement of his body felt like there was so much more to discover. Like there was an endless array of Matthew she still needed to plunge into and search out, and she needed more than one day to do it. Bernie grabbed on tight and tried to hold on.

Her clothes were off now, as well as his, and the heat between their bodies was like lava, the feeling of him coasting over her curves and settling in to all the right spots. Bernie had the distinct feeling that it was going to harden on her, something permanent in every pore that had room for this feeling from Matthew. She wasn't going to be able to forget it. Ever. This moment, this trip, the feel of their bodies together—because something had changed.

His lips were like semiconductors, taking that heat and making it rise inside her so that it stretched in her chest and swirled tight in her abdomen. She cursed her boot and her bum ankle because she wanted to be able to do so much more. As the heat became too much for her to bear, mixed with the desire for even more of it, in every secret nook hidden in her body, she gasped and whispered in his ear, "I don't want this to end."

He paused and looked into her eyes, and for a moment she worried she'd said it too soon. But then his face became soft, and his eyes seemed to glitter. "Me either." He kissed her then, and she shuddered beneath him. Never had two words made her feel so whole.

He gasped in her mouth and opened his eyes, and their foreheads met, his slowly rocking back and forth on hers. "Oh, Bernie. What have you done to me?"

His grin was like the kind of smile she'd only seen when people felt pure bliss. Big and goofy, not caring about what anyone thought because they were so joyful they couldn't help themselves. "You're smiling!" she said. "I love your smile. I want to make you smile more. And bigger."

He half laughed. "You're crazy. But it's not hard with you. I think you retrained me into smiling again."

"You have such a handsome, but serious, face, and your smile just makes something unexpected happen. Like you become this fun kid."

"A fun kid?" He groaned. "That's not what I was going for in this moment."

"Like a really hot fun kid?" She cringed and shook her head. That wasn't what she was going for either. "I just mean your personality shines through when you smile. Your inner Matthew. I'm glad you're smiling for me." She kissed him.

"There's something about you, Bernie. I can't keep myself from smiling."

God help her: she was melting again.

"Or doing other things either." His eyes darkened, and he bent back down.

Her whole body craved him as she saw the look on his face and felt how his body responded physically to what hers was saying on the inside. "Please. I want to do everything with you." And she pulled him to her.

CHAPTER 28

"Food is so good when it's not in a compartmentalized tray. Or rehydrated," Bernie said as she closed her eyes and cut into another bite of her pancake.

"Or with all the hospital smells marring it." Matthew shook his head. The particular bouquet of the hospital, the cleaning products, the sterility—even the burnt electrical smell of those bright-ass lights seemed to be stuck in his nose.

"Yes. So true. And there are no views like this." Bernie gestured to the windows that flanked one wall of the restaurant. "It's like everything here is positioned with some kind of phenomenal view. Just so beautiful. It makes everything better."

He hummed. Although he was pretty sure the view had nothing to do with how phenomenal what had happened in their hotel room last night was. He wished he could capture what he'd experienced in there and bottle it up. Remember exactly how that had felt for later. He couldn't believe that in just a week, he was starting to feel for Bernie what he'd never felt for anyone before. He was trying to rationalize it, because it did not make sense. How could what they had be so fun and so sexy at the same time? Like playing hoops with his neighborhood team and then making out. It just didn't make sense.

The only way it made sense was the magical elixir called Alaska. They were apart from everything. They had these beautiful surroundings. It was idyllic.

But then all the other logic took over. It was not idyllic. They'd been dirty and frustrated with each other. She'd broken her ankle. He hadn't had much sleep. And yet, he still had this weird soaring feeling in his chest when he looked in her eyes, which always seemed to be sparkling. Or at her lips. Those lips that fit him so perfectly, that made him want to savor every moment they were together. That made him want to lurch across the table and take them with his now. Like some uncivilized sex heathen in this five-star brunch joint. He had to clear his mind.

"So did you ever call your mom, by the way?" he asked.

"Um . . . yes?" She smiled sheepishly, not even trying to hide her lie.

"Why won't you call her? I'm sure she wants to know what happened to you. Plus, you can have a video call with your dog. I'm sure he's concerned as well." James Brown. He laughed. Really, who gave their dog a last name? Bernie, that was who.

"She'll freak out and insist on coming up here. Trust me, she's the kind of person who would just go to the airport without telling me and get on the next plane, even if I told her not to. Then she'd find some way to track down my phone and find us in bed and burst open the door and attempt to do her weird coddling thing. Just, no. She's not going to ruin my trip."

"What's a weird coddling thing?"

"Where she acts like I'm not an adult and have no idea what's best for me. And that *she* does."

"Moms are just like that sometimes."

"I don't know how to explain it." Bernie sighed and looked out toward the window. "Ever since my dad died, my mom has become this whole other person. Like she was just waiting for it or something. After the funeral, she started making arrangements to move out and go live her dreams on a farm. And then telling me how to live mine. It's fucked up."

"Sounds like you might resent her a little."

Bernie's head whipped back to his, and he wasn't sure if the look in her eyes was aggressive or thoughtful.

Matthew held up his hands in surrender. "I'm only saying that because I am the king of parental resentment."

She paused and slowly nodded. "Maybe I am a little resentful. Like how she's always telling me to be more like my aunt Bernice. She's cursed me with a name I don't want and expects me to be a person that I can't be."

"But Bernie, I think I might be with your mom here," he said, not shrinking back when her eyes got big like cannons that wanted to launch at him. "From what you've told me, you are more like your aunt Bernice than you think. As if it's in your nature, and you're just ignoring it."

Her eyes ceased firing, and she looked down at her plate and sighed. "I think what really bothers me is that when she says those things, it implies I'm not like my dad. I'm half of him too!"

"I can't see anything about you that would be embracing an accountant's soul. I mean, don't get me wrong, I'm sure your dad was a great guy, but that kind of reasonable-type character doesn't apply to you. Accountants are like the cows of the world, and you're more like a rabid squirrel."

Bernie started coughing as she choked on her bacon.

"I mean that as a compliment, by the way. Are you okay?"

She nodded and took a drink of water. "*Rabid* squirrel?"

"I just meant there are pragmatic people like tax assessors and accountants who perform practical and much-needed tasks in our day-to-day world. Like cows who give us practical nourishing substance."

"Oh my God, I got the analogy. But *rabid* squirrel?"

"I mean, you're cute and funny and squirrely and wild. And you named your dog James Brown. No tax assessor–type person would do that."

She took a big drink of her juice. "Yeah, a cow would name their dog something like Dan."

Matthew laughed. "I don't know, Dan is a pretty weird-ass name for a dog. Maybe like Fluffy."

"Okay, we can agree to disagree. I still like Dan for the name of a cow's dog."

"That's because you are a rabid squirrel." He tapped his finger to her nose on the last word because he couldn't jump over the table to kiss her. "But seriously, maybe you should just ask your mom about it. If she hasn't talked about it, maybe she's just too sad to. You never know. People deal with their emotions so differently."

"Hmm, maybe. Speaking of parental units and drama, what are you going to do about your dad?"

Matthew shook his head and leaned back in his chair, taking his time with the biggest drink of coffee he could. He had the decision like a ball of light right behind his forehead, this glowing thing of what he wanted to do, but could he? The words took shape in his head. What would Bernie say?

"Maybe I'm a victim of the name curse too. You know, my dad goes by Matt, and I'm named after him."

"But you're not like him at all!" Bernie jumped in. "At least from what you've told me."

"Maybe I don't have his bad habits, but sometimes I wonder, though." Over time, he'd thought about some of the bizarre jokes his dad used to make when he was a kid, and with reluctance, he realized where he got his sense of humor from.

"You shouldn't feel forced to give him an organ, just because you have genes in common. You should do what you think is right."

"I've thought about it a lot the past few days. It was hard not to, sitting around a hospital. My dad was an asshole to me, even if now he's a reformed asshole. But there was something you said to me that made me wrestle with my own thoughts."

"By the way, just so you know, I think your animal is a narwhal. So when you tell me you're wrestling with a decision, I see you as a narwhal wrestling with a luchador." She smiled sweetly. "The rabid squirrel just wanted to get that in."

"Narwhal?"

"But please go on, tell me how I influenced you."

He kept finding himself smiling these huge goofy smiles at almost her every word. Even when thinking about his dad. It was like Bernie had weaved some sort of weird magic into him. "You asked if I could live with myself if I didn't do it, and something worse happened to him. I don't think I could."

"Oh yeah, I did say that." She looked down at her own coffee and took a sip. "How are you feeling about it?"

"I think it's the right thing to do." Even just saying the words out loud, he knew it was right. He felt like he was glowing inside with speaking this revelation for the first time.

"I think it's very brave and very generous. I mean that."

"It's just a spare vital organ, right?"

"Exactly. Who needs a little ol' extra kidney lying around?" She shrugged.

"Hopefully not me."

"You're healthy and strong, and all the nurses will be giving you extra attention because you're so hot, so you'll be fine."

He coughed a laugh. Was he really going to say to her what he'd been thinking? It was now or never, and he hoped she wouldn't freak out and jump in front of another bear or anything. "I was hoping that whenever it happens, maybe you would be the one giving me extra attention while I was in the hospital. You know, payback and all?"

Bernie pressed her lips together, and her eyes got big. "Really? You want me to come to LA?"

"I mean, if you still have that extra vacation time you don't know what to do with." Shit, he had gone too far. They'd known each other a week, and he was asking her to come hang out with him during his surgery.

"Wow, Matthew." Her eyes fluttered as she looked around her like she'd lost something.

He'd put himself out there, and of course she didn't want to sit at his hospital bedside. Their entire relationship was currently based on a hospital bed. Relationship? Did he just imagine that? Clearly he was thinking way too deeply about her. "You know, never mind. I shouldn't have said anything."

"No, I mean, I would love to come. Of course I want to be with you through that. Is that crazy?"

"Really?" He might be in some kind of shock. His heart was racing, but his body was frozen. "No, I can't imagine anyone else I want there. Maybe my mom, but she does not do weird coddling."

"I don't want to assume anything, but I like you, Matthew." Bernie's face turned pink. "And I was wondering what would happen, you know, after tomorrow. I have a flight to Portland on Sunday. You have a flight to LA. We both have our lives in separate places. You have your TV show pilot you're working on . . . but I will miss you."

"Yeah, same. We can figure something out. It's a short flight." Was it crazy that Matthew was already wondering if her job could somehow transition to LA?

"So this project you're working on . . ." She cleared her throat. "Would it be crazy to ask if you could work on it from Portland in the meantime?"

Matthew couldn't stop the grin from taking over his face. Maybe Bernie was feeling exactly that same I-don't-want-this-feeling-to-end-tomorrow rush. "Yeah?"

"Does that mean, 'Yeah, I can work on it from Portland,' or 'Yeah, you are actually insane for even asking me that'?"

He shook his head frantically. "No, I mean yes. I could work on it from Portland. For at least a little while. That's a great idea. Maybe I can just fly back with you."

"Really?"

He thought Bernie was ready to squeal, which made him laugh. God, he couldn't help himself around her, smiling all the freaking time.

"Yeah, why not? I can call later and check."

"Do you think you could tolerate me and my scooter for a while?"

"As long as we take turns riding it." He grinned.

"Deal." She stuck out her hand and he shook it but didn't really want to let it go, so he lowered their hands and let them linger on the table, his just holding hers.

"Have you been to LA before?"

She shook her head. "I'd like to go, though. I imagine it's just palm trees, vegan restaurants, and fancy people. Or wannabe fancy people."

"That's funny. I would characterize it as shitty traffic, good tacos, and just like all kinds of people. The fancy people, shockingly, are a minority. But maybe there are a lot of wannabes there. Everyone's trying to make something of themselves."

"Well, I love tacos. We'll make a date. I'll come for your surgery, and then maybe something in the realm of presurgery and postcast. So we're both healthy, walkable, and consenting adults."

"Sounds perfect." Matthew was already envisioning Bernie's visit to LA. Where they'd explore all his favorite record shops; eat at the taco place with the orange tree in front; see stand-up comedy at his favorite hole in the wall; make out while looking at his favorite views in Griffith Park; stay in, curled up in his apartment. So many options.

Was this vision a dream, though? How could he be so swept up, hallucinating glimpses of the future with Bernie?

Was it real, or was it just Alaska?

CHAPTER 29

Bernie and Matthew explored the city that afternoon—slowly meandering through the streets, down a paved beach trail surrounded by wildflowers, then to a brewery—and ended the day back at the hotel after Bernie had thoroughly cursed her scooter and ankle. Although Matthew had easily taken her mind off it. Now she lay on the bed, her clothes sprawled around, Matthew's arms cradling her, and she nestled into his chest as if she could burrow inside it. Her leg lay there like a deadweight. If only she could go back in time to prevent the break, what fun she could have with him. But did she really want to, though? That simple act of insane bravery had brought her and Matthew inexplicably together. And who knows what would have happened if they'd continued trekking through Denali. He would have continued his brooding in silence. She would have continued to bitch about him to Shalini and Diana. Or perhaps things would have always ended up this way with them. She had just needed time to find out who he really was.

Her stomach bubbled up some kind of fierce noise. It demanded food.

"Should we eat something?" she asked.

"Yes." Matthew stretched on the bed. "I was just going to say the same thing, but your stomach beat me to it."

"Pizza?"

"Sure. I'll run out and get something." He sighed and hopped up off the bed, a gesture she'd taken for granted so many, many times, and rummaged through his bag.

"What are you doing?"

"I'm convinced I have another clean pair of underwear somewhere in here."

She laughed. "You mean you haven't just been turning them inside out this whole time?"

"I had a final clean set of clothes at the bottom of my bag for the end of the trip. Aha!" His arm shot toward the ceiling as he swung black boxer briefs around his index finger.

"Narwhals do not act like children, by the way." Bernie was shocked that he could still do something that surprised her.

"I'm pretty sure a child would not do what we just did."

"Ew, go get the pizza." She shooed him toward the door with her hand.

"Meat, vegetable, mix it up—what do you want?"

"I'm not picky. I'll eat anything because I'm starving." Apparently pushing herself around on the scooter was hard work.

He kissed her on the forehead before leaving, and even though her stomach was a raving lunatic at the moment, something in her softened. He was such a surprise. He'd changed so much in mere days. She had to wonder if she had unlocked something in him, just as he had unlocked something in her.

She got up and slid her clothes on with the grace of a goat and then scooted toward the window, looking out at the bright Alaskan night-time sky, an eternal twilight. No wonder it was nine o'clock and they hadn't eaten. She still couldn't get used to the twenty-hour days. She sat on the chair by the window, next to Matthew's mess of a bag, and pulled out her phone to call Tabitha. Was she really going to be gone in a day's time?

She dropped her phone and bent down to pick it up off the floor. It had fallen next to Matthew's little notebook, which must have slipped out of his bag while he was on the great underwear-spelunking mission. She picked them both up.

She was going to set it back in his bag, knowing that whatever he'd sketched out for his show ideas, he wanted to keep secret—for whatever reasons he had. But the words staring back at her on the open page, like a title, took her aback:

The Chronicles of Bernie.

The words sat there like a taunt. Heat flooded through her system. She wasn't sure if this was some kind of panicking sensation that was making the hair on her arms feel electrified. Or was it guilt from invading his privacy and now finding out that the thing he was hiding from her was about her? Why would Matthew keep notes about her for his show and hide it from her?

Maybe she was overthinking this, though. Maybe it was all about how great she was. But the words he'd said earlier rang out in her head—*antihero*, and "like the kind of character who's funny because you feel sorry for them."

She turned the page, hoping that somehow this book was about something else. Not about her as an antihero. Maybe it was about her, the woman he'd made feel so adored over the past few days.

Narcissistic wannabe city girl attempts to make her way through the wilderness.

Cute but with an angry expression on her face all the time, you can't look for too long without wanting to punch something.

A klutz to the highest degree, she is completely unable to function on her own.

A helpless baby who needs someone to explain how fire works.

A biting tongue that will lash out at anyone who confronts her.

Bernie's nose began to itch, the burning sensation seeking the bridge of her nose, the tears welling up in her eyes. Her hopes fried. Somehow, somewhere deep inside, she'd thought maybe that *The Chronicles of Bernie* would be stalkerish at the worst, but amusing at the least. This was hateful. No one had said things like this about her. Ever. It hurt. So much. Like each sentence stabbed her in the chest with its cruel words. Not only was he using this evil sketch of her for his script, apparently, but it wasn't even funny. It was mean. Like ten times worse than eighth-grade mean girls mean. She'd been sleeping with him, and he'd harbored these thoughts about her all along.

These notes were from just days ago. She'd seen him scribbling away in that book the first night they'd set up camp. She took a deep breath, even as her face turned hotter as she started crying, wiping her eyes on her sleeve. Maybe it got better. Maybe the first few pages were, like, from day one, when they'd gotten off on the wrong foot. What would she have said about him? She tried to harness her internal rational brain, lassoing it into thinking clearly.

She flipped the page.

She is scared of everyone and annoys each person to their core because of her inability to function.

The perfect antihero—has some kind of complex over her name because she can't be who her parents want her to be.

Bernie paused. She hadn't told him about Great-Aunt Bernice until days into their hike, when she thought they were becoming friendlier with each other. Even then he was making notes about her, little hate-fueled judgments about her character. To be used for a TV show? He was going to broadcast this horrible interpretation of herself on television? To harness her secret fears and insecurities and splay them on-screen for the world?

She flipped forward to the beginning of the book. "Sheila and Trevor take on the trail" was written with a few notes about them too.

Lost meets Portlandia.

Misfit crew of hikers who all have their own issues—couple who are twin dressers and simultaneously speak, retired couple who are obsessed with sex, etc.

Two tour guides, but you can't figure out if they're lovers or brother and sister.

Ew.

Matthew had written things about everyone. Who was he?

Yesterday he was still writing down ideas, even after he'd kissed her. When she had asked him if he'd come to Portland with her, she'd assumed the confused look on his face was him thinking through travel and work logistics. But in actuality, he was likely calculating the benefits of observing Bernie in her native habitat. And now it made sense why he had come on the helicopter too. He was just using this time to know her better so he could use all the aspects of Bernie for his character sketch.

The feeling of disgust took over her entire body, with eerie little chills cascading into every pore. She felt so dirty, so betrayed, so used by him. Here, she'd just been thinking how Matthew had changed in just a few days, but that was not it. At all. He was the same asshole she'd met on day one, and she'd fallen for his pretty, shaven face. The only reason he came with her after she'd broken her ankle was to fill out his idea of her.

She was full on sobbing now. She'd been so, so stupid. To think she could have some carefree affair, scare a bear, traipse about on an adventure for a week. Well, this was proof, if anything, that she couldn't be like her great-aunt Bernice. Great-Aunt Bernice never would have let a man take advantage of her like this.

She flipped back to the section about her, apparently because she was also weak, stupid, and a masochist.

Thinks she can be some secret adventurer but there is no way in hell.

She sat there numb for a while, looking around the room at the camping gear she'd bought in some feeble hope that she could change and try to embark upon some adventure. Matthew had seen completely through her. Out the window, where Denali peaked over the other mountains, she tried to imagine her great-aunt climbing up its monstrous sloping snowcapped sides. She could only imagine the choice words she'd have for her namesake today. Why had Bernie even tried? She wiped at the tears that were drying up on her face.

Yep. Matthew had called it already.

The door opened, and Matthew came in. "Dinner is served."

She looked up, and he set the box down on the bed. "What's wrong? What happened?" His eyes went to her lap, and, when he saw the notebook, all he said was, "Shit."

CHAPTER 30

Matthew froze. This looked bad. Really bad.

"I know this looks bad. But I can explain."

"Looks bad? This little book fell on the floor, and when I picked it up, it was open to a page called *The Chronicles of Bernie*. I would love to hear you explain your way out of this." Bernie's voice was a roar. He'd never quite heard it get to that volume, even as her frustration with him had peaked on the trail.

"Bernie, I—" He couldn't even finish his statement.

"Bad is all this is. I can't believe I fell for your act." She shook her head, and her gaze drifted off to the corner of the room as she wiped her eyes on her sleeve.

"Act? No, there's no act."

"Oh, there must be an act. Because if this is just who you are"—she held up the notebook—"then it makes it worse."

"Bernie, no, listen to me," he said as he rounded the end of the bed and squatted in front of her. "This is all a misunderstanding."

"Oh, really." She thumbed through the pages. "Is this a misunderstanding? 'Scene idea: She gets super excited while reading a romance novel in her tent and tries to seduce the guy who obviously can't stand her.'" She looked back at him and crossed her arms. "Hmm?"

Matthew winced. God, had he really written that on paper? He exhaled. "I know, it sounds horrible. It's just inspiration."

"No, you know what's horrible? That I let my guard down for you, even though I thought you were a total asshole, and because you were being so nice and funny, we hooked up. I should have known better. People don't change overnight. Or, in our case, over a helicopter ride."

"Bernie, it's not like I changed—"

She huffed out a laugh that choked in her throat.

"I mean, we changed."

"Speak for yourself—I have never changed. I'm the same damn person you met on day one who you wrote this horrible shit about, and I'm the same person who . . ." She tucked her head toward her shoulder and hid her face with her hands. Her shoulders shook, and all Matthew could hear was the soft panting of her sobs.

God, he felt horrible. Seeing her like this, knowing how upset and hurt she must be, felt like a knife was piercing his chest. "Bernie, please stop crying. Yes, I wrote those things, but they were a sketch. They weren't you. I just had this idea of someone who didn't know how to camp and stuff, and I thought it would make a good show. They started out as you and then just built up."

"Because I'm a perfect antihero? The kind of person people feel sorry for. Great. Yeah, thanks for that explanation, Matthew. I feel so much better now."

"No, that's not what I meant." He sighed. How could he explain it? "It's inspired. It's not you necessarily. They're just ideas I sometimes base on reality. I swear!"

She flipped the pages and held his journal up. "It has my name right here. It has Sheila's and Trevor's names here even. Do you expect me to believe that?"

"Yes! I mean, I know it all looks bad, but I really like you, Bernie. I would never want something like this stupid idea journal to come between us. It doesn't mean anything."

"Yeah, it doesn't mean anything to you, because no one wrote a book about all your imperfections and flaws and made fun of you and thought up how you couldn't deal with life!" She threw the book at him, but it fell to the floor, and she reached for the scooter and rolled over to her bag, throwing her stuff in it.

"Wait, what are you doing?" he asked.

"I'm getting the hell out of here."

"You have a broken ankle, and you can't walk."

"I'll figure it out. Trust me, nothing could stop me from escaping you as soon as possible."

He went beside her and placed his hand on her arm. "Please don't. We can work this out."

She shook his hand off so fast that Matthew jerked to the right to avoid getting hit. "Oh no, we can't. I'm not your antimuse or however you think of me. You'll just have to figure out how to write your stupid pilot script without using me anymore." She fastened her backpack in what he was sure was record time and threw it on her back and made her way to the door.

He jumped in front of her. "Bernie, I'm sorry! It was stupid. Please don't leave." He was groveling, for God's sake. Surely she wouldn't just go like this.

"Get out of my way." Her eyes were pink and glazed from crying. What had he done?

"I am seriously so sorry. I hate that anything I did made you feel this way."

"Like document my incompetence? My most embarrassing moments? Move."

"No! I was inspired by you and the trip and wanted to use it as the basis for my next script, but I didn't want to freak you out. It's not *really* you."

"Right," she huffed as she wiped at her eyes.

"I should have told you. I get that now. It would have prevented all of this."

"You really think that?" Bernie's lips pressed together like she was holding something else back. She just looked at him, and he could feel the fury behind her eyes, mixed with hurt. It hit him deep in his chest. Now an ache pulsed there, and he didn't know how to make this situation better.

She reached for the door, almost rolling over his foot in the process, but he jumped back.

"Where are you going?" he asked in a panic.

"None of your business. Don't follow me." She rolled down the hall to the elevator and hit the button, making a point to look straight at the elevator door.

Matthew resisted running after her. Maybe she just needed time. He'd call her in a few hours, he'd explain, he'd beg her forgiveness, and maybe she'd see his side. The elevator dinged and she rolled in. He sighed and closed the door, hitting his forehead on the doorjamb. Then he collapsed on the bed.

That stupid, stupid book. His even more stupid idea. What had he been thinking? But the truth was that little things Bernie did had inspired some of it, and maybe the idea of her had inspired it. But the ideas in the book had evolved. It had become something else—a mix of her, and Sheila and Trevor, and even just the idea of someone he'd thought Bernie was before he discovered she was so much more. She was a constant surprise. He hadn't wanted to tell her that she was the inspiration for his new idea because he didn't want to scare her off, but maybe that had been the wrong approach.

It was the random things that she'd said that had spawned little nuggets of ideas he'd written down. The negativity he'd scrawled on that first day was more a reflection of himself than of Bernie. He'd been in a horrible state of mind. He'd been dour, bitter, feeling like his soul had been sucked out recently. With the crappy work and the dilemma over his father—they had created a shell that he hadn't realized existed.

Until he met Bernie, and the Matthew he'd once really enjoyed hanging out with had emerged again, made all the better by her presence.

"Fuck!" he screamed into his hands. He'd really messed it up this time. He'd been fantasizing a future with her and had made her erupt in tears, forcing that look of hate in her eyes that was clearly directed at him. She had to forgive him. The only way he could even stomach the idea of his dad's kidney donation was because of her. She made him want to do things, create things, made him see what he really needed to do. And now she was gone.

He just needed to tell her that. Explain that somehow in this crazy world together, they made sense. That even if it was only a week they'd spent with each other, he'd never felt this ache inside his chest at just the mere idea of her not being in his future.

But what if she wouldn't answer his calls and he couldn't explain and he never saw her again?

He jumped off the bed, grabbed his hotel key, and ran to the elevator. He'd catch her downstairs. Maybe she was just getting another room. Maybe an Uber. But he'd get down on his knees and cry if he had too.

The elevator finally came and then took forever getting to the lobby. It stopped at every floor, where someone was always getting on or off. His whole body was vibrating. Tingling with nerves and anxiety. When it arrived in the lobby, he looked around everywhere, but she wasn't there. He ran outside and she wasn't there either. Defeated, he walked back inside and stopped at the front desk.

"Hi, I was with another person, a woman; she was on one of those scooter things with a giant hiking pack? Did she get another room?"

"Excuse me?" the woman behind the desk said.

"I'm just wondering if she got another room. She left ours, and I'm trying to find her."

"Uh, sir, we can't give out that kind of information about guests."

"So she is here!" His hands slapped the desk.

The receptionist raised her eyebrows. "Uh, no, I didn't say that. I'm just saying we can't give out information about other guests. Whether they're here or they left. To protect them." The woman put too much stress on the word *protect* and shot him almost the same calculated darts of suspicion Bernie had given him. He probably looked manic, and she was trying to decide whether he was an abusive spouse or a serial killer.

Desperation welled up inside him, like a roar that he had to get out. He had to make this woman understand. Hadn't she ever been in love and messed up? He swallowed. Love?

"I just messed up and I really like this girl and I don't know where she is. I'm not like a danger or anything. I swear!"

"Sir, please . . ." Her voice indicated this was a polite finale to their conversation, and her sigh was imbued with subtle exasperation.

He paused, unsure of what his next move would be. But it would be to call her. Maybe he could explain once he'd figured it out himself. He sighed, completely aware that his shoulders had collapsed like a defeated man's. "Of course, I get it. Thank you."

He walked back up the hall and hit the elevator button, hoping that Bernie wasn't gone for good.

◆ ◆ ◆

Bernie settled into her new room, which was fortunately on the ground floor, almost as far as she could get from Matthew and his evil scribblings. She shrugged out of her pack and laid it on the bed before collapsing beside it.

What an asshole. Even as she thought the words, she felt something prick her chest. The one time she'd believed she'd found someone, it was a humiliating disaster. How could she have thought she could be some crazy, free adventurer for a week, have a love affair, and fantasize about a future with a man she couldn't stand only a few days before?

It sounded like something her aunt Bernice would have done, but her great-aunt would have done it with shrewdness and style, wearing a fantastic hat in a cloud of intoxicating perfume created just for her, the man unable to resist her. She wouldn't have gotten her heart battered like Bernie had. In fact, she was pretty sure her great-aunt had embarked on some kind of impulsive love affair on vacation, but with a much more impressive outcome, per usual. She remembered sitting on the porch with her great-auntie when she was in high school. Bernie had just broken up with her boyfriend, who'd kissed someone on his spring break family vacation, and she had cried over it nonstop for a week.

Aunt Bernice sipped her bloody mary on the back porch and told Bernie, "Listen, you will have so many of these Pauls—"

"His name was Peter," Bernie corrected her.

"Peter, Paul—they're inconsequential because they're practice boys."

"Practice boys?" Bernie had said the phrase wondering how many times she would have to go through this achy, sad, crying-to-her-friends experience in her life.

"Yes. You'll have so many. And you never know when love is going to strike. It can take all shapes and sizes, and seize all your feelings, so you won't even know what you're feeling when you feel it. Take Jean-Philippe, for example."

"Who's Jean-Philippe?" Bernie had asked.

"Jean-Philippe was my hate-to-love-you lover. I loathed the man immensely."

Bernie was still strung up on the fact her eighty-year-old great-aunt had used the word *lover* when she got that far-off look in her eye, in a way Bernie imagined Bernice was transporting herself to some other place and time with wavy lines and a soft focus to blur out reality and travel along some space-time continuum to really capture the essence of her storytelling.

She squinted as she began. "I was in Paris, and Jean-Philippe was in my art class. I was the only American in it, and even though my French was okay, he would constantly correct my pronunciation, scoff at me to his friends, and walk behind my drawings and make this little *huh* noise. You know, it's that particular French way they do that. Just makes you feel like an imbecile." She made the noise and took a long drag off her straw. "But one day we both found ourselves in the studio late and started arguing over something, maybe the turpentine—I don't remember—but then all of a sudden we were kissing, basically ravaging each other on the platform where the model sits."

"Okay . . ." Bernie drew out the word like she could stall what her aunt was going to say next. She was not quite ready to hear about the next stage of her sexual exploits.

"And we were together for years after that. Honestly, I thought that I hated him. But it was really love in disguise. And sometimes the emotion is just so intense you don't know how to identify it."

"Okay." Bernie was biting at her lip and nodding slowly, wondering how she could change the subject, when her mom came outside and asked her to help with dinner. Saved!

Bernie groaned at the memory as she lay on the bed. Well, love in disguise was certainly what it had been. She couldn't even do a hate-to-love-you lover like her great-aunt could. Bernie's lover had somehow homed in on every insecurity she had, surfaced the internal battle she'd been trying to fight her entire life, and then documented its sad demise on the page.

Her phone buzzed beside her, and she picked it up. Matthew? What the hell? Like she would even acknowledge him after what had happened. She hung up and stared at the phone. Maybe it was time to put plan B into action. She had to call her mom.

She groaned and dialed the number.

"Bernie!" her mom said. "How are you? Finally got cell service?"

"Yeah, I did." She swallowed. This call might not go exactly as planned. What was her mom going to say when she found out that she'd not only had service for days but also had broken her ankle and never called her?

"So how's the trip? Did you see any wild animals? I can't wait to see your pictures."

"Oh yeah, we did. In fact, I saw a bear."

"Really? Up close?"

"Yep, pretty close. But you learn how to scare them off." She had to change the subject. "How's James Brown?"

"Oh, he's so happy, running around everywhere. He loves to just lie around in the flowers. It's so cute. So tell me about this bear. It didn't get too close, did it?"

"No." Bernie squeezed her eyes shut. "Actually, it's a funny story. I was scaring the bear away and fell into a creek and broke my ankle, so I maybe need you to come to the airport, or at least could you bring James Brown up to Portland? I can't drive."

"Bernie! Oh my God, are you okay? You broke your ankle? You poor thing, and near a bear? And a creek?"

"It really wasn't that big of a deal, I swear—"

"Did you have to finish the trail, or what happened? Did they do surgery?"

Bernie blew out a big exhale. If she could just get a word in. "No, they airlifted me out, and I'm just in a cast. They said for maybe a month."

"Airlifted? That sounds serious! I'm coming to get you. Are you in Anchorage? I'll find a flight so I can be there in the morning."

Briefly, just briefly, Bernie imagined how, if she were on speaker and Matthew were there, she could totally shoot him an I-told-you-so grin. Then promptly dismissed it. "You don't need to come up here; I have a backpack and one of those scooter things. And I have Uber. I'm good. But I can't drive to Bend now, so if you can just bring my dog up, that would be great."

"But how will you walk him around and take care of yourself and cook and clean and work and all those things?"

"I'll figure it out—this happens to people all the time."

"And you have stairs! I'm coming up there, and I'm going to help you."

Panic drew Bernie's entire body alert. Her eyebrows pulled, nerves crackled at her pores, the hairs on her arm all standing up and calling "Mayday! Mayday!"

"Uh, Mom, you don't need to do that."

"You may not want me in your space, but you'll be glad of it. Trust me."

"No, it's really okay. I'm just going to see if I can get an earlier flight out tomorrow. I don't need to be here any longer. By the time you get here, I'll already be gone, you know?" Because there was no way Bernie was going to the trekking-group dinner tomorrow night. She would love to see the friends she'd made on the hike, but no way was she going anywhere near Matthew. And the longer she stayed in this hotel, the more chances she had of seeing him.

"Are you sure?"

"Yes."

"Well, I'll only not come to Anchorage if you promise I can pick you up at the airport and help you out when you're back."

Bernie's mouth opened. She could see the next month of her life flash in front of her. Her mother treating her like a child, giving her unsolicited advice on everything from how to cook pasta to why it was important only to use vinegar and water to clean, and really, how could Bernie buy spray bottles full of chemicals? Interrupting her work calls and playing her Bruce Hornsby too loud. Needlessly touching Bernie's hair, sighing, and then walking away. Why did she do that? Probably because she was horrified Bernie had dyed her hair. "More chemicals!" she could hear her mom say, if she asked.

But then her mom could also cook. Bernie could convince her to make all her favorites. That was the only way she would approve of motherly coddling. And then she would probably clean the house. Help feed James Brown so Bernie wouldn't have to scoot from one end of the kitchen to the other nonstop. And maybe she was right about the stairs.

"Okay, well, maybe that would be helpful for just a couple of days," Bernie admitted to her mom, as well as to herself.

"Oh, it will be fun, Bernie! Let me know what time your new flight comes in, and James Brown and I will meet you at the airport."

"Okay, thanks, Mom. I'm going to go to sleep now. I know it's late for you too."

"Okay, hon, bye. Love you!"

"You too." Bernie hung up the phone and immediately called Tabitha on FaceTime to tell the tale of Denali and how everything had gone horribly wrong.

Although it was too late to hang up when she realized this, Bernie did not look right for a video call. At all.

"Berns!" Tabitha answered. "Oh dear. What have they done to you up in Alaska?"

"Stop it." Bernie forced a sad laugh. Now that she was off the phone with her mom, she could finally just let it all out with her best friend.

"Seriously, though, are you okay?"

Bernie pressed her lips together and shook her head, trying to keep from crying as she told Tabitha everything. Her friend's eyes got big, then bigger, her mouth opening in shock when Bernie told her about the notebook, and her head retracted into her neck at just the right moment.

"That fucking bastard. I always thought that show with the dog was stupid anyway, even though you liked it. Fuck him."

"I know."

"I just have no words. I'm flabbergasted. I'm not even sure I've ever used that word before—that's how flabbergasted I am. He seemed so . . . I don't know, good? Good for you, at least. He had me fooled too. When I briefly spoke to him on the phone, I was like, 'Oh my God, this is the man for Bernie!'" Tabitha's teeth gritted together. "I mean, I didn't really think that. Sorry!"

Bernie groaned, and her head accidentally slapped the headboard. She hated that Tabitha had thought the same thing in mere minutes that Bernie had taken days to realize. "God, I have been such a fool."

"We've all been there. Remember Ramon?"

Bernie conjured up Tabitha's boyfriend from a few years ago. "He was always a douchebag, though. He was like a hockey jock. Always staring at his own muscles like he was checking himself out."

"Well, to be fair, they were nice muscles. But I thought he was so kind, and then he was . . ."

"A douchebag."

"Exactly."

Bernie laughed. Tabitha had been blind to all of Ramon's flaws, which were mostly personality related, from the moment she met him until the moment another girl answered his phone. Bernie had known he was an ass from the second he'd puffed up his chest and looked casually around the room instead of at her friend when they'd been out in public, hanging out.

"Well, it was his loss. Besides, you've got Duke now."

"Yeah, exactly." Her head tilted to the side, and she got a sappy smile on her face. "So what are you going to do?"

"When I get off the phone with you, I'm going to see if I can get an early flight tomorrow and then escape. And my mom is going to come help me for a short period of time."

"Oh, that should be interesting."

"Short, miniscule. Exactly as long as I can take it. If I have to crawl up the stairs on one leg to fetch my favorite clothes, so be it."

"I can help you, don't worry."

"Thanks, Tabs, I appreciate it. But I know you have your own life too." Her friend yawned in the camera while simultaneously shaking her head in protest. "It's late, go to bed. I just wanted to give you the deets, and also vent."

"Of course. I'm so sorry this happened. It just sucks so much."

"I know. But I'll see you soon. We'll cast some spells on him while drinking too many margaritas."

"Yesss!"

Bernie blew a kiss to the phone and hung up. Outside her window it still looked like it could be five a.m. or midnight. One more night in this godforsaken place that didn't get dark. How could she have thought it was magical only mere hours ago?

She was going to call the airline when a text came in.

Please call me. Please please please. I don't want you to be upset with me and I know we can work this out.

Work this out? Work out what? Work out exactly why she let him use her? Or why she hadn't seen it before? Or how he could still use the idea of her for his TV show because he needed a few more details?

She was stranded in Alaska, by herself, with a broken ankle and a cast, and she couldn't even escape him if he found her.

Stop calling and texting me. You're not even a chameleon. You're a snake.

CHAPTER 31

The next morning Bernie called an Uber and packed her bags. The airline had surprisingly been accommodating to her change request when she told them she'd broken her ankle. Now she just had to make sure that she didn't see Matthew on the way out the door.

She scooted down the hall, peeking around all the corners, making sure that he hadn't figured out she'd stayed in the same place, and in which room. When she got to reception, though, instead of Matthew she found the rest of the hiking group checking in.

"Bernie!" Diana shrieked and then ran to her, giving her a big hug. "Oh my God, we missed you! How are you doing?"

"Well . . ." Bernie gestured to her scooter and the cast.

Shalini joined her partner's side. "So it *was* a break. Well, it's a good thing they could take care of it. And we still get to catch up!"

"Oh, actually, I'm leaving now."

The rest of the group had crowded around, and a collective moan erupted from them that made Bernie laugh. "Well, it does suck that I can't see you all tonight for the dinner, but I just wanted to get out of here because of my ankle and everything."

"That's such a bummer," Trevor said, looking genuinely disappointed.

"Well, give us your email and phone number and stuff so we can at least stay in touch!" Diana said.

"Yeah, of course. I'd love that."

They swapped phone numbers, and as the others went to the reception desk, Shalini whispered, "Where's Matthew?"

"I don't know and I don't care," Bernie said flatly and then put a big fake smile on her face.

"Oh no!" Diana said, leaning back. "What happened?"

"It's a long story. But maybe we can have a virtual happy hour when you all get back, and I can tell you."

"That sucks. I'm usually so good at these matchmaking things," Shalini said to Diana, clearly confused.

Bernie's phone buzzed, alerting her that the driver had arrived. She had made new friends, and now she felt like she was abandoning them. Maybe it had been a little rushed to move up her flight and skip the dinner. But then, imagining sitting in the same room with Matthew made her cringe.

"I have to go, but seriously, let's keep in touch. I want to hear all about the rest of the hike. Happy hour next week?"

"Uh, yeah, we will even shower first."

"Oh my God, I cannot wait for my shower," Diana groaned.

They laughed and had a group hug, and then Bernie said goodbye to the rest of the group, a sad little nest settling in her heart. The feeling that something unfinished was lurking about unresolved. She didn't know if it was the new friends, the hike, or Matthew.

◆ ◆ ◆

Matthew had hardly slept. He couldn't believe she'd found the book. Had read all those things he'd written. To have her think they were directly about her was unsettling. If he'd read those things about himself, if she'd written them down about him on day one, when they were at total odds, he'd feel broken now. Maybe more broken than he already was.

Even if he and Bernie weren't officially a couple, he'd never been this shattered over a breakup. He'd never been so upset that someone was mad at him. And he'd definitely never felt so terrible about making someone cry.

And where was Bernie now? He'd walked around town, hoping he might see her, stopping at the places they'd been to—the coffee shop, the brewery, the brunch place—just to see if she might have gone back to one. But nothing. His last hope was that she'd come to the dinner tonight.

As he got ready, he exhaled at the man staring back at him. Who did he want to be, and who had he become over the past week? This guy he'd become while spending time with Bernie was the man he wanted to be, and he hadn't seen him in a while. He reminded him of better things. Doing what he loved, embracing life, scripting the kind of TV shows that Bernie liked, not being bogged down with a series of cheesy pilots that he knew were going nowhere even as he wrote them. It had to have been her, and them together, as one. Something about her influence made him be the person he wanted to be. The one he liked.

As he made his way to the restaurant, his nerves fired up in his stomach, and he hoped that she had come.

The receptionist greeted him and showed him to a room in the back, where the hiking crowd sat, cleaned up, showered, and with one seat left. Just one seat for him. Bernie was not there. Something fell inside him, knowing that she must have told them she wasn't coming.

The group got quiet, and everyone looked at him, and then Diana shouted, "Oh my God, it's Matthew! I didn't even recognize you! You're beardless!"

A few others shouted his name. Generally the group had that elated, ebullient glow of finishing their hike, whereas Matthew weakly smiled and tried to seem cheerful at seeing them as well. Harold and

Becky looked a bit more exhausted than the others, and Jay's half wave toward him mimicked the way Matthew felt on the inside from seeing that Bernie wasn't there. Trevor came up and shook his hand and gave him one of those back-clap-hug things, telling him he was a hero for helping Bernie. Matthew wanted to laugh in his face but instead just thanked him and sat in the vacant chair across from Diana. But he wanted to jump up and run back to his room as soon as he'd sat down. He just knew that he was going to be in for some questioning by the way she and Shalini were following him with their gaze, like predators tracking their dinner.

The server brought him a menu, and he ordered a beer. As soon as he looked up, Diana smiled one of those smiles that wasn't really a smile, but like she was disguising a mouthful of razor-sharp teeth, ready to sink into him.

"So . . . what happened with you and Bernie?" she asked.

"Uh . . . well . . ." How could he even explain what had happened?

"When we asked her where you were, she did not seem thrilled, so we need to know if we hate you or not," Shalini said, and then casually took a drink of wine, as if she had just told him that the salmon was great and he should order it.

"You saw her? Where? Is she coming?" he asked, completely aware he seemed a little too eager.

"No, she went back to Portland this afternoon. We saw her going to the airport."

"Fuck." There it was. He sank his head into his hands and just stared at the table. He'd hurt her so much she'd left.

"What happened with you two? You seem . . . upset." Diana looked uncomfortable as she studied him.

"I messed up."

"I knew it. So you did get together!" Shalini said, and then turned to Diana. "I'm always right about these things."

"What did you do?" Diana asked.

Matthew told her an abbreviated version of the story. "But I only keep the idea journal as inspiration—it's not real. But she read the first few pages. I was in a foul mood at the beginning of the trip, and it really came off on the page. It's funny because toward the end, all the ideas for the script are about a couple like Trevor and Sheila." He gestured toward them and then realized everyone was now listening intently to his explanation. "Anyway, it wasn't going to be about her in the end, except for the best parts of her."

"Awww, you should tell her that," Gretchen said, and then added, "sorry to eavesdrop, but we've all been speculating about you two ever since you hopped on that helicopter with her."

Matthew huffed a laugh. "Well, she won't answer my calls, and the last text she sent me was not to contact her again."

"But you did abandon your hike and jump on a helicopter for her. She'll forgive you," Becky added.

"I don't think so." The rest of the group hadn't seen Bernie crying over the book, looking like her world had come crumbling down in front of her.

"How much do you like Bernie?" Shalini asked. "To what lengths would you go?"

Matthew sighed. He'd been fantasizing about a future with her. He'd asked her to come help him through a life-altering surgery. He had been trying to figure out how they could see each other, what the commute schedule would look like. He'd even wondered if she would move to LA. And yes, it had seemed crazy, but he couldn't let that potential vision of his future just evaporate.

"Far lengths."

"I'm sure you can figure something out," Jay said with a laugh. "Trust me, *someone* hasn't let me forget that you jumped on a helicopter for a girl."

Gretchen elbowed Jay with a smile and then added in that "Minnesota nice" voice that made every sentence sound like it should start with *Oh dear*, "You just need to make it up to her. We ladies appreciate a big gesture."

Matthew tried to smile at the two of them, still in oddly matching clothes, even though the hike was over. Both of them in red T-shirts, but why?

Make it up to her? How could he do that when she wouldn't talk to him? "I don't know . . . I'm not sure how."

"What if we helped you?" Diana said with a smile, but this time the shark teeth were all gone.

"Really?" Matthew asked.

"Yeah, we're supposed to have a virtual happy hour next week with her, so we could start with that." She shrugged.

"A whole week away?" He sank back into his hand. How could he wait a whole week? "I'm such an idiot."

"Oh my God, you have got it so bad," Diana said with a laugh, and then the whole table held up their drinks in cheers.

"To Matthew. May he get the girl," Sheila said, blessing the toast.

CHAPTER 32

"Bernice, honey?" her mother's voice sang throughout the ground floor. "I mean, Bernie?"

Even though it had been only four days, she was starting to stiffen every time her mom called for her. She told herself, *She just wants to help. She's just being nice. She loves you.* But still, the underlying tension just wouldn't evaporate.

"Yeah, Mom. What's up?" She felt marooned on the sofa. Her personal Gilligan's Island in her own home.

"Do you want a grilled cheese or a BLT or something? You didn't eat lunch."

"Sure. Anything is fine." Since she'd left Anchorage, food had become something she consumed for substance, not for pleasure. She bent down to James Brown, who was lying on the carpet below the sofa, and scratched his ears. She said to him, "Whatever it is, you can have half."

He rolled on his side and gazed up at her. The way his jowls flopped back made him look like he was smiling, as if he knew what she'd said and approved.

She needed to see people other than her mom. She had dinner plans with Tabitha tomorrow, and today she had her happy hour call in an hour with Shalini and Diana, which would be fun. She did want to hear about the rest of the hike, and some venting over Matthew to people who might understand wouldn't hurt either.

She hadn't talked to Tabitha since she'd been back, but she knew as soon as Bernie was over the Matthew topic, they would go straight to the "sell the house" topic. She'd looked through the photos and the listing, but now with her bum ankle she wasn't sure it was the best time to sell it. And what she needed right now, more than ever, was the feeling of home. The safe, secure home she'd grown up in, with its memories and stains, and a moment to really find herself. Because she'd never felt more lost than she did right now.

Her mom brought in a plate with a sandwich. "Here you go. Now actually eat it this time, and don't give it to JB." She nodded at the dog with a frown, as if it was his fault.

"Thanks." She took a bite. "Maybe I should email my manager and see about going back this week."

"What? Why? How are you going to get to work and then get around work?" Her mom sat in the plaid chair that Bernie had been meaning to replace. It was not her style at all. She noted in the pictures Tabitha had taken that the chair had been moved out of the way.

"People do it all the time. There are accessibility laws, you know. Or maybe I can work from home. But I can't just lie around here. It's too . . ." She sighed. Because what she wanted to say was that it gave her too much time to be sad over Matthew. It made her get caught up in her dreams of finally finding a guy she connected with, only to have it end in the worst way possible. Those fantasies of strolling through Hollywood with him and drinking juice and eating at stupid healthy raw restaurants, living an LA lifestyle. Wearing sunglasses all the time. Complaining about traffic. She'd had all those visions when she was in Alaska—too many visions, because apparently they'd clouded her judgment.

Besides, she was fine here. She had her dog, her house, and her job. Why would she want to leave Portland again? Those silly visions of her selling her house and migrating to Los Angeles that she'd flirted with days ago had been ridiculous. Tabitha might be disappointed, but she'd understand. She always did.

"Too what?" Her mom picked up the community newspaper and thumbed through it, then slapped it on her thighs like she was exasperated when Bernie didn't answer, even though her mom looked at the space in front of her instead of actually at Bernie. "I, for one, think it's lovely that we have a chance to spend some time together and I can help you out."

Lovely was not the adjective Bernie would use to describe any kind of situation that had immobilized her. Plus, her mom had seemed uncomfortable ever since she was back in the old house. She didn't even sleep in her former bedroom. She slept in the guest room, which just seemed to prove that her mother couldn't bear to go into the room she'd shared with her father. Bernie hadn't really touched it since she'd moved out, which Tabitha told her was a little Norman Bates-y. But she felt like it was her parents' room and that her mom should be the one to decide what to do with it.

"Yes, I appreciate you coming here," Bernie said, clenching her jaw.

"Of course—you're my daughter."

"Maybe you can clean out what's left in your old bedroom while you're here?"

"What? You haven't done that yet?"

"It's your room."

"Bernie, I got everything I wanted out of there years ago." Her gaze settled on Bernie's plate. "Now eat that before it gets cold."

Bernie sighed and took a bite. Some of her dad's old clothes were still hanging in the closet. Their wedding picture hung on the wall. All her suspicions about her mother's feelings about her dad were fizzing up like a shaken-up bottle of soda that was ready to blow.

Her eyes caught the time on her phone. "Oh, I need a drink. I have a virtual happy hour in a few minutes. Could you get me a glass of wine?"

Her mom raised her eyebrows and then nodded at the sandwich. "You eat half that sandwich, and I'll get you half a glass of wine."

Bernie rolled her eyes and took a bite.

"If you eat the whole sandwich, guess what?" Her mom's voice lifted and coasted on the word *whole* like Bernie was four and wanted some ice cream.

"Ooh, then I get a full glass of wine. Like a big girl." Bernie wrinkled up her nose and didn't bother hiding the snark.

"Exactly." Her mom didn't seem to catch on, though. "I know you're sad about your leg, but that's no excuse not to eat." She got up and went into the kitchen.

Ha. If Bernie were only just sad about her leg. She was sad about Matthew, herself, her leg, missed opportunities, thinking she could be someone she wasn't, letting everyone down, letting herself down, mystified how she could get so wrapped up in a fantasy life, a fantasy man, picturing herself and James Brown in a convertible driving along a cliff-lined coast with the waves and surf music as her soundtrack. And Matthew's secret laughter next to her ear, that she imagined was just for her.

That was what she was sad about.

"Ugh!" She slapped at her forehead. How could she get him out of there?

"Well, don't hit yourself, honey." Her mom stood on the other side of the coffee table with a glass of wine in her hand. Correction, half a glass. "Finish up those last two bites."

Bernie stuffed the whole thing in her mouth and chewed. She stared at her mom and tried to look calm while she hoped she wouldn't choke on it. If her mom was going to act like she was a child masquerading as a grown-up, then so would she.

Her mom started humming the *Jeopardy!* music and then sighed and set the glass down on the table. "Well, I don't need to watch you chew like a horse. I have to run to Sherry's." Sherry was her friend down the street, and she'd agreed to leave Bernie alone while she was having her happy hour.

"Thank you," Bernie said, the words muffled as she was almost done chewing.

Her mom left, and Bernie fired up her laptop. Would a full-on bitch session about Matthew help her mental state or further disintegrate it? She logged into the meeting a few minutes early and, surprise, Shalini and Diana were already there, their two heads pressed together so they both fit in the frame.

"Bernie!" they exclaimed at the same time.

"Hey! I feel so underdressed." Bernie laughed. Shalini and Diana had both clearly just finished work, with their hair fixed and lipstick and eyeliner on. Shalini was wearing a button-up, and Diana was in a soft-looking sweater. And there was Bernie in an old college ringer tee that had an ever-growing hole in the seam of her collar. She straightened up. Maybe they wouldn't notice.

"Well, you *are* an invalid." Shalini dramatically frowned, with Diana nodding.

"Yeah, my mom just left, so I finally have some peace for a moment. It's been intense and also not intense at all the past few days. What about you two? Are you getting back into the swing of things?"

"I'm in that stage of needing a vacation from my vacation, you know?"

"It was hard work. My calves still ache," Shalini added.

"Mmhmm," Bernie agreed, but it was more like a question, because was it? She'd felt so free on that trip, the days blowing by, until they hadn't. "It's weird because I actually have a vacation after my vacation, and I just want to go back to work."

"I would love to have some more vacation to take." Shalini threw her head back in a laugh. "I have an ever-growing list."

Bernie sighed. A week ago she'd been developing a list in her head too. Mostly of all the places everyone in the hiking group had gone and she hadn't, feeling like she needed to catch up. But now . . .

"Enough about that, though—cheers!" Diana said, holding up a beer. "We wanted to dish about what happened with Bernie and the boy and the broken ankle."

"Well . . ." Bernie launched into the story, recapping all the horrific events of the book in detail and skimming over the physical components of those magical two days before the Bernie book had been discovered.

"But he did apologize profusely, though?" Diana asked.

"I don't know. I was mortified." Bernie shook her head and petted James Brown, who had joined her on the sofa now that she was sitting up. "He made me feel just terrible."

"Do you think you could forgive him?" Shalini asked. "Like, if he was really, really sorry?"

Bernie laughed weakly. "Why? You want me to try to reconcile things? He was such an ass."

"But I think he really liked you. Like, a lot."

"Obviously he was just using me." What she wanted to tell them was not to get her hopes up.

"You know, he's one of those creative types, though. He said the Bernie book was just ideas inspired by the trip."

Bernie paused, holding up the wine to her lips. "Oh, you talked to him at the dinner?" She shouldn't have been surprised, especially after she'd planted that little seed with them in the lobby.

"Yes," Shalini said weakly, like she'd been found out, then wrinkled up her nose and shrank back. She reminded her of James Brown when he'd been caught eating a meatball off her mostly ignored spaghetti last night. "He was so upset. Like, sooooo upset."

"I didn't even know he could get upset." Diana shook her head in marvel. "He's like Mr. Calm and Collected."

"Ha." Bernie took a drink to stop herself from asking what Matthew had said about her exactly, because she really, really wanted to know.

"Seriously, I thought for a moment he might cry."

"What?" Now that was funny.

"Yeah, he was really sad about what had happened, and he didn't know how to explain his process or something. That the show was really about two people leading a hiking group or something, not you."

"Hmm, well, that book could have fooled me." She could see the words *incompetent fool* in his handwriting with her eyes closed.

"Maybe you should talk to him."

Bernie considered giving him another chance. Flashbacks of how good she'd felt in his arms, how they'd opened up so freely to each other, how he'd encouraged her and helped her uncover this forgotten adventurous, brave self. But then she contrasted that with how absolutely shitty it had felt to read those words of betrayal staring up at her from the floor. How she felt more crushed now than she had before she'd left on that trip.

"Nope. I'm in enough pain. I don't need any more right now." Bernie finished off her glass. "Let's talk about something else. What else is going on with you two in Seattle?"

Shalini sighed, and Diana started talking about work, and restaurants, and a few of their friends, and then capped off the conversation by asking Bernie how she got around.

"So far I haven't. But I'm venturing out tomorrow. I just haven't been feeling . . . great." Best to leave it vague, because *I've been feeling a little heartbroken after a three-day relationship* would sound absolutely insane.

"What's your address? We want to send you something." Shalini beamed a big smile at her.

"You don't have to do that. I'm fine. My mom's here, and I've got my dog. It's fine."

"No, we do," they both said in their ESP way.

"What's your address?" Diana asked, then scribbled it down as Bernie told her.

"Well, it was so good to see you," Bernie said. "Send me any pictures you have from the trip. I hardly took any."

"Of course!" They said their goodbyes and hung up, after promising to get together next time they were in each other's towns.

Bernie set her laptop down and sighed into the back of the sofa. Somehow she was ready to leave and settle in deeper all at the same time.

◆ ◆ ◆

"I don't know what you're going to do with it, man. She's still upset," Diana said through the phone as Matthew scribbled down Bernie's address.

Shalini jumped in. "Agreed. We're all Team Matthew-Bernie, but she seems a little . . ."

"Broken?" Diana asked.

"Yeah." Shalini's voice sounded a little sad.

"God, I messed up." He sighed into the phone. "Thank you two for your help. I need to fix this."

They said their goodbyes, and he promised to keep them posted. Matthew hung up the phone. Somehow over dinner, he'd convinced them he wasn't a terrible person. Now he just needed to convince Bernie.

She was definitely still upset. Which he knew, since she still wouldn't return his calls or texts. Calls and texts he couldn't stop making, despite her request. But now he had Bernie's address. So what was he going to do with it? She wasn't the kind of girl you sent a dozen roses to, or a box of candy, or a fruit bouquet. And he wasn't necessarily the kind of guy who would send those either.

He sat on his balcony, the sun beaming down on him, another perfect eighty-degree day, and just wished he could go back in time to the day he'd created that stupid notebook and realize it was a bad idea. It was as if all the ideas he'd had on that fateful Sunday when they'd begun the hike and he'd met Bernie were owned by some other man. Some other bitter, angry cretin who had expunged his outer shell and transformed over the course of a week into a happy, pleasant man with fresh ideas and confirmed notions about his future and the tough decisions he had to make. Was that Bernie's doing? He loved the wilderness they'd been submerged into, but it seemed like a difficult notion that the tundra had been rooting into his subconscious.

Hell, he could even begin to understand why Gretchen and Jay wore matching clothes. Maybe he was just nuts. He thought about what they had said about him at dinner. They acted like he was the king of big, romantic gestures. And maybe some dramatic gestures needed to happen. He sat on the patio chair, gazed out at the neighborhood, and thought about all the things they'd been through. The brief journey of their relationship, which felt more like a year than a week.

Jess emerged from her bedroom in pajamas and headed for the coffee. It was one o'clock.

"Uh, good morning?" he said.

"I had to work so late last night. Don't even make me feel bad." Jess worked on a film crew and was currently doing a terrible horror movie of which he'd heard her do at least five zombie monologues in which she mocked the ridiculous dialogue.

"How are the zombies?" he asked.

"Well, Matthew, that's where you're wrong. They're not zombies. Zombies were so last year. These are reanimated aliens from Mars that eat brains, with a penchant for cat brains." Her voice wavered, and she shook her head. "Not just zombies."

"Ugh."

"Yeah, that's exactly how I feel about it. Ugh." She sighed. "I did see some reanimated alien butt yesterday. Surprisingly, the makeup team did a pretty good job on it."

Matthew laughed. That first day in the woods where he'd seen Bernie peeing in the middle of the trail popped up in his head. At that moment he'd felt awkward and embarrassed for the newbie who had no idea what she was doing, but in retrospect it was funny and so, so Bernie of her to do that. He'd offered to show her his ass to even things out, and she'd been mortified at the proposition.

"Hey, Jess, could you do me a weird favor, if you're not busy?"

"What?" she said, scrolling through her phone.

"Could you take a picture of my ass?"

The phone fell out of her hand, and she started coughing and slapping at her chest. "What? Why?"

"I think I might have an idea for how to make things right with the world."

"Does 'the world' mean your girlfriend of three days who you destroyed?" Jess squinted at him as she cocked her head to the side, completely judging him. He'd gotten drunk two nights ago and told her the whole thing as he lay on the sofa like she was his therapist. A snarky therapist who kept reminding him what a jerky thing he'd done. "I always knew those books were going to be the end of you. I can't wait until I find the *Jess the Roommate* book."

"Yes."

"This seems like a very bad idea. Not a dick pic but a butt pic?"

"Well, thank you for being so supportive. It's like an inside joke." Or at least he thought it might be if he could frame it right.

"I'm just saying . . ."

"I know. I fucked up. I've already rubbed it in enough myself."

"But a picture of your butt?"

"Could you just do it?"

She shook her head. "Let me do it before I'm fully conscious, so then I can pretend this is a bad dream. Give me your phone."

Matthew handed her his phone and basically mooned her on the patio, and she took the photo, sticking her arm out as far as she could before handing it back. "I'm afraid I'll never be able to unsee that."

"Thanks. Just pretend it's another zombie butt you came across at work."

His phone rang, and briefly, his heart leaped up as he thought maybe possibly Bernie was ready to talk to him. But it was just his agent, Jude.

"Hey, Matt, how's it going?"

Matthew sighed. How was it that he was still calling him Matt? No one called him Matt, except his dad. Like a stage name. "Hey, it's going."

"So I wanted to follow up on that pilot idea you had. There's currently a hunger for some new comedies, and I'd love to start floating a pitch around in a few weeks, if you have something ready."

He swallowed. "Yes, I can have something ready." He needed to get to work on it. He needed to get his mind off Bernie and the epic failure he'd become the past few days.

"Cool. I need comedy gold. You know what's selling is that quirky, a little bit weird flavor you deliver on so well. This could be your big chance, if you have the idea right."

God help him, but even when Jude mentioned the words *quirky* and *a little bit weird*, he thought of Bernie, in all the best ways possible.

"Maybe a little bit of a love story?" Matthew asked, a nugget of an idea suddenly glowing inside him.

"Love sells. Comedy sells. You know the drill. We're all looking for the next *Friends*. But, like, maybe a weird *Friends*. Like *Twin Peaks* meets *Friends*."

Matthew rolled his eyes. That was a new one. "Yep. Cool. Okay, I have an idea. Give me a week."

"A week is good."

They said goodbye and Matthew hung up.

He jumped up. "I'm heading to the coffee shop to crank out my pilot script."

Jess groaned. "Oh no. You're not going to use that material, are you? I thought you said it was trash?"

"It was. Some of it. But the person I based it on isn't. She's still my inspiration. I should have realized why that was on day one."

Jess scrunched up her face. "I just don't understand how your shitty notes about her and a picture of your ass are going to help. Unless you two have a very weird relationship."

"I don't know if I can explain it yet, but wish me luck!" He bounded into his bedroom, grabbed his laptop, and hoped that this spark of an idea would not only be the thing that would land him a new gig but would also get Bernie back.

CHAPTER 33

"Thank you, tequila." Bernie grabbed the margarita from the server before he could set it down and then took a drink before diving into the basket of chips.

Across from her, Tabitha laughed. "I think the server said his name was Marco, not Tequila."

"And thank you, Marco!" Bernie turned around and called out to the man who was two tables down.

"And he was kind of cute. Just saying . . ." Tabitha shrugged and took a drink of her own.

"Don't try to appease my wounded heart with cute boys wielding cocktails. You know that's my weakness."

Tabitha sighed one of those long, drawn-out sighs that always made Bernie feel a little bit guilty. "Bernie, as far as I can tell, you've never had a weakness when it comes to guys, except for recently."

Bernie took another drink of her margarita to avoid responding.

But a lack of response never stopped Tabitha. "How are you feeling about what happened with Matthew now?"

Bernie felt herself slouch over. It was so hard to explain. How, after the worst breakup she'd ever had—make that, after the briefest relationship she'd ever had—she was still aware of this woeful, sagging space inside her chest. Like a cavity that had been closed off, then opened by whatever had happened to her in Alaska. None of it made sense.

"Maybe it's because I'm giving myself the world's biggest pity party, but I'm still . . . sad. There was Matthew and then my leg and then my mom . . . I mean, all that happened at once, so I think the Matthew effect has been exacerbated by the woe-is-me-ness of it all."

"I can totally see that. I'm bummed for you too. It's just so weird. And then that book?" Tabitha visibly shuddered.

The book. Bernie had thought more than once about the kinds of things she would have written about him the first few days they'd known each other. And those words would have been less than kind. But still, seeing them scrawled out about her, like her worst fears had been dug up and splayed on the page for his amusement, was too much.

Her phone buzzed on the table beside her. Matthew's name appeared on the screen. "He won't give up! Look." She held up her phone so Tabitha could see the alert.

"What does he say?"

"I don't know." She slid her phone across the table. "Feel free to peruse." Because the truth was that Bernie had read every apology and had been on the brink of replying and calling him, since she wanted to hear how it was all a huge misunderstanding, but she didn't trust herself. She'd been a sucker for him before, and clearly she couldn't control herself with him.

Tabitha looked at her phone and covered her mouth with her hand. Bernie could still hear the words "What the fuck?" muffled under her palm. And then she did something like a half cough, half laugh.

"What is it?" Bernie asked. Tabitha's eyes were wide, and she was making such a weird expression.

Her friend's lips pressed together, and she showed the phone screen to Bernie. Two butt cheeks were staring her in the face. "What?" She grabbed the phone.

"Is this his attempt at winning you back, because I'm not going to lie. It's fucking weird."

Bernie looked at the accompanying message.

Remember our first day on the trail? You were so upset, and I'm going to pay you back for all the things between us. Here's the first one. I should have done this then. My ass for yours.

Bernie tried not to laugh, but she did. She remembered that day—how wholly embarrassed, inadequate, and vulnerable she'd felt. Matthew had offered to pull down his pants for her, too, and she'd refused. It was like he was trying to make up for all the things between them.

"'My ass for yours'? I mean, is that a line?" Tabitha shook her head.

"Sort of?" Bernie said. "It's complicated."

"Clearly."

Marco the waiter brought their food, and Tabitha was right: he was cute. He had deep-brown eyes like Matthew. But not the kind she could get lost in. Not the kind she could dip her gaze into and feel like she was swimming in a warm, silky pool.

"Let me see the rest of those texts." Tabitha held out her hand and wiggled her fingers. Bernie complied and dug into her enchilada. Somehow she was feeling hungry again.

Tabitha hummed as she scrolled through the messages. "Well, he definitely seems sorry. Still don't get the butt pic, though. Is that like a new thing guys think girls like? I'll never understand men." She sighed and handed back the phone.

"Would you forgive him?" Bernie asked. Not that she was ready to. When she thought about how hurt she'd felt in that hotel room, it still burned.

"That's only something you can answer, Bernie. It's all about how you feel. Plus, he's in LA. The whole thing is kind of weird."

"Yeah . . . it's like, what's the point?"

"Well, he is the only guy you've ever really liked."

"That's not true."

"He's the only guy who makes you giddy. The only one you've ever been upset about splitting with. Like, he's the only one who affected you. Cracked open the Bernie box of emotions."

Bernie sighed. But what did that mean? The Matthew effect was not necessarily a good thing, was it?

◆　◆　◆

Matthew hadn't heard back from Bernie since he'd sent the picture of his ass. Maybe he shouldn't have expected anything, but he had hoped for at least some kind of smiling emoji back to him. A question mark. Anything. Or maybe it was all a huge mistake.

He shouldn't have expected anything, really. He had to keep going. So he took it to the next level and found himself in REI looking at trekking pants and hoodies. And found something that would do Gretchen and Jay proud.

After explaining to a saleswoman what he was doing (and getting a coo of a response), he tried on one of the teal and midnight-blue pants and hoodies and then dressed a mannequin in the women's department with the corresponding female counterpart outfit. Then he topped it off with a selfie. Conjuring up the ridiculous code word he'd told Bernie, he captioned the photo, *Mr Potato Head! Please respond. I'm finding matching outfits for us. Will you please be my mannequin?* And sent it off.

God help him.

He undressed and redressed the mannequin, thanked the saleswoman (who was giving him heart eyes), and made his way to the coffee shop to continue working on his script. Right when he was opening the door, his phone rang. Had his Mr. Potato Head cry for help worked?

But it was his dad.

With all that had been going on in his head over Bernie, his dad had been pushed to the corners of his mind. He hadn't even told him that he'd decided to donate his kidney to him.

"Hi," Matthew said.

"Hello, son."

Matthew resisted rolling his eyes. He could forgive, but not forget.

"How are you doing?"

"Well . . ." In the background was the noise of an intercom and the occasional beep from some kind of machine. It took him back to the hospital of last week. "It appears that I'm not so good," his dad finished, his voice weak.

"Did something happen?" He'd never heard his dad's voice with that wavering, scratched quality it had just now.

"I had a seizure. I should have recognized the symptoms, honestly, so I should blame myself." He paused. "Fortunately my neighbor came by at the right time and called an ambulance, so I got to the hospital."

"So are you okay now?"

"The doctor did dialysis but told me I don't have much time before they stop functioning completely. And I hate asking you this, but have you made up your mind? I'm far down on the donor list, and the doc, well, he says I need to do this in weeks rather than months." His father's voice cracked, the New Jersey accent from long, long ago bursting through in this plea of desperation.

"Weeks? Like how many weeks?" Something like a chill crawled up Matthew's arm. He'd been so sure he was ready for this in Anchorage. Somehow knowing that Bernie was going to be with him when he did the surgery was going to make it all okay, as crazy as that sounded.

"He said ideally in the next two weeks. I know, it's fast. It's a lot to ask, and this is too much to ask of you. Especially considering what a lousy dad I was." His father sniffed, and Matthew could see himself, when he'd been a kid and his father a young dad. His parents had fought and he'd run off, but eventually he found his dad in the morning crying on the back stoop. When Matthew had sat next to him, his dad tried to wipe the tears away fast, smearing the palms of his hands against his eyes and blinking up at the sun like it could dry them before his son could see.

Just now, he pictured his father doing the same thing: trying to look brave and calm and not panicking about losing his life. Plus, Matthew had made up his mind already.

"Sure. Sure I can do it."

"Really?" His father's voice was breathy, like he hadn't expected Matthew to actually go through with it. "Oh my God. You are a lifesaver, son. Literally. I can't believe it. I owe you so much. A lifetime I'm still trying to make up for."

They talked about the logistics, the hospital in LA they'd already decided on, finalizing a date, how the doctor would call Matthew with expectations about recovery time. And all Matthew could think about was how he needed to finish the script and send it to Bernie as a final apology, just in case things didn't work out.

CHAPTER 34

Bernie looked at the stairs and wondered if she should just use her arms to slide up them backward so she could get the book out of her room she wanted. It might feel easier than asking her mom for yet another minuscule task that normally would take thirty seconds, but for Bernie now took at least ten minutes.

She huffed a cry. She just couldn't take this anymore. It had been a week and a half without the use of her leg, and she didn't care if she was a baby, but it sucked. She'd never been so absolutely dependent as an adult. The stairs to her front door presented a similar challenge to climbing Mount Everest. And plus, the awkward tension with her mom was always present, like a silent, angry third person standing in the room. The words unsaid that stewed in Bernie's brain because she had way too much time to dwell on everything, with nothing else to do.

"Do you want a sandwich or something?"

"No, Mom." As if on cue, her mother knew how to prick her with kindness. Why did it always feel like she had to resent her mom for being nice?

Matthew had said something about this. How her mom probably didn't want to ignore her dad's death, but it was just complicated and that they should talk about it. But how did she just bring up her mother resenting her for not being there for her dad's death and then her mom leaving Portland as soon as she could, and not even sleeping in their old bedroom? Like she was disgusted by Bernie's father, even his memory? It was weird, so weird, that her mom had been back in the house for a week and had said nothing about her dad. It wasn't just in Bernie's head. It couldn't be.

She looked back at the last text she'd gotten from Matthew. She hadn't responded to any of them; she literally had nothing else to do, so sometimes she'd just review them. The apologies, the ass picture, and this last one.

She laughed, a sad, sweet laugh at this photo of Matthew hugging a mannequin with matching outfits. So Gretchen and Jay. Matthew said he'd never wear matching outfits with anyone, and apparently this was his attempt at saying he would for her. Why, of all things, did this make her so desperately sad? Like it was reassuring her that it hadn't just been her who had felt this strong connection between them.

"Ragamuffin," she whispered at the phone. Because if anything, she needed her code word to cry out for help from him right back. Her thumb hovered over the keyboard, ready to type.

"Oh my God, something made you laugh. It's a Christmas miracle!" her mom said, so pleased with herself.

"Ragamuffin" was something her dad used to say to Bernie, every time he'd walk by her, while tousling her hair for no good reason, messing it up, and leaving her to squeal in protest and smooth it back down. Somehow it was these annoying, random things you missed about people. Not necessarily his smile or the shine of his eyes. How he annoyed her by messing up her hair.

"Do you remember how Dad used to mess up my hair and call me Ragamuffin?" Bernie asked her mom.

Maybe the time to bring up the thing that had been unspoken was now. It was almost like Matthew, the preargument Matthew, was there, giving her an encouraging shove.

Her mom looked up from the magazine in her hands and blinked, as if she was unsure how to answer. "Uh, no. Did he do that?"

"Yeah. I was just thinking about when I miss him the most, I think about how he annoyed me. What do you think about?" What Bernie really wanted to ask was, *Do you even miss him at all? Why do you never talk about him? It's fucking weird, Mom!*

Her mother sighed and looked toward the window. "I mean, I can't say." Her head swung down, and she breathed into her chest. Bernie felt her eyes squinting in disbelief, words forming in her lungs, making them hot, like she was ready to expel a stream of verbal attack lava she'd never be able to take back.

"I mean, how can you sum up what you miss about the man you shared your life with? He was the love of my life, and now he's gone and I miss . . . just . . . everything."

Then her mom started crying. Like really crying.

Not what Bernie had been expecting. At all.

"Um. Oh." What did she say now? "Well, why don't you ever talk about him then?" Bernie asked, the calm trickling into her body, the heat dissipating.

"Because this happens." Her mom wiped at her eyes on her sleeve. "Every time. When I'd go to the therapist, when my friends made me talk about him, when the lawyers would call. I can't even sleep in the bedroom because when I walked in there the first day I was back, I just collapsed on the bed and sobbed for like an hour while you were taking a nap. And the comforter was even dusty. You should change the sheets in there sometimes. It's kind of gross. Dust mites must be everywhere."

Bernie huffed out a laugh. "I thought you didn't want to remember him, or . . . something."

"What? How could I forget him?" Her mom shook her head. "He was your father, my husband, an unforgettable man."

"Or . . ." Now Bernie was feeling the tears well up behind her eyes, her nose itching; somehow the words she wanted to say, the words she feared the most, were threatening to take over her voice.

"Or what?" her mom asked softly.

"Or you blamed me for not being here when he died." Bernie tried to will the tears back, but they refused and came tumbling out.

"Bernie, honey . . ." Her mom had finished her sobfest, and now Bernie was starting hers. Her mom scrambled over and sat on the edge of the sofa by her knees. "No one expected what happened—that your father would just not wake up. And your father would never blame you. I didn't blame you. I mean, none of us really got to say goodbye how we wanted to. I think that was the hardest part."

Bernie nodded. "I thought maybe you thought I was a terrible person, just like I was feeling. Because I didn't get here in time; because I never got to say goodbye."

Her mom rubbed at Bernie's good ankle. "I didn't know this was eating you up on the inside. I mean, I'm torn up over it too. Hell, I had to leave the house and move out to the farm, just so I could not be around all the old memories. I'm better now, but I was just so sad seeing everything all the time. It's hard still."

Bernie wiped at her cheeks. "I thought you just wanted to go live the life you always wanted."

"What? Why would you think that?" Her mom's head retracted into her neck. Great, now Bernie had offended her. "Honey, we all deal with grief in our different ways. It's something I've learned from this. I wasn't running away, but your dad always told me that he had the best life he could ever hope for. That he loved you and me so much, and that when he was gone, he wanted me to be happy when I thought about him. And after two months of walking around the corner of the kitchen or the bedroom and expecting to see him, and then . . . well, the reality that he wasn't coming back kept punching me in the gut."

Bernie nodded. She tried to imagine building a life with a partner and then having him gone, with all the little habits and rituals you create together vanishing in a day.

"I mean, maybe it helps you to stay in this house, in Portland, living a quiet life. I just never thought while you were growing up this was how you would be. But maybe it's how you have to deal with losing your dad. For me, it's helped to move out with the other women on the farm."

"I know, you always thought I'd be like Aunt Bernice."

"Well, so did your dad." Her mom laughed wearily. "He always was amazed at how free spirited you were . . . creating some crazy scheme, getting into mischief . . ."

"What?" Bernie asked. This was new. "I always thought I was more like him."

"Really? You were wild as a kid. Always sneaking off with Tabitha and running around; God knows what you were doing." She shook her head and rolled her eyes at the same time, her signature mom move. "But your dad always said that was your spirit, and we had to let you live. That's why we wanted you to go away to school, live out your adventures. He never expected you to come back here and settle down."

"He didn't?" Bernie was mystified.

"I remember one night, while you were away at college, he asked me what I thought he'd miss about you when he was gone, what kind of crazy adventures you'd have. We listed out so many places we thought you'd go, things you might try to do . . . like take food tours through the islands of Thailand or belly dance in Istanbul. It always seemed to give him comfort, imagining all these crazy things you'd do, living your life to the fullest."

It was like a bomb had exploded in Bernie's chest, and she could only stare at the little pieces of debris floating around her like sad confetti in slow motion. Everything she'd thought about her dad and what he'd thought of her, what he'd expected of her, was blown up. Everything she'd thought about who she wanted to be for him disintegrated.

"But he always told me I could come home. That I should come home if I felt lost." It was like a mantra she told herself whenever she felt sad or confused. Her mom must have missed something.

Her mom cocked her head at her. "Honey, home is where you make it. Home can be in your heart, or where you feel complete. I know your dad felt that way too. He always said wherever the three of us were, it felt like home."

Bernie sat in silence soaking this information in. Wasn't home this building that she sat in right now? This place she'd lived her entire childhood in, with its outdated wallpaper, worn carpet tinged with memories, and random old pictures that made her feel safe because she knew what had been breathed into these walls? All the memories she'd shared with her parents sitting at the round oak kitchen table, or holidays spent in the room she sat in now, watching old movies while wrapped up in blankets because this room never seemed to get warm enough. In her mind, her house represented all those memories. That was home.

But she supposed those memories wouldn't fade and disappear just because she moved away from the building she referred to as "home." She'd still had those memories in Alaska when she'd talked to Matthew about her dad. Or when she thought about selling the house. It wasn't as if the house was a prison for those memories, and if she escaped it, they would all vanish when someone new took it over and repainted the walls. Maybe the house was a kind of prison, though. But for her.

She took a deep breath and wiped her eyes. "I was thinking about selling the house. Tabitha encouraged me to, but I—"

"If you're holding on to this house because of your father, I'll tell you one thing: he was never a fan of it."

"What?" Bernie had to shake her head, because she couldn't believe what she was hearing.

"He always hated the way the downstairs bathroom got clogged up because the plumbing is old, and how the heating never gets above sixty-three degrees, and the weird foyer-like space with its posts," her mom said, pointing toward the front door. "Don't you remember how he always hit his head on that one after putting his briefcase down?"

"Sort of." Bernie tried to remember her dad coming home from work, and memories bubbled up. His balding head smacking against the post, and child Bernie laughing at the bad words sputtering out of his mouth. "He used to always curse it, right?"

"That's how I knew he was home." Her mom raised her hands like the gesture should be accompanied with "Ta-da!"

She tried to let these things that her mother was telling her sink in. It was as if everything Bernie once believed as true was being called into question. She'd been so misguided for so long that she failed to recognize that the home he'd always told her to return to when she was lost might not be this three-bedroom structure she sat in now. The one she thought she needed to live in so she wouldn't forget his weird postwork cursing, or the random stain that wouldn't come out of the carpet, or the way he'd laugh when she made him watch Claymation holiday movies, and he'd conjure up all his favorite memories of her as a little kid.

"Wow. This is a lot to take in." Bernie inhaled deeply.

Her mom responded with a sigh. "Honey, I'm realizing that maybe we should have talked about this earlier. A lot earlier. I think I have a tendency to assume you are fine, when maybe you aren't fine. I didn't want to burden you with all my feelings, because you seemed to be dealing with things so much better than me. Like you had moved on, and I just couldn't. I literally had to move away to move on or else I was going to be depressed for the rest of my life. That's why I wanted you to have the house. But maybe you weren't ready, and the house didn't let you move on after all."

Bernie worried her lip, afraid she was going to start crying again. All she could think about was how her dad had thought she was going to live these wild adventures, and she'd essentially stopped living. Period.

Except for the trip to Alaska. And it was true that the trip hadn't been 100 percent amazing, but a lot of good had come out of it. The main thing was that she'd left and had the opportunity to realize that when she'd left, she was still who she was, with the same dear memories she'd always had. In fact, she'd even had the time to consider who she wanted to be. Alaska had turned out to be a surprising gift her mother had given her.

"Mom, I think you might be right." Words she never thought she'd say in a million years.

"Losing someone we love is hard. And different for everyone. But I know that your father, nor myself, would ever want you to stay put when you have the heart of an adventurer. We both knew that, even when you were little. Staying in the house where you grew up is fine for some people. It's what they want, and maybe what they need. But for you, I think it's holding you back."

Bernie nodded, letting it all sink in about how her mom and Tabitha seemed to understand this, when Bernie had been clinging to it like a fairy tale she still wanted to believe in. "Yep. I wonder that too. I think it might be time."

"I have an idea. How much did Tabitha say she could get for the house? I imagine the value has increased quite a bit in the past twenty years," her mom said, with a sly squint in one eye.

"A lot."

"Maybe we can use some of the money and take a real vacation. You get your passport, and we can go to Europe. Do some wacky things your dad can laugh at from the great beyond. Wouldn't that be fun?"

Bernie tried to imagine traveling around Europe with her mom, as her mother skipped down cobblestone roads wearing too many colorful scarves, interrogated vegetable farmers on the source of their produce, and spoke inappropriately to baristas. She croaked out a laugh. *That would be a great script for Matthew to write.* And if she was honest, the idea of a trip to Europe seemed perfect. Just the thing she'd need, once her ankle started reworking. Most of her friends had already been, and Bernie had looked through their photos online with a mix of wistfulness and melancholy. She hated to think of how many trips she'd missed out on already. "Yeah, it would be fun." Bernie smiled at her mom and meant it.

"Great! It's a plan. How about I make us some lemonade to celebrate? With vodka." Her mom patted Bernie's thigh and got off the couch.

Bernie looked at James Brown, on the floor beside her, like he was the only thing she could recognize in this room after that conversation. The furniture she'd grown up with sitting around her now seemed foreign. This sofa she had been lying on for weeks, so not her taste, with its pale flower print. Most pictures on the wall were not even hers, but her mom's old art. Bernie's father had wanted her to live out her life no matter where it took her, and for her to get everything she'd ever wanted.

And what did Bernie want?

Bernie wanted to live. Find her own adventure. And now she could do it for her father.

Her mom brought two pale glasses of lemonade that smelled like vodka and set them down on the table and went out the front door. "Let's see if you have any more fun magazines to look through."

Now Bernie had to question why she got so many magazines and catalogs, half of them seeming to have something to do with travel. Tabitha always made fun of her for it, like she was holding on to paper publications of the past.

Her mom went through the mail and flopped a small stack of it on Bernie's lap. Bernie took a drink of the lemonade and winced. Is that what the farm ladies were drinking all the time? "Damn, that's strong,

Mom." She pulled out a giant envelope from the ones that looked like spam mail and bills. Postmarked Los Angeles.

What was this?

She tore it open at the top and pulled out the stapled sheath of paper.

On the cover page were the words "THE ADVENTURERS," A TELEVISION SCRIPT BY MATTHEW HILDEBRANDT, and scrawled in pen below it, a handwritten note, *a.k.a. The Chronicles of Bernie, but this time, please read the WHOLE thing.* And then a drawn heart.

Matthew had sent her his script. Her heart beat in her chest hard. Her fingers held it carefully, like if she dropped it, it might explode, and she could only deal with so many emotional bombs in a day.

She reached for the glass of vodka with a touch of lemonade and swallowed half of it. Even though it reminded her of some kind of cleaning product, it might be just the thing she needed to purge her soul before she could read the words Matthew had sent to her.

CHAPTER 35

It had been over a week since Matthew had agreed to make the kidney donation, and two days since he had sent Bernie the finished pilot script. Of course, his agent had loved it, calling it all kinds of those Hollywood words Matthew typically cringed at. But he felt like he'd finally done something right since his work on *The Unbreakables*. Something that felt whole and him, and hopefully Bernie would see that as well.

"Mattie, are you sure you have everything you need?" his mom called from the kitchen. She was staying with him until after the surgery, and Jess had offered to crash at her girlfriend's place until he was recovered.

"Mom, it's just a visit with the doctor to discuss . . . plans?" He didn't know what they had to discuss with his dad and his doctor, but Matthew hadn't met his dad's surgeon and thought it would at least be a good thing if he looked the person in the eye who would be removing his vital organ.

He walked into the kitchen, where his mom worried over a stain on the counter, trying to scrub it out. Her shoulder-length hair streaked with silvery strands waved and shook as an entire unit as she rubbed at one of Jess's turmeric stains.

"Mom, don't worry about that."

"I have to do something to not worry about you." She threw the sponge in the sink and sank back against the counter.

"Well, I'll be fine." He tried to make his voice sound positive, but the bitterness cracked at the edges. When he was in Alaska with Bernie, this all seemed to be a good plan. But now, things felt changed. She wasn't here. He'd fucked up. She was in Portland and hated him. He was alone and still blamed himself for what had happened.

"I know, but . . ." His mom shook her head and sighed.

He knew exactly what was going through her mind. The same things that had gone through his.

"Just because Dad was a bad father doesn't mean I can just let him die. Do you know how long people sit around on donor lists?"

She huffed, "Well, when you put it like that."

"I mean, that's how it is. I couldn't live with myself if I didn't do what I could. Besides, I have a whole other right kidney. I'll be fine. That other kidney is just going to miss its pal, left kidney. It will get over it. Just a small grieving period."

"But the complications!"

"We'll talk to the surgeon about it today. I'm healthy, and it's going to be fine. I've already been assured the complications and risks are minimal."

She shook her head and opened her mouth. He thought she was going to say something else, but she just walked into the bathroom and shut the door. He just hoped she wasn't crying over what was going to be nothing.

Matthew pulled out his phone and looked at the series of texts he'd sent Bernie. Maybe he should tell her. But would she think he was trying to make her feel guilty about not responding? He really wanted to know if she'd gotten his script.

He started typing, but before he hit send, he waffled. Maybe wait a day. Maybe it hadn't arrived. Because surely after she'd read it, she'd say something to him. He hadn't poured his heart into a script just for his agent and an attempt at another show. He'd done it for her. But would she get that?

His mom emerged from the bathroom, shaking her head, like she was trying to inhale fresh, clean air to remove the hurt he could tell was still filling her up. She'd gone into the bathroom to hide her tears from him, which was obvious, with her red nose and cheeks.

"Ready to go?" he asked.

"Yes. Let's. I'm sorry. I should be proud of you for what you're doing. Even though he doesn't deserve it."

"I know, Mom." Matthew sighed. "But he's sorry. He's tried to make it up to me for years. Honestly, he's a different person now."

She nodded tightly. "When the love of your life betrays you like he did to me, sometimes that love turns into the exact opposite. I'm sorry. I shouldn't bring you into it." It made Matthew wonder how much his dad had tried to make up for his carelessness with her heart.

They drove to the hospital and were sitting in the waiting room when his dad arrived.

"Late as usual," his mother said, muttering under her breath.

Matthew looked at his watch. "By two minutes. Please, Mom, try to get along for my sake."

His dad gave a hesitant wave and walked over to them. His slight frame and overall tiredness caught Matthew every time he saw him. His dad was sick. It was so apparent on the outside; he had to wonder what he felt like on the inside.

"Hey, Dad." Matthew stood, always feeling awkward when they saw each other, wondering how to greet. His dad took him in a hug, stronger than he'd anticipated.

"Thank you, son. Thank you, thank you."

"Sure."

His dad took a step back and examined his ex-wife. Really gave her one of those head-to-toe studies. "Marianne, you look . . ."

She sat back down, apparently changing her mind about how she was going to greet him. Handshake? Hug? A push to the floor? Matthew wasn't sure.

"Hello, Matt."

"I was going to say, 'amazing.'" His dad sighed and sat across from them.

"How long has it been since you've seen each other?" Matthew asked.

"Not long en—" his mom started, but his dad spoke over her and said, "Your high school graduation."

"Wow. So, a while." That was years ago. Matthew could remember the awkwardness of the event, with his dad drunk-groveling to his mom, and his mom's fists thudding on his chest to keep him at bay like the memory had been tattooed into Matthew's brain.

His dad couldn't stop looking at his mom. It was unsettling. His eyes were shiny, like a glow had lit them up that Matthew had never seen before. If he didn't know better, he'd think his dad had the hots for his ex-wife.

"Well, it's really good to see you, Marianne. I know you probably aren't thrilled about seeing me." His dad sounded defeated, and Matthew imagined he had a running video of all their worst moments playing through his head just then. The light in his eyes dimmed, and he started fiddling with the zipper on his jacket. "I can't blame you for it, Marianne. You never replied to any of my letters."

Letters? Had his dad been sending his mom love letters? Apology letters? Now Matthew wanted to know exactly what had transpired between them.

She looked up and studied him for a moment, worrying at her lip, like she was picking and choosing her words carefully.

He added, "I read that forgiveness is associated with a positive emotional state, as compared to unforgiveness. Once you forgive someone, it activates multiple parts of the brain, including the prefrontal cortex, and if you have chronic emotional distress, it can damage your health—everything from sleep to increasing cortisol—"

"Enough, Matt."

Matthew slumped over and sighed. It was going to be a long day.

The nurse came out and called them back just in time, and they headed into the doctor's office. The waiting was painful as Matthew had separate conversations with each of his parents; his dad's doctor entered, and then the surgeon, and his mother had a list of questions ready that she grilled them both on. Matthew hadn't even thought about making a list. The surgeon was terse and to the point, which seemed exactly how you wanted a surgeon to be, compared to his dad's doctor, Dr. Love (that was his real name), who patted his dad on the back like they were old friends. He imagined if Bernie were there, she'd actually say something inappropriate like, "Wait, do you moonlight as a dating-advice doctor for desperate singles on a nighttime radio show? I'm familiar with your work." And they'd all awkwardly laugh.

Dr. Love had a genuine, friendly demeanor. He put his tablet down and just looked at Matthew, his mom, or dad while they were talking, as if their words actually mattered. Matthew imagined Dr. Love would laugh right back if Bernie made fun of his name. Somehow, envisioning this made him feel better about the whole operation.

Except now he was just disappointed that Bernie wouldn't be there. But his mom seemed less shaken. His dad, though, looked sad and guilty somehow.

They parted ways outside, and as they went to the car, his mom said, "I hope this will all be worth it."

For a moment, Matthew thought she was talking about the script and Bernie. But of course she wasn't. She'd heard about the girl he'd met in Alaska and how he had messed up, but he hadn't shared details, mostly because she'd be as disappointed in him as she was in his dad.

"Me too," he said.

CHAPTER 36

The Adventurers
By
Matthew Hildebrandt

COLD OPEN

FADE IN:

EXT. RUSTIC CABIN

BOBBI is standing with a suitcase looking at a rundown cabin. A concerned look comes over her but then she smiles.

BOBBI

Hello new life!

EXT. RUSTIC CABIN

Rustle from inside the cabin. A man seems to be pushed out through the door, stumbles out, and a woman, SUSAN, appears in the door entryway.

SUSAN

And that is the last time you will ever see me do that again! Or get your eggs scrambled.

The man runs off. The woman looks up brightly.

Oh, Bobbi? Hi! Come in, come in.

BOBBI

Uh, Hi. Susan?

Susan nods, waves her in, and Bobbi hesitantly walks toward the cabin.

INT. CABIN

Susan sits at a rickety desk.

SUSAN

You got here just in the nick of time. Good help—can't find them and then can't get them to do what you want in bed.

BOBBI

Oh yeah, sure.

SUSAN

So, we're excited that you're joining us here in Camp Kawakrazee.

BOBBI

Did you say "crazy?" I thought it was craw-zee.

SUSAN

Nope. Everyone thinks that, though. I don't know why. So you're ready to move out here to the wilderness and lead our little gangs of miscreants?

BOBBI

By miscreants you mean campers?

SUSAN

Oh, yes of course. So this is your first time to Alaska?

BOBBI

It is. I've always wanted to move to a small, quaint town and soak up the smell of nature every day. The air is so clean up here.

SUSAN

What was it? You had a bad breakup? You lost your job? Accidentally maimed someone? Those are usually the only reasons people move up here.

BOBBI

No! I mean. Not exactly. Maybe. Yes. Not on the run from the law or anything.

SUSAN

Maiming? That will do it every time. Just ask ol' Jack.

Susan turns to glance at the mounted jackelope on the wall.

Or Harry.

Camera pans to the menacing bear half out of the wall.

Or Josephine.

Camera pans to the butt of a wildcat.

BOBBI

That's an odd one.

SUSAN

Bill wanted to keep the front half for himself. Don't ask.

BOBBI

Bill?

SUSAN

My ex. The second one.

Bobbi nods cautiously.

BOBBI

Well I didn't maim anyone. Or mount them on my wall. Just needed a change of scenery.

SUSAN

(Squints like she doesn't believe her.)

Well, perfect, then! Let me show you to your cabin.

Ext. walk to cabin, trudging suitcases. End at an even more dilapidated cabin than the first one. A tall, lumbering man exits it, carrying a bag. Bobbi frowns at the cabin.

SUSAN

And here is good ol' Mark!

BOBBI

(Holds out her hand to shake.)

Hi, I'm Bobbi.

Mark looks back at cabin and then nods slightly and walks past them.

SUSAN

Oh, don't worry about him. He'll come around sooner or later. He's currently suffering from a broken heart.

Bernie put down the script. Would she ever come around, though? It was her fourth time reading through it. It was obvious what he was doing. Bobbi and Mark? But in this version, Bobbi was brave and funny. Susan was like someone's crazy aunt, and Mark was the brooding coworker whom everyone loved to hate.

She flipped to the middle of the sheath of papers, where her favorite scene was.

BOBBI

So Mark, what do you do around here for fun?

MARK

Oh, you know. Stare at the mountain.

BOBBI

Doesn't that get old?

MARK

Well it's no Mt. Kilimanjaro.

BOBBI

Have you ever been to Mt. Kilimanjaro?

MARK

No.

BOBBI

Okay.

MARK

But I want to. More than anything.

SUSAN

Mount. It's a funny word, isn't it? It reminds me of my ex . . .

Bobbi and Mark both look at her.

SUSAN

He was a ranger, and he used to have these horses. One named
Sam (FADES OUT)

BOBBI (internal monologue)

Okay, I'm stuck with like this horny great aunt Susan and Mr. I'll
brood if I want to. I have a dirty cabin, no wine, no cell service,
and . . .

BOBBI (aloud)

There's a moose!

SUSAN

That's Herbert.

MARK

No, that's Beau.

BOBBI

You've named the mooses?

MARK

The plural form is just moose.

BOBBI rolls her eyes.

SUSAN

I named Beau after my ex because after he died, I caught this one peeping in through my window.

BOBBI

Oh! I'm sorry.

SUSAN

Don't be. I was having a good hair day. All over.

Bobbi looks to Mark for commiseration but he looks away quickly.

BOBBI

Uh, so Mark, tell me about why you like mountains so much.

MARK

What?

BOBBI

Mt. McKinley, Mt. Kilimanjaro—what are some other cool mounts?

SUSAN

Oh, this one time, I heard Mark and Vicki liking some kind of mount. The whole community heard them.

Mark pushes away from table and throws his napkin on the
table and leaves.

BOBBI

What was that?

SUSAN

Oh, that's Mark. He's just sad.

BOBBI

Who's Vicki?

SUSAN

His ex, Vicki. She left him last week for the mayor. You know,
he'd just proposed and then she upgraded for the big time.

BOBBI

Isn't this town only like 200 people?

SUSAN

Exactly. Big time.

Bernie smiled as she put it down. Bobbi was a hero, trapped in a
crazy town. Instead of the notebook where Matthew had made Bernie
seem like the weird one, he'd made himself the asshole and Bernie the
only one who made any sense. He wasn't turning her into some antihero like he'd hinted at. Her faults weren't going to be on display for a
television-viewing audience.

Maybe the notebook contained notes about everything they'd been
going through, not just Bernie's flaws. Because he seemed to appreciate
her like no one else had.

He had been trying to make it up to her—the photos, the texts,
the calls, the script. Maybe it was time to call him. Besides, it had been
almost four weeks since she'd left Alaska, and he still hadn't given up.
And she still missed him. It was ridiculous that a handful of days with
him felt like an eternity compared to the time she'd spent with other

men she'd dated. An eternity that she wanted to settle into, nice and snug.

She picked up the phone. Four weeks without speaking seemed sufficient torture. At least for her.

A woman answered. "Hello?"

"Uh, hi, is this Matthew's phone?" Bernie asked. Her heart thumped in her veins. Was she already too late? Had he given up and moved on? Was he back with his model/actress girlfriend?

"Yes, this is his mother. He can't come to the phone at the moment. Can I take a message?"

"Oh, sure. Could you just tell him this is Bernie and I'm sorry it's taken me so long to get in touch and that I'd like to speak to him?" She resisted adding, "At the next, soonest-possible moment?"

"Sure, honey. He's being prepped for surgery, and—"

"Wait, for the kidney transplant?" The air seemed to get sucked from her lungs, and Bernie almost dropped the phone.

"Yes." His mother's voice hesitated, probably because Bernie had just yelled in her ear.

"I was supposed to be there with him. I told him I would come down for it. Where are you?"

"Uh, at the Cedars-Sinai Medical Center."

"When is he scheduled to have it?"

"I think in an hour, and then the surgery and then recovery."

"Okay, I'll find the earliest flight and come there." Bernie started looking around the room. What did she need to do?

"A flight? Oh, okay. Sure." His mother sounded overwhelmed and confused. Then her tone changed. "Wait, you're the girl from Alaska?"

"I'm a girl from Portland who met him in Alaska, but yes. Is that okay? If I come?"

"Of course. I'm sure he would be very happy to see you."

"Okay, good. I'll just call you when I'm there. Bye."

Bernie hung up the phone. How could she let this happen? Matthew was already doing the surgery without her? And she'd promised she'd be there. Of course this was what happened. She'd made him wait too long—after his apologies, after his texts and calls, the photos and the script. What if he didn't wake up, and the last thoughts he had of her was that she was a stubborn wretch of a girl who didn't care about him, a girl who was selfish and didn't trust her gut? Because if she was honest with herself, Matthew had seen who she was, had even tried to convince her of it, when she'd been in full-blown denial.

It shouldn't have taken a heart-to-heart with her mom and a script spelling out his true intentions for her to believe him. It was as if she had so much untangling of herself to do that she had to make herself truly unravel before she could see clearly. And now that she could see, all that was in her vision was Matthew.

Tears burned behind her eyes. She told him she'd be there, and dammit, she needed to be there. He'd been there for her. Adrenaline flooded her system; she felt like she could almost walk at this point.

Laptop. Tickets. Dog. Mom. Where was her mom?

"Mom!" she yelled so it echoed around the house. The back door shut.

"What? Are you okay? I was outside and heard you through the house."

"I'm going to LA. Can you stay here and watch James Brown?"

"Honey, you can't fly to LA—I'm here taking care of you."

"It's fine. I did it in Anchorage. Rolled around all by myself. I'll just take a backpack. A small one." She searched for flights on her phone. There was one leaving in three hours she could make. "Seriously, I'm leaving in three hours. I should be there when he wakes up."

"What? Who? That boy you met in Alaska?"

"Yes. I'm buying the tickets. Clicking the 'Purchase' button. And it's done." She turned to her mom. "Can you please help me pack a bag?"

"Honey, your leg!"

"I'm fine. I can do it."

"I'm not comfortable just letting you go."

"You have to let me. I made a promise. I'll crawl upstairs if I have to."

Her mother stood, giving her that raised-eyebrow, one-side-of-her-cheek-sucked-in look she hadn't seen since she was a teenager. "Fine."

"Pack me something that looks cute!" she called up the stairs. "And maybe some sexy underwear!"

"Bernie!" her mother admonished from the top of the stairs. "Oh my God. You're just like your great-aunt, you know?" she said, obviously annoyed, shaking her head. But Bernie caught a little self-satisfied smirk on her face as she disappeared on the landing.

CHAPTER 37

Matthew felt something tight on his hand. And something tickle it. Like he was holding something. Something firm but soft. The surgery must be over, but it was as if he was living in the clouds, and behind his eyes, the colors of the clouds were changing. Soft blue. Midnight blue. Glowing yellow. Dark blue again.

But there were voices from somewhere. Soft voices, murmuring like they were under a big furry blanket. He must have survived. But now a piece of him was gone. He tried to imagine the space in his abdomen where it once was. There was some soreness there, an achy feeling. Would he miss a piece of himself that had been carved out by the surgeon?

"Mr. Kidney?" The words seemed as if they came from somewhere else, but it felt like his mouth might have moved.

The gentle cloudlike grip on his hand squeezed again. "Matthew? Matthew, are you awake?"

Maybe he did die, and he was waking up in some kind of afterlife where a replica of Bernie was there. Because that for real sounded like Bernie's voice.

He tried to force his eyes open so he could see. But they were so heavy. Like in those old movies where they put thick coins on a dead person's eyelids to keep them from opening back up like a zombie. Where was he? The light was bright. Back to glowing sun ray and away from calming, deep-sea dark blue.

"Let's turn the lights down."

Was that his mom? His mom and Bernie had followed him into the cloudlike afterlife? He frowned at this idea. If the surgery had killed him, he could at least just have Bernie alone to himself.

Dark blue again. He tried to force his eyes open with the will of a crowbar. God, he had to pee. He couldn't be dead if he had to pee, right? There wasn't excrement in heaven. That just wouldn't be right.

His eyes opened to slits, and the shadowy light of the hospital room was there. And Bernie. Why was Bernie there? Maybe he wasn't dead but hallucinating?

"Matthew!" She hovered over him, and her hand was the thing on his hand.

"Bernie? Why are you here?" His voice was a hoarse whisper, and he cleared his throat.

"Well, hello to you too!" But she laughed.

"This happens a lot when they wake up from the anesthesia," the nurse said quietly.

"I can hear you." Matthew tried to stretch his lips open. His words sounded underwater, like they wanted to slip back into that deep-blue sea.

The dull pain in his abdomen pulsed, growing more apparent with each breath. Mr. Kidney. Had he really said that out loud?

He blinked and really looked at Bernie now. She was there. Really there. That big, bright smile on her face, her eyes doing that glittering thing they did. Her leg still in a cast. The nurse said she'd get the doctor.

"How are you feeling, Mattie?" his mom asked.

"I'm okay. Just need to wake up."

"Good." His mom patted his thigh, likely because Bernie was still clutching his hand. He tried to squeeze it, but his hand was weak. "Do you need anything?" his mom asked.

He shook his head because it was easier than speaking. Also he felt like he might cry. Was that weird? It must have been the anesthesia. He really didn't want to cry in front of Bernie.

"I'm going to get some coffee down the hall. I'll be back in a moment." She looked from Matthew to Bernie, sighed, and walked out the door.

"You came."

"Yeah. I read your script like five times and then thought I'd punished you enough. And when I called, your mom said you were getting ready for surgery, and then I just got on the next plane and came down." She adjusted in her seat. "I literally just got here right before you woke up."

"Seriously? Like you left this morning? Er . . . what time is it?"

"Yep. Luckily the hospital isn't far from the airport." She looked at the clock on the wall. "It's like six o'clock. But geez, the traffic."

"Spoken like a true Angeleno."

She laughed. "I love it here. There are palm trees, and it's so bright and everyone seems happy all the time."

"You've been here for like thirty minutes." He laughed. "But I'm glad you like it."

"Well, sometimes you just know from the start."

"And sometimes you don't." He sighed. "Listen, I'm sorry again, about—"

"Shh. Don't worry about it. We'll talk later." She paused. "I really liked the script."

"Thanks."

"Has anything happened with it?"

"Not yet. My agent is shopping it around. I was trying to finish it before the surgery."

"Why didn't you tell me you were having the surgery?"

"Well, my dad was told he needed to do it sooner than later, and then you hadn't responded to me at all, and I didn't want to guilt you into forgiving me. Honestly, I didn't think you'd come. I thought I'd ruined my life."

Her eyebrows shot up, and her eyes got wide. "Ruined your life? Wow."

"Yeah, pretty much. I couldn't stop thinking about you. This is not the drugs talking, by the way."

"I couldn't stop thinking about you either." Her fingers stroked his hand.

"I would kiss you, but I'm pretty sure I have surgery breath, if that's a thing."

She laughed and bent down and kissed him lightly on the lips.

"Also, if I start, I don't know if I can control myself, and I don't know what is doctor approved."

"We're always finding ourselves in the hospital, huh?" she said with a laugh.

A knock tapped at the door, and the doctor walked in, followed by his mom, peeping around the corner. It was Dr. Love.

"How's the patient doing?" he asked.

Matthew sighed and squeezed Bernie's hand. "Much better now."

"Good, your dad just woke up, and it looks like the transplant was a success!"

◆ ◆ ◆

"So there is espresso in the LA hospital. I thought there would only be fresh-squeezed juice and matcha," Bernie said, sipping on her latte. The latte she and Matthew's mom, Marianne, had awkwardly journeyed to find. They were walking/rolling back to Matthew's room after taking an accidental tour of the facility trying to locate it.

Bernie had wanted to reciprocate by playing Matthew's caregiver role. She wanted to help him like he'd helped her in Anchorage, but Bernie was more like a third wheel with three more wheels under her, but neither Matthew nor his mom seemed to mind.

"It was very sweet for you to come see Matthew in the hospital. He was really sad before the surgery, and I can tell from the moment he saw you he perked right up," Marianne said.

"That's nice of you to say. I promised him in Alaska I would be here for it . . . I just . . ." What could Bernie say to explain without diving into the details of how her son had broken her heart?

"Oh, I heard about the book. His roommate told me about it." She shook her head.

"You know?"

"Those stupid mini journal things of his." Marianne stopped in the middle of the hallway and turned to Bernie. "Do you know one day I found one when I was visiting called *The Mom Book*, and of course, well, I opened it. And it was all these weird things he'd written down about a mom character for a show he was writing. And there were things that had actually happened in our family. Like dialogue between his father and me. Or the process I used to do my hair. Things I'd said I really wish I hadn't. But then half of it was stuff I didn't recognize, just random thoughts about moms, I guess." She did a little shiver and started walking again. "Those idea books. Always causing problems."

"So you've been the victim of his idea books, too, then." Bernie and Matthew hadn't talked about what exactly had happened yet, but she couldn't believe he'd made one with his mom in it.

"Oh yeah. We had a little talk about that one. He said he just keeps them because he never knows when inspiration is going to hit him, and he doesn't want to miss it. But still. Maybe call them something else, Matthew, huh?" She laughed.

"Yeah, like *The Most Boring Book of Random Stuff Ever That No One Would Ever Want to Look Inside and Read*."

"Exactly. Or *My Bowel Diary*."

Bernie cackled. "Oh, that's a good one. I would definitely not open that up."

They reached the door to Matthew's room, both of them laughing. Matthew squinted and looked back and forth between them.

Bernie set down his coffee. "Oh, don't worry. We're totally laughing at your expense."

"I can only imagine. My mom and my gi—" He stopped short, and Bernie felt herself blush. He cleared his throat. "I'm sure you two could trade stories about what a jackass I am for days."

Had Matthew been ready to call her his girlfriend? She sat down and tried to decide how she felt about that. She felt good. It felt right.

"Well, I think I'm going to check on how your father is doing and see if he's up for a visit in a bit," Marianne said and then left the room, closing the door behind her.

"So, how are you feeling?" Bernie asked.

"Like an asshole. But like an asshole that hopes you will forgive him because he's an idiot and very sorry."

"I meant about your missing kidney. 'Mr. Kidney,' as I believe you called him when you were delirious?"

"I think if I knew we were good, then I could focus on Mr. Kidney's MIA status."

"Oh, I see how it is. You don't want to guilt me into forgiving you, but Mr. Kidney has no such qualms." But she smiled at him to let him know she was joking.

"I know it's going to sound insane, but I've been so upset the past few weeks. And not just about having to do this surgery. But that I just totally fucked up with you. I think when I met you, I was so miserable with work and my dad, and all these things weighing me down. Then there you were, light as air, not giving a care about anything, and I wished I could be like you. Because I've never been like that. But then . . . it's so weird. Like when we left on that helicopter and I just wanted to make sure you were okay, and that darkness I was existing in sort of dissipated. Like you let me into your lightness. Does that sound crazy?"

"Yes. Are you sure it's not the drugs talking?" Seeing the worried look on Matthew's face made her clarify. "I mean, it sounds crazy because I'm not light and carefree. Or at least I wasn't. I was so scared to go on that trip and leave Portland. I didn't realize how I was internalizing my dad's death. But being around you, and being on the trip, brought out the real me I hadn't seen in years. So, I think you drew whatever you needed to out of me." She rolled herself up to the bed from the chair she'd been sitting on.

"Really?"

"Yeah, I think so." Bernie bent down to kiss him, hovering over his lips. How did he still smell like the Matthew she missed, postsurgery, in a hospital bed?

"You know," he whispered, "I think you're saying that we both saved each other."

Bernie hummed.

"Which is like the most clichéd shit ever." He smiled.

"Shut up." She kissed him, missing the feel of his lips on hers like the greatest thirst, like a warm bath, like a hot, sexy blanket covering the two of them as everything twitched inside her.

The door opened and Bernie shot back, wiping at her mouth as if she could hide the evidence of them making out in a hospital bed.

A woman appeared in the door, her lithe body strung tight as if she was deciding whether to stay or go. "Whoops!"

Matthew flopped back on the bed. "Your timing as always is impeccable."

The woman smirked and threw a bouquet of flowers on him. "Yeah, and these are for you, dummy." She turned to Bernie. "You can't be Bernie, can you?"

"Uh, yeah." Who was this force of a woman, and how did she know who she was?

"Oh my God. Did you forgive this dickhead?" She laughed.

So maybe she knew not just who Bernie was . . . "Uh, maybe. Do you think I shouldn't?"

"Nah, let him wallow in his misery. Let that inspire him, am I right?"

"Geez, Jess!" Matthew sighed. "Bernie, this is my roommate."

"I'm not just his roommate, but also his *friend* who has seen him basically cry himself to sleep every night since he got back from Alaska."

This was interesting. "Oh? Please do tell."

"I was not crying," Matthew insisted, like a brave toddler trying to cover up a lie that he was just sniffling instead.

"Pouting then? Acting like the world had fallen apart around him and he was helpless to do anything?"

"Well, it felt like it had." Matthew's voice got quiet. "I think that's enough."

"Awww," Jess cooed ironically. "Just kidding. But seriously, this girl is so cute, you should hang on to her." Jess winked at Bernie.

"I'm trying to. That's what I was attempting to do when you barged in."

Bernie couldn't help but laugh at these two. They were like their own Abbott and Costello show.

"So sorry I wanted to see you. And maybe now embarrass you." She laughed.

"Thanks for the flowers," Matthew said.

It was a gorgeous bouquet. Wild, winding purple daisies and pink peonies and white allium flowers all strung together terrifically.

"They're beautiful," Bernie said, admiring them.

"Not as beautiful as you." Matthew swung his head up and looked at her with the equivalent of male doe eyes, blinking.

Bernie and Jess cooed at the same time.

"Just trying to see how clichéd I can actually be in one day." Matthew grinned. "I'm just trying to even it up. Make things better."

Bernie felt warm and soft all over and squeezed his hand again. "I think we already have."

CHAPTER 38

A few days later, Matthew was discharged from the hospital. The doctor had told him he needed to walk and move around, get used to his new body sans kidney. He and Bernie stopped by his dad's room to see how he was doing before they left. When they walked in, his mom was there, and they were laughing. Laughing! He hadn't seen his mom even smile within five minutes of mentioning his dad for the past fifteen years, and now she was laughing with the person she referred to as "the man who destroyed my life."

"Uh, hi, you two." Matthew cleared his throat. "How are you feeling?" He looked at his dad.

"Pretty good. Some soreness, probably like you. I'm taking immunosuppressive medications along with some painkillers, and so far there's no indication of acute rejection. Although that can happen anytime. Apparently up to thirty percent of patients will experience some degree of organ rejection, but I'm hoping because you're my son, that won't happen."

"Let's hope that my kidney genes recognize their father genes."

His dad worried his lips together. They were trembling. He then wiped at his eyes. "It's all thanks to you, son. I can't make this up to you, no matter what I do. You've given me a chance at life. A new life. A life that I want to live right this time."

"Oh, well . . . it's f-fine," Matthew stammered. He didn't know how to react to his father. He was like a new man. A man who cared about his family. A man who cried seemingly all the time now.

His mother passed his dad a tissue from her purse, but his father just grabbed onto her hand and held it there, clutching it like her touch was all he needed. And for whatever reason, she didn't pull away.

What was happening?

"Come here, Matthew." His dad gestured to him, and Matthew hobbled toward him with the distinct feeling that shit was about to get real. His dad never used his full first name.

As Matthew stood beside his bed, his father took his hand, the free one that wasn't holding his mother's. "I was a terrible father to you. You know that I know that. I don't deserve all the kindness you've shown me the past few years, but I want to make up for it. I want to make it up to your mom too." He glanced at her with a sappy smile that was becoming a familiar look on his dad.

"Okay," Matthew said, willing the awkwardness away. "Also, this is Bernie. I don't think you've met."

"Ah yes. Your mother told me about her."

Bernie waved from near the door. "Hi. Nice to meet you. Glad you're feeling good. Or the surgery worked. Maybe *good* isn't the best word." She rolled back and forth on her scooter a bit, which must have been the equivalent of shifting back and forth in an awkward situation.

"Matthew, you be nice to this one. Don't do anything I ever did." His dad laughed weakly.

"Okay. Roger that. Well, we're going to go to my apartment and also breathe some nonhospital air."

"Okay, honey. I'll call you later, see how you're doing," his mom said. "Bye, Bernie!"

"Bye!"

They left and then at the same time both said, "Well, that was awkward."

Matthew laughed. "I know."

"I think your mom and dad—something is going on there. Rekindling the old flame?"

"I just can't imagine."

"Stranger things have happened. Like us?" Bernie stopped him in the hallway and kissed him properly for the first time. So properly he wondered how strict the two-week mark was that the doctor had told him to wait before having sex.

"And also, now I know where you get it from." Bernie laughed.

"Get *what* from?" God help him if she was going to compare him to his father.

She put one hand on her hip and the other gripped onto her chin as she tilted her head up toward the ceiling. "By my estimation, the likelihood of a kidney transplant is seventy percent without any acute nonbinary rejection syndrome, with a twenty-five percent chance of rejection syndrome. The additional five percent is my son's kidney poking me in retribution, as often a bear does to a honeycomb. Such as in the case of the infamous Pooh Bear, once he has been stung." She finished her weird nasally voice and then burst out laughing.

"Oh yeah, you're funny, all right." He shook his head and tried his best to shuffle ahead of her so she couldn't see his smile. How had he never noticed that before?

◆ ◆ ◆

After convalescing at Matthew's apartment for three days with his mom awkwardly helping both of them, Bernie and Matthew were finally free, walking and scooting, in his neighborhood, Silver Lake. Slowly.

"Coffee?" he said as they passed by his favorite café.

"Always." He gently sunk down in one of the outside chairs, his abdomen still sensitive. Bernie parked her scooter and hopscotched into her seat.

"We're quite the pair." He laughed.

"Oh, don't I know it. Mr. Kidney and Miss Scooter."

The server came outside to take their order, and Bernie breathed deeply as she left, looking around. "You know, I really wish I'd been able to drive down here with James Brown. He'd like this. It's exactly the kind of street he'd enjoy. I bet he'd get pet a lot. And the weather is perfect."

"That would be fun. Why don't you do that?"

"Last time I visited the doctor, he said I'd probably have my cast off in two weeks. Max."

"So, road trip? When do you have to get back to work?" A little unsettling grumble in his chest. She'd forgiven him, but now what? He felt like he'd just gotten her back, but she still lived far away.

"Well, I was thinking about that. I don't see why my job can't be done from anywhere, honestly. I don't really need to go into the office, so I thought I'd ask my manager if she'd let me just work remotely."

"Oh?" This was interesting.

"Yeah. That trip to Alaska made me realize something, after all. I've been spending way too much time hiding in Portland. I used to want to go away, explore the world, and I just stopped. I liked being free and on my own, away from all that was familiar. And why not start with checking out LA?"

"You know, Jess loves dogs," Matthew said. "And she spends half her nights at her girlfriend's place anyway . . ."

"Matthew, are you saying I can stay with you and see if LA is just the thing that I need?"

"I'm saying you can stay with me and see if I'm the thing that you want." He laughed.

"Oh, I'm pretty sure I already know that." She sighed and looked down at her lap. "So you don't think it's too crazy if I just road trip it down here with my dog and crash with you for a while?"

"Uh, no. I think it's delightful. Wonderful. Amazing. I'm so excited at the prospect."

"We did share very close quarters for a week. And Tabitha will be ecstatic that I'll be out of my old house. I've decided to finally sell it."

"This sounds almost like a semipermanent kind of move, huh?" This day was getting better and better. Could it possibly be that the vision he'd had in Alaska of Bernie moving to LA was finally coming true?

"It's definitely time for a change." She shrugged.

"To sweeten the deal, my apartment is bigger than five square feet and has more than a bedroom. And working plumbing. Two bathrooms even. A huge selling point."

"It is. And your bed is way more comfortable than the ground. No matter how much moss is covering it."

"I will get moss for my bed, if that's what it takes."

"Well, not to get too ahead of myself, but I might have looked into a hike up Mount Kilimanjaro."

"Really?" he asked. How had she remembered that was his dream trip?

"Yeah, flights to Tanzania are like super cheap right now. I thought . . . if you were interested . . ."

"Let's do it."

"Yeah?" she asked, her eyes bright and glittery.

The server set their cups down on the table and then scurried off.

"I had actually been considering doing it sometime after this surgery, as sort of a celebration of life."

"Let's definitely celebrate life. To life!" She held her cup up, and they clinked them together.

"Maybe to our life?" Matthew said. "I'm really excited about the idea that you might be moving to LA. And then also going on an amazing trip with me."

"Me too."

"We should call Shalini and Diana and give them the news."

"What?" Bernie looked at him suspiciously, but with a smile.

"They might have given me your address."

"Ah. I was wondering how you got it. I thought you just did some internet stalking."

"They told me I was an asshole but knew I cared about you a lot. So they might have been part of the apology orchestration."

"I see. Those sneaky ladies. Maybe we can have a hiking reunion. See if the others want to join us?"

"Maybe. Although I'm selfish. I kind of want you all to myself for a while."

"I could be down with that. As long as you let James Brown snuggle with us now and then."

"He is allowed snuggle privileges for one night out of the week."

"Two, and we'll call it a deal." She held out her hand for a shake. He laughed and took it.

"I love it when you laugh," she said.

"I just love you." The words came out of his mouth before he realized what he'd just said. The look on his face must have shown exactly that because Bernie laughed.

"Don't worry. I think I love you too." Her cheeks flashed pink, a smile crept up on her face, and then she leaned over to kiss him.

"I'm so glad you started channeling your inner aunt Bernice."

"Me too. But can we not talk about her when we're making out?"

"Never again." He kissed her once more, any pain he had diminishing as the pure pleasure from having Bernie in his life eclipsed anything that had come before this moment.

EPILOGUE

Five months later

Bernie climbed up the last few rocks, her trekking pole digging into the earth to pull her to the top. And once she was there, she breathed in the cool wind that whipped around her, whistling across the top of Mount Kilimanjaro.

A few rocks crumbled below, then a similar exhale blew out from her right. "We did it!" Matthew sighed. His arm came around her shoulder, and they stood staring out from the plateau of mocha-colored earth and gazed around them. An ice wall sank into the mountain to their left, but otherwise clouds cut through the bright-blue sky with bleary streaks.

"And no one broke anything!" she couldn't resist adding. It was the first major hike they'd done since their big Alaskan trip, and while her doctor had assured her that her ankle would be fine six months after she'd broken it, at times she couldn't help anticipating some kind of calamitous disaster befalling her.

But that was the old Bernie. New Bernie tried to rein in the confidence she'd been accumulating since she'd left Portland and moved to LA. She had a new, and much more fun, marketing job that was less about data and more about creative solutions that she was actually excited about; she and Matthew had moved in together officially, after Jess had moved in with her partner; and not only was she in Africa, but she would be going to Europe this summer with her mom in the promised I-finally-sold-the-house trip. And she'd been messaging with Shalini and Diana about organizing a Denali 2.0 do-over.

And maybe she missed Portland and Tabitha at times, and she missed the house she'd grown up in, but she took comfort in the fact that she really did feel at home now. She felt at home with Matthew in their apartment. She felt at home when she visited her mom at the farm. And she felt at home when she thought about her dad and all the fond memories they'd had. She had to admit that her mom was right. Home was where you made it.

"This is quite the start to the new year, isn't it?" Matthew kissed the top of her hair, and she smiled up at him.

"It is. So far in January, I've seen a giraffe, at least two kinds of monkeys, and my favorite—the bush baby! Plus your new TV show, inspired by *moi*, just got sold. I would say it's been a pretty good year so far."

"I'd say so. And we'll see more animals when we go on our safari in the Serengeti when we get back down."

Every time Bernie thought about rattling around in a jeep watching for wild animals in a place she'd only seen on TV, she felt a giddiness spread through her. "I know!" Even after climbing almost forty miles up the mountain, she was still excited about what awaited them when they descended.

"You know what would make the start to this year even more fantastic?" he asked.

Bernie could think of so many things. "A beer to have on top of this mountain? A shower to wash off all the dirt that's caked on my body? A rhinoceros to walk up here and ask, 'Well, good day, Bernie, can I get you a cup of tea?'" She laughed and looked at Matthew, who was giving her one of his signature toothy grins.

"Well, any of those things do sound fantastic, especially the beer, but I had something else in mind." He worried at his lip, and Bernie realized they might be having a very serious moment.

"Oh?"

"I thought a great way to start off the year would be if you agreed to be my wife." Matthew fumbled in his pocket and pulled out a tiny box.

"Oh my God, you've been carrying that with you the whole time?" Bernie's hands went to her face. Her entire body, which had felt ragged moments ago, when she'd forced herself to the top after seven days of climbing, woke up. Now it was full-on alive, her blood pumping in her veins, her eyes feeling electric in the wind. A squeal piped out of her.

"Um, yeah. So what do you think? You know I have a reputation as the king of romantic gestures to keep up with?" One of his eyes squinted at her playfully, and his teeth tugged at his bottom lip.

"Of course I'll marry you, you fool!" She practically leaped on him, and he stumbled backward, laughing. A proposal at the top of Mount Kilimanjaro? That might have set a new standard.

He embraced her left hand. She hadn't even looked at the ring, but there it was, simple and exquisite. He slid it on and squeezed her hands in his.

She kissed him and Matthew pulled back, letting out a giant, "Yahoo!" from the top of the mountain. Bernie joined in, mustering up all the breath she could to let out a sound that would match his.

"I should have known you'd do something like this." She shook her head at him.

"I've got to keep my game up. Can't have you not being surprised. You surprise me every day."

"And I hope we keep surprising each other for the rest of our lives." Bernie held up her water bottle in cheers. "And to Great-Aunt Bernice, wherever you are, may you watch over us on our hopefully many adventures."

Matthew clanked his thin steel water bottle against hers. "So now it's blessings from Aunt Bernice and not a curse?" His eyebrow shot up in suspicion.

After everything that had happened, Bernie had a slightly different perspective on Aunt Bernice, her love for adventure, and even her name. Maybe it did feel more like a blessing now. "Well, if it weren't for her, we never would have been forced to share our tent. Without her name, who knows what would have happened?"

"Oh, I don't think a name could have kept us apart." Matthew bent down and kissed her again as his mouth sank onto hers, and she smiled into his lips, imagining all the moments they'd have like this. In fantastic places together, whether it was standing on top of a mountain, scuba diving in the sea, or trekking through the middle of a desert. The world was waiting for both of them. Waiting for all the adventure Bernie could ever dream of, living her life to her fullest.

ACKNOWLEDGMENTS

There are always so many people to thank when you write a book, whether they're the people who handle the logistics of getting the actual book published, the support system you lean on throughout, or those special people who review your manuscript and tell you what's working well and what needs some serious help. I want to start out by thanking Kimberly Brower, my agent, who always has such an amazing editorial eye and helped me finesse this book into the story it always wanted to be. And thank you to Lauren Plude for taking another chance on me, and to Selina McLemore for providing feedback and story edits along the way. You all are such a joy to work with.

Also, big thanks to the whole team at Montlake, from Lauren Grange and the copyediting team of pros—Bill Siever, Carolyn Allard, and Heather Buzila—to the graphic design team led by Kris Beecroft for their fun work on the cover. And I don't want to forget the marketing and PR team—Erin Mooney, and especially Jessica Preeg—who are superstars.

Huge thanks, of course, go to my husband, Prabhu, who gives me time and still has the patience for allowing me to write undisturbed. I'm glad we've found in each other that love for spending time in the outdoors together. Even though we don't rough it in tents—we are definitely glampers—so much of the spirit and energy we have when we're immersed in nature inspired this book. And always, thank you for being the catalyst for every happily ever after I write about.

This story, like so many others, was conjured up one night in Austin over margaritas. Thanks to my friend Marty Ross, who told me the tale of his hiking trip in Denali, where two strangers had to share a tent and, by the end, were voluntarily sharing a cabin together. It's proof that romance book tropes do happen in real life. Thank you for reading the book and ensuring that my Denali moments were authentic.

Big thanks to Julia Lee, who was the first person to read this book and to give me her thoughts on the journey of Bernie and Matthew—I always appreciate your perspective and critique, your friendship, and all the writing chats over the past few years. And I can't forget Katie Webb Kneisley, my oldest friend and constant shenanigan chaser, for always being supportive and for inspiring a lot of the moments between Tabitha and Bernie.

Lastly, my love for the great outdoors was really fostered in my teens, when my parents loaded my nightmare teenage self and my sister into a conversion van towing a camper and journeyed out west for two months. There is so much beauty in the landscape here in the United States, and I feel very lucky to have seen so much of it at a young age. So thanks for enduring those two months, Mom and Dad. It was totally worth it!

ABOUT THE AUTHOR

Brooke Burroughs is an award-winning writer of fun love stories about women with a heart for adventure. Brooke lives in Austin, Texas, with her husband, whom she met on one of her own real-life adventures living in India. When she's not writing, she conducts experiments in vegetarian cooking, performs with a Bollywood dance troupe, travels whenever she can, and is frequently seen at the dog park with her Great Dane, which is often mistaken for a horse.